*Until
Your
Heart
Stops*

UNTIL YOUR HEART STOPS

T. M. McNally

VILLARD BOOKS
New York 1993

Portions of this novel were written with the assistance of a Presidential Fellowship provided by Murray State University and the Committee on Institutional Studies and Research. The author would also like to thank, once again, the Hotchkiss School Summer Program.

Library of Congress Cataloging-in-Publication Data

McNally, T. M.
Until your heart stops / T. M. McNally.
p.   cm.
ISBN 0-679-41826-1
I. Title.
PS3563.C38816U5   1993
813'.54—dc20   92-50490
Manufactured in the United States of America
9 8 7 6 5 4 3 2
First edition

To the living

Heaven was no safer.

Ovid, *Metamorphoses*

Contents

I

Fahrenheit

It begins with knowing. With mystery, and never knowing exactly why the weather changes. It begins with Walker Miller dying unexpectedly on a hot October night: ninety-eight degrees, and falling.

Walker Miller had friends, he was a polite boy with big feet, and just a few hours before it happens, Joe Jazinski sits waiting in an air-conditioned waiting room, holding a magazine for women and leafing slowly through the pages. Joe's nine-year-old brother, Spencer, is seeing their family doctor. This past summer, while riding his bicycle, Spencer was hit by a car. Spencer carries a seven-inch stainless-steel plate in his leg, screwed into the femur, where it will remain until the bone knits. The car was going forty-seven miles per hour and the plate is longer than Spencer's two hands put together. His leg is set in a cast which reaches up past his hip, and he travels everywhere in his wheelchair; sometimes, when he is feeling brave, Spencer says that he likes being pushed around. Soon he will be officially permitted to use crutches, and already Spencer is practicing when he thinks Joe is not nearby. He falls down often. As for today's visit, this is merely a routine requirement for Boy Scout camp. Next summer Troop

364 is planning to hike down the Grand Canyon. The doctors guess by then the crutches will be unnecessary.

Joe is reading an advertisement on feminine hygiene. After he drives Spencer home, Joe is supposed to pick up his girlfriend, Edith McCaw, at school. Edith has swim practice every day, and until that's over, Joe doesn't have anything that he is supposed to do. Normally, he'd be at practice himself, in the upstairs gym, working out with one of the bigger freshmen. Mr. Morrison likes to break the new guys in slowly. Sometimes, Morrison is nicer than he seems. Today, for example, when Joe asked for the afternoon off, all Morrison said was, "Practice."

He meant *You're always going to have to practice,* which is what he always says. That, and *Life is not a watermelon.* Joe doesn't recognize the picture of the woman in the magazine. She seems wholesome and strangely unfamiliar; she looks as if she goes to church, or is about to have chidren with her husband, who also goes to church—a tall building with lots of bells and stained glass. She looks different than the women in the magazines Joe is more likely to browse through, like *Sports Illustrated, Car and Driver,* or *Vogue.* She looks as if she might be from Iowa, and she doesn't look at all like Edith, who is Catholic, and who Joe knows is the most beautiful girl he has ever seen. He has even seen a girl naked, taking a shower, who wasn't half as beautiful as Edith. Sometimes, he can't believe he even knows her. *Edith,* he'll tell himself, when he's not thinking. *Edith.*

Unlike the wrestling gym, which Morrison always keeps set in the nineties, the reception room feels cold and remarkably quiet. The vent overhead makes Joe shiver and wish he had something else to look at. When Spencer finally rolls through the door, the receptionist, dressed in a white uniform and blue cardigan, makes a sweet whistle.

"Hey, cutie," she says.

"Hi," Spencer says, waving. "I'm fine."

In his wheelchair, Spencer appears dwarfed, his arms thin as axle rods. He is pale, too, because he hasn't spent much time outside. Instead, he reads books. Recently Spencer has grown interested in space exploration. He sits in his room with animal wallpaper, reading his books, watching educational TV, which means no commercials or violence, and all day long Joe knows that Spencer is waiting for Joe to come home so they can do something. Spencer usually helps Mrs. Amato cook dinner, but that's not the same thing. Now, here in Dr. Ripley's office, sitting in his wheelchair and smiling at the receptionist, Spencer is holding on to his doll—a large stuffed moose. One of its legs is splinted by a tongue depressor.

"So," Joe says, "you get to go?"

"You betcha," he says, nodding. "Dr. Ripley says I need a tent." Nodding Mr. Moose's head, Spencer says, *Me too!*

Dr. Ripley wanders through the open door. Since the Jazinskis moved to Scottsdale, ten years ago, Dr. Ripley has given Joe three physicals and an occasional prescription for penicillin, during strep season, but Joe still feels uncomfortable around people you have to pay to make you feel better. Dr. Ripley is wearing his stethoscope and sneakers; he asks Joe if he's rooting for Chicago.

"Nah," Joe says, instantly wishing he were. Now Dr. Ripley will want to know what team he *is* rooting for, and Joe hasn't looked at a *Sports Illustrated* in months, since the last time he brought Spencer to see the doctor. Joe doesn't even know what sport they are talking about.

"Denver," Joe says. "Dad says Denver looks pretty good."

"Tell Brad to give me a call," Dr. Ripley says.

Sometimes, on weekends when he is home, Brad Jazinski will play racquetball with Dr. Ripley, and Joe wonders if this is why Dr. Ripley wants their father to give him a call. Before, Dr. Ripley and his wife would come over for dinner on weekends. After Joe's mother left, Dr. Ripley started prescribing lots of Valium, and Halcion, which Joe's father keeps in the cupboard by the kitchen plates and saltshaker. Joe thinks Dr. Ripley might want his father to call because he's got some new investment idea. Or maybe something is wrong with Spencer. Maybe something is wrong with the plate in his leg, or the screws—a loose screw coming out of the bone.

Joe used to think an accident—something which doesn't happen on purpose—might not be so bad: a cast, maybe, with lots of girls like Diana Vanderstock and Carol Cunningham asking about what happened, signing *Love Ya* above their names in loopy purple ink; they'd draw pictures of toes on the cast. But now, at his age, Joe's old enough to know what pain is really for. Accidents are only meaningful if you're young, a kid under nine or ten, or if they happen to someone else. When Walker Miller's mother killed herself, last year, it was the same thing. Everyone wanted to know all about it, and Walker said it was one of those things that just happen. It's a fact Joe understands not to mean really anything, except that maybe pain is something you're supposed to remember because of the way it hurts—ice held up against a sprain, or too much heat.

In the elevator, Spencer says, "Get ready, Mr. Moose!"

Ready! says Mr. Moose.

In Arizona, fourteen floors is considered excessive, almost like Chicago, and Joe knows they'll make this trip again and again because Spencer likes playing in elevators, and because this is *Fourteen whole floors!* . . . But now the doors are opening into the lobby; an old man is leaning against an ashtray, breathing. He is breathing through a tube in his nose, and an old woman—maybe his wife, or sister—is hanging on to his green oxygen tank and a travel atlas. Joe thinks they look lost. The woman's eyes are tired and sad.

Spencer holds up Mr. Moose, who says, *Lady with a baby. Make way!*

Outside, the weather is hot, the white parking lot hot enough for cooking sausage and eggs. Joe and Spencer like cereal, which is what they always eat. The air is still and dark—a final monsoon just now beginning to gather. By October, the weather is supposed to cool; in Arizona, a storm can last for days. Today the sky is heavy and close, *nimbus*—a new word Joe has learned in A.P. English, with Walker Miller, before he freaked out.

"Dr. Ripley's the coolest doctor in the world," Spencer says. "When I'm a doctor, I'm gonna be just like that. Cool."

"I thought you were going to be an astronaut."

"Yeah. Uh-huh. I am. Or president. By the time I'm a doctor, they'll need doctors and people in space, too. I'll have my operating room on the moon, where gravity's only one seventh of what it is here. On the moon you can play basketball even if you're fat."

Spencer is talking about Donald Bloomquist, his only friend, who is fat. When Spencer was hit by a car just two blocks from home, he was with Donald, who panicked and rode to his own house for help. Donald has short legs, and by the time he arrived home, he was out of breath. He had to use his blue asthma inhaler before he could get the words out.

Accident! There's been an accident!

Spencer was thrown onto a yard full of granite, where a brass sprinkler fitting nearly sliced off his ear. The sprinklers were running on an automatic timer; the bicycle, an orange-and-blue BMX, flew into a saguaro. The man driving the car began to move Spencer, but stopped, afraid of damaging what might already be broken: Spencer's neck, or his spine, which could truly have been broken—something slender and neatly snapped in half. The man stood in front of the sprinkler head, deflecting the water, trying to keep Spencer dry while waiting for someone to show up who knew what he was doing. He took off his shoe and slid it over the sprinkler head. When the ambulance arrived, the man was wearing one shoe and his pants were soaked. The paramedics lifted Spencer into the ambulance and drove away; Donald Bloomquist's mother, also fat, left a note on the Jazinskis' front door, another on the gate leading to the pool. In each note she explained that she didn't know Spencer's father's number at work, and in each note she explained where Spencer was—Scottsdale Memorial. Mrs. Amato had the day off, Brad Jazinski was in Buffalo, New York, and by the time Joe came home it was after midnight. In the driveway, asleep in his car, sat Donald Bloomquist's father. Mr. Bloomquist had recently lost eighty-three pounds on a special diet involving lots of grapefruit, which made him sleepy. The notes were still hanging where his wife had left them.

"He has a Corvette," Spencer says, meaning Dr. Ripley.

Joe's car is a modified General Motors station wagon formerly in the employ of Green and Pleasant Pastures, *The Friendliest Cemetery in the Entire Valley of the Sun!* Joe bought the hearse last year at an auction just after he passed his driving test. He had made only one mistake, in parallel parking, and his father had agreed to pay insurance; because Joe's grades are good, he received a ten-percent discount. The car is the color of gray primer because Joe has been fixing it up. His father calls this a *learning experience.* The front seat has a sheepskin cover, and the stereo has four speakers. On weekends, Joe parks in his father's spot in the garage, sanding off the paint with a power sander. Joe has been reading books about body repair, though his father wants him to be a broker, not a lawyer.

His mom writes either way, it's fine with her. Joe figures another month at the rate he's going and he can begin rebuilding the engine, if he wants to. He has no idea what that really means, to *rebuild an engine,* but it's something he wants to know how to do. Spencer tumbles into the front seat. Once inside, he powers down the window and begins going through the tapes, picking out the music, because he's *riding shotgun.* He's going by the pictures.

"How 'bout these guys!" he says, holding up a tape. The plastic case has been warped by the sun. In August, while visiting Walker Miller at the psycho ward, Joe left the case sitting on the dash.

"Sure," Joe says.

"Yeah?"

"Yeah, sure."

"Do you have any reggae?"

"Nope."

"Boy, Joe—everybody's got reggae."

"Not me," Joe says. He pulls the long car onto Indian School and says, "The fast way? Or the really fast way?"

"Dad says you should buy me ice cream and take me to the library. Mr. Moose wants to get some books."

"Is he hungry, too?"

"Nah," Spencer says, giggling. "Just me."

Spencer says that word, *Nah,* just like their father; they have all learned to speak the same way. Near Scottsdale Road, they pass Mr. Jazinski's office. His car is in the parking lot, where it usually is even when he's not there, because he takes a limo to the airport *in order not to drive.* Actually, Joe likes to drive, and today his father is going to Austin. Recently Joe's been spending a lot of time considering careers, and what he's supposed to do with the rest of his life if he wants to be successful. Walker Miller says he wants to be a rock star, and that he's going to change his name to Vic. Not to *Vic Miller,* or *Vic Walker,* or *Walker Vic Miller.* Just to *Vic.*

The public library, which is set in a park full of fountains and long white buildings, was designed by a guy who used to hang out with Frank Lloyd Wright. The grass is wet: the sprinklers are watering the lawns of the Department of Motor Vehicles and the community theater and the edges of all the long white sidewalks leading into the air-conditioned buildings. Inside the library, the volunteer women smile at Spencer. The women wear pink smocks and buttons that read SHHH! READERS AT WORK! Their job is to sort out all the heavy books and keep people silent.

Inside her glass office, where people are allowed to talk, sits Howie Bently's mother—LIBRARIAN OF ACQUISITIONS. The Bentlys live north of Shea, near Gold Dust High, and Howie is in Joe's A.P. English class, taught by Mr. Rolf the Drunk. A.P. English is for double credit, two years for two hours a day; each week they write a theme, and on Tuesdays Mr. Rolf tells them individually what's wrong with each theme. The themes have to be typed, and after the conference the theme has to be rewritten, and then typed all over again. Joe types with his fingers and uses his father's computer. "By the time you graduate," says Mr. Rolf, "only six of you shall remain." Mr. Rolf also says, "Everything that lives is holy." When Joe can't find anything good to write about, he trades ideas with Howie, and Mr. Rolf can always tell.

"He's a loon," Walker would whisper. "He's getting loony!"

Walker once wrote an essay about Iva Polanski, and it remains the only student essay Mr. Rolf has ever read aloud. Walker said later that there were too many details, and that parts were made up. Still, Mr. Rolf liked the details. "So many adjectives," he said, glowing. "So many possibilities!" This was just after Walker began to freak out. At the Safeway where he worked. People said he threw a shopping cart on top of a car, then he went inside and started throwing fruit at all the customers. Now, of course, it seems like a long time ago.

In her office, surrounded by glass walls, Mrs. Bently is reading a book that has pictures of lots of other books inside. Her eyeglasses are half-moons, the stems connected to a silver chain made by Indians. She doesn't look up. The volunteers are pushing away an empty cart, and Spencer is saying, "That way," pointing in the direction he wants to go. To the books on space.

Joe leaves him and wanders over to the magazines, which are mostly dull. After too many complaints, the library discontinued its subscriptions to photography magazines. Joe likes to look at naked women, even if they are only pictures. If he were a professional photographer, and not a lawyer, he could take all the pictures he wanted; he could take pictures of naked girls and have a good excuse to look. Edith would be beautiful, because that's what she is, *beautiful,* even if she is almost blind. Ms. Williams, the swim coach, used to pose nude for magazines. Joe likes to look through *Vogue,* especially the advertisements, but he knows he shouldn't be looking through a magazine like that. Everyone will think he is a pervert.

Joe strolls over to Mrs. Bently's window, knocks, and says, "Hi, Mrs. Bently."

She looks up and smiles, adjusting her glasses. She motions for him to step inside and says, "What, no practice today?"

"How's everything going?" he says. Her desk is full of papers. He wonders if she's really going to read them all. "I brought Spence," he says, explaining. "He likes to look at the space books."

"How's he feeling?"

"Oh, you know. Fine." It's the kind of question a mother would ask. After Walker Miller was institutionalized, in the spring, Joe became Howie Bently's best friend. Actually, Joe thinks, it's a question anyone might ask, but when it comes from a mother, it makes more sense. "Fine," he says to Mrs. Bently. "He wants to play basketball. On the moon."

Joe hasn't talked with his mother in over two years; he's not even sure anymore what she looks like. Walker Miller's mother killed herself in a Jacuzzi, and Joe's mother bought a new car and took a long drive. She said she was just going out to get her hair fixed. Now Walker Miller is in the psycho ward and Joe has no idea what he's supposed to say to anyone.

Mrs. Bently laughs, concerned, like a teacher. She asks Joe to have a seat. The chair is empty, pale blue, and Joe says he needs to get going, and he knows he's waiting for her to say something about Howie, about himself, about Walker Miller, who's coming home next week from the Superstition Mountain Care Facility . . . *Walker, Howie, and the Jazz* . . . but he's not sure what Mrs. Bently, a mother, is supposed to say next, except maybe *Yes, Walker's coming home soon, everything's going to be fine. Just wait and see. . . .* But it's not really working, and Joe thinks about Edith, his girlfriend, who is beautiful: she will be waiting for him in the parking lot, squinting at all the cars going by and looking for his, the long gray car with the rubbed-off paint, waiting for Joe to show up just on time, and now Spencer is wheeling in from behind, skidding, banging into the door. Joe steps aside to make way.

"Hiya, Mrs. Bently!"

"Hi, Spencer!"

On Spencer's lap sit three heavy books, and Mr. Moose on top, and now Spencer's looking all around the room, thinking. He's scratching at his ear, the one that had stitches, and says, "How big's the Grand Canyon."

It's a question, Joe thinks. It means he wants to know.

Edith . . .

Joe and Edith bought Mr. Moose the day after the accident. In July, on a Thursday, hotter than July: one hundred and fifteen degrees. They spent the afternoon at Fashion Square, inside the air-conditioning, squeezing stuffed animals in stores large enough to require escalators. Bears, dogs, ducks—Joe wanted to pick something out that people wouldn't think belonged to a wimp. At one store, he tossed a purple elephant across the aisle to Edith and hit her square in the face; her glasses skittered across the wooden floor, knocking loose a lens. Joe thought she had been looking, and he felt bad for a long time, and then they came across the moose . . . *Look, Joe. It's Mr. Moose!* . . . who had long flexible antlers, a green scarf and a thick leather nose. It was Edith's idea to give the moose a splint and to bandage one of the horns to look like Spencer's ear, which now had seven stitches; when Edith was in hospitals, she explained, that's what people did for her. Joe paid for the moose with his father's credit card, *for emergencies,* and on the way to the hospital they stopped at an optical store to fix Edith's glasses. At the hospital, they watched Spencer sleep. His body was full of fluids and drugs; he was still foggy from the anesthetic. Donald Bloomquist's mother had also come to visit, though she had left Donald at home to *think about what had happened.* Mrs. Bloomquist bought Joe and Edith ice cream sundaes in the cafeteria while they waited for Spencer to feel better, which Joe soon realized was going to take months. The night before, the doctors had talked to their father in Buffalo, New York, documents had been faxed back and forth, and Joe had learned about the special brace, and the ankle, which was also broken. But what Joe remembers most is watching his brother lying in a huge bed, swallowed up by all the blankets and sheets— the back of the bed elevated, the middle bent to accommodate the swollen leg and the loose gown and all the white sheets, like clouds—and knowing that Spencer has come this close. This close to disappearing completely, leaving behind only the bones, which eventually turn to dust. Even the sky is full of dust, and the quiet: the absolute quiet of the hospital, as if it were a church, or a grave. There was a window with a blue view and Edith put Mr. Moose in the crook of Spencer's arm, and Joe stood there, looking out at the view while Edith adjusted the doll. Standing there, looking out the window, he thought about snow and the way it used to look. In Chicago, and the way it could snow, and what it meant to really feel cold.

Six weeks after Spencer's accident, Walker Miller was moved to the Superstition Mountain Care Facility, and there the doctors permitted him to receive visitors, like a king, because he was coming along so nicely. The weather was cooler, but humid, now into the heart of the August monsoons. Joe and Edith and Howie took Joe's car and drove to Mesa and parked in a place for VISITORS.

Howie said, "That means we can leave when we want."

From outside, the hospital looked like a recently built hacienda. In front of the large wooden doors, Howie turned and pointed to Joe's hearse. "Hey," he said. "People may be getting the wrong idea."

Walker had never seen Joe's car; he'd been institutionalized that long. Once inside, they followed the signs. A man big enough to play football took their belongings, including a bag of pretzels and Edith's purse. His shoulders filled the doorways. They went past locked doors, down a hall with purple-and-orange walls, following the arrows painted onto the walls in cheerful colors. Inside one room, a woman was yelling at a man with a beard, saying the man was full of crap, what did he really know about pain? What did he really know about what it means to feel pain? Everyone wore normal clothes and Joe was uncertain just who the patients, those in pain, were supposed to be. Even the nurses looked as if they could have been in pain. People here were all alike, Joe thought. *Fucked up.*

"I can't believe it," Walker said, beaming. "I can't even believe it!"

They were standing in his room, looking out a window which held a view of the Superstitions. In the light they reminded Joe of the mountains in those books about hobbits and dwarves and men who rode galloping black horses. Walker's clothes lay scattered throughout the room. A hotel room, Joe thought. *Nobody's really meant to stay.* On the nightstand stood a jar full of quarters—

forty or fifty dollars' worth—and there was a painting of a saguaro in the moonlight, and now Walker was explaining that he was in the Adolescent Ward—drugs, alcohol, depression. Actually, this was the Razor Ward, which meant he was allowed only certain items: clothes, but no belts; soda pop, but no glasses. Only cans and paper cups.

"It's like they think I just can't wait to nuke myself," he said.

He was wearing shorts and a T-shirt, and his hair hadn't been washed in weeks; it hung down his face like long, wet grass. His face had broken out—his nose and forehead covered with blackheads—and he spoke frantically, the way people do when they live too long by themselves. He took pills three times a day to keep him level, he said, which made him kind of jittery.

"Especially when I get nervous," he said. "But don't worry, you guys don't make me nervous." He stopped, took a breath.

"Still, it's weird. I mean, I feel different. Every time, for example, I think I know what I'm going to do, I do something different." He kneeled on one leg to tie a purple shoelace and said, looking up, "Like when I look at the sky. I used to, you know, think I knew what I knew I'd think. But now I look up at the sky and I think, Wow, there's the sky, but I don't think about what I used to. I can't even remember what I used to think. I just know it's different."

He stood and laughed, differently than he used to, and said, "Want a Coke?"

They walked down a hall with more arrows pointing them into a room filled with Ping-Pong tables and pink vinyl couches. Inside the room was a bunch of fucked-up kids talking. Walker said, pointing to a Ping-Pong table, "I'm getting pretty good." He said, dropping quarters into the soda machine, "Coke, snow, blow . . . It's the new big deal. We learn a lot about it in Psychodrama."

"Psychodrama?"

"Yeah. You know, acting. Ryan says I got what it takes to be an actor. You know that? Me. An actor, that's a wrap. Take five."

Edith said, "You could be in the school play."

"I don't know, actually. I want to be a rock star. But Ryan

says it's how lots of actors get started, in Psychodrama, because what you do is act out your psyche. I mean, you think you're worried about the sky, or something, so you pretend you're the sky."

He looked out at the sky and said, "I'm the sky, you go, and I'm gonna fuck you over. The great thing about being here is you can cuss all you want. Even the doctors do it. The language of the soul, Ryan calls it. Cuss cuss cuss, so cuss, okay, the sky, that's me—I'm full of lightning and wind, I'm bigger than you, than anything you've ever felt, and Ryan says, 'Yeah, yeah. Go with it, Walker. Tell me how you really *feel*!'" He looked at his feet, which were huge.

They took their Cokes and walked outside onto the hot lawn. Walker said, "I'm talking a lot, aren't I?"

"No," Edith said. "It's interesting. Really." She was squinting, because she had new contacts, and she still wasn't used to them. Sometimes, she'd grab Joe's arm and lean real close.

"Who's that?" Howie asked, looking at a girl. She had yellow shaved hair.

"They think I'm nuts 'cause of my mother," Walker said. "I tell 'em my mother was nuts. Not me. She's the loon downtown."

"When do you get out?" Joe asked.

"Out? I don't know. The thing about your psyche is you never get out. You've got to live with it. You've got to learn to clean your own garage."

"No," Edith said. "When can you go home?"

"I know, I know. Home home home. Yeah. But don't you see? You never get home. Home is where the psyche lies. That's home. Here," he said, pointing to his temple. "Here, with all the drama."

The girl with yellow shaved hair, wearing torn jeans and a flannel shirt tied at the waist, walked across the grass. You could see her navel, and her sleeves were rolled up, and on her arms were tattoos—they looked like lizards. Her shirt was buttoned low, and it was big; it was Walker's shirt, Joe knew, and you could see sweat rolling down the center of her chest. On her chest was a green-and-red lizard burrowing inside of her, and when she leaned over to light a cigarette, Joe realized that if he kept looking, then he was going to see an entire breast—and the dark part, there in the center.

"Hi," she said, putting out her match, sitting down on the grass. "I'm Cathy. Are these your friends, Walker?"

"Yeah," Walker said. "My friends. Decided to come down and see the nuthouse. The bonkers gone bonked. All that."

"We're not really bonkers," Cathy said. "We're perplexed. Walker's disturbed about the sky." She let out a stream of smoke and looked like an intellectual. She said, "He thinks his mother's in it."

"I never said that."

"Oh, he doesn't need to. It all comes out in the wash, you know. I'm Cathy," she said, turning to Edith and holding out her hand. "Cathy. With a C."

Cathy leaned again, and Joe saw it, by accident. It was pink and tender, swollen. He knew she had wanted him to see it.

"Hi," Edith said, squinting.

"I'm from Cleveland, really," Cathy said. "But not anymore." She turned to Joe and said, "So how do you like the place?"

"I don't know," Joe said. He could see Howie looking down her shirt, smiling. "It seems nice."

"Do you get much free time?" Howie asked, smiling.

This time Joe didn't look. He wondered if Walker knew that she was doing this, if she was showing off her tattoos or her body or if she just wanted to embarrass them.

Walker reached over and put his finger on her chest. "Cathy likes lizards," he said, touching it. "Pretty weird, if you ask me."

"Actually," she said, "we get lots of time. Like today. Meal time, social time, talk time, doctor time. We have just as much time as anybody else. Twenty-four hours a day, same as anybody." She held Walker's hand, which was still touching her chest, and smiled. "I used to have this iguana. When I was a kid. His name was Ig."

"Ig," Walker said, nodding.

"Yeah, kind of short for iguana. Walker thinks they're going to send him home soon."

"Yeah?" said Howie.

"Yeah," Walker said. "Pretty soon. Depends I guess on what my dad says. Sometimes it's really hard to concentrate."

Cathy pointed to Walker's watch, the one his mother had given him just before she died. She explained that he was able to wear it now because he had confronted his pain.

"I never used to wear it," Walker said. "It has my name on the back and everything."

And now Cathy was telling stories about Cleveland and Des Moines and, later, L.A.; she'd been almost everywhere, at least by Ohio standards, and she told them more stories than they could possibly remember. After a while, Cathy left to find a nurse . . . *medication time* . . . and they all rose and left their spot on the grass and began walking across the lawn toward the main corridor. The football player was keeping an eye on things, and it was too hot outside in the sun, anyway. Their Cokes had turned warm as coffee. Walker was going slowly now, stretching out the visit, kicking at the grass with his sneakers. Size thirteen, for really big feet.

"Don't let them fool you guys," Walker said softly. "The folks here are weird. Cathy, she's weird. She's a loon, I'll tell you. I could tell you stories about those lizards . . . but that's unsupportive. Everything here's supportive. It's like family, you see. As long as you're here, you're supposed to be supportive. But yeah, things here are pretty out of whack."

"We should go," Joe said. "Edith has practice."

"I kind of like it, really. It's not bad, I mean." He shoved his hand into his pocket, reaching for more quarters. "You guys want another Coke?"

"No thanks."

"Yeah. Yeah yeah. Ms. Williams says she's going to come visit. She even sent me a card. Tell her I said hi, okay?"

"Okay," Joe said.

"Yeah," Edith said. "Sure, Walker."

"And Mr. Rolf. He still senile?"

"Walker," Howie said. "You should do what they say, you know? You should get yourself cured and get the hell out of here."

Outside, on the way to the car, Edith carried her purse and the pretzels they had brought. They all sat in the front seat of Joe's car and Howie turned on the radio. The tape case had melted in the sun. Joe drove fast, to show what the car could really do even if the engine might need to be rebuilt. He never did tell Walker about his car, and he remembered wanting to, and by the time he thought of something to say, driving, listening to the radio, they were almost at school and a conversation would have taken too long to say anything. Instead, it was easier to let it go. To listen to the radio and to think about the weather, which was hot—late August, when you knew fall was on the way and everything was going to cool down in October. You could leave things on your dash and everything was going to be like starting over, the way it did every year, like school, or sports, or something else you didn't have to think very hard about. In the parking lot, Howie said good-bye and sprinted off across the asphalt. Sitting there in the car, the engine idling, Joe took Edith's hand and held it. Her knuckles were smooth as stones.

"Joe," she said, blinking. "What were those things on her arms?"

"Tattoos," he said. "Probably fake."

"Oh. I'm gonna be late."

When she kissed him unexpectedly, he let her go.

On the day they picked out Mr. Moose, the day it was one hundred and fifteen degrees, Edith explained to Joe that zero degrees was what you always started with. She'd learned about it in Chemistry, from Mr. Horn, who always dressed like a nerd; she explained that to get to *zero,* you had to mix snow with salt, because the two things together were what made Fahrenheit, which was also the name of the guy who invented temperature. It seemed weird, *snow and salt,* but it almost made sense, too, and it was the first time that she had ever done that: kissed him without any special reason. Just reaching over and doing it, without her glasses brushing up against his eye because now she's wearing contacts.

After ice cream, Joe drives Spencer home. Spencer ordered a Tin Roof, his favorite, and now his stomach is full, swollen like a pregnant lady, and Spencer keeps thumping himself on the way home, saying, "I ate too much. Boy." Joe laughs, the first time, because he hasn't eaten anything. He's still trying to cut weight; next month, Morrison wants him to wrestle at 145. Joe's stomach feels empty and full of acid, and he can feel the acid, eating away, making him all the more lean, while Spencer keeps thumping his stomach and talking, playing with the power window, until Joe finally stops listening. He knows that Spencer wants someone to talk to, but what do you talk about with a nine-year-old kid? Joe can't think of anything, and for a while he feels bad. Sometimes, if he makes himself feel bad for long enough, he can actually make himself feel better. It's a peculiar experience.

Faster, says Mr. Moose. *I want you to go faster!*

At home, Spencer wants to play pool.

"I have to go," Joe says.

"Nah, come on. Just one. Five whole dollars!"

"You don't have five whole dollars."

"Dad does."

"A quick one. I win, you have to help sand."

Joe's planning to work on the car Saturday, and he knows Spencer is going to help anyway. Friday there's a dance, the Halloween dance, but Joe has never been to a dance, and he knows Edith wants to go, and he still hasn't told her anything. He thinks that if he goes to the dance, he'll make a fool of himself, either because he won't dance, which he won't because he doesn't know how, or because he will dance, and if he does that then he will truly make a fool of himself.

Joe picks up his cue and tells Spencer to *rack 'em* while he turns on MTV. There's a commercial selling shoes and physical fitness, and then someone is on, singing. Dancing, too, of course, because you can't sing if you can't dance. If Walker Miller is really going to be a rock star, he's going to have to learn some moves; he'll have to take some lessons and grow his hair long and get some tattoos. Joe watches the dancing woman to see if she is really singing. You can't fake the dancing part, anybody can lip-sync, and sometimes it all looks so fake—these people pretending to mean something they really don't. Or the way they pretend to be pissed off—angry, as if being angry made you strong.

Definitely, Joe thinks. The woman on the TV is faking it.

On the break, Joe sinks two stripes, then cleans away two more; Spencer doesn't stand a chance. Joe steps out of the way while Spencer wheels up his chair, aiming, the cue a rifle about to go off anywhere. Spencer misses the cue the first time, and Joe says, "Okay, try again," which Spencer does. This time, Spencer hits the ball, and it rolls slowly across the table. In law school their father used to hustle on weekends for cash, he's that good. He worked in steel mills. He's shot pool almost everywhere, and their mom used to call him "Chubs" . . . *Chubs Jazinski* . . . he's so skinny, and even now that she's gone, no one is allowed to use his cue.

"Chubs," she would say, "when are you going to go on TV?"

The woman on the TV is still singing in her underwear. That night, when Joe came home and found Mr. Bloomquist in the driveway, asleep at the wheel, Joe knew it was something bad. He thought something bad had happened to their father, and when Mr. Bloomquist said, rubbing the sleep out of his face, "Spencer, he's had an accident," Joe wasn't sure whom to call. He thought first about Spencer, peeing in his pants, which he did sometimes when he laughed too hard . . . *He's had an accident* . . . *Well?* . . . and his father was in Miami, or Buffalo, he couldn't remember, and Joe called the hospital and gave a nurse the phone numbers his father had left on the refrigerator. He called his father's hotel, which was in Buffalo, and then he called Howie and asked him to come over and wait for messages. Bad news, wait by the phone. Then Joe drove to the hospital in his father's car because this wasn't a normal week, because his father had left his car at home and this car had a telephone inside, and because this was an emergency. He'd never driven his father's car beyond the driveway. Spencer had to have surgery. In the hospital parking lot, he tried to call Edith.

"Don't you know what time it is?" her father said.

"It's Joe," Joe said. "I'm sorry—"

"Look, Joe. It's late. Call me at work. Tomorrow. Okay, Joe?"

Across the parking lot, Joe could see two men being led through the doors by cops. One of the men had blood pouring down his face, and in his skin were pieces of glass, glinting under the lights.

"I want to talk to Edith," Joe said. "Not you."

"Joe who?"

"Joe Jazinski. I'm sorry—"

"Sorry. Sorry. Indeed, I believe you are. Thing is, it's late, Joe. Why don't you give Edie a call tomorrow? During business hours. That's a boy," Edith's father said, and then he hung up the phone.

Joe sat in his father's car looking at the phone. He had only met Edith's father once, and he suddenly realized that he didn't know anything at all about her. He went into the lobby of the waiting room and stood by the telephone. He felt stupid and decided that he would never call her again. He could hear the cops flirting with nurses. On the couch he read through the magazines, waiting, and when Howie came in, explaining that his mother was watching the phone, taking messages, explaining that this was where the action was . . . *Here* . . . in a room full of people having emergencies, he asked Joe if he wanted to go for a quick ride in Mr. Bently's car. The car was still new, and Joe said, "Later," and when he woke up, Howie was sound asleep. Joe's father was on a flight to Phoenix and Spencer was out of imminent danger. By the time Joe got home, Edith had left seven messages on the answering machine, and he was tired. He was really, really tired. It was something he'd never felt before.

Imminent danger is where you end up when you're not paying attention; it's when you have to start bridging if you're not going to let yourself be pinned. Now, looking at the pool table, aiming, Joe scratches the cue on the eight, on purpose, because one of the rules of Chubs Jazinski is never to win unless you absolutely need to. Only their mom ever called him Chubs.

"I got to go, Spence," Joe says, and he knows something is wrong—a sadness, deep and uncomfortable, the aches he gets in his legs at night . . . *growing pains*. The kind deep in the bone, when you know it hurts because the bone is still growing. Stretching and making a noise, which is the pain you feel in the middle of the night that goes so deep into the bone. This is what that really means . . . *growing pains* . . . and at night, when the weather is changing fast, Spencer gets sinus headaches; he'll get a headache and cry for hours until he falls asleep. Now Spencer is wheeling across the carpet, and Joe thinks his brother is going to be picked on for the rest of his life. He thinks his brother needs to get outside and that he needs more muscle.

Practice, Morrison will say. *You've got to practice!*

"I win!" Spencer says, pointing with his cue. "I get to help."

Last year, sometimes, instead of hanging out with Donald Bloomquist, the fat kid, Spencer would come home from school and go to his room. There, he'd play with his Legos and sing with the radio, and Joe could hear it sometimes, coming down the hall, and he knew this meant that Donald Bloomquist had gone home, or to the doctor to take his allergy shots, and he knew that it was only a matter of time before Spencer would come down the hall with a newly constructed helicopter or moon truck and start asking questions or explaining. Joe knew Spencer was thinking about their mom, who left to get her hair fixed, and he wanted to tell Spencer it's no big deal. Cope, he wanted to say. *Happens all the time* . . . and he wanted to tell Spencer what their father once told him, outside, by the swimming pool: *In the end, you're all you've ever got.* The sun was setting, burning up the sky, and Joe knows that this is something true, and he has proven it true on the mats when the air in the gym is full of his name . . . *Jazz! Jazz! Jazz!* . . . and he knows that if he wants to, that if he really wants to, then he can just break this guy's neck, just snap it in half. Or alone, even, lifting, all by himself with just him and the weight and watching it move. He knows that this is true, and he wants Spencer to let him go. Read a book, he wants to say. Watch Madonna, but I got to go.

"Spence," he says, "I really gotta go."

Mr. Rolf, the Drunk, and assistant swim coach, once told a story to his A.P. English class. He told the story in the third person, meaning *impersonally,* and it's the only time Mr. Rolf has ever said anything about himself. It was a story about how his son had died in a boating accident and how Mr. Rolf used to be a man who loved the sea. Mr. Rolf was a professor, at a real college, and he loved the sea. Then his son died in a boating accident, and Mr. Rolf's wife decided to hate Mr. Rolf because he had loved the sea, and now Mr. Rolf lived alone in Phoenix, Arizona, where there was no sea. "He is," Mr. Rolf said, in the third person, "a man still clearly possessed," and then he smiled, sadly, and Joe realized Mr. Rolf knew more than he was telling. Then Mr. Rolf kicked at his chair, yanked on his beard and announced, "Now you must write me a theme! You must write me the theme of your lives!"

Joe drives to school. The sun is setting now, turning the sky purple and orange behind him, *west,* in the rearview mirror. The sky is filling up the back of the hearse with light. In the parking lot nearest the gym are faculty cars, which are always older and more damaged than the students' cars. Joe parks in the space marked HANDICAPPED. Sometimes, Roxanne the Retard's mother parks her car there, because Roxanne is retarded. Roxanne carries a tape recorder everywhere she goes; she's practicing to be a journalist and is always asking people questions. A journalist is something Joe doesn't think he wants to be, and now, when he steps out of his hearse, he sees Mrs. Fullerton and Mr. Langousis, both frowning at him. Joe looks back at his car, then at the sign for Roxanne.

HANDICAPPED.

He looks back at the teachers. Maybe they think if they frown long enough, he will move his car without having to be asked. Mrs. Fullerton teaches Government and Economics, both required by the state for graduation. Personally, Joe doesn't think Mrs. Fullerton knows very much about Economics. She is haggard and full of wrinkles, and if Joe misses one more class, or is tardy for three and a half more classes, then he will fail Economics.

"Economics," Mrs. Fullerton says often, "is the study of our economy."

Deciding, Joe reaches for his hip and moans loudly. Behind Mrs. Fullerton he can see Morrison, sitting in his office, watching. Joe moans again and says, "It's bad. It's really, really bad."

Mr. Langousis, who teaches Life Science, says, "Jazinski, you can't park there. How would it be if everyone who got a sore leg parked there? What would happen to all the people with really sore legs?"

Mr. Rolf, Joe knows, would call this a *rhetorical question.* Joe has never had a class with Mr. Langousis, but he does seem unnecessarily friendly with Mrs. Fullerton. Joe falls onto the grass, screaming. In the distance, he can see the long cement ramp leading up to the second floor, and a group of students is beginning to form—freshmen, mostly, waiting for their rides.

"What's wrong with the Jazz?" says Mitchell Hemly, a gay kid with lots of acne Joe has been nice to because Edith likes him. "He okay?"

"Get up, Jazinski," says Mrs. Fullerton. "Stop doing that right now!"

And now Morrison is running across the lawn. He's standing over Joe, saying, "Easy, Jazz . . . Easy," and he's squeezing at his hip like a doctor. His hands know just where to go.

Morrison winks, and Joe is biting hard at his lip. Morrison helps Joe to his feet and says to Mr. Langousis, "McGregor slammed him yesterday. Bad."

Morrison's shaking his head, slowly, and now Joe is moaning again, saying, "Oh, Coach. Does this mean the Novocain? God, can't we try the whirlpool first?"

"He still can't park there," says Mrs. Fullerton. "He's not permanently disabled!"

Joe moans. "Coach, I can't stand it!"

"Maybe just this once," says Mr. Langousis.

"For the team, Andre."

"Someone could always move it for him," says Mrs. Fullerton. "Why does he have to drive that kind of car? It's disrespectful!"

But now they are moving toward the gym, and Joe is limping badly and beginning to scream all over again. Before they reach the main door, he falls to the ground. He does this a second time, only now he is laughing, saying, "Oh, God, not the knife! I can't have surgery!" and they can hear everyone else laughing, and Mrs. Fullerton and Mr. Langousis are still standing there on the sidewalk, together, staring at Joe's car.

Inside the gym, Joe and Morrison listen to the wrestlers running laps.

"Stairs," Morrison says, pointing to the ceiling.

"What about my leg?"

"You got to practice," Morrison says. "Give me sixty."

Novocain in the bone is the same as in your teeth, only more acute; it's the kind of pain the body is likely to remember. Joe had it once in his ankle, before a match with Phoenix Union, after he had bruised it playing Frisbee. "I'll break him down fast," Joe told Dr. Ripley. "Once we're on the mat, who cares about my ankle?" Dr. Ripley thought it would be okay *just this once*. He stuck the needle into Joe's foot. The needle was long as a fresh pencil with an eraser, and Joe could feel it going through the muscle of his foot, and he wanted to scream, though of course he did not do that. Later, he couldn't feel a thing, not his entire foot, and when Morrison taped him up, he threatened to throw Joe off the team. Even then, Joe knew Morrison was just pretending. This was during Joe's sophomore year, when Joe was just starting to realize how good he could really be. Once, he even wrote a theme about it—wrestling, and the Novocain—for Mr. Rolf, and Mr. Rolf wrote back, after marking all the grammar, *The severe nature of the pain is neither fully explored nor adequately realized. Try again.*

In the locker room, Joe weighs himself in, as Morrison says, *buck naked*—149. Joe's not sure where the remaining four pounds are supposed to come from. The only excess weight on his body seems to sprout from loins; his cock feels swollen and necessary. He tucks himself into his running shorts and pretends to ignore the feeling—the cold skin of his hand on his cock, because if he thinks about it, he'll get a hard-on, and the locker room is not the place for hard-ons. Still, just thinking about trying not to think about it initiates the ache, the swelling in his stomach spreading up into the chest. He has three hairs on his chest . . . *Only three?* . . . and the locker room is filling up with wrestlers finishing their laps, and now Joe is trying to think about his feet—the way they feel here on the cold, wet tile.

"Yo, Jazz," calls McGregor. "Stroking it?"

McGregor weighs in at 193. After a workout on the mats, his skin is livid.

Joe says, "Fuck you." He stretches his calves. He puts on his sweats, and then his vinyls; he laces up his running shoes. Morrison won't allow stairs in wrestling shoes. "It kills the shins," he says. Joe grabs his headgear, because with the headgear on, even his ears will sweat.

On the way out he passes Howie Bently. Howie is guiding two exhausted freshmen into the locker room, his hands behind their shoulders, steering them through the wooden doors. "How's Spence?" Howie says.

" 'Kay. Coach wants me to do some stairs."

"I'm Howie," Howie says. "I know everything."

A sophomore, Colin Houston, is on the scale. Everyone knows that after Joe graduates, Houston will be the next hotshot. Houston is on the scale, adjusting the weights, saying, "I fuck like a buck," and slapping the cheeks of his ass.

Morrison comes through the door. "Houston!" he yells. "Keep Jazz honest."

"Coach!"

"Somebody's got to," Morrison says, almost smiling, but not quite. He looks at Joe and says, "What are you waiting for, hipster?"

Outside the locker room, Joe heads for the first flight, which leads to the wrestling gym, across from the observation deck of the pool, where Edith is working out with the swim team. Houston, wearing only sneakers and shorts, joins Joe by the third lap. On the twelfth, Edith is floating near the side of the pool, looking right up at them, though Joe knows she can't possibly see who they are. Just two wrestlers running stairs. Joe feels like calling out, saying *Hi!* . . . But the feeling drifts: he likes being around Edith without her knowing; sometimes, she looks different, almost sad. By lap forty, he's feeling spent, and Houston is setting the pace. They take the stairs three at a time going up, they sprint through the mats in the wrestling gym, across the bleachers over the pool, and on the way down they lift themselves on the banisters, floating down the stairs—using their arms, saving the legs. In the basketball gym, they do a slow jog, preparing for the next climb. Every half lap or so, Joe opens the sleeves of his jersey, allowing the sweat to drain out. It falls onto the floor in puddles. The pool is empty now; Edith has gone inside to shower, where girls shower, *naked,* and Joe knows she'll be waiting for him outside with Howie, by the car, maybe, talking with Ms. Williams. There won't be enough light for Edith to read by; and it's getting late, Morrison's in his office, brooding, looking over the cool lawn, the long cement ramp cutting across the grass; he's making up the roster. Edith and Howie are sitting on the hood of the hearse, maybe, and at home Spencer is reading a book full of pictures describing the Grand Canyon, and the moon, singing to himself, dreaming of pizza and Oreos and Joe is feeling fine: his heart is full of blood, and pumping: he's got his second wind. Houston falls behind and Joe laps him, fast, and now while he's sprinting, flying over the soft rubber mats, he trips himself up—his body coming down hard, slamming the mat. He lifts himself up, looks around the empty room, hitching his breath. The room feels hot enough to die in.

Morrison isn't in his office. Except for a stray shower, the locker room is quiet; the room smells of sweat and disinfectant. In the main gym, Houston is standing by the door, looking outside where people in summer clothes are gathering on the lawn. It's so much hotter than it's supposed to be.

"What?" says Joe.

"Oh, man," says Houston, not moving, just leaning against the door. "Oh, man."

Outside, Joe can hear voices screaming.

Call an ambulance!

It's Morrison, and now Houston turns and sprints into the office. Ms. Williams is on her knees, in front of a body, screaming *Get away! Get away!* and Morrison is trying to push people out of the way, swimmers and wrestlers, but the people keep coming on. Mr. Rolf is standing still, looking at the sky, weeping, and the people keep coming out of buildings and cars, and Ms. Williams keeps screaming.

"He's wasted," says McGregor, pointing.

"Who?"

"Miller, the crazy fuck. That's who."

"For Christ's sake!" Ms. Williams screams. "You do not want to see this!"

And now Joe sees it, the body and parts behind Ms. Williams. There is no face, just muscle and blood and bone, but he recognizes the shirt—a large flannel shirt, and the sneakers, and there are quarters falling from the pockets. Dollars' and dollars' worth of quarters, and Ms. Williams is screaming and Morrison is pushing people away. All these people and all these bodies and Joe needs air, his head is swimming, his knees weak and in need of collapse. He's holding on to his headgear and Ms. Williams's blouse is covered with blood, she's covering the bad parts with a towel, a bright yellow towel mopping up the blood . . . and her swimsuit, falling onto the grass. It's blue and has green stripes, and an ambulance is driving across the lawn, and now the cruisers are coming, driving through the lot, past Joe's car, past the shop building and Joe can feel the sweat dripping from his vinyls, the wind blowing in from behind and making the sweat freeze even though it's so hot he can't even breathe, and he's thinking that never before has he understood the meaning of so many lights. He's sitting on his heels, head between his knees, reaching for air. The sky is full of lights and air, and somewhere, somewhere he knows that Edith is nearby, and now he feels himself lifting. He is lifting himself up and walking through the air and he is listening to all the voices.

Edith . . . Oh God, Edith.

What I Look Like; What I Taste Like in Your Mouth

What frightens her is knowing. Walker Miller, before he killed himself, attended Gold Dust High. He was seventeen years old, and he killed himself, and she knows what it looked like.

Her eyesight is deficient, a birth defect, *toxoplasmosis*, caused by a parasite that entered her eyes through the placenta, encouraging them to frost: her vision is perpetually distorted by small patches of white. To see anything, she must first try to see around the edges of her blindness. The left eye is clearer than the right, which compensates and aches from excessive strain; and she has grown, she tells herself, to live with this: what she sees is what there is. Meanwhile, her vision continues to improve; after a while, a little bit slowly becomes clearer. When she was five, her ophthalmologist prescribed eyeglasses heavy as a book and exploratory surgery. Later, in junior high, another ophthalmologist dramatically modified her prescription. And last spring, while Walker Miller was beginning to freak out, she had more surgery to strengthen the muscles in her right eye, the one that wanders. For two months she looked as if she had drifted into dangerous territory—South Phoenix, or Detroit; she looked as if she'd been punched a dozen times in the very same place. She cried often, because she felt ugly, and blind, and finally she stopped crying when she realized it wasn't ever going to change anything. Weeks passed, and her face grew increasingly less swollen and sore, and eventually, she understood that she could see more now than she had ever thought possible. And it frightened her, the world unfolding, and all the things that she was going to see.

Now she can even wear contacts three times a week. Today in A.P. History, Mr. Nadolny is discussing *the Age of Brinkmanship*. Written up on the board, though she can't possibly see it, is the phrase MORE BANG FOR THE BUCK, which means, Mr. Nadolny has explained, that it is less expensive to make a bomb than it is to make an army.

And why is that important in a democracy?

"Communism is not the enemy," says Mr. Nadolny. "The enemy is us. This is the Decade of Momentum."

Even Mr. Rolf might agree; it would make a good theme, maybe: *The Decade of Momentum*. Nobody is writing down what Mr. Nadolny has said. Not a word, because the bell is about to go, and everybody knows it won't be on the next test anyway. Meanwhile, the climate control has gone haywire and the entire school is freezing. At the bell, the class gathers itself and rushes into the hallway, and Mr. Nadolny is standing behind his desk, thinking all alone. In the hallway, Mitchell Hemly is going the wrong way, holding his books in front of his crotch, looking at the ground, shuffling. Usually, Edith worries about Mitchell Hemly asking her out, and having to say no, and now she's hugging her books, thinking about that: *momentum,* and where it takes you; or *adrenaline,* which is supposed to do the same thing. The hall is full of people, most of whom say hello, to which she always says something back even though she's not always sure exactly whom she's talking to. Sometimes she can tell by the voices, or by the shapes some people make. Howie Bently is tall, and he uses his knees when he walks, and Joe is short and square, his muscles stiff as trees. She sees them in front of her now—Howie, bouncing, and Joe, who *saunters*—they are a slow blur of nice colors, and she can tell who they are by the way they walk, and by the way people move to get out of their way.

She's walking with Carol Cunningham, her best friend, and near the gymnasium, Roxanne, the retarded girl, is holding out her tape recorder. She's asking people questions about cucumbers and broccoli; vegetables, Edith thinks. Carol steers them away, and Edith can make out Roxanne, talking into her machine, making notes because nobody is talking to her. Finally, once released into the enormous gymnasium, which smells like basketballs and apples, the congestion begins to thin. People are rising into the bleachers, and Carol is reaching for Edith's arm, saying, "Where?"

Edith knows that Joe and Howie will sit with the wrestlers, but she doesn't know if Joe wants her to sit with them. Edith has a note she has written to Joe in her pocket, and she reminds herself to slide it inside his locker after assembly. Carol Cunningham has been Edith's best friend since Edith transferred in. Last spring, after Edith's surgery, while Edith was lying in bed, with the lights out, crying, Carol had sex for the first time. Carol is the only girl with red hair Edith has ever known; at first, Edith didn't think Carol would even like her. Carol's hair reaches all the way down her spine and never seems to look heavy, or hot, though Edith knows it's both. During swim practice, Carol has to tie it up in a knot, and still it weighs her down. Even so, it's beautiful. Beautiful and long. Sometimes Edith wonders why Joe doesn't like her instead.

"There," Edith says, pointing. She has no idea where she is pointing, but she can hear Roxanne talking, and it makes Edith feel bad—standing so close to somebody whose feelings are always being hurt, especially when that person is retarded.

Edith follows Carol and they climb three rows of bleachers; they end up sitting next to some freshmen boys, maybe sophomores, but if they are sophomores, no one knows who they really are. One of the boys has a calculator, he probably gets beat up a lot, and she wants to say *Hi* to him so he'll stop being so nervous, and because she is sitting right beside him, but then she thinks she'll probably just make him more nervous. When boys get nervous, they sweat vinegar and ammonia and break out.

"This is all about Walker," Carol says.

"What?" Edith says.

"The assembly. They don't want us to think he did the right thing. They want us to think it was a tragedy."

"Tragedy involves choice," Edith says. It's something Mr. Rolf always says. She says, "It was stupid. It was stupid and now everybody knows it."

"He was an asshole!" says the boy sitting next to Edith. "A real dick!"

When Mr. Buckner taps on the microphone, a group of guys yell, "It's working!"

"What?" says Mr. Buckner, meaning he knows exactly who they are.

Even if Mr. Buckner does try to be friendly, he expels people all the time; his voice is suddenly louder than the gym. Sitting in chairs behind the lectern are a woman, Ms. Williams; Mrs. Henderson, the nurse, who's wearing white clothes; and Ms. Owens, who is young enough to look like Edith. Ms. Owens wears jeans and does college placement advising, and Mr. Buckner never wears a suit. He wears light green pants and an aloha shirt because he used to live in the Bahamas. Also, he wants to show he's friendly. When people wear the right clothes, they think they'll fit in, even if the clothes don't fit. Edith thinks everything about this is entirely wrong. She thinks she is going to be sick.

"You guys have something to say?" Mr. Buckner says.

The assembly waits, and now Mr. Buckner is clearing his throat, sounding sad, and explaining, talking about lots of things, indirectly, like parents, explaining . . . *that recently a tragedy has struck the lives of all* . . . and now Edith is standing, trying to make her way down the bleachers, because tragedy involves choice, and because she doesn't want to be here and have to listen to all this. She should have never worn this skirt, the guys in front are turning now, she's moving down the steps, gingerly, careful to land on each step and knowing that at any moment she could be falling down the rest, down all the steps into the middle of the gym. Once on the floor, the pretty wooden floor with blue lines, she begins to walk along the edges of the gym, in front of the bleachers, hugging her books, and now she stops. She stops and looks at where Mr. Buckner is supposed to be standing in front of a microphone: from this distance, she knows he knows who she is. Even if his voice has stopped, he knows who she is . . . *Edith McCaw, the girl who saw everything* . . . and now when she begins to run, running toward the light which will eventually read EXIT, she knows that she is crying. She is crying, and scared, and all she can hear are the sounds of her feet, and her voice, crying, and lifting her across the still, wooden floor.

What she wants to feel is warm. Instead, she holds herself over the toilet, retching. When she feels herself finally empty, she flushes. She sits on the floor, her hands gathering the folds of her skirt, shivering. On the door of the bathroom stall, in thick, wide letters, she reads WALKER MILLER LIVES!

The bathroom door opens; she hears a voice. "Edith? Are you in here?"

"In here."

She can make out the pumps, beneath the stall door, which is shaking. She reaches up to flip the latch and Ms. Williams steps inside.

"Oh, Edith! Are you okay?"

She's crying again, even if she doesn't mean to; sometimes, there's just no way to stop, like running downhill, or getting sick in the first place. Her mouth tastes like vomit. She wipes at her mouth, looks for her glasses and stares up at Ms. Williams. When you have Ms. Williams for three or more classes, or are on the swim team, you get to call her Jenna. Now Jenna is leaning down, facing her, wiping Edith's cheek.

"Can you stand?"

"He was supposed to be okay," Edith says. "And nobody knows why!"

She wraps her arms around Jenna, crying. Jenna's sweater is full of perfume, and now Jenna is on her knees, holding her. Edith can feel her teacher's arms, which she knows are strong; Edith knows it's not her fault. *It's not my fault* . . . and her mom, who doesn't understand, says it's not Edith's fault. If she tells herself she wants to, she knows she will stop crying, because faults are where earthquakes come from, in San Francisco, and nobody knows how they even got there. She stops now . . . *for good.*

Standing, she goes to the sink. Together they are rinsing her face, like sisters. Edith wishes she had a sister. It's something she's never known she's wanted, and the water is ice, she can't stop shivering, even if it's not that cold.

"Rinse your mouth," Jenna says. "There. Feel better?"

"No."

Jenna reaches into her pocket, a big pocket on the side of her dress, and hands Edith her glasses. "Let me run you home," she says.

Outside, by the parking lot, the desert is cool and recently rinsed; not a storm, not yet, just a rinse for now to cool things off. Even so, the temperature has dropped twenty-seven degrees in less than twenty-four hours. Her father says it's because of the environment that everything . . . *the weather?* . . . is so extreme: drought in California and Georgia; fires in Wyoming; tornadoes in Illinois, and hurricanes blowing off the coast of everywhere. Ten years, he says, and things are really going to start to burn. Right now, the skies over Mummy Mountain are swollen and bruised, and the parking lot is full of sad gray water. Edith's shoes are soaked, and as she and Jenna pass Joe's car in the parking lot, Edith remembers her note and tucks it beneath a windshield wiper. The note says, *Have a great day. I can do anything tomorrow* . . . and she has signed it with a heart, in purple ink, and her initials, *EM.* She has never used the word *love* in any of her notes to Joe, only her parents call her *Edie,* and she didn't want to seem pushy about the dance since Joe's never brought it up. She thinks Walker Miller is dead, and now they may never talk about it; she thinks her skin has been drained of all its blood, that's why she feels so cold. Her skin feels exactly like the sky.

Selfish.

Jenna drives a small blue car. On the third try, it starts. "We'll need to wait a moment," Jenna says, looking through the windshield. "It sure is chilly. Thin blood," she says, laughing. "My blood keeps thinning out with all this heat. When it gets cold, I swear my body goes into shock!"

The glass is the color of the sky, and the lawn in front of them, and the places where last night the ambulance and police cars drove across the lawn. When students drive across the lawn, they are instantly expelled by Mr. Buckner, though this, of course, has never happened.

This has never happened, she thinks. She holds her knees and waits for them to stop shaking. She knows it's not that cold. She's lived in Michigan. Edith says, concentrating, "Tomorrow's Halloween."

"Are you going to the dance?"

"I don't know. I guess."

"I love Halloween," Jenna says. "All those costumes. When else can you get all dressed up without having people know who you are?"

"I don't know."

"In college, once, I went as the Abominable Snowman. You know, Bigfoot? I wrapped myself in toilet paper until I could hardly move. Hundreds of rolls. I wore my boyfriend's bowling shoes. He'd borrowed them, you know. From the bowling alley." Jenna holds out her hands and says, "This big. They were huge!"

Edith thinks Jenna is trying to make her feel better, like a sister, and says, "If I go, I guess I'll have to dress up."

"That's the fun part," Jenna says. "Doubletree?"

"Yeah. Right before Tatum."

Once they start driving, through neighborhoods and a golf course, they don't have to worry about talking so much; they always have the radio, and the scenery, to keep them occupied. When a song comes on that Jenna likes, she rocks her shoulders, both hands on the wheel, humming. Edith thinks she looks funny, and she tells herself she wants to be more like Ms. Williams, who likes Halloween. When a person wears a costume, only the person inside gets to know who she really is. Costumes make everybody equal, like democracy.

"The cops," Edith says, pointing. "My dad always gets tickets."

They turn onto Via de los Flores, a street which has been named after flowers, because of the way they smell, and now they drive into the cul-de-sac—a French word—which is full of new houses, all of which are stuccoed white. While Edith's family was still living in Michigan, her mom would give instructions to the builders over the phone, standing in the kitchen, usually during meals. The house is long and the property is landscaped very nicely: yucca plants, and bougainvillea, and three paloverde, where hummingbirds live. The hummingbirds are small and tender, faster than light. Her father's car sits parked in the driveway beside the cholla.

Jenna pulls the car out of gear, and it grinds a little. She says, "You have my number?"

"Yeah. Sure."

"Anything happens—you call, okay? You call and I'll come right over."

"I'm sorry," Edith says. "Thanks."

"Anything, Edith. I mean it. We've had a big shock."

"I know. Thanks."

She closes the door, walks around past the garage and in through the kitchen. Jenna's car takes a while to drive off. Inside, on the kitchen table, is a slice of cold pizza in a box. Her mother is at work and won't be home until seven because of traffic. Edith takes the pizza . . . *pepperoni* . . . and goes into the family room. She turns on the stereo and calls, "Dad! I'm home!"

Her father comes rushing down the bedroom hall, wearing slacks and an unbuttoned shirt. His hair has recently been wet; it's streaked with the marks of his comb, the tortoiseshell comb her mom bought for Father's Day. He said he really liked it.

"I got sick," she says, stepping inside the kitchen.

"Are you all right?"

"Yeah. Ms. Williams brought me home." She puts the pizza back in the box and opens the refrigerator. Inside are two Cokes and a bottle of sparkling water. She takes a Coke, opens it, and drinks a third of it down fast. Sometimes, a Coke can fill her up for days.

"I just came home for a dip," says her father. "Just a quickie."

"It's awful cold. Mom's at work?"

"Indeed, at work. Home after seven. The traffic is terrible." He says, "I turned the heat on yesterday."

He means the heat in the Jacuzzi, not the house; the house is freezing. She walks past her father, down the hall and into her room and turns on her radio. She turns it to the same station as the stereo in the living room, KSTM, *The Storm,* and listens to Angelica. Angelica has a new song by someone who's been around. Edith loves Angelica's voice, so certain and calm. Edith has called Angelica three times, asking her to play requests, and every single time Angelica is nice. Once, while discussing nuclear war, a rock star asked Angelica what she would do if she knew the world was going to end, maybe even tomorrow, and Angelica said, "Plant a tree. I think I'd go plant a tree."

It didn't seem to make much sense, especially when there were so many other possibilities. But Edith thinks about that often, planting a tree in spite of what's someday going to happen, and Angelica is playing a song by someone who really does know how to sing. It's a sad song, and pretty, but it makes Edith feel sad, too. She slides beneath the down comforter her mom gave her last Christmas because it matched her eyes . . . *green* . . . even if they didn't work right, and now outside her door are voices, and she's concentrating hard on the music, trying not to listen. The voices are hushed, urgent—the voices of men talking to one another. Now a fist raps gently at her door, and a voice, opening the door just enough to speak through . . . *Edie, I'm off. See you tonight* . . . while the music is passing, her face to the pillow and she is feigning sleep. She's trying not to breathe. When her father shuts the door, when the door finally closes shut, Edith listens to the thunderstorm. Thunder and rain coming over the radio into her room, and Angelica, so smooth and perfectly calm, riding over the storm.

This is Angelica. . . . KSTM, Apache Junction . . .

•••

Outside where Edith sat on the wall with Howie Bently and Ms. Williams, the sky was beginning to fall. Ms. Williams said she was waiting for Ray—Mr. Morrison, who spoke with an accent—to finish up inside. Everyone knew about them, though Ms. Williams and Mr. Morrison pretended there was nothing really to know. It was the same way a senior would go out with a freshman: quietly, in case it didn't work out. Edith thought it was cute, the way Mr. Morrison would show up at swim practice, just to say hello.

Earlier, while Joe was running stairs, while she stood outside Mr. Morrison's office, Edith could hear Mr. Morrison and Ms. Williams quarreling; you could tell by the way their voices kept trying not to yell, and the questions they kept trying to make. There was a crash: books falling, and then Ms. Williams stepping through the doorway, closing the door softly, trying not to make a sound.

"Edith!"

"Hi," Edith said. "I'm just waiting for Joe."

"Outside. Let's wait outside," Jenna said. She was holding her towel rolled up in her hands, with her swimsuit inside. Her hands were shaking fast.

Outside, the moon was rising, and they sat with Howie, the three of them on the wall watching everybody who was waiting for their rides. Some kids were playing hacky-sack on the lawn. Later, Howie, Edith and Joe were going to go to the Dairy Queen, where Edith would have a chocolate shake and Joe and Howie would drink ice water. Then they'd drop Howie off, and Edith and Joe would drive somewhere nearby for a while. There were so many places to drive, so many roads, and she was thinking about where they might drive when Walker Miller came walking across the lawn, right past Joe's car, because Joe had parked in the place for Roxanne, the retarded girl, who was officially handicapped. At first Edith wasn't sure just who he was.

"Walker!" said Jenna, pleased. "It's Walker Miller!"

But he looked strange. He was carrying something wrapped

in cloth, and then he sat on the grass, twenty feet away from them. The grass was wet from the sprinklers, and it was hot; Edith could feel her legs sweating against the brick wall, and the sweat sliding down the backs of her knees. Walker was sitting cross-legged on the wet grass, and then he said, looking up, "You never know what you're going to miss."

Howie jumped off the wall, and Walker said, "No. Don't."

"Don't *what*, Walker?" Jenna said, rising. Her voice was different, but she said, "It's so good to see you!"

"No," Walker said, shaking his head. "No."

"Walker, come over here. Come over here. We'll go to the Dairy Queen. Why don't you come with us?"

"No."

"He's got a gun," whispered Howie. "Underneath."

"What?" said Jenna, turning. "What?"

"No," said Walker. "I'm sorry."

"Walker!"

He reached, unfolded the cloth and pulled out a gun. It was black and heavy, and he took it and put it up against his ear. Edith could feel the muscles in her legs twitching, and she could hear Howie, almost whispering, "Don't do that, Walker. Come on, now! Don't do that!"

"Don't look," Walker said. "I'm sorry. Just don't look, then."

He put the gun to his eye, and Edith tried not to look. Howie was breathing hard and Jenna put her hand on Edith's shoulder and squeezed.

"Call an ambulance," Jenna said, so softly she didn't need to whisper, and Edith and Howie turned, because she must have squeezed them both, and then they started running. She could hear Jenna talking now, saying nice things, fading. *Walker*, she heard, and then from inside the locker area, by the pay phones, Howie was dialing, and now he was talking, and yelling *Come on! Come on! Come on!* and then *Yeah. An emergency. Gold Dust High, by the gym! By the fucking gym!* and she thought he was going to cry, or explode, and he had to wait on the phone for more questions, standing there with the phone, waiting.

"Howie," she said, shaking, "he won't do it, will he?"

"Nah."

And for a moment, a brief moment, she felt as if he really wasn't going to. She left Howie and walked out through the tunnel of the lockers, out onto the lawn full of sprinkler heads and short trees. The gym was all the way across the lawn, and when she first moved here, to Arizona, all the way from Michigan, this was where she used to eat her lunch: away from the sun by all the lockers. She would sit by her locker and read a book while she ate her lunch, because she didn't know anyone, and because she was *new*. It was hard enough to find anyone to sit with even when she did know people—all those bodies in all those clothes changing every single day—and her father was going to stop doing what he was doing, *a fresh start,* and her mother was going to forgive him, *for love,* and they were going to live in Paradise Valley, Arizona, where the sun would always shine. Edith learned to eat lunch by herself, away from the sun, near her locker, and then she met Carol Cunningham, and the next year became this year, and the season started all over again and now she could swim. She could swim for hours with people who knew how to swim. Like Jenna Williams, who taught her to swim blind, to feel for the wall because waiting for it just slowed you up, and she could feel her stroke becoming smoother. She could feel herself smoothing out the kinks, the wrinkles and dents, and Jenna would say, sometimes, *You could do it, Edith. You could really do it,* and the lockers, the lockers which were always cold and dark, tucked under and away from the sun, and Carol, suggesting they move to a tree . . . *Hey, let's go somewhere else, yeah?* . . . and the tree, a frail little pine stuck on the edge of the lawn by Fine Arts, next to the gym, and the dealers doing coke behind the boiler room . . . the kids from Band, and Chorus, and Walker Miller, who was in Chorus, and she could see them even now: Jenna, and Walker Miller, standing on the lawn, only here they didn't look like who they were supposed to be. They looked like two people in a picture after the sun has gone away. Two bodies which could have belonged to anybody standing beneath a hot October moon. The moon was pale and white and nearly round, and she was watching the moon, and the light, and the explosion which was loud enough to kill it.

Sometimes, when the light is right, the full moon looks like the Host, which is the body of Christ—transubstantiation. The light has to be just right, and there can't be any clouds, but sometimes they really do look the same. It's as if you could honestly hold either on the back of your tongue—the moon, or the Host, just now beginning to dissolve, and now when she rolls over in her bed, her pillows snug beneath her arms, she begins to recognize her mother's voice.

Edie? Are you up?

"I'm dreaming," she says, sitting up. "What?"

Somewhere, from beyond the pool of light spilling into her room, her mother says, "Phone."

Someone has turned off the radio, and she's still in her school clothes. She reaches for her glasses and scrambles out of bed in case she might be late. The phone is hanging down the wall by the bookcases in the hallway. Until last year, she had to share the phone with her older brother, Anderson . . . *Late for what?* . . . but Anderson has gone away to college in Boston.

"Hello?"

"Hiya!"

"Hi, Spencer! How are you?"

"Good. Joe wants to know if you'll come baby-sit me. He says I need a baby-sitter. He has to go to Howie's."

"Sure, I think."

"He says he'll pay. He's on his way to pick you up. He said you were sick or something."

"No, I'm fine. Fine. I'll see you in a while."

In the kitchen, Ellen, Edith's mother, says, "No. I think you should stay home. Get some rest."

Ellen is standing with her back against the sink, drinking sparkling water from a green bottle. She is still in her work clothes, her business suit; school clothes make you look like a girl, but business clothes make you look like a man. It's something else that makes no sense.

Edith says, "Please, Mom?"

Ellen shrugs. She feels Edith's forehead, the way she used to; Ellen's hand is cold from the bottled water. When Joe's car pulls into the driveway, Ellen says, "Have you seen your father?"

"No."

"Home by eleven, kiddo. I mean it."

"Tell Joe I'm changing."

"Please?"

"Please?"

"You're changing," Ellen says. "I'll be sure to tell him."

Edith can't find the jeans she wants, the pair she bought three summers ago in a department store in Michigan, so she stays in her skirt which is just a little wrinkled. She takes off her sweater and her skin shivers in the cold. Somebody needs to turn on the heat in the *house*. She considers her bra, but keeps it, because according to her mother, age comes quick enough even if you don't have very much. Edith thinks she has enough to fill a wineglass, which always makes her feel shy and suddenly nervous at the same time. Anderson says that's all a guy ever needs, enough to fill a wineglass . . . *a wineglass* . . . and she puts on a hooded sweatshirt, BOSTON UNIVERSITY, her favorite, because Boston University is a place where people read poetry and drink wine; it's the place where her brother, Anderson, lives with his girlfriend, Laurie Something, who wants to be a model. In the bathroom, Edith puts her mouth to the tap, twice, and now she's brushing her teeth hard. Down the hall, in the kitchen, Joe is talking with her mother, and the water is cold. She splashes her face; she slides a brush through her short hair. Carol Cunningham has to use conditioner every night, and Carol even knows what it's like: sex, and what it feels like. In the hall, Edith remembers her earrings, and she's taking them off just in case Joe kisses her ear a lot. He's standing rock-still, holding a glass of Coke, awfully embarrassed.

"Hi," she says, blushing.

"Hey," he says.

"Thanks, Mom," she says, kissing Ellen's cheek. Her mom smells like the perfume grandmothers wear, like flowers and dust, and Edith says, "I'm fine. See you!"

"Be careful."

Once in the car, Joe kisses her. His mouth tastes a little like salt, and Coke, and she thinks the inside of his mouth is big enough to fill a wineglass. She puts her hand on her breast, kissing him, making calculations. She looks into the black space of her closed eyes, and the light which happens if you close them tight; pressure on the retina will cause you to see something you never knew existed, and if she does it right, she doesn't even know she's doing it.

Joe pulls away and says, "Ms. Williams said you were sick."

"I'm fine, really. Just a cold."

"Howie's a wreck. I mean, he's bad. I thought maybe you could watch Spencer, just this once. I'm not supposed—"

"It's fine," she said. "He called already. It'll be fun."

"It's okay if you're sick or something."

She laughs and starts going through the tapes. Halfway to Joe's house, she finally decides and puts one into the stereo. The music is fast, the way Joe drives, the kind of music she likes to dance to. Sometimes, she dances by herself in her room with the lights off, and Joe is driving with the window down the way he always does. She thinks maybe he is claustrophobic because he has to wrestle, maybe, and roll himself up in all those mats just to make weight. She thinks the open window is what's making her shiver; she turns on the heater, and the air begins blowing from the vent, rising up her skirt. The air feels warm and soft as an expensive sweater.

In the driveway, Joe says, "I'm just going to take Howie to a movie or something. Maybe drink some beer. He's all fucked up."

"Okay."

"Spencer says he wants to make dinner. Watch out," Joe says, laughing, and then he kisses her again. He kisses her hard this time, and she can feel her hand on his leg and she is squeezing it, hard, because Joe is kissing her hard, and then a light comes on and she can feel it pouring in through the corners. And Spencer, in his wheelchair, banging at the car window.

"Come on!" Spencer is saying. "Come on!"

She wonders if Walker Miller ever got to know just what it feels like. She pushed Spencer up the ramp, through the garage door and into the house. Spencer had already started making chicken, Shake 'n Bake, because Mrs. Amato, the Jazinskis' housekeeper, had shown him how. Spencer explained to Edith how you shake it, and how you put it in the oven, knocking three times on the oven door, just like Mrs. Amato, *to bake it,* and how after they were going to have chocolate ice cream with chocolate sauce and raspberries.

She let Spencer teach her to play pool, and then chess; Edith wasn't particularly good at either. Spencer kept telling her how to move the pieces. After chess, television, and then to bed, but Spencer didn't want to go to bed. If you go to bed, you have to be all by yourself, and Spencer kept wheeling around in his chair in the living room, saying, "Look, I'm a space car!"

"You have to get into your pj's, Mr. Space Car."

She helped him slide into his bottoms, the cast taking up most of the leg. When she moved his leg too far, it hurt, and Spencer said, "Ow!" But then he said, "Nah, it's fine," and Edith knew she must have moved something the wrong way—the bones, and the way they were supposed to be lining up. After a bone broke, it knit itself back into place, and the broken part became stronger than the rest. In the television room she let Spencer watch a movie. He fell asleep before the second car chase, and she covered him with a blanket, in his chair, his leg propped, where he sat sucking his thumb, drooling. He looked like Joe when Joe didn't know anyone was looking at him. She was wheeling Spencer toward his bedroom when the doorbell rang.

It was Mrs. Bently, standing in the door. Howie had called; the boys had a flat tire and weren't going to be home until late. Could she give Edith a ride home?

"Boys," Mrs. Bently said. "It's good they're such friends. How are *you?*"

"Fine," Edith said. She thought she was supposed to say *Come in,* but this wasn't her house. She said, "I'm just putting Spencer to bed."

"Here," Mrs. Bently said. "Let me help."

Mrs. Bently stepped inside. She picked Spencer up out of the chair and carried him down the hall to his room; she didn't even stagger, she was that strong. Spencer's bed was full of pillows, and his bedspread was covered with spaceships and planets. Mrs. Bently tucked Mr. Moose under Spencer's arm while Edith stood back and watched.

This is what moms do, Edith thought. *Even librarians.*

Again Mrs. Bently said, "How are you, Edith?"

"Fine."

"Fine? I wonder. I wonder if we'll ever be fine. It's so difficult sometimes. . . ."

"Uh-huh."

"So difficult . . ."

With Spencer put to bed, Mrs. Bently didn't have anything to do. She began looking at the bookshelves in the living room, glancing over the titles. The Jazinskis had a million books. Mrs. Bently said, finally, "Let me take you home."

First Mrs. Bently left a note for Spencer, just in case he woke . . . *Be right back, honey* . . . and in the car she took the same route as Joe, only much more slowly, and she kept both hands on the steering wheel, like Ms. Williams, and she listened to classical music on the radio. Edith knew she had heard the song before, but she didn't know who it was. Most people loved Beethoven, probably because he was deaf. In the driveway, Mrs. Bently said, "Do you want me to explain? To your parents? It's kind of late and I don't mind."

In Boston, where Anderson lives, there is no curfew and people drink wine. "No," Edith said. "That's okay."

"Joe," said Mrs. Bently. "He's such a polite boy. So determined. So steady."

"I guess, yeah."

Edith had never thought about Joe like that. Determined, and steady; she'd never even seen him angry once. He never even said anything mean. If he didn't like somebody, he just wouldn't talk to him, or Roxanne, the retarded girl, who wrote mean things about Joe in the school paper because she wanted him to like her. She wanted attention, like Mitchell Hemly, who was always saying stupid things in A.P. History. When Joe got angry, Edith realized, she never even knew.

Once, when she asked him about his mom, all he said was, *I don't know. I think she lives in New York . . .* and she thinks he must look like her, his mother, though Edith has no idea what Joe's mother looks like. Mr. Jazinski looks like Joe with gray hair; she's seen his picture, on the table in the Jazinskis' living room, but there is no picture of Joe's mom. It's as if she's disappeared, as if she never existed, which is impossible: Edith has put her hand on Joe's leg, she's let Joe touch her breast. Sometimes, Edith hopes her parents get divorced, too.

Right now she is in the cafeteria waiting for Joe, her boyfriend, who never gets angry. He's with Howie Bently across the picnic area, in front of the snack bar, and she wonders what he really wants to do about the dance. She wonders if he's mad at her and if she doesn't even know it.

"Here," Joe says, handing her a Coke. He is drinking ice water.

"Thanks."

"I'm gonna go," Howie says.

"What?" Joe says.

"Screw Economics. Screw it. I'm going home. Tell Fullerton I got real sick just thinking about her."

"She's gonna nuke you," Joe says. "And then you'll really have to join the navy."

"I don't give a fuck," Howie says. "I'm outta here. See ya, Edith." And now Howie's walking between the picnic tables. The cement under the tables is sticky with soda and catsup and flies; Edith prefers to avoid the entire area. The picnic area smells like hot dogs and cookies that have chemicals inside to make them smell homemade, and hamburgers, and Howie is walking between the tables, flexing his knees, bouncing.

Mitchell Hemly, the kid with acne, bumps into Howie, and now Howie grabs him by the collar. He pushes Mitchell up against the lockers and Mitchell's hot dog tips. Edith can't see it clearly, but Mitchell is still holding on to the bun, and she knows that Howie's being an asshole.

"Why's he doing that?" she says to Joe.

"He's pissed, I guess." Joe takes a drink from his ice water and says, "Thanks. About last night. Spencer really likes you."

"Did you fix your tire?"

"What?"

"Your tire. Mrs. Bent—"

"Nah. Howie just said something so she wouldn't worry. I've got almost new tires. They're radials."

She looks over at Howie, thinking. Howie's arm is raised, his hand cocked in a fist. When she looked back, she really did expect it to be over with, and Johnson, a tall senior who always smells like pot and cigarettes, is grabbing Howie's arm—shoving him, back and forth. Mitchell Hemly is out of the way now, looking at his hot-dog bun, which is empty, and Johnson is taller even than Howie. *Bigger.* He's wearing motorcycle boots.

Joe says, "Howie's gonna waste him."

"Huh?"

"Come on. Let's go."

He walks into the gathering crowd, slowly; Edith thought he meant somewhere else. She follows Joe past Diana Vanderstock, who carries birth-control pills inside her purse, which she empties it out at least twice a month, during Chemistry, because she wants people to know. Edith thinks Joe is walking the way he walks before a match when he is coming onto the mats: slowly, so everyone is sure to see him. His hands are deep in his jeans, and now he's standing up on his toes, looking, and Johnson is saying to Howie Bently, "Lighten up, asshole."

Howie looks at Joe and smiles. Howie's holding his hands behind his back, grinning. He says, "What?"

Johnson says, "Fuck you, dickwad. Fuck—"

And Howie lets go. His fist flies out from behind his back, then the other, then twenty more. In the time it takes Edith to take a breath, Johnson is lying on the ground covering his face; when he tries to get up, Howie lets go again. Then again. He won't let Johnson get any higher than his knees, and he's saying to Johnson, *What?* and pounding away at his face . . . *What?* . . . and he's shaking so hard he can't keep still, he's bouncing on his toes, bending his knees. Springs, she thinks . . . *adrenaline* . . . because that's what makes the body spring, and there are cigarettes all over the floor, and catsup, and Howie's still shaking, his veins flooded with adrenaline.

"What?" he screams.

"Nothing."

"I'm outta here," Howie says to Joe. "And I know fucking everything!"

He takes off at a run. He's taking off past the picnic tables and the lockers with everybody watching.

Joe steps into the center and offers Johnson his hand, probably because it's hard not to be nice to somebody after he's just been beaten up.

Johnson says, "Fuck you, Jazz."

Joe laughs and says, "Yeah. Sure."

Joe turns and faces Edith, and she can feel her body shaking.

"He shouldn't have done that," she says.

"What?"

She turns and walks back to where she was sitting before

anything ever happened. Before she met Carol Cunningham, before her last operation, before she started wearing contacts three times a week; before she met Joe and started running by his house every day. Carol will be in class now, and Edith's books are by the yucca, and last summer Carol had sex for the very first time. Her parents were having the yard redone and she was sitting by the pool. First, the landscapers had to lay plastic on the ground, to keep weeds from growing, and then the granite, tons and tons of granite, and there was a Mexican, spreading granite in a fan all over her yard. The granite was the color of roses, and the Mexican's crew left early for another job, and Carol asked the man . . . *He must have been twenty. He was really twenty, only he didn't have any hair, except, you know* . . . and she asked the man if he wanted a glass of iced tea. *Si!* said the man, smiling, and Carol always started giggling at this part—the way he said that word, *Si!*—and she gave him the iced tea and then she asked him if he wanted to jump into the pool, it was so hot, and the man took off his boots . . . *He wasn't wearing any socks, even* . . . and his pants, his long green pants, and then he jumped into the pool, naked, and when he climbed out of the water his skin was dripping with oil, or sweat, because the water wouldn't even go into his skin. It kept rolling off his skin and then he looked at Carol, beaming, looking right at her. He was pointing now, and he jumped back into the water, and when Carol dove in, she knew this was going to be it . . . *I just knew that this is what it was going to be like. I never even took off my swimsuit. He didn't even kiss me. Not once* . . . and sometimes, when she's by herself, or even in class, Edith can't stop thinking about that: being in a pool with a man with thin brown skin who doesn't even speak your own language. Carol said she made him come all over her swimsuit, *not inside,* and still some got inside and she knew *for six weeks* she was going to be pregnant. *I just knew!* And every day she just knew, even after she got her period; then she read through her biology textbook, the parts on reproduction . . . *You know, fertilization? Genetics?* . . . and then she worried only half as much. Still, she never had to worry, everything turned out all right, and now, standing in front of her locker, thinking about it, Edith thinks she's still shaking and that Joe never tells her anything she wants to know. Her hands are shaking, and she can't get her combination to go right, and Joe is standing there behind her.

"Hey," he is saying. "Hey, thanks again. About last night, I mean."

"Sure," she says. "Anytime."

She thinks if he wanted to, then he could put his hands around her waist right here. He could slide his hands up inside her sweater.

"Yeah," Joe says. "Thanks."

But he doesn't, and a man could give you AIDS. He could even rape you. But if he speaks a foreign language, the one thing he can never do is tell anyone who matters. *Si,* the man had said. *Si,* and before Edith shuts her locker, she looks to see if everything she needs is still inside it.

Edith opens the door.

Trick'er treat!

Outside stand Jimmy and Kelly and Robert Henderson and somebody else. They live in a cul-de-sac two blocks away and are dressed tonight, according to the sign their parents have made, as HEAVY METAL ROCKERS! Kelly's hair is green, and Robert, the youngest, who isn't yet in school, wears a black studded dog collar. The collar used to belong to the Henderson's rottweiler, Biff, who kept wandering out of the neighborhood onto Tatum Boulevard, which has four lanes.

Edith says, "But you have to do a trick!"

Ellen is standing behind Edith and Carol. Ellen says, "Yes, you must do a trick, you Heavy Metal Rockers!"

"Mrs. McCaw," says Robert. "I know a trick!"

He begins to sing "Hound Dog," by Elvis Presley, and after a few seconds he forgets the words and simply shakes his pelvis. Ellen claps, Carol is laughing, and Edith passes out the chocolate bars. Behind the paloverde on the curb stand two adults. Probably, they inspect all the candy when they get home, the way Ellen used to when they lived in Michigan and Edith still went trick-or-treating.

After the Hendersons leave, and the quiet kid nobody recognized, Carol says, "We should go out."

"Where?" says Edith.

"We could go to the dance."

"Why don't you go to the dance?" Ellen says. "It's such a perfect night for a dance!" Ellen has been sipping wine, and now she begins humming a song that was popular decades ago.

"Walker's service is tomorrow," Edith says. "I have to give a speech."

"You can still go to the dance," says Ellen. "You can go stag. I wonder where that comes from, *stag*."

"Deer," says Carol. "It has to do with hunting."

"It's so ugly," Ellen says, laughing. "You two go and I'll watch out for the Munchkins."

When Edith and Anderson were babies, they were *Munchkins.* Now they're old enough to be *stags*. In the bathroom, Carol and Edith help each other dress. They wear Mr. McCaw's shirts and ties with their own jeans. They each wear a sport coat. Edith has the houndstooth, Carol the one with leather patches on the elbows. Edith's never seen her father wear the one with leather patches. Carol takes a pair of scissors and snips a lock of hair from her bangs, which are red, *flaming,* and she binds the lock with transparent tape. She fastens it to her lip.

"Here," she says, handing Edith the tape. "You too."

By the time they enter the kitchen, they look like two girls trying to look like two boys with fake mustaches. Ellen is watching the television in the den; Carol opens the refrigerator. She finds two carrots, in the vegetable bin, and giggles. When she puts one of the carrots inside her jeans, it reaches halfway down her thigh.

"Now we're really stags," Carol says.

Outside, the moon is a hole in the sky, pouring out the light. At school, in the parking lot which is full of cars, they can hear the music beating through the air. A car door is opening and the air smells briefly like rubbing alcohol; once inside the gym, the lights are low and the room is full of bodies. Edith doesn't know where Joe is, and she wonders if he even came. *Stag?* Maybe he came with Howie, so why didn't he tell her he was even coming? It is absolutely impossible, she thinks, to say that word without always getting the wrong idea. *Coming.*

The band is loud and not very good, but still it's live, and this makes music good no matter how bad it sounds. The gym is full of music rushing through the air and Edith wants to dance. She and Carol stand by the bleachers among people not dressed up. Most are drinking punch, listening to the music, pretending they don't want to dance. Carol won't dance, no matter who asks, and Edith thinks she must be afraid of looking bad, even if her hair *is* flaming. It's not as if anybody is going to be able to put it out. Dancing, and if you're really good-looking, perfect, like Diana Vanderstock, then it doesn't matter how badly you do it; the guys will still all pay attention. Spinning overhead is the disco ball, the one installed for every single dance, and nearby, Lacy is dancing by herself. Lacy, with yellow-white hair and black clothes—black ankle boots, black tights, a short black skirt and a black maillot, dancing to the speed of light—Lacy is full of *adrenaline* and everybody knows she's going to be famous. Sometimes, Edith thinks she's never seen anything so beautiful.

The disco ball is spinning, the music beating even faster. The lights make Edith dizzy and she loves them, the lights spinning through the gym; even when you're blind, you can still make out the source of light, and in front of her a gorilla holds out its paw to shake.

The gorilla looks at its paw, shrugs, and holds it out again.

Edith laughs; she takes the paw, shakes. The gorilla punches her in the arm, friendly-like, the way gorillas are supposed to be, and then the gorilla begins to dance. It dances slowly away from her, waving; if Joe were here right now, just about to say something, Edith wouldn't know what to say. For a moment, she doesn't even want him to be here. It's an idea which almost makes her feel good; the carrot is slipping down her jeans, and she reaches inside, sliding it up, wondering if this is what guys have to do all the time when they get hard-ons and don't want anybody else to know. They have to readjust, like when you're falling out of your bra, though that hardly ever happens to Edith. *And even if you do, so what?* . . . but with guys it's different. They always look so ashamed, and the music is faster now, faster and a girl in the band is singing a song about love and sex, and doing it just that way, and more love, *oooh,* and Edith takes Carol's arm.

"Come on," she says into Carol's ear. "Let's dance."

Carol, after hesitating, twice, says, "Okay . . ."

They make their way into the crowd of dancing ghosts and football players and firemen, and now they begin to dance. Shyly at first—two tender toes, dipped into the water, gauging the temperature. Edith thinks the water is just fine. And black. Black as moonbeams with your eyes closed tight; if Walker Miller were here, he could be here, too, dancing like a crazy man. He could be here dancing and no one would even know that he was really crazy, and she's going to give a speech, tomorrow, and everybody's going to be listening. The carrot is slipping, and when she reaches into her jeans to pull it out, she thinks it was a stupid thing to do—putting a carrot inside her pants. It's something someone else might do, because it's so obvious and crazy, because a carrot is just a vegetable and because Edith doesn't want to be a stag. She slips the carrot inside the pocket of her sport coat, the place where men carry checkbooks, and credit cards, and the lights are faster now: she can't see a thing, dancing is what you do best when you know nobody is even watching, and if she could be anywhere, right now, anywhere doing anything she ever wanted, then this is where she'd be. Here, moving, like Lacy, the girl who's going to be famous all by herself and doesn't even care if anybody ever knows.

Faster, Edith thinks, moving, because this is almost perfect, as almost perfect as it ever gets.

Fast.

She's lucky, she's never had to watch her weight. When Spencer was hit by a car, she didn't know what to say, and Mrs.

Bloomquist, who is very fat, bought her an ice cream sundae in the cafeteria at Scottsdale Memorial. Joe wasn't saying anything, either, and she still didn't know him very well. He was this guy who never said very much and walked slowly as if his knees always hurt. Later she learned it was his ankles, and not his knees, and that he wanted people to know he wasn't afraid of anything. He walked as if he'd been riding a horse all day, which always made her think he was kind of sore from so much riding.

This during her first summer in Arizona: the ground was too hot to walk on barefoot, even at night. The sky was simply too hot; the sweat would evaporate right into the air, leaving behind only the salt. The men who worked outside wore hats, and they wore gloves in order to pick things up—a wrench, or a brick, a pair of pliers. You could see them building houses everywhere. In the afternoons, when the days finally began to cool, Joe lifted weights under the porch of his house. The houses were built low to the ground, where it was coolest, even if the ground did burn your feet. In Arizona, you built a six-foot wall around your house to establish privacy, and after running, Edith would always run straight to the pool and dive in and take her clothes off. Water was a way of life here, even if there wasn't much, and during her run she'd stop by the Jazinskis' house where Howie Bently and Joe would be in the back lifting weights. She knew she really liked Joe when she started running by his house every day.

In the hospital, she tucked Mr. Moose under Spencer's arm. Joe kept apologizing for breaking her glasses, in the department store, when he threw the stuffed elephant at her and hit her in the face. And Edith kept apologizing about the way her father had hung up on him. "He's like that," she said. "He doesn't like to talk to people on the phone"; though she knew that wasn't why her father had hung up on Joe. She knew her father thought Joe was someone else, and her father apologized only to her mother, for certain things, over and over again, which seemed to be more and more the thing people did when they still wanted to like each other. Apologize, in case the other thinks you did something on purpose, like breaking your glasses, and decides not to like you anymore. If you apologized long enough, you could make anybody feel better over anything, even if it killed you.

I'm sorry, Walker Miller said, before he killed himself. *I'm really sorry.*

After they left Spencer in the hospital, they sat in Joe's car in the parking lot and began to kiss. It was unbearably hot, and Joe turned on the car and started up the air-conditioning and kissed the salt from her lips. They kept kissing and Edith took off her glasses. She set them on the dash, and Joe said, "Are they okay now?"

"Fine," she said, squinting.

Away from the sun, her chest was dripping with sweat, and Joe put his hand on her breast. He just reached out and did that, and looked at her, and his hand, and she thought it strange the way a hand could feel so strange on her breast.

Then he said, "I've got to pick up my dad. At the airport."

And that's when she knew he liked her . . . *for real . . . this is for real!* . . . because he took his hand back and kissed her on the forehead. Then he put the car into gear, which lurched, and what troubles her now is that if he liked her so much, back then when it was so unbelievably hot in his car, how come she doesn't even know where he is? How come he never asks her any questions?

Why won't he even talk to me?

Outside, in the backyard, her mother is sitting in the Jacuzzi: a small, blue-lit pond, filling up the air with steam. Steam is similar to clouds, or fog—the result of water mixed together with warm air. Her mother is naked, and sad, because no one knows when her husband is coming home. He has gone away again. *A ghost,* Edith thinks. *He keeps on vanishing. . . .*

Her mother drinks from her green bottle of mineral water, and says, sadly, "How was the dance?"

"Okay."

"Here," says her mother, patting the deck. "Sit."

Edith sits on her mother's bathrobe, a pink cotton robe made out of bath towels. She crosses her legs and folds her hands into her lap—a Catholic schoolgirl, out of uniform. Edith watches the steam rise into the air, and she can feel it, washing over her face. The steam feels good against the cool parts of her skin. It makes her face feel clean, like the clean smell of chlorine, which she loves, and it surprises her that here in Arizona where it's always supposed to be so hot, it surprises her that sometimes she can feel so cold. As cold as she ever felt in Michigan. In Michigan, her father was an Existentialist and worked in the city; each day he drove his sports car to work and back. At work he talked to people with career problems. A counselor.

"It's so cold," Edith says. "It gets in your bones."

"Not in here," says her mom, skimming her hand across the surface. "Why don't you come in?"

"Nah."

Ellen splashes her now, friendly; probably, she'd make a great sister, but Ellen is her mom. She could never be a sister. Edith thinks this is too bad, and she wishes that Anderson, who lives in Boston, with his girlfriend and he's not even twenty . . . she wishes Anderson were here to talk to. She wonders if her mother has ever had an affair with someone else. You can't have an affair, she thinks, if it's not with someone else.

"I don't know," she says to her mom. "I don't think Joe likes me anymore."

And just as she says it, just as the words come spilling out of her mouth, she prays it isn't true. Tomorrow, when she goes to Walker Miller's memorial service and gives her speech, *Adrenaline, and What It Means to Live,* she's going to pray for Walker Miller's soul. She's going to pray for Walker Miller, and her mother, who's lapsed, and Spencer, because he's too small to live all by himself. She's going to pray for Ms. Williams and Carol Cunningham, her best friend, and Anderson, and Laurie Something who's not even twenty. She's going to pray for everyone she loves and doesn't even know.

"Oh, Edie . . ." says her mother, patting her knee. "Edie . . ."

She thinks her mother's hand is going to leave a dark print, there on her knee, and she can feel her mother's voice, it's so familiar and close.

When you stand near the ocean and look at it, sometimes you can't tell where the water ends and where the sky begins, and when Edith wakes, she knows the fight is bad. She's been asleep for hours. Turning in bed, she stares up at her ceiling, and the sky, it's that big. Even the stars are big, no matter how small they look, and she can hear her mother, screaming, and her father, apologizing, and then there is the sound of shattered glass, and more screaming. Her mother's voice is full of anger and fear, enough to fill a sea, and that's how Edith knows this fight is bad. Because her mother never sounds afraid, especially when she's angry. Her father is speaking now, trying to be calm, and objective, because he's a counselor, until he finally gives up and *Yes, fuck it! Fuck it! Fuck you! Fuck the whole entire deal!* and then the door, the front door slamming shut. Her father's sports car fires up, it pulls out of the driveway, fast, and her mother is crying. Her mother is crying hard. This, Edith thinks, the sound of mourning, and in the Bible, when people are sad, they beat at their breast and tear their hair. Edith can't imagine beating herself, especially there where everything's so tender, but she knows her mother's going to be up for a long time. Most likely, her mother won't sleep at all, and in the morning, the glass will have all been swept away, and Edith will have to look around the kitchen to see what's missing. Last spring, after Edith's eye surgery, when she lay in bed feeling ugly, and crying, her mother would come into her room. She would sit on the edge of Edith's bed and let her cry. Edith knows she's not old enough to watch her mother cry, and outside, beyond her window, the sky is bigger than anything she thinks she will ever get to know. It's big enough to get lost in, and she imagines the sounds of her mother's voice, rising up into the sky the way water fills a pool. The way wine will fill your mouth. The way anger, once it passes into the blood, will cause the heart to swell until it bursts.

The Services of Need

After a great divorce, or flood, love always lingers on—the covenant of God. Sometimes we see the evidence bridging across the sky, an unexpected letter slipped into the day, the script deeply familiar and close for having traveled so great a distance.

Even a cloudburst will do. In Pinetop, three weeks ago, they had decided this wasn't going to work. It was nice enough to try, things had been okay, but there was something faintly incestuous about it all: teaching by its very nature was something you brought home with you day after day, until the days turned into semesters and, later, years. It wasn't something you necessarily wanted to marry into. The rule had always been that they would form their own lives outside of school, outside coaching and classes and students, but to go outside their lives as public-school educators left very little for either to form—with the exception of their ideas, the fine result of experience and need, which never seemed to agree. And form, as in all things, brought about shape. Form was something to be admired, the grace with which you carried yourself through time and space, through water and air—a dialectic of resistance and relief. When Walker Miller shot himself in the eye with a .45 caliber automatic, he died, according to the paramedics, instantly, and what troubles her now is the measure and give and take of an instant. Alone and by itself, without other instants with which to cleave, an instant becomes enduring as a photograph. Once isolated, it will last a lifetime, and the problem with time is that time never stops, and when it does stop, someday, it's all finally going to stop: a final, shuddering wail, while the muscles twitch and the lungs release that final spasm of need—this, the last gesture of faith, here in her bed.

"Okay," she says, flinching. "Okay."

And when he does come, if only for an instant, she knows that he will feel as if he's dead.

In the morning, while Ray's still asleep, whimpering, fighting off his demons, Jenna feels the day grow bright outside her window. Ray's hands are fists, smashed into the pillows. It is the morning, she will tell herself, which gives us hope. She wants merely to watch the sky. And she feels the beginnings of a migraine—in her left eye, already hazy with light. The light is localized and specific, but she is familiar with the pattern. The light is just waiting for the right moment to greet her fully, and then it will implode, which seems impossible. It seems entirely impossible that anything can happen. That night, when she came home, her clothes smeared with blood and grass, she had felt bewildered—a stray looking at the sun, blinking. With people nearby, she knew how she was expected to behave. She was a teacher, taking instruction, giving instruction; she was a fluid part of the great chain of being. But at home, her apartment swollen from the heat, and empty, she knew that she needed to be of use, and she knew she could only water her plants so many times before they began to drown. And it was quiet, quiet as a dream, a movie with a silent screen. She sat in the kitchen reading the want ads. Eventually, in the morning, she rose out of her kitchen chair and made a cup of coffee. She had a slice of toast with peach preserves. She drank a glass of water, vomited, and later, a lifetime later, with Ray, detached and equally in need of relief, she had felt it her need to relieve him. And so she had pulled him back into her life, into her body, like a song.

Do you think people who kill themselves are crazy, Ms. Williams?

Walker, of course not. I think they're sad. I think—

Yeah, well, I think they're crazy. I think they're fucking crazy!

And she remembers taking a bath. She remembers trying to wash the blood from her hair and being out of shampoo. To get through the day, she will need to cut the headache short. In the kitchen, she reaches for her Fiorinal; she washes down two with a tall glass of water. She drinks another glass of water. Then another. Scattered across the living room floor are the parts of her Halloween costume—the gorilla suit—and Ray's clothes. For the dance, Ray dressed like Robert Horn, who teaches Chemistry and Bowling.

She thinks if there once was a rainbow, the sun has by now burned it up, and the weekend is full of people drinking in the sunlight. She puts on her swimsuit, a maroon Speedo, and steps cautiously down the seven flights to the pool. There, she points her lounge chair west, away from the sun. She waves to her neighbor, Bill, a black man with skin rich as saddle soap. He knows her by name and has lived in this same apartment complex, Indian Shadows, for nearly two years, and she understands, regretfully, that he is gay. As he smiles at her, she admires the length of his body—water on a dark sea, rippling. To confuse would-be intruders, Bill and Jenna keep a spare key over each other's porch light.

Jenna soaks her towel in the pool, wrings out the excess water, and lies back to cover her eyes. The water feels cool and black, and she can feel the sun pouring through her skin; she allows her hand to skim along the slope of her hip. The voices from the pool are eager, the palm trees rustling, the local traffic busy and fast. Her skin is a body of nerves, and if she cries, she knows that the pain will spread: it will spread into both eyes and across the crown of her skull, the blood throbbing to the rhythm of her heart, because once released, there is no pulling back.

When she visited Walker at the Superstition Mountain Care Facility, she had thought that this, too, would pass. Walker told her about the games they played during rec time: Ping-Pong, and hearts. Sometimes they played volleyball, which he claimed to be getting pretty good at. Last spring, at school and on a fluke request, she had taught a coed course called Sports for Life. Walker was in that class, and they played volleyball, badminton and tennis: games which involved the use of nets. On the lawn at the Superstition Mountain Care Facility, sitting under a tree, Walker told Jenna that he didn't really think about his mother as much as all the doctors seemed to want him to.

"You know," he said, "they think everything explains everything. You know, like one plus one equals why you're going nuts. Only I'm not nuts, Ms. Williams. I mean, sometimes I get mad, sure. You know, really, really mad, and I don't know why. But I'm not crazy!"

"Of course you're not."

He calmed himself. He said, faithfully, "I know where all my apples are. That's what Ryan says. He says I know where all my apples are. In a great big barrel," Walker said, holding out his hands. "Ryan says it's a good sign."

"That's wonderful, Walker. Really—"

"Here," he said, shoving out his wrist. She thought she was supposed to look for scars.

"No," he said, unhooking the band of his wristwatch. "Here."

He passed her the watch. "My mom," he said, "she gave it to me just before . . . you know. She put my name on back. It says *Love, Mom.* Ryan says this means I'm learning how to confront my pain, because she's dead. Because I'm wearing this watch. I told him the reason I never wore it before was because I was afraid of breaking it. You know, banging it up and breaking it so I could never give it to my children or anything, and Ryan said, 'Exactly,' like he knows everything. 'Exactly,' he said."

"It's a lovely watch, Walker. So simple and nice."

"I don't know," he said. "It seems like I just never get to say the right things."

She smiled. "I know what you mean. Sometimes—"

"It's a symbol," he said, pointing at the watch. "That's what

Ryan says. He says it's a symbol of the passage of life—a watch. 'See what I mean, Walker? You *watch* your life pass right on by. Get it?' "

Jenna handed the watch back to Walker, who blinked, tightly, as if he'd just remembered something he was afraid to. He shook his head.

"Walker?"

"Nothing," he said, relaxing. "Just a shiver, you know. They make me feel tired, though. Really tired." He looked at his huge feet and said, "The food's not very good. Sometimes we sneak out and go to McDonald's. Don't tell anyone, okay?"

"Okay."

"Okay," he said, nodding. "Want a Coke?"

Before she left, he bought her a Coke; his pockets were stuffed full of quarters. "You know," he said, pushing the button, "it may look pretty, Ms. Williams, but it really is a dangerous place. I know that now, you know? Thanks for coming. It was great. Thanks."

She reached to squeeze his shoulder, fondly, but he ducked.

On the one-year anniversary of his mother's death, Walker Miller left the hospital without permission; months later, Jenna would learn that Walker had told his friend Cathy, after giving her his watch, that he was just going out for burgers, and then he never came back. His mother had died in her Jacuzzi after swallowing a bottle of Percocet and then slitting open the veins in her thighs. Later, in the spring, Walker signed up for Sports for Life and Chorus. He was kicked out of Chorus, and later fired from his job at a grocery store for attacking a carful of kids with a shopping cart—in the parking lot, while carrying out Jenna's groceries. Then he ran inside the supermarket, to the produce section, and started hosing down the customers. He told her that he had been protecting her honor.

After Jenna returned to school, after assembly, she met Cal Buckner in his office. He was sitting on the edge of his desk, being young. On top of his filing cabinet sat a silver disco ball, big as a basketball, or globe. Margaret Knudson, Cal's secretary, stepped into his office and set a box of chocolate-covered cherries on Jenna's lap.

"Chocolate always helps," Margaret said.

When Margaret left, leaving the door open so she could listen, Cal said, "Maybe you should take some time off. Can you make it for the memorial service? For the kids?"

"Of course."

"Good," he said, and when she caught his eye, she noticed, not for the first time, that he wanted to sleep with her. He avoided her eye, lit a cigarette, looked at his coffee cup—SUN DEVILS. He flicked his ashes into the cup and said, "Ray says he's got a good team this year. He says they may just beat Cholla. That'd be a first."

"I don't know."

He put the cigarette out, dipping it into the coffee cup. "Joyce," he said, laughing, meaning his wife. "Joyce says if I start smoking again she's going to move out. Ray says—"

"Ray and I are on different terms now, Cal."

Cal shifted uneasily. Clearly, he had prided himself on knowing that Jenna and Ray had been on terms in the first place. "I'm sorry," he said. "Or whatever it is you're supposed to say."

"It's fine, really."

"What do you know about Howie Bently?"

She took a breath and looked at the picture of Cal's wife on the desk; Joyce Buckner was wearing a yellow sundress and white shoes. The disco ball was made of tiny square mirrors.

Jenna said, "He wasn't in class today. It was his father's gun. Walker took it from his garage. He brought it back from Korea or someplace."

"I think we need to keep an eye on him. And Jazinski, too. They were his best friends. Just in case they start showing signs."

"Okay—"

"We don't want this to become a fad," Cal said. "This is not goddamn L.A., or Minneapolis. I don't mind a little cocaine in my school, a little after-school drinking, but I'm not about to have my school on the goddamn TV." He reached for his cigarettes. "Once these kids start knocking themselves off, you never know. . . . It's like dominoes. We need to contain it." He lit another cigarette and said, exhaling, "Jesus, I sound like goddamn Harry Truman."

She laughed, and suddenly felt bad. She told herself to think about Walker Miller and to pay attention. She thought about Walker Miller and blanched.

"Are you sure you don't want to take a week?"

"Yes," she said, standing, uncertainly. She looked at the chocolates, put on her polite but not inviting smile, and thought she was going to faint. "I need to make a quiz," she said, leaning into the doorframe. "But I'll be there. At the service."

"I know," Cal said. He looked puzzled. He said, "That's supposed to be a compliment." He blushed and reached for his coffee, took a sip and spat.

"I won't tell Joyce a thing," she said, meaning the cigarettes. She hoped he would laugh, to ease the unexpected innuendo, which he did. On the way down the hall, toward her office, she saw Ray walking into the faculty men's. He caught her eye and paused, deciding to wave, and she stepped into an empty classroom. Her knees were weak. She wanted to sleep and she didn't want to sleep. The classroom smelled like chalk and new carpet, and at the window she had a view of the lawn. The lawns were green and fresh from the sprinklers, and the students were eating lunch, talking about Walker Miller, gathering in groups. She heard the classroom door shut behind her and panicked all over again.

"What are you doing?" Ray said, his voice soft and slightly foreign; he was from Kentucky, where people spoke differently. "You okay?"

"I'm looking at the kids."

"The kids are going to be fine."

"No," she said. "They're not. No one's going to be fine. They're going to sit out there on that lawn until they grow up and decide they don't know what we've done. And then there's going to be all hell to pay. There's going to be bloody hell to pay and we'll have done nothing to let them know it's going to happen!"

He was standing by her now. She could smell the skin on his neck, honey and oil, motor oil, before it's put inside the engine. She could feel the hair on his arm brush her skin.

"They're going to be fine," he said.

"The dumb ones, maybe." If she let herself, she was going to lose it, which would change the meaning of everything she said. She said, bracing herself, "It's our fault."

"No."

"Yes, it is, Ray. It's everybody's!"

"You just happened to be there, Jen. It could have been anyone. It could have been Fullerton, or Owens."

"Remember Sammy?"

"Yeah."

"Sammy, before all that. Before. High school. His friend Bobby Seevers, he was supposed to take me out. We were going to see a movie. He was supposed to pick me up in his dad's MG, it was a big deal, but he didn't. He never even showed. Later I get a call from one of my friends saying the word is out. I've done it with Bobby Seevers at Nickel View. I'm a slut."

Ray put his hands into his pockets, leaning into them. They'd been careful not to touch each other for weeks.

"And for the rest of my life, Ray. For the rest of my life I knew it was going to be true. I knew it was going to be true and everyone knew it."

"You were sixteen."

"They," she said, pointing out the window. "They are sixteen!"

"That's right," he said. "They're sixteen. They'll get over it."

"And you know what she wanted, Ray? Angie Volkskye? You know what she wanted to know?"

"No."

"She wanted to know just how it was. She wanted to know just how fucking good it was."

She never did it with Bobby Seevers; rather, Bobby Seevers must have done it to himself and, later, Angie Volkskye. But before people knew that Jenna was a slut, they thought she was gay—a lesbo, as it were, because she lived with her aunt Nicky, who lived with her lover, Claire. Years later, while in college and living with her boyfriend, Sammy Coughlin, Jenna posed partially nude for a photographer who published her photograph in a July issue of a men's magazine. After Sammy went tripping into the ocean, and drowned, the magazine sent her a check for 350 dollars. It is a small photograph under a large heading, "California Volley," and Jenna is wearing a white bikini, only the bra is in her hand, and she appears to be smiling at someone behind the camera. She no longer owns a bikini, but now, getting dressed for Walker Miller's service, she worries everybody knows she wears a bikini, a white bikini, and that her skin is always perfect and tan, because in the picture she is tan, and the blemishes—the mole on her breast, the coffee stains on her teeth—have been airbrushed away. Nicky and Claire thought it was lovely; they put a copy on the refrigerator, and whenever Jenna went home to visit, there she was, posing on the icebox, smiling. At night they would all gather in the living room to read aloud, and Jenna would try not to think about Sammy, who had drowned somewhere in the Pacific. Now her aunt Nicky lives alone in Sedona, Arizona, and Claire has been dead for years.

The service for Walker Miller is informal and full of guitars. After each brief presentation, the participants sing a song. Halfway through, they listen to a song without words, meaningful music with feeling, during a slide show: pictures of the sky, of the Sonora desert; pictures of Walker with his friends, his mother and father; a picture of the chorus, Gold Dust Singers, out of which he was kicked; a picture of Walker in his supermarket uniform, smiling; and finally, a parting shot, gloriously sad, of the Grand Canyon at dusk. Now Marcia Taylor reads a sonnet from Western Civilization, *No man is an island,* and then another poem, closer to home . . . *After great pain . . . stupor . . . the letting go . . .* and Marcia Taylor is wiping her eyes before she's halfway through. Marcia Taylor loves Emily Dickinson, she loves her students, she loved Walker Miller even if she never knew him. The sanctuary is full of students and parents and teachers, including Mrs. Henderson, the nurse, whose dog has recently died. Jenna is sitting with Ray, in the second row, the two of them conspicuous and polite.

She is wearing sunglasses now; even the vague light of the sanctuary hurts her eyes. Together, the Fiorinal and headache have made her light-headed and weak, and in the front row, beside Cal and Joyce Buckner, sits Michael Owens, the undercover cop—a girl with a bow in her hair. Beside her sits Captain Miller, not in uniform, a thin man burdened with graying hair, sloping shoulders and grief. Last year, his wife; this year, his son. And now Howie Bently is walking up to the pulpit, wearing slacks and a sport coat and a bola tie. He's so grown up, and Jenna thinks Howie Bently is truly handsome. She thinks she will have to remember this: the light, which hurts her eyes, and the way Howie is striding toward the altar—a reminder for when she is grading papers, for when she is attending faculty meetings. She will have to remember what's important.

At the pulpit, Howie looks slowly over the congregation. He drops his hands into his pockets, rocks on his heels, and says, "Walker Miller was my friend."

And now Howie is leaving them, all of them, walking down the aisle, down the long aisle and through the narthex and out the door. It takes a moment for the door to close shut behind him, to squeeze shut the white cone of light spilling into the church.

There is another song, and then it is Edith's turn. Ray drops his hand onto Jenna's thigh and squeezes lightly. Tenderly, she thinks, but she wants Ray to remove his hand, it bothers her skin; she lifts his hand and sets it onto his leg. He takes a breath, collecting himself, shifting his weight. When he shifts, the entire pew rocks and people look annoyed, while Edith stands bravely, talking about things that make us afraid. Edith can't see the paper she has carried with her, and so she stops trying to read from it, and now she's simply speaking, looking past the congregation and saying that we have to be brave, we have to face it, Walker's death . . . *in order not to be afraid. We have to use our adrenaline* . . . and Jenna prays for

Edith, too . . . *Please, God . . . Please* . . . knowing that God's smart enough to figure out what she means without anybody ever having to say it. When Edith finishes speaking, the people in the church applaud, politely, and Edith begins to cry.

Outside, in the courtyard with punch and cookies, several students are crying unabashedly. The adults gather in a line to offer their respects to Captain Miller, retired, who sits in a lawn chair drinking a cup of tea, smiling patiently; obviously, he is on medication. Jim Lawson, a young Episcopalian priest from Saint Christopher's, is talking with a group of teachers and Michael Owens, the undercover cop; they are listening to a story about Walker Miller: the time he and Howie and Joe snuck into the girl's locker room, after school on a Friday, and the security guard, Wiz, ended up locking them inside. The boys had to wait through the weekend before anybody discovered they were missing. When Jenna found them, two days later, they said they were hungry.

People are laughing. While Ray guides Jenna by the elbow into the shade of a lemon tree, Cal and Joyce Buckner approach.

"Ray! Jenna!" calls Cal. "So good to see you two!"

"It was a good service," Ray says. "It was good for the kids."

"Hell, it was good for me," Cal says. "You'd never think a screwball kid like that could have so many friends."

Jenna blinks impatiently and says, "Hello, Cal. Joyce."

"Those are lovely glasses," Joyce says. "I simply can't live in Arizona without good sunglasses. In the Bahamas—"

"Through a glass darkly," says Cal. "Eh?"

"What?" says Ray.

"In the Bahamas," Joyce says, "it's the same thing. All that water."

Cal is handsome; in his tie and blue blazer, he looks ten years younger. He asks whether Ray knows anything about Jazinski.

"Jazinski?" says Joyce.

"Jazz. The wrestler. All-state last year."

"And Howie," says Ray.

"Howie and the Jazz," Cal says proudly.

"They're okay. Jazinski still needs to cut weight."

"Cal could stand to cut a little weight himself," Joyce says, patting Cal's stomach. "All that good cooking, right, honey?"

Across the lawn, Captain Miller is talking with Edith. Captain Miller is nodding, distractedly, and Jenna realizes that Edith is wearing a black dress. Another first, Jenna thinks. First love. First car. First black dress. Although she will never be able to drive legally, Edith is still taking Driver's Ed. Edith is in Ray's class.

"Excuse me," Jenna says. She leaves Ray talking with Cal and Joyce and starts across the lawn, carefully, her knees uncertain and oddly loose. She wants to say something to Walker's father, she wants to say something to Edith, but she keeps coming back to the pain in her eyes—the sheer, terrific pain. Halfway across the lawn, she feels the need to scream. She avoids Captain Miller's eyes, turns, and walks as slowly as she can into the vast parking lot, and she understands now that she is afraid of Captain Miller, and the pain in her eyes, and what it is that he might possibly say to her.

In the parking lot the cars are warm and bright under the late afternoon sun. There is a view of the mountains. The sky is blue. She walks by a paloverde buzzing with hummingbirds; a bird hovers in the air among the branches, its chest glistening, bright as Christmas, but she doesn't stop to admire the bird. Instead she keeps on and once she locates Ray's car, she opens the door, rolls down the window, and sits inside on the warm vinyl seat. She leaves the door open. She rubs her temples, squeezes them tightly, so tightly that her hand begins to ache, until she begins to feel a slowly arriving presence.

"Hey, Ms. Williams."

"Howie?"

She glances up at Howie Bently, still in his coat and bola tie. He is standing in front of the sun and light is pouring over the edges of his clothes. "What'cha doing?" he asks.

"I'm sorry?"

"You okay?"

"What? Yes. I have a headache. That's all."

"Do you need some aspirins?"

"Howie," she says. "What are you doing out here?"

"I don't know. I was gonna give Edith a ride home. In case Joe doesn't show up."

"Joe," Jenna says.

"Yeah, you know. The Jazz." He shrugs and looks at the car. "This your car?"

She nods to avoid further conversation and realizes that Howie must know that this is Ray's car, because Ray drives it to all the away meets and because Howie wrestles and Ray coaches wrestling and because everybody knows absolutely everything there is to know.

"Walker," Howie says. "He really liked you. He said you were a lot like his mom. He used to talk about you a lot."

"Howie," she says, lifting her head. "Are you okay?"

"Sure," he says. "What do you mean? 'Course I'm okay."

"I mean, are you sure you are okay?"

Life makes her weak. On the way home, she can hardly think. She thinks she may never speak again, and she tries to keep her voice inside to keep from explaining just the way she feels. In order to speak, you first have to breathe, and Ray is talking to her now, in the parking lot of Indian Shadows. He keeps the car in gear, his foot depressing the clutch.

He is saying, "So, a lot happens."

"What?"

"A lot happens, I guess. Some kid blows his brains out and everything happens."

"What are you talking about?"

"But nothing's really changed, has it? I mean, okay, Walker's dead. We're still dead, too. Aren't we?"

"Maybe we should just give it a rest."

"Yeah," Ray says. "A breather. Thing is, I thought we were going to have dinner and figure some things out. Instead, *Bang,* and nothing's changed. Not a thing. And what am I supposed to do, next week, when you call me up? I mean, what am I supposed to say to you?"

"Thanks," she says, opening the door. "I mean, okay. See you."

"I've done this before," he says, looking at her. "I don't like it, Jen. You should know this."

"Okay, Ray. Bye."

She shuts the door, stumbles. On the way up the stairs, slowly, working the handrail up the seven flights of stairs, she can see her neighbor's lights; tonight, Bill is home again. Home on a Saturday night. If she didn't have a headache, she wouldn't want to be home, either, though probably she would still be here at home. Maybe not, they were going to have dinner. Then again, maybe not, it's fucked up, bad, and by the time she reaches the walkway, aiming for her door, she can feel Ray pounding up the stairs behind her.

"Hey," he says, taking her arm. "I'm sorry, Jen."

She pulls her arm away. "Ray," she says. "Please. I can't."

"It's okay," he says, going through his keys. He opens her door. Inside, the air is fresh and cool, smelling faintly of oranges and overwatered plants.

"What can I do?" he says.

"Pills," she says, pointing to the kitchen, simultaneously realizing that she has to vomit. "No, wait," she says.

She drops her glasses onto the carpet and stumbles into the bathroom, where she is sick, and the blood expands. She thinks she's going to hemorrhage and she vomits again, and cries. She stands, flushes, wipes her face. She lets her dress fall around her ankles, her underwear. Her bra dangles from her shoulders, and she brushes at it, only it won't let go, and she cries again *No! Goddamn it! No!* and she's screaming, she's gasping and turning on the shower, clumsily, stepping inside and beginning to rinse. The water is cold and hurts her skin, which is hot, and as the water warms, her skin begins to cool. In this life there is simply no longer any balance, and now she's stepping outside, slipping into her kimono, glancing off the walls. Still, she's bending to pick up her clothes, dragging them into her bedroom where she lets them go inside the closet. She shuts the closet door to keep things neat, and Ray is sitting on the edge of her bed, the sheets pulled back, holding a glass of water with two hands. He rises, steps out of her way, gives her the Fiorinal and passes her the water. He has opened up the window and closed the blinds. The room is full of shadows and the hum of city traffic and the steady persistent bass of her neighbor's stereo. She swallows, finishing only half the water, and she lies on her back, her spine stiff as the God's truth, trying not to breathe, because if she breathes again then she will have to live a lie because she can't live like this ever. *Never* . . . and now she tries to breathe, slowly.

"Hey," Ray says, so quietly it hurts; he is too big a man to try to be quiet. He sets a cool washcloth on her forehead. "I set some more in the freezer."

"Thanks," she says, barely.

"Just feel better, Jen. Feel better. I'll check on you later."

"No," she says. "No . . ."

She can hear her neighbor's stereo through the walls: music, fundamentally uninvited. She thinks Ray must be gone and she lies with her arms by her sides, her fingers splayed, a hopeful attempt to flush the migraine through her swollen fingertips. Just as a door is closing, she remembers that she needs to say something . . . *what?* . . . but Ray is heading out the door. She can feel the weight of his body pounding down the stairs outside, and after a while, she stops listening for his car because she knows it's just a matter of time before he drives away. She knows it's just a matter of time before she drifts away.

She's been someplace far away, she feels sloppy and diffused. The bass is throbbing, steadily, mixed with the slow sounds of men and love pumping through the walls of her apartment. At times she suspects she knows the music, though this too she must imagine for herself, which she doesn't for fear of starting up the pain: if she can keep her mind quiet, her mind will rest. When she places her hand against the wall, she can feel it vibrating, and she neither thinks nor understands but simply knows it must be late, or early, because the light in her room is still and gray and because the highway is very quiet. As long as she never moves again, she tells herself, quietly, then she will never feel a thing.

She thinks that without pain, the body has nothing left to lose. After she drove Edith home, she returned to school and cleaned out Walker Miller's locker. She asked Wiz, a retired cop from Florida, to break open the lock; it was the type of request he enjoyed fulfilling.

"This the one?" Wiz asked. He was wearing a golf jacket to keep out the wind.

"Yes."

He took his bolt cutters, two feet long, and snapped the lock. His cheeks looked fit to burst, which she thought just might, and inside were Walker's things: books, notebooks, a pair of huge sneakers, a yellow windbreaker. She was pulling out the books, piling them into Wiz's hands, when a notebook slipped from the pile. The notebook fell to the ground, partly open, and out slipped a photograph. They both stood there, looking at the picture—a woman's pubes, a red polished fingernail languishing amid the flesh.

"Hey," Wiz said, stooping, holding up the picture. "Look at that! The kid's a little pervert, eh?"

She snapped it from his hand and tucked the picture inside a folder. "Thanks," she said, gathering the books. "Thanks a lot, Wiz."

"Anytime. Anytime, Miss . . ."

She hurried through the dark locker area to the lawn past the gym. There were tire tracks gouged into the lawn from all the traffic. The janitors had sprayed sand over the area to encourage the lawn to heal, and the day was still and dark—recently rinsed, unexpectedly cool. There were kids wandering around the wet lawns, cutting classes; and a boy and a girl, against the boiler room, the boy leaning his body deep into the girl, practicing.

In her car Jenna looked at the spiral notebooks—worn and

littered with messages: *Karen, 7:30 . . . Remember essay, dumb-shit! . . . Help. Help Help Help.* Walker's handwriting was round and heavy like a girl's, and she opened the folder and removed the picture. The photograph had been folded repeatedly into squares the size of half-dollars, and Wiz had seen only one side: behind the woman's splayed legs, on the other side, is Jenna Williams wearing half a white bikini.

The public teacher, she thinks, sitting in the car. She is sitting in her car, looking at all the distance, and she wants to laugh and cry both. Because she could have been anyone, really. She thinks she could have been anyone, and the girl looking up at her is so very far away. She's so far away and small.

"Hello," said Captain Miller, at the door.

He wore sunglasses, Bermuda shorts and no shirt. He looked cold. The sun had gone away with the heat and the rain. Most likely, with those glasses on, he could hardly see a thing.

"I brought Walker's things," Jenna said. "From his locker."

"Yes, yes. Please come in."

He led her through the house, which was dark, not a single lamp switched on, and onto the back porch, where he offered her a lounge chair. The lounge chairs were pointed west, where the sun should be, and they were covered with dust, which had settled on them after the recent rain. She sat on the chair and felt the dirt seeping into her dress. On the lid of a gas grill sat a bottle of vodka and a spray bottle full of window cleaner.

"Been cleaning things up," he said. "Windows, walls. It's good to keep things clean. Shipshape," he said, stepping back inside. "Be right out."

I can change my mind, she thought. *I can make up my mind all over again.*

Captain Miller returned, bringing her a glass of iced tea, as if it were summer. He sat in his chair. He crossed his pale legs and smiled, glancing at the notebooks and sneakers on her lap. She reached for her tea.

"Would you like some?" Captain Miller asked, pouring vodka into his glass.

"No. Thank you."

"Walker said you were his favorite teacher," he said, shifting awkwardly. Clearly he had been drinking, though he did not appear to be drunk. He was glazed. He looked at the lawn and sighed.

"I think he had a crush on me," Jenna said. "You know, a schoolboy crush."

"When his mother died, I think we should have moved. I think I'm going to move to Bozeman. I've never been to Montana. All that grass, and the snow!"

"His things," she said, wanting to make a point. She gestured to the notebooks. "I saw some of them, unintentionally. I didn't want to disturb them. I mean, he was your son. I'm sorry if this isn't coming out right—"

"If you lean too far to port, you're going to start doing circles."

"What?"

"Just say it."

"His homework," she said. "The things he wrote to himself. I can take them with me. I can take them, but I thought I should let you decide. You see?"

"I see just fine. I think we should have moved sooner, that's all."

"You see, it might be painful. He was sad, your son. Not that it's anybody's fault. He was just sad and confused."

Captain Miller set down his glass and reached for the vodka. "Have you ever been hunting?" he asked.

"No."

"Me neither. Fishing. I've done a lot of fishing. It's supposed to be enjoyable, though. There're still a lot of things to shoot at in Montana."

I tried, she thought. *I really tried.* Standing, she said, "If I can help, please call. I knew your son. Not well, but we talked sometimes." She looked at Captain Miller's pale skin, the loose folds over the stomach. "I should go."

"It was nice of you," he said, looking at the pool. "Nice of you to step ashore."

"It's only because I'm still fairly young. It's very normal. The boys get carried away sometimes."

"I'm sorry," he said, turning to face her. "I've forgotten your name."

"Jenna."

"Jenna," he said, turning back to the lawn. "Ms. Jenna Williams. Walker was very fond of you." He lifted his drink, a toast to the lawn and his swimming pool. "These kinds of things," he said, "they cause a lot of collateral damage."

She saw her way out through the dark halls; once inside her car, she told herself she'd done the right thing—truth, and the way you looked it in the eye when you were ready. She fitted the key into her ignition and glanced at the house. From the outside, it was a pretty house, decorated with flowers and plants.

The heavy wooden door swung open. Captain Miller, striding across the granite lawn. It was a long lawn, and he was barefoot, carrying his drink in one hand, waving a white cloth with the other.

"Casualties!" he called. "We got to report some casualties!"

"Pardon?"

He was in the street now, in front of her car. He began to wash her windshield with his drink, pouring his drink over the windshield and smearing it with the rag—a pair of boys' briefs.

"You know what death is, Ms. Jenna Williams? You know what death really is?"

He bumped around her car as she stepped outside, the engine running.

"Captain Miller?"

"Like a windshield, if you keep it clean enough."

"I don't—"

"The planet," he said, breathing heavily. "The planet isn't

one big ship. It's one big fleet. A fleet, the size of D day, because if the enemy's bad enough, you're going to have to go to war. You're going to have to invade. Take Inchon, for example. We did a pretty sweet job there. Because we still knew back then. We knew that if you go to war, Ms. Jenna Williams, we knew that then you're gonna have to shoot some guns. You're gonna take some heavy damage and you're gonna have to learn to read the semaphore."

"The what?"

"The semaphore. The guy who waves the flags. The guy who tells you when to fire and where to go. The guy who listens to the big old admiral in the sky." He stuck the rag firmly onto her radio antenna. "A flag," he said. "You got to learn to read the signals."

"Can I get you something?"

"Me? *Me?* I just thought I'd tell you something, Ms. Jenna Williams." He smiled, like Walker. "That's a remarkably long name you've got there." He pointed to the underwear, dangling from the antenna. "That's what I was washing windows with. Makes the best kind of rag—old underwear. Cotton, absorbent. No grease or oil, and you can wash it over and over again."

"Captain—"

"Me, I prefer boxers. All those years in the navy—" He looked at his feet and said, "If you take on too much damage, then you're going to take on water. Hell, look at the Stark. Now days, even a little firecracker can take out an entire goddamn carrier." He withdrew, looked away. "No," he said, hesitating, walking away. "No, no, no."

He finished what was left of his drink and stopped in the road. "You know," he said, turning, "I spent twenty years of my life on a fucking ship. A fucking sub tender, Ms. Jenna Williams. We thought it'd be nice here. We thought this was a place we could figure out who the hell we were. Me and my wife, Lucy. She even looked like you. She wanted to be Joni Mitchell. I met her in college, after a hockey game, and she said she admired my slap shot. My slap shot, you know? I used to play hockey. Hockey! And then I spent twenty goddamn years of my life on a ship, and not once, not once did anything bad ever happen to my family ever. Hell, I had dinner with George Bush, back when he was with the CIA. The CIA and so, yeah, sure, we'd take on some ballast, same as anybody. But Mary Smith Almighty . . . Mary Smith Almighty."

"I'm sorry," she said. "I very, very sorry."

"Go home," he said, waving. "Go home, Ms. Jenna Williams. Go home and live a good life."

He was walking home now, gingerly, across his granite yard, his feet suddenly tender and sore. At the door, he stopped to see if she was still there. The rag fluttered on her antenna, and he stood there, and then he snapped his hand into the air. He stood motionless, saluting.

She thought he might never move again, and she fingered the folded-up piece of paper there in the pocket of her dress.

"Face it," Ray would say, later. "Love is sloppy."

Last February, on the eve of Martin Luther King's birthday, her neighbor Bill stopped by with a bottle of wine. They drank a toast and she decided to take a personal day; if the state of Arizona would not allow for a holiday, then she would have to make her own. Sometimes she feels irresponsible and lost. She rises now to wash her face. In the bathroom, she washes her face and she remembers that Ray has placed some washcloths in the freezer. In the kitchen, she opens the freezer door. There, on top of a frozen green washcloth, sits Ray's key to her apartment, glazed in thin ice.

She doesn't know what to do with it. Next door, the stereo has stopped, and there is an argument. She tries not to listen. If Ray were here, he wouldn't even argue. He'd say, *I can read the writing on the wall. Okay, it's been swell. . . .* She sets the key on the toaster oven. She holds the cloth to her forehead and takes one more Fiorinal, for preventive purposes; Ray is upset, and she will need to avoid chocolate for a week, to avoid coffee and tea, and she will need to talk to him soon. She's been a bitch, an irresponsible bitch, and while her head feels better, she feels ethereal and weak, drifting within the locked confines of her apartment. Free-floating, which is a comforting feeling, sometimes.

Until now. And the voices next door, screaming.

The wall by her couch shudders. Glass, breaking. A window or door. She opens her front door, peeping from behind the chain, and sees a man sprawled naked on the cement walkway. He sits with his back to the railing among pieces and sheets of glass. His arm is swimming in blood. Jenna's neighbor Bill is shouting, tugging on his jeans and shouting, "John! John! Please!"

"I can't get up," John says.

"Please," Bill says to Jenna. "Call a doctor!"

"You mean an ambulance," says John. "But don't. Just get me a towel."

Jenna runs into her bathroom and grabs a few towels; on the way back, she puts on her thongs. John takes a towel to cover himself; he is still sitting on the landing, almost comfortably. *Shock,* she tells herself. She raises his arm and applies a towel. The gash spreads from his elbow to his wrist.

"Move your fingers," she says.

"What?"

"Try and move your fingers."

"I am," he says.

The fingers aren't moving. Her robe has fallen open. Blood is running down her arm into the open sleeve of her kimono, and she's sitting on her heels, drawing together her robe with one hand, holding the man's arm with the other. She says to Bill, "You've got to get him to the hospital."

Others are opening their doors, having a look. Two cruisers are in the parking lot. A cop is coming up the stairs.

"I didn't mean it," Bill says. "I didn't mean it!"

"Of course," John says. "I can't move my goddamn fingers."

"Can you drive?" Jenna says to Bill.

"I'm drunk."

The cop puts on a pair of long yellow gloves. He reaches for

John's arm, and John says, "I slipped. I was standing on the coffee table and I just slipped. I fell right through!"

"It's okay," says the cop loudly. He says to John, "You're bleeding pretty fast." The cop looks up at Jenna and says, "Do you have any more towels, ma'am?"

Jenna finds one more. On the way out, she shuts her door, instinctively, and Bill is picking up the big pieces of glass. He's trying to be helpful and to atone. The cop has wrapped a belt around John's arm.

"Do you want to press charges, John?"

"God, no."

"We're going to run you down to emergency, John. You're going to be okay."

The cop and another are helping John stand, guiding him down the stairs. Bill looks at the glass covering the walkway. Seven stories below, the light in the pool is filling up the water.

Jenna says to Bill, "I can drive you. To the hospital."

"I'm so fucking drunk," he says. "I never get drunk."

"It's okay," she says. "Let me change first."

The door is locked, and Bill says, "Here," reaching above his lamp, passing her the key.

She takes the key, steps inside and says, "Meet me at the car, okay? I'll be real quick."

What she loves most about teaching is the kids. Ray, she tells herself, is a good teacher; he knows why it's important, and she knows that Ray is smarter than he thinks. She knows that Ray understands things that she doesn't want to be true, and sometimes, after showering and looking at herself in the mirror, or walking down the sidewalk to the grocery store, the deviants driving by yelling and calling her names . . . *Hey, bitch. I want to fuck your tits!* . . . sometimes she knows he may be right. She knows the need for muscle and restraint, the need for needing to be strong and maybe even unforgiving. But if he is right, if he is right about all these things that he believes in, then what about what she wants to believe in? Where is that going to leave her?

In the waiting room, Bill says History was his worst subject. "Really," he says. "I always got bored."

"Yeah, I guess that's the trick. To make it not boring."

The waiting room is full of bright lights and yellow chairs. Jenna is wearing her sunglasses, jeans and a sweatshirt. They're at Maricopa County, and two Mexicans are sitting on the other side of the room; neither wears a shirt, and they are arguing about something quietly in Spanish while watching the television.

Bill says, "How's that guy? That big guy I see sometimes?"

"Ray?"

"You know. The walls are thin, that's all. I figure if I can hear you . . . well, you know. It used to make me nervous. I've known John seven, eight months now. I didn't want him to go home."

"Oh," she said. "Yeah."

"See, thing is, he's married."

She doesn't know what to say; she's never slept with a married man, though she has been unfaithful to a lover. Somehow it all seems twisted. The men in front of the television have stopped talking. One of them is drifting off to sleep.

"I just can't believe it happens," Bill says. "One minute, everything's swell . . . and the next, I don't know. I don't know. I don't know how stuff like that happens."

Bill stands and steps over to coffee machine. He wipes his mouth and says, shaking his head, "I don't know. I don't know."

Later, after he's called to the desk, Bill returns, saying, "John's going to be here for a while. Nerve damage, so they think they're going to have to do something."

"Can I help?"

"Hey, thanks. But no. Thanks. I think I'm going to hang out, but thanks a lot." He opens his wallet and says, "I'll get a cab. It's okay."

"There are no cabs."

"Then I'll call someone. It's fine, really." He opens his wallet and takes out a ten-dollar bill. "Here," he says, handing it to her.

"No, Bill. It's fine."

"Please, Jenna. Please. Just take it."

The moon is full, looking like the eye of God, who only rises now to look, fully, once or twice a month, and then only at night. She is home now. She has returned her spare key over Bill's lamp, she has swept up the loose pieces of glass, she has even poured herself a glass of wine, and now she is sitting on the tip of the diving board. She's overlooking the pool—a large pool glowing in the soft blue light of chlorinated water. When she looks down over the edge, she can see herself, her feet dangling near the water, and the shadows she makes against the bottom of the pool.

Last night, at the dance, in her gorilla suit, she wandered around the kids and watched them dance—Lacy, the girl who's always by herself, dancing, and the others. Jenna watched them sneak outside to drink a beer, a shot; apparently, a lot of coke was being exchanged behind the boiler room. After, the kids would return to the gym, smelling musky and warm, dark with the mysterious promise of authority. Once a kid begins to break the rules, she has to start making up her own.

Inside her costume, Jenna grew sweaty and hot—the sweat running down her legs, her fingertips and knees. Ray was dressed like a nerd.

"Is that you?" he said to her.

She pretended not to hear him. She scratched her head.

"Is that you?"

She shrugged. He put his hand onto her shoulder and squeezed. Then she took his hand from her shoulder and held it in her paw, thinking, though Ray couldn't possibly see what she was thinking. She took her free paw and cupped him.

"Jesus."

She began to nod, *Yes.* On the way home, she took off her mask in order to see properly, and Ray followed, his lights cutting a path in her rearview mirror. In the carport, she leaned against her car and waited for him to park, her arms resting across the roof of her car. The area was well lit, and when he stepped out of his car, she held her finger to her lips.

"What?"

"Shhh."

She led him upstairs, where she poured them each a glass of mineral water, because Ray didn't drink. She poured them each a glass of water and she considered telling Ray about the underwear, and the semaphore, and Captain Miller, and about what she was supposed to do for the fleet. She assumed she'd wash the underwear the next time she did her laundry, maybe use it for a rag to dust with, to clean her windows. She knew that in the morning she was going to have to say something.

Ray cut her off. He lifted up his glass, his glass greeting her own, and said, "Face it. Love is sloppy."

"No," she said, shaking her head. "No."

And now, sitting on the board, when she shakes her head, *No*, she watches her shadow ripple across the still blue water. The migraine has finally passed, she has finished her wine, and she thinks that the only thing sloppy about love is the way you never can contain it: once it's going, it runs into your life like a river or disease, like a terrifying secret. And once in love she knows it is possible to tread and sink both, buoyancy becomes relative to weight and the amount of oxygen in the body, and what she wants to feel is the way she feels sometimes when she knows she is entirely by herself but someone near is here and still in reach. Not exhibitionism, but intimacy, the communal isolation of the soul: the way loving once begun will begin to engender its own private heat until she comes by herself in the arms of her lover.

Or he in yours.

The water is ice. And as she swims the length of the pool, she feels blessedly a part of it. Here she can hear only the water, and her heart pumping steadily beneath the nerves of her skin, and she is in the water, pulling herself through the water and someone, someone who has been unable to sleep . . . *maybe someone is overlooking the pool?* . . . someone who is holding a drink, watching her swim, just waiting for the day to rise, because she knows somebody must be watching over her . . . *Somebody, something* . . . and when she rises, up through the water and into the air, she knows it will be like starting over. It will be like starting over and she will have to find her sweatshirt, and her jeans, and she knows that she will be starting over once again.

Slowly, she thinks. And so in need of grace.

Falling

We can only be afraid of that which we know to be possible, and in a world without order, in a world where anything is possible, then everything becomes equally probable—a stray bullet coming home, the promise for understanding why, a sudden realization that maybe you are in fact incapable of knowing love.

When Ray leaves Jenna's apartment, he takes the stairs two at a time, down the seven flights, down the cement-and-steel stairs he can feel flexing beneath the weight of his body. If he can move fast enough, then he won't have to think about where he's going, but inside his car, catching his breath, he has time to think, and to put his key into the ignition; he has time to hit the clutch. The car is too small, his shoulders ache: knots, leading into the back of his neck, and he thinks this should be telling him something. If Walker Miller had never shot himself, maybe they would have worked things out. Maybe, if he hadn't blown it in Pinetop . . . *maybe* . . . and now it's over. It's over because if it's not over then it's going to keep going on, she's going to call him up, or ask him how's it going, in the hallway, and the way she does that . . . *How's it going?*

I just don't think it's going to work, Ray. . . .

"Fuck her," he says. "Fuck her all to hell."

In the gym, he wears shorts and sneakers and a T-shirt; he's climbing the stairs into the wrestling room, which is hot, a room full of blood-red mats soft as a mouth. He starts with the rope—up, then down, and up again. The rope is burning into the skin of his hands which are callused and thick as doors. The gym is silent—the silence of the gaping mats below him, stirred only by his breathing, which he uses to gauge the rhythm of his ascent, and the rope, creaking under the strain of his weight.

Today there is no pattern, on the bench he pushes it hard. Between sets he does flies with a pair of fifties. He does sit-ups on the incline; he works his lats and traps and delts until his torso begins truly to burn: he's tearing down the muscles, flushing out the toxins; if the burn is hot enough, he knows he's done some good. His pecs are twitching, exhausted, and he's already feeling disappointed and spent. He wants his body to be capable of doing more, and already he is feeling the need for rest. In twenty-four hours, he can lift again; rest encourages the muscles to grow and repair. It's something he's taught Jazinski, which is why Jazinski is so good, but Jazinski is also smart, smarter than Ray, and fast: Jazinski has speed, and he's going to be able to do anything he wants. He's going to go off to a fancy private college and be smart and get laid by any girl he ever looks at. He's going to walk into a room full of people and people are going to say, *Hey it's the Jazz! The Jazz!* who Ray knows is going to be tested again and again because the Jazz is strong and smart, and because that's worse than being just strong.

He thinks he has never been smart, just strong, and he understands this imbalance to explain just why it is he coaches wrestling—a sport he was never really any good at—and why he teaches Driver's Ed. Because you can screw up a kid's life by not teaching him enough, or too much; if you say the wrong things, you're going to cause some harm; and while he may not be smart like Nathan Rolf or Cal Buckner . . . *like Jenna* . . . he does know how to try and be safe, which is the whole intent of Driver's Ed, the most popular course at Gold Dust High. He teaches five classes a day. He had wanted to teach Wood Shop and Auto Mechanics, with the derelicts, but Gold Dust High doesn't even have a wood shop. It's that kind of school. *Perfect.*

Truth is hard. It's something he read in college, Humanities 201, with a hundred and twenty-seven other people, all of whom were still under the legal age to drink. If they weren't real careful, they might not pass this class. They read philosophers, and Ray, sitting in the second row, like a dweeb, pushing twenty-six and working with a crew of wetbacks during weekends, bartending at night, because he knew he needed to keep himself busy, because he was waiting, just waiting to be enlightened . . . this is what he thought. He thought, *Truth is hard,* because he knew exactly what the guy had meant. He meant that you've got to be strong enough to never let it break you, and he meant that nobody ever escapes, and if you wanted to be weak, you could always blame somebody else. If you made yourself feel bad enough, you could convince yourself of anything, like:

—*I made him pull the trigger;*

—*I posed naked in a magazine he used to whack off to;*

—*If I hadn't posed naked in a magazine, he wouldn't have gone crazy and stolen a .45 from Howie Bently's garage and shot himself twenty feet in front of me.*

And Ray knows what he knows. He knows, for example, that a magazine is just a place where you store your ammunition, one shell at a time, and he knows that Jenna wants to blame herself for Walker's suicide. If she can make herself feel bad enough, then maybe nobody else will, which means she's going to have to blame everything else within reach. *It's our fault, Ray. It's all of ours!*

"And that means me," he's telling himself, running. "That means me."

In Humanities 201, his class read a couple essays about the Modern World, all one hundred and twenty-seven students, and one guy, Sartre, said, *You are what you do.* If you kill yourself, then you are a suicide; if you do a lot of curls, your biceps will be strong. All you have to do is make up your mind what it is you want to change, and do it, and watch your body grow. Lifting, and if you look into the mirror, you can watch your body grow right in front of you, and reading Sartre, Ray thought this guy was saying everything he already knew. He thought, *How'd he know?*

For a while it made Ray think he might not be so dumb after all, because he thought about the world the same way a famous philosopher did, and this guy was French. In class Ray would even smile up at his professor, a crazy guy with wild hair who looked like a teenager; the professor was supposed to be brilliant, because he was so young and crazy, and would come into class and ask what they were supposed to talk about, it beat the hell out of him. Now Ray understands the world to be capable of making inexplicable connections: transatlantic cables, automatic bank tellers, and history books—all those history books sitting on all those dusty shelves just waiting to be read. The crazy guy with electric hair told Ray to read some other books, and Ray started reading all these books his professor told him to, at night, because that's when Ray needed something to do most. He was going to expand his mind; he had decided that he wanted to be smart, even if he knew it wasn't likely because it wasn't in his genes.

In the army Ray had learned about ammunition and blame and what it meant to drift through the sky at night until you fell into a tree, or a cliff, with the weight of your gear pulling you deep inside a territory recently stocked with munitions and supplies. His division, famous for always being airborne, had nearly been decimated; they had been following orders; once Ray learned everything he was going to learn by taking orders, he ditched out. When it came time to reenlist into the division famous for often being airborne, and once nearly decimated in a foreign conflict, the 101st, Ray closed his bank account. He said good-bye to the famous division and bought himself a pair of surfing shorts. Once, over a territory fraught with wood ticks and federal regulations, Ray had pushed a nervous PFC through the gate.

"Go," he'd told him. "Go."

And Ray had watched the kid falling through the middle of the sky. He was falling through the middle of the night, wearing his night vision and looking at the sky. The night vision made the night seem quiet and unreal—a view of everything the enemy or civilian could never really see, we were that sophisticated a force, accomplished and full of technological wizardry. Because we could see the enemy, and the enemy was blind.

At the time Ray told himself they were just going through maneuvers. They were still going by the book, and if he were smart, he would never have joined the famous division which had once been nearly decimated in a foreign conflict; instead, he would have returned home and gone to the local state university and become a salesman. Instead, he went to college knowing what he wanted: he wanted to be a teacher, because teachers were supposed to be smart, and he wanted to go far away from where he was. He read books at night, which is when he always read his books, trying to make himself smart, the way Abe Lincoln had, and after Ray told his crazy teacher with enthusiastic hair where he came from, a border state, his teacher took him out for coffee and gave him a list of books to read.

Ray has read a lot of books. To get to Arizona, he followed a highway, all interstate, because the world was full of possibilities that could take your breath away, like scenery, and by the time he hit Flagstaff, he knew he was someplace far away. He was in a land which spoke with a different accent—the vowels more open and relaxed—and he took his time, driving down the mountains, looking at the scenery. He drove into Tempe and found a job. His first stop: a bar along the river bottom. He worked at the bar, nights, and during the days he did rough carpentry, and then later he ran a crew of wetbacks installing automatic sprinkler systems: digging trenches, laying out the PVC, screwing on the sprinkler heads and getting very tan. He was responsible for making things grow, and he seemed to like it, thinking, *This is what it's like to teach.* He signed up at the university for Composition 101 and Fundamentals of Math, he was that dumb, and he sat in plastic chairs next to eighteen-year-olds who wore clothes which cost hundreds of dollars. His instructors spent a lot of time setting up their visual aids.

He let his hair grow long, then shaved it off; he decided he didn't like things getting in his eyes. Summers, he worked hard, and *Yeah, he'd seen some things,* he'd say, disguising his accent in the hallway while waiting for a class, holding his books and being polite. He learned to disguise his accent and maybe he'd tell some frat boy or girl wearing perfume and a necklace from Nicaragua something about himself, in order to explain his age and not to seem so deformed, something like *Yeah. I used to live in Tennessee.* Or *Yeah, I knocked around for a while. You know, the Caribbean. Central America. Then I figured out what I wanted. . . . You know.*

He learned. He learned that in polite circles it was better to *travel* than to *knock around.* He learned that if you spoke with a foreign accent in Arizona, it didn't mean that you were stupid; it meant you were from a foreign place, same as anybody. Sometimes, he'd play his accent up for a girl he'd met, and he learned that if he ever wanted to get laid, he should never, never talk about the army. Still, he didn't get laid very often, and there seemed an inordinate amount of effort involved each time: saying the right things, pretending to be a better person than you knew you were, and all that explanation. He dated a sophomore for two months until she fell in love with her professor, the brilliant crazy guy with disturbed hair.

It made sense, really, and just one week after turning thirty, Ray was offered a job at the school where he had done his student teaching, in Economics, with Belinda Fullerton. He learned to follow her lesson plans while she ran errands or met with Andre Langousis in the parking lot. It wasn't much different than being in the military; he spent a lot of time taking attendance. He showed a lot of movies, it didn't take him long to figure out how to work the projector, and when it was over, Belinda Fullerton wrote him a letter of recommendation which was so terrible, so fundamentally scathing, that the principal, Cal Buckner, called him up and said, "We need somebody for Driver's Ed. Interested?"

"Sure."

"I'll see what I can do. Wrestling, right? You used to wrestle?"

"Yeah. In high school."

"Bingo," Cal said. "I'll see what I can do."

Later, during the formal interview, Cal asked Ray about the army. As a vice-principal, Cal Buckner had lived in the Bahamas. *Paradise,* he called it. He pointed at his aloha shirt, because he still missed living in paradise. He said to Ray, settling in, "So why do you want to teach?"

"Because I've been in the army," Ray said, adjusting his blue tie.

He thought that would be it; he could call it a loss and get back to work. Instead, Cal said, "It's a pretty swishy school. Those who should probably go into the army become drug dealers instead. Lots of expensive cars. Still, it's a good school." He lit a cigarette and said, "Nothing like new blood. You'll have to drive around a lot, doing Driver's Ed, but the cars all have air-conditioning."

And Ray got the job, and he didn't talk about his past, the army, which Jenna called immoral and pernicious and insidious. Sometimes, when she wanted to prove her point, she'd use words he wasn't familiar with.

"Patriotism is no longer relevant," she said in Pinetop, Arizona. They'd rented a cabin in the mountains to get away from the heat, and it was the kind of weekend neither of them could afford. It was early in the evening, and they were in bed, sitting up and watching CNN, which was still preoccupied with the anniversary of Tiananmen Square. Apparently, later that night, the decade of the eighties was going to be on trial, and it was going to be asked some hard questions.

Jenna said, "It's no longer relevant. It's become inimical to the spirit of men and women."

He said, "Meaning?"

"Meaning patriotism is as arcane as the Ten Commandments." She said this in her teacher voice, but not quite; it seemed to have an even more precise edge. "It's Old Testament," she said. "Christ turned ten rules into two. But patriotism wants just one that ignores both. Patriotism, as if all you have to do is love your country in order to justify murder and exploitation. Love it or leave it—as if anything's ever that easy." She pointed at the television. "That," she said, pointing at a tank. "That's the army doing that. The army!"

"It's a different country," he said. "What's wrong with being loyal to your country?"

"It means build a bunch of factories in Mexico because the labor is too cheap to know any better. Because in the name of patriotism you can sell guns for oil, just like Ollie North. He's a hero, for Christ's sake! What patriotism really means is that it's perfectly okay to go after anybody who wants to own their own mineral rights. Their cocaine, or their oil."

"You're from California," Ray said. "You wouldn't understand."

"Alien and Sedition Acts—1798, Ray. It's been done before. The McCarthy Trials? You're the one who doesn't understand. You joined the army because you didn't understand."

"I joined the army because it was something I could be good at."

"What? Killing people?"

He got out of bed and picked up his glass. He went into the bathroom and took a leak. After, in the small kitchenette, he ran the tap, waiting for the water to cool. He filled himself a glass. The floors were wood, and he could feel the grit beneath the balls of his feet. The air in the cabin was heavy, the ripe sweat of pine, and when he stepped back into the room, she was sitting naked on the bed, cross-legged, looking at the television. She'd turned the sound completely off.

He leaned his head against the wall and said, "If you don't want to understand, then you don't have to."

She looked up at him, trying to be polite. "You're different than me, Ray."

"I hope so."

"I mean, I'm not sure I believe in these differences. You believe in things I don't."

"What I believe," he said, "is that there are certain things in this world that you don't want to exist. Except they do exist and

I've seen them. I've seen a woman in Managua shove a pistol up inside her just to make a buck. A fucking buck, Jen. You can talk love fest all you want, but if we didn't have tanks in Europe for forty years, there wouldn't be any goddamn Europe. If we didn't have all these poor little dumbshits running around our borders writing home to Mom and Dad, we wouldn't have any goddamn borders to write home about. If a country wants to lay down and get fucked, another's sure to come on by and take its pants off."

"That colloquial humor," she said. "It becomes you."

"Why are you being so bitchy?"

"I am not a bitch, Ray. Do not call me a bitch."

"I didn't call you a bitch. I want to know what's wrong. I want to know why the hell we're fighting about things that take place on the TV. I want to know what the hell this has to do with us."

She dropped the remote. She reached for a pillow and hugged it. On the television, which was silent, stood a bottle of sparkling water with two yellow flowers inside it; last night, before they went to bed, she had dropped an aspirin into the bottle. Water had dripped across the dust on the television, and now she sat hugging her knees while he drew his finger across the dust on the screen.

"Look," he said, still trying. "I'm not going to be perfect. But I want to try. I mean I'll try if you want me to."

She met his eye, and for a moment he was almost hopeful. "I'm sorry," she said.

Looking at her, bracing himself, he wondered whom she was trying to convince.

She sat looking at her toes. "I just don't think it's going to work, Ray. I just don't want this to be anything more than it has."

Standing there, with the wind kicking up through his chest, he felt bloody and sore. So unbelievably stupid, standing there, buck naked, thinking he should have known better.

"Okay," he said, telling himself it was. "Okay."

He looked across the room for his pants. He couldn't find his pants, he knocked his shin against the bed frame, looking for his pants, and that's when he hit the bottle. He hit the bottle hard and the flowers inside and he sent it all flying across the goddamn room.

"That's what I mean," she said, beginning to cry. "That's exactly what I mean!"

Outside the day is moody and uncertain, as if still considering which way to turn, when everybody who's ever been there already knows the answer: it's going to turn into night.

Michael Owens, the undercover cop, looks as if she's sixteen, but inside her purse she carries a badge and, the kids say, a .38. The kids all know she's a cop. She talks to the kids, she gets to know them, and on College Day, with all the representatives from all the colleges all dressed up like salesmen, especially the women—because they are professional, wearing nylons and sensible shoes—on College Day, Michael Owens organizes the tables and tells which kids to go visit which tables. Because most of the kids are ineligible for any significant amount of financial aid, Gold Dust High School is a big hit with private-college admissions offices. Last year, though she never made any drug busts, Michael Owens received the first annual Southwest Public High School College Guidance Counselor of the Year Award, administered by the Private College Council on Higher Education and the Association of Private Colleges for Higher Education. There's a plaque in the hallway, outside her office, and since her arrival, the cocaine traffic has become increasingly discreet. Jenna, in one of her idealistic fits, will refer to cops as fascists, especially those who give her parking tickets.

A fascist, Ray thinks, is what Jenna will call somebody she is mad at, someone who she is afraid will not like her, or who tells her where she can and cannot park. Before Walker Miller blew himself away, like dust, Jenna even called Ray a fascist.

"Sometimes you are such a fascist," she said. She looked beautiful, and he laughed.

It was such a stupid thing for her to say; this afternoon, at the memorial service for Walker Miller, she was absolutely silent. He watched her walk across the lawn, unsteadily, walking over the soft grass and aiming for the parking lot, where he knew she was going to wait for him by his car. He knew she had a headache. Her headaches could last for days, and he was watching her walk across the lawn under the sun while he stood caught between Cal Buckner and his wife, Joyce. He was listening to Cal Buckner ask him a lot of questions.

"Ray," Cal was saying, "I want you to keep your eyes open."

"Howie," Ray said, nodding, watching Jenna recede into the parking lot. "Howie and Jazinski."

"I think Jenna should take some time off," Cal said. "A week or two. We can get a sub. Why don't you talk to her?"

"I'm sure she'd love a vacation," said Joyce. "Maybe you could take one together, now that . . . You know, now that things are patched up?"

"It's not my job, Cal. There's not a hell of a lot I'm going to be able to say."

Jeffrey Nadolny, History, and Robert Horn, Chemistry and Bowling, joined them. Ray saw Michael Owens, at the punch table, talking to a priest. She was holding on to her purse, talking, and Cal's wife, Joyce, was nodding, and now Michael Owens caught Ray's eye and smiled.

Ray excused himself.

Michael said to Ray, in front of a saguaro, "I'm sorry."

"What?"

"About things. The way things happened. It's nobody's fault, you know."

"I know it's nobody's fault."

She winced and looked past his shoulder, avoiding his eyes.

"I mean, I know," he said. "Thanks." He said, feeling obligated to repair the bridge. "How's the captain?"

"At sea," she said. "Completely drugged. It's not the kind of thing that helps. He used to come to our group, at Saint Christopher's. You know Jim . . . ? Father Lawson? We have a social. Maybe you'd like to come?"

"I don't know," he said, nodding. He told himself to quit looking or she was going to take it the wrong way. Standing on her toes, waving, she called to the priest, Lawson. Ray watched a ripple run through the shape of her blouse. Her blouse was made of silk; somewhere, she probably had a trust fund. All of this was taking much too long.

The priest said, approaching slowly, "You're Ray? Ray Morrison?"

"Ray Morrison," he said, nodding. He wasn't certain if priests found it necessary to shake hands. The services, he'd imagined, were all alike. They had a lot of rules; you behaved properly and weren't supposed to question authority.

"The wrestling coach?" asked the priest.

"Among other things, but I've really got to be going—"

"He's thinking of coming to our group," Michael said. And then to Ray, "Thursday nights. This week, it's *Casablanca*."

"I remember the day," the priest said. "You wore gray. The Germans wore blue."

Michael said, laughing, "Isn't it the other way around? The colors?"

Ray figured they were speaking in code, something meaningful and humorous. He shifted his weight.

The priest said, "It's not like it sounds, Ray. We have a good time. Drink some wine and get together. Sometimes we talk about what it means to be single in a secular world. To live alone . . . that kind of thing."

"I'll think about it," Ray said. Across the lawn, Diana Vanderstock smiled brightly to him. She was waving, flipping her hair.

"Bring Jenna," Michael said uncertainly. "Most of us aren't in couples." She turned to the priest and said, "At least most of us—"

"I've really got to go," Ray said, scanning the parking lot. He couldn't remember where he'd parked.

"Please," Ray said to Michael, to Lawson. "Give my best to the navy. You know . . ."

He turned away, walking through the crowd of kids. He could feel the kids watching him, and he knew he was going to have to talk to Jenna, and he knew she had a headache; he knew, too, he should have never come. Ceremonies were for the ceremonial, the army or the church. They were for people who collected together in groups for company to talk about how miserable they felt. AA for the responsible type. He saw Howie Bently standing by himself beneath a paloverde.

"Hey, Coach."

"Howie?"

"Hey. Just hanging out, you know."

"You said the right thing, Howie. Inside there. You spoke the truth. You and Jazinski, I want to see you two on Monday, okay? You all come in early and we'll get this division thing lined up."

" 'Kay."

Howie stood there, looking at his boots, digging at the granite with the points of his toes. The boots made Howie look even taller than he was.

Ray said, "What?"

"You think he would have known better, you know? You think Walker would have known better than to do that." Howie shrugged and said, "Walker, he was a lone scout. He shouldn't have gone off alone like that." Howie glanced at the parking lot and said, "I think Ms. Williams is waiting for you. In your car. I think she isn't feeling so good."

"First thing, Howie," Ray said, squeezing his arm. "First thing. We all are going to talk."

When Jenna called Ray a fascist, just before Walker Miller blew himself to Mars, which wasn't necessarily a very long way off, they were quarreling in his office. He laughed, because she looked so lovely, saying that, and then he said, "No. That's one thing I'm pretty sure I'm not."

Jenna had knocked over a pile of books, angry and embarrassed at being laughed at, and left his office. She left the office and waited outside for him because they were going out to dinner. She said she wanted to make up. In high school, in Kentucky, Ray used to *make out,* and he was sitting at his desk going over the rosters, trying not to think about what he knew he was, and what Jenna knew he was, and why she had become so upset. Because she hadn't meant to hurt him that way, making him say that . . . *No. That's one thing I'm pretty sure I'm not* . . . and because she had made him say it, anyway, because that is what she really was afraid of. The idea struck him, brightly—they were each afraid of the same thing, because even if you made up your mind, nothing was ever certain; one day at a time, forever, and he stewed longer than he should have, his back to the window, thinking about what that meant . . . *It's not the army, it's me* . . . and then he heard the shot. It was a sound he hadn't heard in years—a .45 automatic, standard army issue. He thought a truck had backfired. He thought, *That sounded like a .45,* and this is what he is: a thirty-five-year-old schoolteacher, responsible to no one but himself, and absolutely terrified of what he knows is coming next. He thinks the day is almost over; people do what they must even when they know better.

Truth is hard. He has forgotten his homework, and even though he knows he's not about to grade it, he turns to the simulator—a white trailer, the kind he grew up in, with his daddy, Merle, only this one is longer and has more paint. The trailer is parked on the edge of the lot, and he jogs up the steps, finds his keys, and enters. Inside he hits the light switch. The long room is full of empty stations: cars, olive-green interiors with dashboards and steering wheels left over from the sixties, twenty-nine of them, though number thirteen has been out of commission for months. He was once trained to drive a tank the same way, by faking it, in case of emergencies.

In the back, behind the projector, he locates his driving exams. The lowest, of course, belongs to Edith McCaw, who can't see the screen, let alone the streets she is supposed to drive on. Yesterday, she blazed through a school zone doing 115 m.p.h. In the sixties, people still thought you should be able to go as fast as you like, cars were built for comfort and speed, and while Edith is always remembering to use her blinker, she's also always turning into a factory or tree, depending upon which scenario the kids happen to be following: *A Country Drive: The Risks of Two-Lane*

Passing, or *Urban Traffic: Learning the Escape Routes.* Still, Edith scores the highest on the written work; even if she can't drive, she seems to know a lot about it. She has signed up twice for *On the Road,* the practicum part of the course, where Ray drives around Phoenix with his students in a modified Ford Futura. He has a brake on the passenger side, which he often uses, and on the roof, a sign: CAUTION, STUDENT DRIVER. Ray has yet to figure out whom the sign is actually designed to caution, and he thinks again, and not for the first time today, that some things just aren't fair—like who gets to drive, and who doesn't. He thinks Edith is going to get an *A* in the course, anyway, and he takes the papers, and his grade book; he hits the light and walks out through the dark, vacant metal building. He's got his keys, the lights are out, all the simulators are safely parked, and he's telling himself that some things just aren't fair. Edith is legally blind, and there's only so much you can change, so many things you can really change because even if you are what you do, truth is hard as glass.

The River Bottom is dark and full of smoke.

Freddy, the owner, a fat guy from New Jersey with connections, calls to the bouncer. The bouncer is a washed-out college-football type slipping into the soft decline of his late twenties.

"Okay!" Freddy yells. "Ray!"

The bouncer waives the cover, puffs out his chest, and says, "Have a nice day."

"Thanks," Ray says.

Ray reaches across the bar and shakes Freddy's hand. The hand is dripping with dishwater, and now Freddy is clapping Ray on the shoulder, saying, "Jeezum. By jeezum, it's good to see ya, Ray. How's things? How's things going?"

"Good. Things are just good."

"J.D. and Bud," Freddy says. "Coming up." He wanders down the bar and fetches a mug; he sets up a shot glass and begins to pours. "Jeezum," he says. "Things just ain't the same, Mr. Professor, I tell the girls. Mr. Professor, since ya left, the place just ain't the same!" Freddy pours himself a double and says, "Here's to education!"

Ray hesitates just long enough to make the wait meaningful; he doesn't have to do this, even though he's going to, which he does.

The bar proper is stocked with a few regulars, and eventually the music starts. The music is loud: guitars and leather, drums, and a screaming androgyne, screaming. In the mirror over the bar, Ray watches the girls parade out of the dressing room, which is the same room in which Freddy stores the empty kegs, and they come onto the stage, all six or seven, wandering haphazardly with the music. The girls are in tops and G-strings, most appear to be under thirty, but one, one he recognizes from before, Olivia, she's got to be pushing forty. Last time Ray was here, Olivia was Freddy's squeeze; she ran the girls and made out the schedule. She was responsible for new talent.

"Ray!" she calls, though Ray can't hear her. He watches her recognize him and half step, half tumble off the four-foot stage, and now she's coming to him, stiletto heels and all. Ray turns on his stool and catches her as she nearly stumbles into him. She smells like a bottle of perfume with a nicotine base. He tries not to sneeze.

"Hey," he yells. "How are things?"

"What?"

"How are things?" he yells, sneezing.

"Freddy," she yells, "turn that fucking thing down!" Reaching for a beer, she says, "I'm a partner!"

"Yeah?"

She points to her hand—to a ring with a diamond the size of a blister. Ray thinks it's not the kind of thing a girl usually wears in a place like this. He says, "Congratulations!"

"Last summer. Freddy and me. Just by jeezum flew to Vegas and did it. Took in a couple shows, you know. Got to keep up with the competition!"

Ray's never been to Vegas. He's also never been to a strip

joint much different than the River Bottom. Still, it's a nice place
to drink a beer, see the sights. When he first came to Tempe, years
ago, he walked in and ordered a beer, and Freddy said, "You're
huge! I'll give you a job, you're that huge."

He liked Freddy. Together they drank a lot of beer. Ray could
clear a bar fast, and sitting there, reading his Education books
under the light by the cash register, listening, sipping on a glass of
bourbon, he made the place seem safe even if the parking lot was
perpetually lethal—a lot of stabbings and whatnot. And he thinks,
really, that it's good to be in a place where people still remember
you, even if they are just the owners—Freddy, and Olivia, whom
Ray used to call Margaret because that's her real name. He thinks
everyone else is gone, though, which is fine by him; the girls were
sweet and lonely and always running out of time. They never had
enough money. They did a lot of coke because it made the nights
go fast, and they were a lot like the girls he used to date in
Mayfield, Kentucky, only now they were wearing more expensive
underwear. Usually, they stayed six months, or nine, and then
moved to a different bar, or maybe they went on to L.A., where
they were going to take acting lessons. *Hollywood.* Once, Ray
brought his crazy brilliant professor with independent hair, who
said, looking at the girls, "This is the only place in America where
it is truly possible for a woman to still exploit a man. The system
fucks the girl, and the girl fucks the man who makes the system.
Without ever even touching him!" The professor raised his glass,
pointing. "Poetry," he said, smiling. "Poetry in commerce."

Ray's pretty certain he was the only Occupational Safety
Education major who worked in a titty bar. The bar is filling up
now: men out of work, just now bracing for the day, which is
night, or men just getting off from work and still in the process of
trying to avoid it—here, at the River Bottom, where the women
are sweet and scantily clad. The table dances are going. A second
stage behind the pool tables has opened up. A black-haired girl in
cowboy boots is working on a salesman—encyclopedias, or vac-
uum cleaners. Her hand's on his shoulder, her bikini top in his lap;
her heavy breasts are swaying three, maybe four inches from his

nose, and he's breathing her in, all of her, thinking maybe some-day he'll remember what this was really like, while he's busy servicing his wife, who maybe once looked beautiful. The dancer is far from beautiful, but she is mostly naked.

Four beers later, in the toilet, Ray is standing next to an Indian who's fumbling with his fly. Ray watches a college kid tuck in his shirt. The kid checks his profile in the aluminum foil hanging over the sink, fixes his hair, primps. The kid sees Ray grinning and tries to act tough—lights a cigarette, flicks the match into the urinal, coughs. The kid grunts, and Ray keeps grinning because he's too far committed now. As things stand now, he's pissing out seventeen months worth of sobriety; he's standing by a Native American who can't figure out his fly; he's feeling the need to celebrate and be friendly. If Jenna knew he was here, hanging on to his dick, beginning to sway, she'd never want to talk to him again.

Back at his spot at the bar, a girl has taken the stool beside him. She's in a loose yellow tank—a muscle shirt, he tells him-self—and she's wearing an imitation pair of two-hundred-dollar sneakers. The aerobics costume. The girl is thin and pretty, her face still relatively undamaged, and when she leans forward, Ray can see the beginning of a tattoo deep in the center of her chest. It looks like a lizard or worm.

"Hey," she says, punching his shoulder. "Freddy says you're a professor!"

"Not quite."

"I'm Cathy. Cathy. With a C. I'm a stripper."

"Hey, Cathy with a C. How's business?"

"Okay," she says. "Okay." She's clapping for a girl finishing up her set on stage. The air is suddenly quiet, and she's clapping.

The girl in cowboy boots yells, "Get 'em out of your pants!"

A few men begin to clap, along with all the girls, hooting. Ray sees the college kid, across the smoke with all his friends, and nods. Ray tells himself he's being friendly . . . *easygoing* . . . like back home.

"That's better," Cathy says to Ray. She calls, "Freddy! Gimme a 7UP."

Ray says, "Another set."

Freddy says, "You got it, Professor."

"He thinks I'm a professor," Ray says to Cathy. "He thinks if I'm a professor, by jeezum, it'll make his place a nice place."

"Uh-huh."

"A long time ago," Ray says. "A long time ago I used to work here." He smiles, looking at the shot in his hand, and tells himself to shut up. Cathy with a C has tattoos on her forearms. They look like lizards.

"Oh," he says, swallowing the shot. "How sweet it is." He sets the glass onto the bar, and says, " 'Nother one." He says to the girl, "Sometimes I talk too much."

"It's nice," she says. "It's nice to talk to a guy who doesn't want to fuck you."

How does she know?

She pushes aside her 7UP, extinguishes her cigarette, and says, "It's nice. But I gotta make some money, you know?"

He says, pointing to the college kid with groomed hair, "That kid, he's just waiting for you."

"Thanks," she says, patting Ray's arm. "You're sweet, Professor. You got nice arms, too. But that's not the kind of woman who's going to love you back."

"Huh?"

She smiles, pointing to his whiskey, and walks away.

He's watching her walk away. After three, maybe four and a half beats, she's got the college kid taking out his wallet. The room is full of bodies and the sweet smell of beer, the bitter taste of nicotine cutting through the smoke: like gasoline, and the way it will linger on your hands. Or a woman, the way she smells drifting away on your hands, no longer a fire hazard . . . *the kind who won't love you back* . . . and the room is swollen with women and men, the ratio uneven and necessarily complete. At the door, the bouncer is talking to two guys in leathers—one a Mohawk, another with a beard. The bouncer's telling them to have a nice day and to take off their leathers, and Ray knows the guys are going to give the bouncer a hard time. He's just not convincing, and the Mohawk is posing, and the guy with the beard is jawing, giving the bouncer a hard time, which makes the bouncer nervous. Beneath the bar Freddy has a sawed-off twelve-gauge pump, by the beer cooler. Now the bouncer is standing up from his stool, flexing his pecs, pressing.

Ray turns toward Cathy with a C. He raises a toast to the fine shape of her ass—and a Pegasus, bright as a rainbow, the wings brushing against her cheek. The college kid with friends is blushing; he never expected to pop a rod, to really want to do it; he thought it might be fun, slumming, just to see what it's like, only now he's finding out what it's like, popping a rod in Cathy's field of vision. Olivia-Margaret's up on stage, and Freddy is whistling, because he loves his wife, this woman who still fits herself inside her very first G-string, however snugly, and Ray understands that he is finally here . . . *here* . . . and he understands once again that here anything is always possible. He's thinking if the bouncer doesn't relax, any minute the Mohawk's going to lay him out. The Mohawk's scanning, considering the possibility; things are looking good, any minute . . . but now the beard is saying something to the Mohawk . . . *It's not that big of a deal, Moe. Come on, let's get a beer and fuck 'em later* . . . and they're sliding off their jackets. They're sliding them off and leaving them with the bouncer, and instructions, and the bouncer's setting them there beneath his stool, waving them by, saying *Have a nice day* and now Ray gets a look. The big guy really has a Mohawk, and an earring the size of a toe, the big one, and now the short guy with the beard is pointing to a table near the center of the stage. A man who sells encyclopedias or appliances is sitting alone at the table, admiring the snugly fitted design of Margaret-Olivia, and when the bikers sit at his table, the beard, who's the bully, this little guy with the beard who thinks he's Teddy Roosevelt, fine friend of Chief Mohawk . . . *Bully!* . . . now TR stubs out a butt in the ashtray, and the man who works in a department store . . . *appliances?* . . . now the man is rising, laying a bill upon the stage, receding into the dark.

TR picks up his chair and straddles it, his back to the bar. Ray finishes off his beer and calls to Freddy.

"Where'd you get that guy?" Ray says.

"What?"

"Your doorman."

"He shows up on time," Freddy says. "He doesn't fuck with the girls."

"Give me another," Ray says.

While Freddy pours a shot, the bourbon swelling up the glass, pouring over the rim, he looks at Ray sadly. Now Freddy draws two beers, one for himself, and Ray says, "What?"

"You fall down recently?"

"Recently," Ray says, laughing, and he can hear Teddy Roosevelt yelling at the cowgirl with black hair. He's yelling . . . *Bully! Bully!* . . . and Ray says, pointing into the mirror behind the bar, "That guy, the little guy with his back."

Freddy strains, looking.

"Behind the frat boys," Ray says. "Near the stage."

"Where?"

"By the Indian!"

"Yeah. Okay, I got it."

"He's carrying."

"You sure?"

"Revolver, something big."

Cathy with a C is coming up behind, carrying a tray of empties, placing an order . . . *Two Buds and a Mic!* . . . and Freddy's going to the cooler, fetching the beers.

Cathy with a C turns to Ray and says, "And just what does the professor want?"

Ray thinks she's smarter than she looks; he thinks she's seen some things. He smiles, lifting his glass. "A good excuse," he says, tipping his shot. "Just one."

• • •

In the army, Ray had never seen real combat, though he had been dropped into Grenada along with thousands of others. There they were in excess, overkill, just waiting to make a statement. And he'd been to Nicaragua, training rebels. He didn't fire at a single living target, but he'd seen this kind of thing before: Walker Miller, and holding back the crowd of kids, trying to keep the kids from seeing what they didn't need to. And Jenna, screaming, *You do not want to see this!* and covering up the mess with her yellow towel, and her damp swimsuit, falling out. All the while Ray had tried to keep the kids from knowing what it looked like.

But maybe they should have seen it. The chunk of skull, for example, because maybe you should know what it really looks like and the shit you're going to leave behind—the loose and scattered parts that people you think still love you are going to try to not remember while they're picking up the pieces.

Robert Horn, who teaches Chemistry and Bowling, now wears a bulletproof vest to school underneath his lab coat; apparently, he is concerned about an accidental discharge pointed in his direction. In his Driver's Ed courses, Ray shows the students terror films—badly produced films narrated by world-weary highway patrolman Sergeant Jack. He's the kind of guy who cares but nonetheless confronts tragedy every day of his working life, which accounts for the tone of Sergeant Jack's world-weary voice, narrating. He often shakes his head sadly while visiting the maimed in various hospitals, listening to their stories, and the idea is, if you show kids what it looks like to go flying through a windshield, maybe then they will wear their seat belts. Maybe they'll wear their seat belts and drive slow and keep their hands to themselves, or better yet the steering wheel. It's amazing the things people do while driving down the highway, maybe the kids will at least start to pay attention, but the films are black-and-white. Sergeant Jack has a baggy crotch, the blood is gray, and the heads rolling across the highway are obviously plastic, like the plastic bowling balls Robert Horn uses during Bowling, with the kids in the gym rolling the plastic balls across the gym and aiming for the plastic pins. Nothing ever sounds right, and maybe what Ray should have done was pick up Walker Miller's body, just pick it up by the belt and hang it on a hook. Jenna had wanted to put it in a closet and keep it out of sight, and he thinks he did exactly what Jenna wanted: trying to keep it all out of sight beneath the floodlights with everybody screaming—the really bad parts neatly edited by Jenna's yellow towel, and her swimsuit off to the side, a decoy, while they waited for the paramedics. They stood there waiting for someone to tell them what to do, and now he thinks they should have run it up a flagpole.

Here, this is what it looks like. Take a good, hard look.

Rules, he tells himself, looking in the mirror. You gotta break the rules. And hearts. And bones . . . *Bones* . . . which are the easiest to break. Watching Mohawk and Mr. President hassle the college kid with friends, Ray thinks it's getting now to be about the right time. He thinks there are two ways to kill yourself: the fast way, and the slow way, and he thinks either is fine if you can keep it to yourself, which is impossible. His father, Merle Robert Morrison . . . *Merle-Bob* . . . has been working on the slow way for decades: any reason, anytime. Anytime, Ray thinks. Anytime now and things are going to break. It's the kind of thing he's learned to predict—the weather, even if he never can explain the feeling, or why he's here trying not to face it.

Cathy with a C is doing another table dance, peeling off her muscle shirt, and a girl in a leopard-skin outfit is up there on the stage, straddling the floor, watching herself in the mirror. She moves better than most, and the mirror is filmed with grease and handprints, and she's watching herself in the mirror, moving. Now she's taking off her top, a shirt she has to lift her arms to raise, watching herself, and she sees Ray, watching her watch herself, and she blushes. Cathy's dancing for the college kid's friends, and Mohawk and Mr. President, the bully Teddy Roosevelt, these two lost leaders looking for their leathers . . . TR and the Mohawk, they're busy watching, and now the Commander in Chief is scratching at his ass, his shirt beginning to hike, revealing a .38 . . . *And?* . . . Now, Ray thinks. *Now.*

"Freddy," he says. "Give me a roll of quarters."

The drawer pops, Freddy rolls the quarters across the bar, and Freddy's moving down the bar to the cooler. Ray's going up to the stage, the quarters in one fist, a five-spot in the other, because the girl up there really does know how to move—watching herself like that, moving. The girl is lying on her back now, bridging, stretching the muscles in her neck, and now she's accepting the five-spot Ray is feeding into her mouth. Her stomach is layered with stretch marks, the honest truth, and Ray watches TR strike—his hand on Cathy's ass, and Cathy's hand, swinging, coming across a frat boy's face, and two other frat boys on the floor bluffing for a fight. Margaret-Olivia, in the dressing room, has hit the switch. The music stops.

With everything this quiet, everything becomes equally clear, even the smoke. And somehow, amid all the quiet and smoke and perfume, and the beer, spilling, somehow Ray understands that he is holding Teddy Roosevelt's arm, twisting it just so and snatching the .38 from his waist. Holding the president's arm, Ray knows that he is going to break it. The girl on stage is reaching silently for a stray bill held by an outstretched hand. Ray's twisting the arm that's ready to snap. The Mohawk's taking a swing, swinging wide and short, and when Ray connects, the first time, he knows he's split the skull. The frat boys are lining up against the wall, and Freddy is pointing the shotgun, which is fully loaded, and even now, Ray understands that if he wanted to, he could stop. He could stop and let it all blow over, call it a loss, an accidental drunk. Even with the knife, the bright flickering knife long as a man's cock, and now Ray knows that he is going to waste him. He's going to waste him hard and worse, Ray knows exactly how he's going to do it. Because he's been here before, and because he knows what is coming next.

On the field, in the wrestling room—the most important thing was to learn to take a fall. To treat it like a hurricane or a tornado because, simply, the weather is a hell of a lot bigger than you are ever going to be. There's not much you're going to be able to do to stop it, no matter how much you lift, and what you have to do is learn to let it take you—a woman, kind enough to rock you elsewhere; you have to let her take you where she will and watch her let you go. You're going to have to keep your knees bent, and once you hit the ground, you're going to have try and duck and roll, and you're going to have to keep on rolling with the fall. You're going to have to roll and keep on rolling and maybe, if you're lucky, maybe the storm will blow on by. Maybe she'll blow on by and maybe you'll get back on your own two feet.

It's the kind of thing he needs to explain to Jenna. Driving, carefully, because Ray understands the dangers of influence, he drives to Jenna's apartment. His side is burning and he holds the dressing, applying pressure until he needs to shift into third and, later, fourth. The cut is longer than his middle finger, along his oblique, trimming the fat from his body, and love . . . *love* . . . he thinks, driving. Love means a woman can have a man, but a man can only have beer; otherwise, one is sexist. Meanwhile Ray's driving, taking brief swigs from his beer, thinking he's never done anything stupid unless it had to do with a woman or a bottle. Right now he's keeping one eye shut, following the lines along the highway. He's driving forty-two miles an hour, he thinks, and he's been using his blinker when he remembers that this is something he's supposed to do. The streets are empty except for the occasional cop, passing by at sixty, running through the lights; or a pickup already headed off to work, some new job site on the other side of town, or Ahwatukee, because folks who are normal have all gone into their homes with nice appliances, into their husbands and wives, and now he's listening to the radio, switching to the other eye, which isn't quite as tired, hanging on to his side with the beer caught there between his thighs. He reaches for a fresh beer in order to not disturb the one cooling him off, almost. It feels so cool between his legs. Then again, if he cut off his prick and bled to death, if he yanked out his liver, then maybe he wouldn't go around fucking things up. He's making a left, onto a street named after flowers, pulling into the apartment complex, Indian Shadows. He's yet to see either an Indian or an Indian's shadow here;

someone should report this to the management—false advertising, like salvation. The cars are all asleep, too, and he's in the HANDI-CAPPED, parking, figuring out the clutch, what gear he's supposed to be in.

At least I'm not retarded.

The stairs are steep. He thinks the butterfly might hold. If he had stitches, he'd have to start explaining because he's been here before, and he knows knife wounds are reported to the police, some fine print in the Hippocratic oath, and when he was sitting in the back room, before he truly began to sink, there in the back with all the coffee, he discovered that maybe it was time he started to even himself out. Margaret-Olivia and Freddy, and Cathy with a *C,* and the girl with leopard skin—a private party, postclosing, while he showed Olivia-Margaret how to make a butterfly from duct tape. Before applying the butterfly, he asked Cathy to pour a shot of bourbon into the wound, and while she did he stood holding on to the points of his elbows, anchoring himself, while the whiskey washed through the edges of his body. It felt like dying without ever dying, just standing there and watching it happen to you while you died. Later, he felt slightly resurrected, and they sat around the back room on empty kegs, listening to country music, repeating parts of the story . . . *And then, whammo! . . . Heh heh heh . . .* and the women changed into normal clothes and looked like women, instead of strippers, all jeans and loose shirts, and now there was left only the need to get through the night. He drank more bourbon and beer, and some bourbon in the coffee, playing chemist, and after a while he knew that tomorrow would be Sunday, and he knew that on Sunday he was going to want something to keep himself from dying all over again. He knew that he was going to have to go through it all over again and figure out his tactics, and he was wondering why he was going to have to go through it all again. Why he had given in, though he didn't talk about giving in because he felt so good, so beloved and melancholic, and so he listened to the voices. He held a bar towel to his side, over the duct tape, and began to sink.

Cathy, the stripper with a C, asked him if he wanted to shoot a game of pool; it was true, she did have a lizard in the center of her chest. She asked him if maybe he wanted a ride home.

"You gotta get yourself repaired," she said. "You gotta get yourself repaired real good, Professor. I can help, you know. I know how to help."

Later, just before Ray left, Kyle, or Lyle, came in through the back. He was the leopard skin's man. The girl kissed the man and introduced Ray, who said hello politely. The man was just leaving for a day of work and responsible behavior; he wanted to drive his wife home: each night, this is what they did, and looking at them, at the man and the girl who watched herself in the mirror smeared with fingerprints and grease, Ray knew that they were in love. It made him feel tired.

"I gotta go," Ray said finally. "It's time."

"Ray," Freddy said. He wrapped his arm around Ray's shoulder and said, "Ray. Ray. By jeezum, Ray."

"Freddy."

"That's what I mean, Ray. We're like blood, you know. Like father and son. Anytime, Ray. Anytime. We're even thinking of expanding. You're family," Freddy said, looking at Margaret-Olivia. "Jeezum, ain't he, doll! He's just like family!"

Olivia-Margaret nodded; she kissed Ray on the cheek. When she stepped back, she admired the blistering ring on her finger.

"Honest," Cathy said. "I can take you home."

"No, really," Ray said. "I'll just kick the shit out of the cops, too."

Nobody laughed, and he thought somebody should. It was kind of funny. He could go to prison for seven years and rest.

The stairs are steep now, all seven flights, but he's still moving forward. He's climbing up the stairs, drunk enough to understand that he is in control. It's all under control. He's weak, from having lost it, of course, but now he's got it back. He has it back, and now, ascending the final flight, he thinks he's got some things to tell her. She's got a headache, and he's got to let her know

. . . *Not tonight, Ray. I've got a headache* . . . but maybe she doesn't have a headache, it's been such a long time . . . not tonight, but forever. It's been forever and a day, and inside, the lights are on. The lights are on and he is standing here, knocking.

Next door, the apartment has no window. The wind is filling the drapes; if he wanted to, he could just step inside through the open wall. There's glass, sticking in the edges, and he could step inside and go to sleep, there, on that long, pretty couch. It's so pretty it is blue, and there's a television, and CNN asking a lot of hard questions. He turns back to Jenna's door, knocking, and next door somebody has forgotten to shut an awfully big window. Turning around, he has a look at the pool.

And there she is: a vision of herself. She is standing on the ledge of the pool, pulling her sweatshirt over her head. Now she is slipping out of her jeans. She is standing there, naked, looking at the pool. She is looking at the pool and he can see her, almost clearly if he shuts one eye, because she is down there standing by the water. Looking up, he sees the moon between a hill of clouds, and he follows the light of the moon back into the water, into the small of her back, and the pool. She is diving into the pool, and he can almost hear the water, and the noise her body makes, diving.

He finishes his beer and tosses it through the open window, onto the couch. He reaches for the beam holding up the railing and the roof. He's standing on the railing, balancing, using his hands and adjusting himself. He reaches for the roof, swings himself on up. He doesn't even almost slip, except once, and he lifts himself up onto the roof of Indian Shadows. From here he has a view of the entire city. It's clean as the water in the pool. The city lights stretch for miles, and he is standing on the roof, looking at the water, and this woman swimming through the water, and he knows that inside the water it is cool, cool as the sky and blue; he's beginning to measure the distance. It's not much, he's seen a lot more, and now, stepping back because this is something he's been trained to do, he's giving himself room. He's testing the wind, checking the breeze. He's giving himself plenty of room and now he's running, running into the sky which always, always fails to hold him.

For a moment, it's something that feels familiar, being airborne, and he's sailing through the sky knowing that he is going to land wide of his mark. He's forgotten to account for the wind, he's telling himself to bend his knees and roll, he's telling himself this time he's got to be saved, because he's screwed up, and he's not going to be saved, not this time because *this is it. You can only hit bottom for so long. You're going to have to try and breathe. . . .*

The surface, just waiting to be broken. And Jenna, screaming.

He wipes the water from his eyes, and he understands that he has hit something pretty hard. The water is full of blood—his fingers and hand, wiping away the blood. Somewhere he's popped an artery, and the water's still here, swelling at the edges. An unexpected wave. Jenna's stopped screaming.

"Look at me," he says. "Look at me!"

She slaps him. She slaps him hard and he remembers what this must have felt like. All around him, lights, just coming on. People checking the locks, peeking out from behind the drapes. He can't make out the faces.

Jenna says, "Get out."

"Look at me!"

She slaps him again. He takes her arms, because he could snap her in half, *two,* and now she's crying and he knows that she is never going to be able to forgive him. He knows it's hopeless and he wants her to know he knows this. He wants to say *I know what I did, I'm not stupid . . .* and he wants to say he's sorry and he wants to stop crying.

It's not the army, it's you. . . .

"It's not your fault," he says. "I'm sorry. Goddamn it, I'm sorry!"

He lets her go and swims to the ledge. He's holding himself by the ledge, trying to remember how to breathe because the water's freezing, turning to ice, and now she's swimming over to him. She is swimming over to him and now she turns him by the shoulders.

"Ray," she says, wiping the blood from his face. Steam is rising from her body, into the air, because even ice can be warmer than air, and she is wiping the blood away from his eyes.

"It's not your fault," he says. "It's not your fault!"

"No?" she says. "Then whose is it?"

II

Simulation

Blood is thicker than skin. Blood feeds the bones, lying just beneath the surface, while skin feeds the love you learn to taste and swallow even if it is the very first time. Even if it is the very first kiss.

Edith has white skin, which seems the wrong color, as wrong as *black* or *yellow* or *brown*. *Flesh* is the color of white skin, but not really, and blood is the same everywhere. It comes from the veins. Her father's arm is set in a *splint,* and the tips of his fingers are purple and blue. He slipped in his office, working late and trying to hang a plant; he drove his fist through his office window. He had to drive to the hospital because of all the nerve damage, and he says he can't feel things in his fingers anymore. Sitting in his chair, eating peanuts with his good hand, he's watching the Thanksgiving football game. The team from L.A. used to live in Oakland, and until just a few moments ago, Edith thought Oakland was a place in Oklahoma.

"Have you been there?" she asks her father.

"It's a town, like any other. In '69. No, '70. In 1970, I flew into LAX—that's Los Angeles. I flew in with your mother. We were on our honeymoon. On our way to Hawaii."

Edith wants to know if he's been to Oklahoma, but she says, "Where you had Anderson."

"Well, at least where we started Anderson."

"That's what I mean."

"Indeed."

"Can you feel your fingers?"

"Yes," he says, reaching for the peanuts. "They simply don't move very well."

Edith thinks this is like her eye—the one with the damaged and badly repaired muscles. The muscles in her arms make her look bigger than she is, and Joe says she's the strongest girl he knows. He says he likes her triceps, which are the long muscles in the back of her arms. She likes Joe's quadriceps, and the way they make his jeans swell, and his lats, and the ones leading up to his neck—the deltoids and traps. Last week, out at Fountain Hills, he picked her up by the arms and lifted her over his head, and when her sweater lifted he kissed her stomach, and then her navel. The stars were thick as cream and Joe was holding her up in the sky. If she had been thirsty, she could have had a drink; every time they do something, it's always new. She thinks about what's going to happen next, always, and then Joe kissed her belly button. Four months ago, she never would have dreamed this possible.

She wondered if Joe could tell she had her period, like dogs, and the way they always seem to know. Her mother has PMS and it makes her moody. Last week, she asked Edith if she needed to go on the Pill.

"Mom!"

They were in the car, on the way to Dillard's After Thanksgiving Day Sale, the biggest shopping day of the year. Already there were Christmas trees on the streetlights, and candy canes, and her mother, Ellen, said, "Edith, don't be a prude. The Pill," she added, driving too fast. "It prevents accidents."

Later, at the coffee shop, Edith said, sipping at her chocolate soda, "It gives you cancer."

Ellen drank coffee, she lit a cigarette. Beside Ellen in the booth sat their After Thanksgiving Day Sale packages. Edith had two new bras, the type that clips in the front, her first, and a navy cashmere sweater, also her first. The sweater cost over two hundred dollars, but her mother said it was on sale, not to worry. She said it was a mother's duty to buy her girl her first cashmere sweater. Ellen had said, "Here, feel."

Edith had never felt anything like it. She thought about wearing it against her skin and the way it would make her skin feel. Now she looked up at her mother, across the coffee-shop table, who was looking for the ashtray.

Her mother said, "Everything gives you cancer, Edie. You've got to be careful." She said, "Is Joe careful?"

"Mom—"

"Boys make girls pregnant, no matter how good they are. And sick. We're going to get you some condoms. Does Joe have condoms?"

Edith looked at her soda. She didn't know if Joe had condoms.

"That's okay. That's fine. But someday there's going to be a boy—maybe Joe, maybe somebody else. It doesn't matter. It's different now, you kids. People doing it every half hour on the television. You'd think that's all people did. You'd think they never got sore. You'd think it's easy. And it is," she said, reaching for her coffee. "It is easy. But it isn't, either."

"I know that."

"I mean nothing good is ever easy. Nothing."

"Oh," Edith said. It was something her father always said, too. She said, "What about Dad?"

"We're talking about you, not Dad."

Edith thought they should be talking about Dad, and what he had been doing. She thought she wasn't the person they should be worried about right now. She had never even touched anything.

"My mom," Ellen said, "Grandma Jean. You know what she told me about sex?"

"No. What."

"She said, 'Take a lot of baths, read in bed, and don't give yourself to any man unless he thinks you're beautiful.' " Ellen laughed and said, "She was what you call modern."

Edith's not certain why this is so modern; when she takes a bath, sometimes she'll stay for hours. She finished her soda and looked at her shopping bag. She wanted to put her sweater on, and she wanted to have a good reason to wear it; sometimes she wanted to be alone, and sometimes she didn't.

She pushed the soda glass away and Ellen said, "You're beautiful, Edie. You could break a boy's heart, I swear to God."

But if she were beautiful, she'd have hair like Carol Cunningham's, which is flaming. She'd have guys looking at her all the time, like Diana Vanderstock, posing, letting them look; or else she'd wear black clothes like Lacy the Dancer and never even think about it. Now, sitting here by her father, who's watching the halftime parade, which is taking place far away from Oklahoma, Edith thinks that while she may not be beautiful, she can still break somebody's heart. All somebody has to do is love you, and even ugly people get married and have children. Hurting someone, she thinks, is how you test somebody's love; it's what her father does, only it seems dangerous and wrong. All you have to do is ask, but instead you go around and hurt people to make yourself feel better: the things you say, back and forth. The way you slam the door. Mostly, she wants to know if she should be worrying.

Carol is driving. She is driving her father's Bronco because it is big and because her father doesn't think Carol can get hurt driving a big car as long as Carol wears her seat belt. Last year, on Tatum, a fancy pickup truck drove over a cliff. It was going too fast; a boy was driving, Robin Mendelberg, who was showing off for his girlfriend, Suzy Dribble. If Suzy Dribble hadn't been so pretty, people would have made fun of her name; she was lucky, being pretty, and they were driving too fast and went over the cliff and died. They found cocaine in Robin Mendelberg's pockets, now the speed limit is thirty-five, and cops wait on each side of the bend with radar guns. After, Mr. Buckner said something over the

P.A., and every year, Edith thinks, every year somebody new is dying.

In the supermarket parking lot, Carol puts the Bronco into *P* and says, "Okay?"

"Okay," says Edith.

They walk inside, past the hair salon that takes care of the old ladies—the blue-haired specials; they walk through the aisles of groceries and into the space reserved for appliances, televisions, and alarm clocks that talk. They go past the radar beams into the music section. Edith has forty dollars in the pocket of her jeans, and she and Carol go through the CDs and look for ones on sale. Edith's father still has a stack of eight-tracks, sitting on a shelf next to the albums, but the eight-track player doesn't work anymore. When Edith and Anderson were little, they listened to music by the Carpenters. Karen Carpenter died because she was anorexic. When she sang, it was always pretty and lonely, even if she was on an eight-track, going *click* in between the songs, and then she starved herself to death. She used to play the drums, too—skin and bones, singing. Edith's father says he always had a crush on Karen Carpenter, which makes absolutely no sense, even if he did get married, and Edith doesn't even have a CD player.

If she finds one she likes, though, she can always get the same on cassette which is cheaper anyway. She can always get something for Joe. On the CDs, the pictures are bigger. They're so bright and pretty.

"Come on," Carol says.

Edith leaves the G's in the Rock 'n' Roll aisle and follows Carol back through the radar and into Pharmaceuticals, across Toys, and east to the Condom Display. They stand at a distance, pretending merely to be curious, on their way maybe to pick out some toothpaste or shampoo, only from this distance Edith can't make anything out. All she sees is boxes with pictures of moody sunsets.

"Lubricated," Carol whispers. "That means they go on easy."

"Lubricated with what?"

"Oil. They come in assorted colors."

Edith thinks this is weird; she steps closer to the display, suddenly realizing this isn't weird, it's stupid—coming to this store. She no longer feels like a mature woman about to buy any ordinary household item; instead, she feels like Roxanne, the retarded girl, dropping half her sandwich into her lap during lunch. Her entire neighborhood, including Roxanne's mother, shops at this store. Sometimes you see their car parked out front in the HANDICAPPED. They should have gone to a supermarket in Glendale or Wickenberg; in college, you can buy condoms in the dormitories, from machines, one at a time. Anderson says some guys buy five or seven all at the same time, meaning himself, because he lives with his girlfriend, Laurie Something, who isn't even twenty. FORM FITTING, she reads, squinting. SAFETY IN LOVE. A WOMAN'S PLEASURE. Anderson, when Edith was a kid, said condoms were a lot like balloons, only people didn't want to blow them up.

She reaches into the rack and selects a box containing a VARIETY OF STYLES—a baker's dozen, like cookies. Carol picks the same box, and now they return to the music section, nonchalant, whistling, along the way looking at the toys in Toys. They're carrying their small boxes with the pictures of moody sunsets turned inside against their hips, bouncing along. Edith picks out a tape with a picture of the Pacific Ocean on the cover, then turns and heads to the checkout stands—all thirty-seven. The store is bigger than an airport, and along the way she picks up a pack of chewing gum, telling herself this is just like any other shopping day, friends and shoppers . . . ASSORTED GOODS: FOR FEELING IN LINE . . . and now, at the checkout, a boy she doesn't know with acne like Walker Miller's is ringing up her purchases. He spends too long looking at the condoms, because the electronic register won't pick up the price, and now he has to punch in all the numbers. He's punching in the numbers, slowly, with his finger, and she realizes that he is embarrassed. He is shaking and the tips of his ears are flushed crimson.

"My husband," Edith says. "You know . . ."

Carol is giggling, and while Edith waits, the boy picks up

Carol's box, looks, and panics—all those numbers. He pokes at the keyboard with two of his fingers, to be efficient, and now he's scanning Carol's shampoo and tampons, and Carol is going through her wallet. She is almost ninety cents short; tampons actually cost a lot of money. Behind her a woman full of groceries and children, because she didn't use condoms, is pressing with her cart. The checkout boy's ears are full of blood, waiting, and Carol is going through her change. Carol pushes the cart away from her, into the negligent lady, and says, "Do you mind?"

Any moment, and Carol will either cry or laugh, Edith can't tell which. She passes Carol a dollar bill and sees Mrs. Fullerton, the Economics teacher, coming through the front doors. She's wearing yellow tights and lots of silver chains.

Edith thinks the grocery store is a good place for someone the size of Mrs. Fullerton to visit often. Maybe Mrs. Fullerton is going to buy some condoms, too. And bologna, and a fifty-pound bag of new potatoes, and Carol is tugging at Edith's sleeve now, laughing, and Edith knows the embarrassed boy thinks Carol is laughing right at him. The boy says, "Have a nice day," because if he doesn't he'll be fired, and Edith feels sad. His ears are so red and hot.

"Thank you," Edith says.

"Hi, Mrs. Fullerton!" Carols says, waving.

Mrs. Fullerton looks, blinks. "Hello," she says.

Carol runs on ahead of Edith, through the electric doors, outside into the parking lot. Edith wonders if Mrs. Fullerton is going to think they are on drugs—cocaine, which does the same thing adrenaline does, only cocaine kills you. She thinks Mrs. Fullerton is going to blow away and that Mrs. Fullerton doesn't seem to know who Edith is. Mrs. Fullerton, who is having an affair with Mr. Langousis, Edith's Life Science teacher, is standing behind her empty shopping cart staring at a girl with thick glasses in a supermarket the size of an international airport, and now Mrs. Fullerton is going to fill her grocery cart with products.

"I'm just visiting," Edith says, heading for the doors.

Once outside, she tries to remember where they parked. She

stands on the curb, holding her condoms which make love safe, looking, and she is watching all the cars go by. All in all, there are probably seven billion, and from this distance they all seem to have four wheels. They all have four wheels and look the same.

They're late for practice and Ms. Williams is mad.

"You're late," she says, in the locker room.

In the water Edith wants to make up for being late. Mr. Rolf blows a whistle, which he always does, and she swims hard and fast: thirty free, the standard warm-up. After, they're going to do suicide sprints, and the water is cool and smooth. When she reaches for her first turn, she pivots early and loses her speed, the wall is too far away and she has to begin her stroke early—a car, in the wrong gear, chugging uphill in the rain. Water is dripping in through her goggles, the chlorine is sweet and she's going to make up for being late. She's going to make up and swim until Ms. Williams is no longer angry, until she can call her Jenna all over again, though it's pretty clear Ms. Williams has been angry for quite a while. She and Mr. Morrison have broken up, and Mr. Morrison won't talk to anybody; he's always striding down the hallways, looking at the walls, or the floor. When Ms. Williams and Mr. Morrison meet in the hall, they don't even smile at each other, though Mr. Morrison always says hello. *Hey,* he says, sounding like he's from Alabama, and then he keeps walking down the hallway, pretending he's really going somewhere else because he never even sleeps. That's exactly how he looks: as if he never even sleeps.

Stroke!

To the left, Ms. Williams is pacing the deck, following Edith. She's pacing the deck in her suit, blue as a dark sky, and she's yelling at Edith—*Push It Push It Push It*—and when Edith reaches for the wall, preparing to turn, a hand bites into her arm and pulls.

She's blowing water from her nose, sputtering. "What?"

"Your head," Jenna says. "You're dragging your head. Get your head up!"

"Okay."

"Look into the water. Get your head up and you'll cut half an hour. Get your head up, Edith!"

"It gets in my eyes."

Jenna reaches for Edith's goggles. She grabs and pulls, yanking the strap from behind her ears, her hair. Looking up, Edith can barely see the outline.

"You think that matters! You think it even matters! Get your head up. Swim *into* the water. And quit favoring your right."

"I'm not."

Jenna swings into the water. Edith thinks that Jenna's going to hit her. Instead, Jenna stands waist-deep and tells Edith to stretch out. She holds Edith's body level, and her hands are warm, because she's angry, and the heat from her fingers is going through the skin of Edith's suit. Edith tries to listen and to float still.

"Breathe from your left," Jenna says. "Okay, your right."

Edith starts to turn to her right, but before her jaw even begins to clear the water, she feels Jenna let her go. Edith finds her feet while Jenna pivots behind her, grabbing her neck and turning her head to the right.

"There. You feel that? Did you feel that?"

"Yes."

"There. Every time. Every time you glitch. You glitch. You smooth out that glitch, Edith. You've got to smooth it out and keep your eyes level."

Edith turns so she can see who's talking, but she can't see a thing—just the blue which is Jenna's swimsuit—and Edith knows that Jenna's angry, and she knows that Jenna's beautiful. She's staring at Jenna and thinking that she hates her. She's telling herself she hates this person who's yelling at her just because she's late, no matter how beautiful she is, and everybody else is finishing up. They're lining up beneath the blocks, listening to Jenna explain how much Jenna hates her. Mr. Rolf, even, who's telling people things, is listening. They're all listening and watching Ms. Williams.

"You're late. You're not concentrating. What do you want?"

"Nothing."

"Nothing? You want nothing?"

"No."

"Then get out. Get out of here, Edith, and don't come back until you know just what it is you want."

Jenna swings up onto the deck, the water pouring off her suit, and yells, *Blocks! Line up!* and now everyone is lining up. Even if Edith didn't leave, she'd still have to finish her warm-up with everybody watching. The boys are standing around shivering with their arms crossed because they have less fat, and the girls are standing beside them holding their hands on their hips. Edith is pulling herself out of the pool, and Carol says, "Hey. Hey?"

When Edith turns to look, Ms. Williams doesn't even notice. She's busy setting up the clock. In the locker room, with the door open, Edith can hear the swimmers making their dives into the water—and the water, churning. Normally, when Edith dives from the block, she stretches out her body and tries to make it long; by now, the team is halfway across to the other side, and every time she dives, Edith thinks this time she just might do it perfectly. Under the shower, rinsing her suit, she tells herself she hates Jenna . . . *I hate her* . . . and she is wringing out her suit. She's standing beneath the shower because she isn't going to cry, because every time you dive you always have another chance to make it perfect, and from outside she can hear the voices, and Mr. Rolf, whistling, and the water churning up the pool which will always sting your eyes until they start to bleed.

The condoms are *clear,* which means they are the color of flesh, whatever that color happens to be. Joe's arms and shoulders are tan, brown like deerskin fading into the center of his chest, which is always pale; she doesn't know what color the rest of his body is, though probably it's the same as his mouth. Anderson says that lips are the color of everything that matters. All you have to do is look at someone's mouth. She has felt it, Joe's mouth, and what the color looks like swelling beneath his jeans. His jeans are blue, the same as her father's fingers, because they are swollen with blood, and she doesn't know what anything really feels like. The jeans are thick cotton, sometimes almost white, from all the washing.

In her closet, at the bottom, by a box that says EDIE'S B-ROOM, she finds her old ice skates from Michigan. She doesn't ice-skate anymore because she lives in Arizona, where there is no ice, and she puts the condoms into her skates, tucks them beneath the tongue, and she thinks that someday it is going to happen. Last week, before they went to Fountain Hills, they went to a party out in the desert. The party took place near 126th—a boondocker, which meant kegs in the back of pickup trucks and off-road lights pointed into the sky. There were kids from Phoenix College, and Scottsdale Community High, which is really Scottsdale Community College; the name for Phoenix College is FK, though it took Edith a long time to get the joke. The desert was full of all these people from all these places. Off to the east were new homes, big ones which cost millions of dollars, and Joe parked near somebody's driveway away from all the cars and noise. He was checking out the territory.

"Five years ago," Joe said, "all this was desert. You didn't have to drive so far to have a party."

Five years ago, she thought, Joe was twelve. They approached the party slowly. People were wandering around drinking beer from plastic cups. After a while, Joe was drinking beer and talking to Howie Bently and McGregor and some guys from FK who used to wrestle at Gold Dust High. Edith listened to the music and looked at the sky. It was pretty, full of stars and lights, and the valley below, Mesa, where the Mormons live and sleep with fifty wives. The wives wear special underwear, which most people never see, and Edith doesn't know what they believe in.

"Hey," Howie Bently said.

"Hi, Howie."

"How's it going?"

"Okay. It's nice out here. It's nice tonight."

"Yeah," Howie said. "Walker and me, we used to come out

here a lot. He really liked it a lot. We'd come out here and drive around, you know. We'd drive around and stuff. It was pretty good."

Joe came walking over with McGregor, who was huge, and Colin Houston.

"Hey, Ed," said McGregor.

"Edith," Edith said.

"So fuck," McGregor said. "Like, where's all your friends?"

"Beats me," Colin Houston said, shrugging. Everybody looked at Colin. He was lighting up a joint. Edith loved the way that smelled—*marijuana*.

Joe left to get more beer, and some girls were dancing in the back of a pickup truck. In one car, parked, Edith could hear a girl screaming. Colin was sitting on the ground, Indian style, smoking his joint. His peace joint, he called it. Sometimes he'd look up and smile. Howie asked if anybody had any blow, and then he wandered away. She didn't know where Joe was, he could be anywhere, and when Howie came back, he asked Edith if she wanted to do a line, which she didn't, because she was afraid of what drugs would do to you, even though she always wanted to do some, just to see. Howie opened a small package of foil. He wet his finger, put some on his finger and told her to snarl.

"What?"

"Come on, like you hate me."

"But I don't hate you, Howie," she said, flirting.

"No, come on. Just pretend."

She tried to snarl, and now he was rubbing his finger along her gums. She could feel his finger inside her mouth; this was just enough to give a taste. Like chalk, and his finger, and after a while it made her want to kiss. It made her mouth alive and she wanted to kiss for seven hours. Then Howie used his McDonald's spoon, the kind you stir your coffee with, and snorted. She stood there, thinking, fingering her mouth.

"Like sex," Howie said. "You know—"

"You know Carol?" she asked Howie.

"Carol?"

"Yeah. You know, Carol Cunningham?"

"Yeah. Sure. Red hair."

"Flaming."

"She's real nice. You sure you don't want to try some?"

"Try what?" Colin said.

"Nice what?" said McGregor. "That's what I want to know. Nice what?"

"Mellow out," Howie said.

"Hair. Nice hair," Colin said, nodding. "Real red."

"Fuck you, Bently," McGregor said. "Eat—"

"Hey," said Colin, holding up his joint. "Hey!"

"Hey—" said Joe, jogging up to them. He didn't even have a beer. He took Edith by the shoulder and looked at Howie. "Come on."

"What?"

"Cops. Come on!"

They ran. Slowly at first, a loose pace along the edges of the lights. Once into the shadows, she could feel Howie, his hand on her shoulder where Joe's hand had been, guiding her along because she couldn't see anything for all the dark. They were running along the edges when the siren hit, splitting the sky, and the floodlights coming on across the street, lighting up the sky, and the cruisers—all five or six. She could hear McGregor, panting, *Oh fuck Oh fuck Oh fuck,* and Colin Houston, laughing, and farther away the girls in the pickup truck began to scream. The sirens stopped and a cop was giving commands into a bullhorn . . . *Do not move! Do not run away! Stay where you are!* . . . and they were running, through all the mesquite and cholla, and the thorns, across a creek bed and down a gully into Mesa, where the Mormons lived, miles off.

She could make out a wall cutting through the desert—white stucco, tall as Howie, marking off somebody's property and glowing in the moonlight—and she knew that she was going to go up and over, following Joe and Howie, who both stayed at the top to help her over. They reached for her arms, and when she turned around, to look, she couldn't see a thing.

"Colin," she said. "Where's Colin and McGregor?"

"Come on!"

She was pulling at their arms, pulling herself up onto the wall, the wall scraping at the soft parts under her arms. She straddled the wall and began to swing down. Once on the ground, they sat very still, breathing.

They were in a large backyard—big as a soccer field—and in front of them stood a tall chain link fence for tennis. She could see lights, and a swimming pool, bright as day.

"I knew it," said Joe. "I fucking knew it."

"So," said Howie, laughing. "So we almost got busted." He reached into his army coat, pulled out two beers and sprayed them open. "How 'bout it?" he said, holding one out.

"Fuck," Joe said. "FK—all those dicks from fucking FK—"

Edith reached over and kissed Joe's neck. She kissed his neck, tasting like salt and the way he smelled, and listened to Howie laugh.

"Almost," Howie was saying. "We almost pulled a Walker Miller!"

"Almost," she said, thinking maybe she was drunk, though she knew she could run for miles. She never felt out of breath, and she couldn't tell if she was drunk. Instead, she felt almost breathless.

In her room, reading over her History notes, waiting for Joe to show up, she thinks she doesn't know what she is doing. She's supposed to be reading her notes, which are all about Vietnam and the feminist movement, though she's not paying much attention to either. All that is history; in the sixties, people began to make the country what it is.

Broke, says her father.

A land of democratic impulse, says Mr. Nadolny. *If everyone is equal, then everyone is equal. . . .*

Pretty wild, if you ask me, Walker Miller said, once.

When the doorbell rings, she knows it's Joe. Standing in the hallway, she watches her father talk to him.

"Hello, Jim."

"Hey, Mr. McCaw. How's your arm?"

"Edie!" her father calls. "Your beau's here!"

She stays in the hall, almost hiding. She's listening to her father interrogate her date. He's busy thinking up the questions. He says, "You guys going out tonight?"

"Yeah. You know," Joe says. "Maybe we'll go see a movie."

"What movie?"

"Whatever," Joe says. "I mean, what's showing."

"Got your car painted, eh?"

"Yeah," Joe says. "Almost. It's just the primer. I still got to do the other side. From here it looks done, I guess."

Now her father's running out of questions; he's talking about what's taking Edith so long. Looking at his back, and the way his shoulders move when he talks, she thinks that her father must have had to do this, too. He must have had to talk to parents and explain all these kinds of things. Her father thinks she's sleeping with Joe—*fucking*—because that's what everybody does. She pictures her father going through her desk, her closet, reading through her diary and finding her condoms in the well of her ice skates. For a moment, she almost decides to bring some.

How many?

"Edith?" says her father.

"Hi!" she says, kissing Joe on the cheek.

He blushes, because she's kissed him here in front of her father. Now she kisses him on the mouth.

"You kids be careful," says her father.

"Okay," Joe says, blushing.

"No," says her father. "Not okay. Be careful. There are crazy people out there." Her father points outside with two of his purple fingers. "Out there," he says, "there are some crazy goddamned people. People that'll kill you if you even blink. You be careful, that's all. You be real careful. I mean, I don't even know you, Jim."

"Bye, Dad."

She takes Joe's arm and waits for her father to shut the door, but he doesn't. They walk across the granite to Joe's car, parked behind the yuccas, and she can feel Joe shaking because he's so nervous. He says, softly, "Carol said you got in trouble today. With Ms. Williams."

"Nah. Not really."

When the door behind her finally closes, she thinks it's about time. It's about time she quit swimming and grew up. She thinks the door is closed and that means her father knows exactly what she is going to do. In the car, watching Joe put his key into the ignition, she feels giddy and dangerous.

"So, Jim," she says, laughing. "What are we going to do?"

Fourteen miles east of Scottsdale Road, up Shea Boulevard, up along the rim of the valley past 124th Street, sits Fountain Hills—a housing development famous for its artificial lake and fountain. The fountain, which erupts every hour, on the hour, is the largest fountain in the country, maybe even the world. It shoots hundreds of thousands of gallons of water up into the desert sky and people from Berlin and Rio de Janeiro all come to see it. From miles away, they can see the fountain shooting up into the sky, and the rainbow it makes, after, and this is the place Edith and Joe go most often—to Fountain Hills, because there it is easy to park and not be disturbed. The place is even patrolled by security. The security people drive around the lake slowly and shoot their spotlights across the lawns, lighting up the sky just overhead, and they are nice and never shoot the light inside your car. Instead, they just let the lights sail overhead, letting people know they're always close.

While Joe drives out of the city, Edith watches the lights ripple along the hood of his long car. The hood is long and the new paint is full of ripples which make the light resemble seawater—gray and very, very dark. At night the city is beautiful, like a postcard, and she's watching the light. Joe's beating his palm to the music, his palm bouncing off the dash; he's driving the huge car with just one hand. In Driver's Ed, using the simulators, they have to drive with their hands at ten and two o'clock, but Edith knows only old people really drive this way. Once, when Edith told her mother she shouldn't drive this way, her mother said, "Okay," and then turned up the radio. When her mother wants to think about things, she always says, "Okay."

That way, Edith thinks, everything really is: everything's fine and going to be okay. All Edith's life her mother has said if she hadn't eaten meat, maybe . . . maybe then the parasite—*toxoplasma*—would never have snuck into her body, which then snuck inside Edith's body. She has seen pictures of fetuses, looking like small people with their eyes shut tight, and sometimes Edith imagines herself in a small pool of water, someplace deep inside her mother, keeping her eyes shut tight to keep all the bad things from outside getting in—disease, parasites, things that afflict the cornea and make you blind.

"In real cities," says her mother, "people don't drive, anyway. It's too much of a hassle."

Mr. Morrison always says that life is not a watermelon, and a hassle is something difficult. It's the kind of word teachers use when they want to show their students how much they really understand things, and outside, beyond the windshield of Joe's car, is all of Arizona—the sky, the dust, and all the people driving. Her father, when he wants to get on her good side, says maybe he will buy her a car, anyway, and she knows he's only promising because it's not something that's ever going to happen. Today, in the simulators, while trying to parallel park, she ran over a cocker spaniel. She never even saw it, but she knew Mr. Morrison was back in his booth, adjusting the focus, taking notes.

"The dog!" he yelled to the class. "Watch out for the dog!"

Joe says to her now, in the car driving east toward Fountain Hills, "What's wrong?"

"What?"

"What's the matter?"

"I killed a dog today. In Driver's Ed."

Joe turns and smiles. "The cocker spaniel?"

"Yeah."

"Ever notice how they always use little dogs? You don't ever seen any Great Danes. No Saint Bernards."

She takes his hand and looks at it. His hand is covered with calluses from lifting weights; the cracks are filled with gray paint, from the car, and she thinks about all the places his hand has been and all the places it is going to be: it's going to hold his very own credit card, and laundry detergent, and law books, because Joe will probably be a lawyer like his dad. Either that or a broker. It's going to polish shoes, and every day, every day for the rest of his life, he's going to run his fingers through his hair. He's going to hold the steering wheel of all the different cars he's going to drive, and each year, he's going to be introduced to people he doesn't know yet. He's going to do all the things everybody gets to do only she doesn't know what they are. Gypsies know, and can tell you just by looking at the cracks in your hand, and closing her eyes, holding his hand, she thinks there are so many things left for them to do. So many places still to go.

That night, the night they were chased by the police into the millionaire's backyard, sitting against a wall and drinking the last of Howie's beers, she sat with her arm around Joe's waist and kissed his neck, and she soon realized that they weren't alone. McGregor and Colin Houston managed to make it to the highway, where they were given a ride home by someone from Scottsdale Community High, but sitting there in the yard, finishing their beers, Edith and Joe and Howie began to hear voices, and then the voices came outside onto the patio, which was lit, and the voices carried across the dry air the way they might across a still lake . . . *far* . . . and here they were, still as salt, listening: a woman, laughing, happy and full of music; and a man, also happy, and then the splash of water. The man and the woman splashing in the pool. Edith sat very still, not moving, listening to the voices and the bodies splashing in the pool. *Watch!* said the man, on the diving board, diving into the pool—and the woman, laughing. Edith wondered if they were married or if they were cheating on other people they already loved, or if maybe they were just normal people swimming in the middle of the night in a house which belonged to a millionaire. In the darkness, she could hear Howie breathing. She could feel the cocaine on her gums, her mouth watering, and she squeezed her arm around Joe's waist and whispered into his ear, "Hey. What are they doing?"

"Swimming," he whispered back.

"They're swimming," Howie said, almost loudly. "But, really. Really, guys, this is nothing."

"But what are they going to do?" she whispered, and now she squeezed Joe tighter, and she put her free hand in his lap and realized he was hard as a book—the spine that holds the pages all together, and she thought it must hurt, having it be that way with no place for it to go. It was something she had only read about, and now she sat there, resting her hand along the ridges of his cock.

"But what are they going to do, Joe?"

When the voices stopped, she knew what the people in the pool were going to do. The woman stopped singing, and now there was only the sound of the water and the air all of them kept breathing . . . an occasional ripple of water . . . and Howie, crawling forward on his stomach. He looked like someone in a movie. He was making noise, more noise than anything she'd ever heard before, and her hand was here, on her boyfriend's lap, and she wanted to be inside that pool, too.

Now, opening her eyes, a week later, she is looking through the window, watchful as if slipping into a dream. She is watching the stray, wandering searchlight of a patrolling guard—the spotlight filling up the landscape, the lawns and the water skimming out across the lake. The dark sky and all that grass and the light passing slowly overhead: a beacon, giving off directions, and Joe with his hand beneath her sweater, unhooking the clasp, and her body, spilling out into his hand—the rough spots of his hand against her skin which could be almost water. The light is wandering through the sky, pale as her skin looking for a place to land, and when she kisses Joe, concentrating, sometimes she tells herself she loves him. She thinks his mouth's a drug, and she's moving his hand now over her skin, her navel, into the waist of her jeans, and when her jeans rip open, the fabric ripped apart together by their hands, it sounds like fireworks—when they explode, and the sound they always make, exploding.

After, in the back of the hearse, she looks at his body naked for the very first time. She sits Indian style looking at his body, running her fingers over the bones in his hips, the thin path of hair leading to his navel, and she thinks he was conceived in a womb, too, same as everybody. His nipples are small as a girl's, and bodies, before they grow, are bodies full of muscle and blood and, later, semen. She's thirsty and remembers the pool, and the chlorine that keeps the water clean, and she can't believe the way she feels because she's never been so certain and so terrified in all her life. Because she knows this must be love. This, and knowing what it is and being afraid of what you have to say, after, and Joe's mouth, his mouth and the way he let her body feed him. The human body is a mystery. It's ninety percent water, the rest is merely stuff that floats along and holds it all together—your skin and your hair, your knees, and now, from across the water, she hears the fountain rising: the engines inside the middle of the lake, igniting, and all the lights turned on for all the world to see. They are listening to the water rise, rising up into the air until the water becomes foam and the foam becomes a rainbow. The mist is going to be carried away with the breeze, places she's certain now she wants to go, and now she knows she's really scared because she knows the water's cold. It's cold as ice and looking at the fountain, and Joe, and the white skin of her chest brushing along the dark skin of his arm, she thinks what she really wants most right now is just a glass of water to clear her throat.

"I'm so happy," she says, finally, kissing him. "But can we go?"

Skin is the largest human organ: then comes the digestive tract, which gives you energy, and the lungs, which provide the body with oxygen . . . and the heart, circulating all that oxygen through the bloodstream. She's going to be a doctor now. She's just decided, because nothing makes more sense to her now than figuring out the way the body works and how she's going to try and make it last forever.

Next week, Spencer goes into the hospital to have the plate in his leg removed. If she were a specialist, like a bone doctor, then she could make Spencer feel better. She wonders if bone doctors have to have good eyesight and realizes, belatedly, that of course they do. They have to see all those little cracks in the bone. She could never be a doctor. The way she kills dogs, she couldn't even be a vet. Maybe a horse doctor, because horses are big, and she thinks she'll need to pick out something realistic. Until today, Edith has always thought Oakland was a place in Oklahoma; she even thought she was going to be a swim coach.

"What are you thinking?" Joe says, in the driveway.

"Nothing."

They stand there, beneath the paloverde, not talking, just thinking and holding on to each other until it's ten minutes past her curfew, and then fifteen.

She says, "I've got to go."

"I know."

"Are you really going to be a lawyer?"

"I don't know. Probably a broker. They make more."

"So you'll have to go to broker school, yeah?"

"Yeah. I guess."

Edith calculates that Joe will be in school for at least seven more years, maybe eight, depending. She thinks eight years is a long way away, but not that long. She thinks eight years ago, she was only nine, but that doesn't seem quite right: that eight years ago she could have been only nine years old.

"In eight years," she says, "I'll be twenty-five."

"What?"

"You'll be twenty-five, too. That's almost thirty, if you think about it." She kisses him and says, "I'll call later, 'kay?"

" 'Kay."

They say good-bye . . . *see ya* . . . three more times before she finally steps inside. The house is still and quiet. She watches Joe drive off and goes into the kitchen for a soda. In the bathroom, she brushes her teeth, twice, and she washes her face, which is swollen and red—the way it looks after too much sleep, or if she has been crying hard. She takes out her contacts.

She pulls on her nightshirt and grabs the phone in the hallway and brings it into her room. She climbs into bed and sets the telephone in her lap. Sometimes she and Joe will talk all night. Sometimes, she wakes up in the morning with the phone by her pillow, or on the floor, and she wonders what they must have talked about. Sometimes, when it's good, they tell each other what they like about each other most, which is the hard part: telling people things they'll be able to hold you to forever. For example, she has recently learned that she has a nice voice, that it sounds nice when she talks. That's something she never knew about herself, and other things that Joe tells her. And the things she will tell Joe, like the way he ties his sneakers, or the way he looks at his toes whenever anybody says anything nice about him. Sometimes, when she knows she's saying nice things that he wants to hear, she imagines him lying in bed, looking at his toes. She wonders if they're under the sheets. She wonders where his hand is and what he's really feeling.

Someday he'll tell her because she's not a girl anymore. She's seventeen years old, and next year she'll be able to vote and live on her own while she goes off to college. Sitting up to dial Joe's number, she hears her father's step treading down the hall. He stops at her door and knocks. She slides the phone beneath her pillow and tries to hide the cord.

"Edie?"

"Yeah?"

"You're home," he says, stepping into the dark room. "I was worried."

"I wasn't late."

"I know. I heard you drive in. I was just worried." Her father rubs at the splint on his hand. He sits on the edge of her bed and pats her knee.

"You okay?"

"Yeah," she says. "Just tired."

"You haven't seen the phone, have you?"

She giggles, falsely, knowing that she's caught. She pulls the phone from beneath the pillow. "I found it here, kind of."

"Your mom's not home yet," he says. "She called and said she was going away for a few days."

"A few days?"

"She may call again."

"We've got call waiting," she says, figuring it out.

"Which won't do much good if you're asleep. Stay off the phone. Get some sleep."

"When's she coming back?"

"Soon, I think. She's awfully upset at me." Her father lights a cigarette, his match a brief torch, lighting up the room and the lines in his face. He shakes out the match and says, "Edie."

"What."

"I love your mother. You probably don't understand this, but I love your mother more than the whole world. I love her the way you love Jim, only more, because I've known your mother more than half my life. And the way you feel, the way you feel nobody else could ever understand how you feel . . . that's how I feel. That's how much I love your mother. And you. How much I love you, too."

"Joe. His name is Joe."

"I don't give a damn what his name is. I love you. And I've promised your mother, it's all going to stop. We don't have to worry anymore because it's all going to stop. Someday, you'll understand this. When—"

"I'm older. When I'm older, Dad."

He turns and smiles, sadly; she thinks she should have known better, and now she's mad for ever being nice. She should have just let him yell at her.

"So this makes it okay?" she says. "This is what make everything fine?"

"What?"

"What you do, Dad?"

"Edith—"

"Yeah, Dad. What you do."

"Don't talk to me like that."

"Like what?"

"Like that. Don't—"

She scrambles out of bed, twisting the telephone cord in her ankles, dragging the phone to the floor. He's sitting on her bed filling up her room with smoke, and everything she owns is because of him. She doesn't own a thing. He's looking at his cigarette, shaking, and she knows she can say anything she wants.

She feels almost giddy, knowing that. "You think that makes it okay?" she yells. "You think it's fine? What you do? You're a faggot, Dad, and I know what you do! I know what you do and if I were Mom I'd tell *you* to leave. Go die of some goddamn disease, Dad. Go—"

"Shut your mouth."

"Yeah? What are you going to do, Dad? Not buy me a car? Kick me out of the house? You gonna tell Mom I called you a fag?"

She runs out of the room, crying, because she can run for miles; she's running down the hallway, onto the porch, and once there she curls up beside the palm trees, weeping, thinking of all the other things she could have told him—what it tasted like, settling there on the back of your tongue, and how while doing it you had to hold your tongue down to keep yourself from gagging, and the way it felt, fitting there inside your throat. The way you had to watch your teeth, and the way his hands felt, holding you down there while you worried about your teeth, and his body, pumping into your throat . . . maybe he could give her some advice? Maybe he could tell her how it's really supposed to be done, and crying, she thinks she doesn't know about all the other parts, about what it's all supposed to mean and she wants someone to be at fault because somebody's got to be at fault. Somebody's got to be to blame because somebody here has been doing something wrong. Somebody, and nothing here is ever going to be the same. Because nothing's real, there's nothing real at all except for what you feel like, and what it feels like, after, and the way you're always going to have to keep it secret.

Let Me Close Your Eyes and Dream

Sleep is afraid of the darkness, which is why we have to close our eyes, and even still it happens. The darkness seeps inside and you have to go inside looking for a way to clear it out.

It happens slowly and you slide right in, your body adjusting to the temperature, slowly, the way a woman will admit you during the early stages. Maybe she's thinking she can save you. Love requires responsibility. It's time to be responsible, and love is blind, and now, sitting on the edge of his bed, his head in his hands, he doesn't know what he wants to be responsible for. The day, maybe, which sooner or later is bound to begin, and for the events during the day in which he will be partially involved, he knows that he will have to appear responsible: he will have to teach his classes and say hello to people in the hallway. He will have to make it through the day.

That night, the night of the deep plunge, Freddy and his bouncer tossed the two men into the back of Freddy's pickup. The men were in bad shape: the Mohawk's breathing was uncertain; most likely, he had a rib sticking through his lung; the other hadn't even twitched since Ray snapped his collarbone. They drove the battered men to the Scottsdale courthouse and dumped them onto the lawn. Then Freddy pinned a twenty-dollar bill onto the Mohawk's jacket. The Mohawk was still conscious, and Freddy said, "For the cab." Then Freddy took the .38—the gun Ray had already emptied, the shells somewhere in the parking lot of the River Bottom—and tucked it into the small man's belt.

He turned to the Mohawk and said, "Can you hear me?" He slapped the man's face. He slapped it again, and said, "Hey, can you hear me?"

The man nodded.

"Can you hear me real good?"

He nodded again.

"We're going to do you a favor here. We're going to see that you get taken care of. That arm, say. That arm that's not moving so good. We're going to get you to the hospital, but let's get one thing clear. You come back here, you ever come back here again, and Miss Cathy's going to scream rape. She's going to scream rape real loud and you just may never get to leave. You know what I'm saying?"

The man nodded, and now Freddy pinched his jaw. "I'm saying you don't know where you've been, asshole. I'm saying don't let me ever see you coming back."

The bouncer was sent to fetch a cab. Ray and Freddy drove around the block and waited behind some palm trees. The Scottsdale police department was less than a hundred yards away, the parking lot was full of blue-and-white cruisers, and Ray stepped out of the truck and stood under the lights looking at the sky. He had a long cut along his flank and was holding a bar towel to his side; he was also drunk, and he was telling himself to breathe.

Later, at the River Bottom, after closing, Cathy with a C said, "If I'm going to say I'm raped, Professor, I'm going to have to have some evidence."

She was changing into her jeans, becoming a different person, and Ray said, "Meaning?"

"I've got to have some proof, that's all."

"If it goes that far," Freddy said, "we're all fucked." He

meant everybody but himself, because Freddy was from New Jersey, and because he had connections. What he really meant was *Ray's fucked.*

"If they come back," said Ray, "they're not coming back with cops."

"You gotta get yourself taken care of," Cathy said. "You gotta get yourself taken care of real good."

Eternity is not knowing what the future's going to bring you, and once the here and now is broken, it's not the kind of thing you're going to be able to fix. You can fix a broken leg, or hand; you fix a cut on the top of your head and wait for it to heal; but you can't fix need and wanting to have it for the rest of your life. You've got to learn to live with it or do without.

Cal Buckner is stepping through his office door. He's wearing his Cubs hat and aloha shirt and he's clapping Ray on the back.

"Ray," Cal says, beaming, and now he's showing Ray into his office, shutting the door, stepping around the table and pulling out a pint of gin. He's pouring a shot of gin into a plastic glass full of orange juice.

Ray nods complicitly, because Cal's sitting behind his desk, smiling unnecessarily, saying, "You know . . . It makes the day seem more bright."

"Uh-huh."

On top of Cal's filing cabinet sits the disco ball which Cal stores in his office to keep kids from stealing it. Ray wants to say something hopeful, but he's too tired to try; this is his annual review, during which he should be fired, and now Cal is going through Ray's file. Ray sits in an uncomfortable chair, his legs partially crossed, resting, cutting off the circulation.

Cal says, sipping, looking up, "Your evaluations are fine, Ray. They're really quite fine."

Ray scratches his head, trying to think of some reasonable excuse; he thinks his hair hurts, and that his eyes are shot, and that probably this is something Buckner's looking at—his shot eyes. Cal Buckner is peering out over his gin and orange juice examining

Ray's shot eyes, because Cal is the kind of guy who can start before breakfast and never even have to worry. He's the principal.

"But some students seem to feel—really, it's not a big deal—"

"But?" Ray says, hopefully.

"Well, it's just the textbooks, Ray. You're supposed to use the textbooks. A certain small percentage of your students last spring didn't seem to feel the textbooks were being utilized to their maximum potential. Of course, it's just a suggestion."

"I didn't pick the textbook."

"Yes, of course. I know. Are we going to win the sectionals?"

Ray sighs; he's not going to be fired yet. "We're going to do okay. Jazinski, maybe—he's doing fine. We'll know after tonight." He scratches at his hair, which still hurts, and looks at Cal. "You're right, of course. I should have realized my students wanted to utilize their textbooks. I'll make a point of it next semester."

Cal's beaming all over again, Ray gives him a wink, they really understand each other. Last week thirty kids were busted off 124th, cocaine and under-age drinking; the papers listed all the names, and it was good news because not a single name in the paper was from Gold Dust High School.

Buckner says, "Yes. I'm sure." He says, "Wonderful."

"After tonight," Ray says, sighing. "We'll know."

"Cholla."

Ray nods, repeating, "Cholla." His side begins to ache. Yesterday, while working out with McGregor, he split open the wound in his side. The skin was just beginning to knit, and blood started spilling into his shirt and all over the mats. McGregor thought he'd done something wrong. McGregor's mother is on the PTA, and the PTA knew what kind of textbooks they were using. They were using a textbook as meaningful and long as any other— each year, a new edition, to keep the kids from buying used ones. Looking at Cal across the desk, Ray wonders just what it is he does, exactly.

What do you do all day?

Cal says, "How was your Thanksgiving?"

"Good," Ray says. "Good. You know."

"Sure," Cal says, nodding. "Joyce and I were going to have you over, for dinner, but we figured you had other plans. You being single again and whatnot."

"Thanks," Ray says, nodding.

"I remember," Buckner says. "I remember, you know?"

"Jesus," Jenna says. "You look like hell."

"Is that a new blouse?"

They are standing in the hall by the drinking fountain; being cordial, Ray tells himself. He tells himself he must look about as fine as he feels. A moment ago, in the faculty men's, he ran into Nathan Rolf. They said hello, standing shoulder to shoulder, talking about the weather while each hung on for dear life to his prick. A man hung over is a man in need of balance, and after washing his hands, Nathan Rolf took out his flask and unscrewed the cap, almost gracefully. Nathan's coat, a houndstooth tweed, clashed with his tie, and Nathan nodded, taking a swig. He passed the flask to Ray, and said, "Hair of the dog?"

Ray thinks the only time a man washes his hands after taking a leak is when another man he works with is looking on. Looking at Jenna, Ray calculates, six, maybe seven more hours. At home he's got a half-pint of cheap bourbon under the sink and four beers in the icebox. After school, he'll have to stop at the store, except he's got a meet tonight with Cholla High which will last forever. Jenna looks at him and smiles the way she smiles.

"Late night, huh?"

"Really," he says, pointing to a button on her blouse. "Really, it's a nice color."

He walks down the hall, aiming for the classroom. If he's not careful, he's going to fall down, which is something he has recently done, and now Jenna runs up behind him. She's tugging on his sleeve.

"Just because things are different," she says. "I mean, just because things didn't work out"—and now she's whispering, the students passing all around them—"I mean, honest, Ray . . . You don't have to be so—"

"Careful," he says. "People will think we're talking."

"We *are* talking."

"What about?"

"We're talking about being civil to each other. We're talking about dealing with all this like normal adults."

"This?" Ray says. "This? Dealing with *this*? And what's *this*, Jen? The Friends Who Fuck Club? The Co-worker Coitus Syndrome? If you talk about *this* long enough, you might convince yourself it's really worth talking about."

"I wish you'd be nice to me again."

He thinks he's never said that word out loud before: *coitus*. He wonders if he's even said it properly. "Yeah. Okay. Well, hey, Jen—"

"What?"

He thinks he should be nice to her; he thinks if you really want to hurt somebody, you should give her something she no longer deserves. He says, avoiding further collision, "Look, I gotta go."

"Did you know Fullerton thinks you're having an affair with Diana Vanderstock?"

He stops—the kids in the hall are still streaming all around—and laughs. Diana Vanderstock is a senior, a cheerleader and on the debate team. Yesterday her car was stuck in gear, the transmission locked in second, and Ray slid underneath and popped it free. He told her to get her clutch checked; the car was twenty years old and worth a fortune, like Diana Vanderstock's parents, and Belinda Fullerton came walking by while Ray was leaning against Diana Vanderstock's car. He was talking to a girl wearing a sweater who held her books up against her chest like a good girl—a girl who stood talking to him, nodding, saying yes to everything he had to say. He saw Fullerton walk by and whisper something to Langousis.

"An affair," he says. "Is that what they call it?"

"That's what she's calling it."

"Does Diana know?"

Jenna laughs nervously. "You shouldn't joke about it. This kind of thing happens all the time. Even here. You've got to be careful, Ray. Careful."

He's heard the story before. The man, some fool named Fennerstrom, was popular and a pretty girl fell in love with him and he went crazy. He drove himself off a cliff, during Christmas, while the girl went skiing with her friends in Utah or Colorado. It was in the papers for months, the love letters and testimonials, and Ray thinks that whenever people don't know what to do, they have to go and kill themselves.

"I've got to go, Jen."

"And," she says, catching him, "Michael Owens wants to know if you are Catholic or Episcopalian." Jenna arches her eyebrow. She shifts the weight onto her hip, the way a woman carries a baby, or the world, because of the way she bends.

It's the kind of move she makes when she wants someone to notice her, and now the bell rings. The hallway is clear, the stream has dried up. *Dried out*—which means something different to normal people, something normal people never tend to think about because when a thing runs dry, no one ever seems to notice. They'll just bring more water into town with trucks. For normal people, things go on as usual.

"What?" he says, shifting.

"Could we have lunch or something? I mean, just to talk?"

"Sure," he says. "Yeah, sure."

His daddy, Merle, used to say life is but a dream, and the nightmare is this: a random series of events which turn out not to be a part of any particular nightmare. The events are real as life itself, equally frightening, big enough to kill you, and there are certain things likely to damage your confidence—the dark, skeletal bones tucked away inside the closet of a binge. Freddy had warned him. "She's a looker, Professor. She's got tattoos. You figure it out."

But tattoos aren't necessarily a bad thing, especially if describing the right portions of the body—a kind of beauty mark, a blemish on the lip of something otherwise and kind. Ray is older now, he's supposed to be wiser, and had he known better, had he read the writing on the wall . . . *the bathroom wall* . . . he would have avoided further contact: had he known better and listened to the polite voice of reason. That voice telling him to go slow, *slow*, the way you prepare for the worst of things: taxes; a hangover; the breakup, before the divorce, when things begin to really break and everything starts turning dangerous and hard.

He thought, Time is a river, and the rivers are drying up. He thought, What doesn't kill you makes you strong, unless it kills you. He thought she looked crazy.

Absolutely crazy . . .

"That guy," she explained. "That big guy with the Mohawk. I live with him, kind of."

They were at Ray's place, on the couch, Thanksgiving Day. She had looked him up in the phone book and brought over fast-food chicken. She stood at his door in a pink dress with a box full of chicken, and said, "Happy Thanksgiving!"

Once inside, she turned on the stereo and wandered around the rooms of his house, asking why he didn't have a TV, and picking up the books, looking at them. Books meant more if you could touch them, and she stood there, flicking through the pages, thinking. She seemed amazed that he would want to read so many dusty books, and on the couch, she looked at the books on his end table, a book about Vietnam, another about drug dealers in Mexico, a novel about very long bridges. Beneath the table was an empty bottle of vodka.

"He was in Vietnam," she said, raising her eyes.

"Naturally," Ray said.

"Yep. The Nam. He has this plate in his head and goes crazy sometimes. Beneath the Mohawk. It's why he doesn't shave the whole thing."

"His head."

"His best friend died in his arms."

"Special Forces?"

"No, the green guys. You know, like that John Wayne movie."

"Yeah," Ray said. "And now he writes songs. He goes to night school and takes classes in poetry. He writes lots and lots of poetry."

"How did you know?" she said brightly.

"How's he feeling, by the way?"

"Freddy would fire me, don't you see? You don't want Freddy to fire me, Professor. Sometimes Louis just gets angry and he really is a nice guy. He's had some problems, that's all. Actually, you'd like him a lot. You have a lot in common, really. He went to his mother's for Thanksgiving."

"I see."

"I thought you might be lonely."

Lonely men do lonely things. Ray popped a fresh beer and thought this had to be better than writing poetry; the crazy brilliant guy with misinformed hair had said Ray must never, never write a poem if he wanted to keep his self-respect. Later, Ray asked Cathy, who looked crazy, if she knew what she was doing—taking off his shirt, sliding out of her dress. In a pink dress, she could have been his daughter, if he had one, and it seemed maybe to be a good idea—a holiday of sorts, though he knew better, too, than to let a strange woman into his house. Strange women wore tattoos. Next thing, she'd be stopping by for breakfast, just to chat, and she'd stop wanting to use condoms, because they were safe . . . *Aren't we, love?* . . . and then she'd be pregnant, and her mother would be flying in from Indiana, to take care of the kids, or New Orleans. She'd be picking out new furniture they could all rent together, and a color television, and so he had asked her.

Do you know what you are doing?

Afterward, buck naked, he asked her again.

"Sure," she said. "I like you."

"What about Chief Thunderclap?"

"Nuh-uh," she said, shaking her head. "His name's Louis."

"Louis," he said. "That's a nice sensitive name for a vet. A real nice name."

She sat up, straddling him, and looked him in the eye. Then the other. She said, "You're divorced, aren't you? I can always tell."

"Never married."

"Then you wanted to be. That's it. Once. You wanted to be divorced."

She reached for a cigarette and said, squeezing him, "If you're divorced, then everything is supposed to make sense. You know how things really are." She exhaled and said, "I think you should get it out of your system. Talk a lot about it. I know all about that kind of stuff."

"Tell me about the chief."

"Louis. His name's Louis. He says if he ever sees you again he's going to kill you. First, he's going to shoot your balls off. Then he's going to watch you bleed."

Ray laughed, and she reached beneath and gave him a squeeze. "That's what he said, Professor. He has an awful lot of anger stored up inside."

He lifted her off and stepped inside the bathroom where he could take a leak and think to himself. Holding himself, he imagined someone aiming for his nuts; kill a man's appetite, and you kill the man. He had eaten too much Thanksgiving chicken, he wanted another beer, and he didn't know how he was supposed to get rid of her. His hands smelled like condoms and sex, and he stood there, hanging onto himself . . . *This is stupid. This is very, very stupid* . . . imagining Louis, somewhere off inside the traffic, a Remington .30-06 in his arms, waiting. Ray knew that if you stood far enough away, you could kill anybody; it was the fundamental premise of war—first the bow and arrow, now the ballistic missile. With all the traffic, Louis could be anywhere, and if not Louis, then maybe the police, waiting, because each day anything could happen. People died all the time. It was a dangerous world and he was becoming more and more dangerous. Things happen, he told himself, and then more things happen.

"I would have told you sooner," Cathy called through the bathroom door. "But I figured you'd just get angry. If you don't know how to control your anger, it never does any good to be angry. It becomes destructive!"

"Out," he said, coming through the door, scratching his head. "I've got to go out. I'm sorry."

"Oh, it's okay. It's not like he suspects anything or anything. I told you, he's visiting his mother. I'd never say a word."

"No," he said. "It's going to get out of hand. Things are going to get out of hand."

She reached for him and held him in her hand. "But it's nice, Professor. It's so nice!"

After he has met his classes, before the meet with Cholla, Cathy is sitting on his desk, cross-legged, the tattoos on her chest blazing in the overhead lighting. She is sitting on his desk going through a stack of writing assignments.

Today he had his kids write an essay on the importance of the over-the-shoulder double check, which meant that while they were writing he could pretend to be teaching them something. Actually, he pretended to read, going through the textbook McGregor's mother helped pick out; it is full of useful illustrations and examples, and for the first time in months, Ray is wondering if he really wants to be a teacher. He's thinking he doesn't really have very much to teach anyone . . . *Do as I say* . . . and now here's this girl, who's got to be under twenty-one, wearing shorts and tattoos. Like his alleged affair with Diana Vanderstock, it's not the kind of thing people are going to want to understand.

She says, "Hi!"

"Somebody let you in?"

"I haven't been to school in years," she says, giggling. "So. This is where you teach?"

He sits on a chair, the one across from the desk where students sometimes sit when they're in trouble. He watches her lift the pile of papers, weighing each. Already she has the makings to be a fine teacher. "Nice handwriting," Cathy says. "This is real pretty."

"What's up?"

"Do you remember me, Ray?"

"What?"

"Do you remember me? Because if you don't, I'm here to make sure that you remember me."

"Uh-huh."

"See, I figure if you remember me, then maybe you'll call me up. Maybe you'll come see me sometimes. Maybe take me out to dinner?"

She sets the papers on the desk and pouts. She says, "I like to go on dates, of course. Nothing fancy—dinner, a movie, maybe. A bottle of wine. Then we go to your place, or my place, except my place is kind of crowded, you know. But we go to a place, anyway, but we can't do that, see, if you don't even remember who the hell I am."

"I don't remember asking you to stop by, Cathy."

"Yeah," she says, nodding. "But Louis does. He's really pissed at you, Ray, for treating me this way." She slides off the desk and stands in front of the window.

Outside, the lawn, and the parking lot, and the place where Walker Miller blew his brains to Pluto. Across the road, across the field owned by a church, men are erecting Christmas decorations on the roof of a house—Santa Claus, animals, a tree made out of lights, a seven-foot candy cane. And the lawn—kids are out there now, waiting for the buses, and Cathy pulls her T-shirt over her head. She is standing in front of him, the lizard swimming into the center of her chest, there through the narrow bone, and she turns now to the open window.

She says, "Ray, did you know your window's wide open?"

"Put your shirt on."

She turns and faces him. She shivers and says, "You really do want to remember me, don't you? Why don't you want to remember me?"

"Put your shirt on, Cathy."

"Say it. Say you want to remember me. Say you want to save me."

She unbuttons her jeans and slides her hand inside. She's working her hand, her eyes, closing, saying, "This is how I remember you, Professor. This is how I think of you all the time and you won't even be polite."

"Cathy," he says. "Cathy, put your fucking clothes on."

"Fucking," she says. "Yeah. Sure, fucking's a real good idea. Isn't it?"

"Please," he says. "Come on."

"I think you're going to forget who I am, Ray. I think you just want to use me. Louis loves it when people watch, you know? He loves to watch them watch. I think I could even come, Professor. Do you want to hear me come?"

He grabs her arms now, spinning her around. "Put—"

"I'll scream," she whispers, so fiercely that it hurts. "I swear to God I'll scream until they think you fucked me first, Professor. Come on, Professor. Fuck me first before I scream."

He lets go her arm and says, "What do you want?"

She unzips him. "Tell me something nice," she says, dropping to her knees. She's on her knees behind the desk and he is looking out the window. He sees Edith McCaw, holding her books, waiting for the bus. He waves, uncertainly, and Edith stares back widely. Across the field a reindeer falls off the roof, the men on the roof watching it sail, testing the wind, and Cathy says, "Say something nice. Say something nice to me right now."

The lawn outside is green and wet. Cal Buckner is taking off his Cubs hat, talking with Langousis, and Diana Vanderstock is holding her books. Edith McCaw is walking away, and Ray says, "What?"

"Everything," Cathy says, taking him.

The crazy brilliant professor with prehistoric hair once told Ray that things get out of hand when you don't know where to put them . . . *Your hands, Ray. Your hands!* . . . and now, Ray thinks, things are truly out of hand.

His students no longer appreciate his neglect of the Driver's Education textbook; his body is going slack; he can't get through a night without first passing out. Things, he tells himself, are spiraling—all in the wrong direction, a stray helicopter out of control, its props aflame. It's time to ditch or figure things out, and he's in the weight room, climbing the rope, waiting for his wrestlers to finish suiting up. Tonight they are going to impress Cal Buckner and the PTA and the Gold Dust Boosters all combined. Tonight his boys are going to kick some ass, and he's climbing the rope in the weight room, telling himself that if he keeps on climbing, if he just keeps climbing, then maybe he'll pull himself on out.

Below him he sees Howie Bently, who's tapping his foot, waiting.

"Coach?"

"Yeah."

"Coach—"

"Hang on."

Ray slides down the rope fast, the rope burning his hands because he's held it; it's something he can understand—the burn in his hands. On the floor, he's sweating out last night's beer, all fifteen. His hands are shaking and he's more nervous and exhausted than a body has a right to be.

Rest. I've got to get some rest.

"Coach?"

"What?"

"Nothing."

"What? What the hell is it?"

"Just that we're waiting, Coach. That's all."

Inside the gymnastics gym, the room white with powder and dust, Ray looks over his team. Like sobriety, wrestling is not a team sport; to live a decent life, you must first convince yourself you want to. Houston is about to say something, and Ray cuts him off. *Wait,* he says, because Ray has learned to wait, and his team is scattered throughout the small powdered gym, the gym for *powderpuffs,* because the boys who do gymnastics are graceful and dry; the wrestlers are *pit lickers,* they know how life sometimes tastes, they know how to survive: by keeping themselves close to the ground, but not too close. Bently is screwing around on the parallel bars, living dangerously; another boy is straddling the horse; and McGregor is doing takedowns with three freshmen, rotating, pumping up the ego. Jazinski is sitting by himself lacing up his shoes.

"Come on in," Ray says, and now he's feeling the need to be useful. He may be screwed up, but this is something he knows that he is good at, like shooting an M-60, or getting himself into trouble. The team gathers, brushing off the dust; if they win tonight, they will lead the entire Southwest conference, which isn't necessarily all that important: simply, after all is said and done, a team can never win.

"Houston?" Ray says.

"What?"

"You okay?"

"I'm okay."

"They're just a bunch of guys," Ray says softly. "Remember that. They're just another bunch of guys who fart and fail History and can't find girlfriends. When in doubt—"

Punt!

"What?"

PUNT!

And now they're up, a slow jog into the gym where they are received by parents and cheerleaders. The thermostat has been turned down to sixty-five, but still the gym is hot. Ray shakes hands with Cholla's coach, a fat guy with a goatee who thinks he'd like to take Ray on, Ray can see it in his eyes, and Ray sees fear as well: deep and necessary fear, the fear of an out-of-shape Math teacher hiding behind the strength of his team, like an officer of the court, or a principal. Maybe he's having an affair with a stripper who likes veterans and tattoos. Maybe he's got a problem with the bottle.

"G'luck," says the coach, grinning widely and Ray under-stands that the man doesn't want to be taken the wrong way. He's the kind of guy who doesn't want to be misunderstood, and he recedes to his corner, quietly, because he's just a Math teacher. And the ref, the volunteer scorekeepers, the parents in the stands—they've all been here before. Diana Vanderstock is filling out her pretty sweater, her earrings modest and bright; and Michael Owens, the Catholic cop, she's hanging on to her purse. She catches Ray's eye, and Ray doesn't see the priest anywhere—Jim Lawson, the guy who shows movies and talks to lonely single people. Roxanne, the retarded girl, is sitting in the front row, holding her tape recorder, listening. Now his team is taking the bench, the loudspeaker announces the first match, the whistle blows.

Ray's sitting on the bench watching a kid get bullied into a clumsy takedown, the ref is calling points, and behind him, when he turns to see the points register on the board, Ray sees Jenna sitting next to Cal Buckner who's tugging at his Cubs cap, giving off signals, frowning coach-like. Ray puts his head into his hands and tells himself that this is just the beginning. That things, as always, are bound to get worse, especially for the skinny kid out on the mats.

"Sit," Ray yells, looking up. "Sit!"

He hears a voice behind him. "Coach?"

It's Michael Owens, carrying her purse.

"Yeah."

"How we doing?"

"What?"

"I never know what the heck's going on with these things," she says.

"It's okay. We're going to do okay." Behind her, he can see Cal Buckner in the stands, pointing, and Jenna, watching Cal's finger. Jenna seems to be paying close attention.

"Really?" says Michael.

"Here," he says, making room for her on the bench. "Go ahead. You can be manager."

It's a suggestion which seems least complicated, and sitting there, watching his team suffer, and win, he's thinking this is not as unpleasant a complication as most people are going to want to think it is. He's thinking he's the coach, and that his team looks pretty good out there. He's thinking that maybe things are going to be okay and that he'll never drink another beer again. He's thinking he saw Jenna smile at him.

Why?

Later, and while there still is hope, while Colin Houston is out on the mats, winning, Ray says to Michael Owens, "Sometimes . . . Sometimes I feel like I'm just one of them."

Freddy sees him coming. He pours Ray a shot and a beer.

Ray's telling himself he's looking for Cathy, though he knows she won't be here. He knows she's going other places. After the meet, she left with Howie Bently, smiling to Ray on her way out, waving, while Ray stood by Michael Owens, trying to appear responsible. Waving like that, in a sweater with real sleeves, Cathy could have been a schoolgirl. Michael asked Ray if he'd like to go out, maybe, get a drink?

Freddy looks at Ray and says, "Things okay?"

"I'm in need of a new career."

"Come to Papa," Freddy says, spreading out his arms. "Jeezum, just come on home."

"Where's the tattooed bimbo?"

"Cathy?"

"Cathy. With a nuclear C. You know what she did today?"

Ray suddenly understands that he's not looking for Cathy; he's looking for her boyfriend, Louis, the big guy with the Mohawk who's going to go recon and take out Ray's nuts. He tells Freddy about Cathy's surprise visit and about her vet boyfriend, though he doesn't reveal the vet's identity—Chief Mohawk, with the plate in his head beneath the Mohawk. Freddy says, "Hey, I thought she was a dyke. I thought she lived with some chick named Yolanda in Buckeye or Ajo. She told me she commuted!"

"I don't get it," Ray says.

It's like something from a bad movie, Ray says, and Freddy nods, knowing exactly which movie he's talking about. A body in heat is capable of the most inexplicable changes; Ray has another beer. He passes on the shot. From now on, he's a beer man only. He's going to get even, because beer evens a body out, keeps it level. Tomorrow, maybe he'll give up beer, too. He's too old to have to keep having to give things up, and the sooner he gives himself up, the sooner he'll be through with it. Then it will be strictly a matter of survival, which is something he's had special training for. *Survival.* Tomorrow, he's going to give a driving lesson.

"I'm a beer man only, Freddy. That's it. Beer only."

"Here's to beer."

And what's he supposed to do? Call the cops? Ask Michael Owens if maybe she'd like to try and keep him safe? He says to Freddy, "You tell that bimbo to stay away from me. I'm serious, Freddy. Things are going to get ugly. Tell her you'll fire her. Tell her I'm crazy, but pass the word. I am too old for this crap."

"You're never too old," Freddy says, laughing.

The smoke is thick and Ray tries to smile. It makes his face hurt, trying. Maybe he should take up smoking instead. He wants to be able to be with somebody for the right reasons. He wants to be rational and to quit feeling like he's not, and maybe Cathy wanted to do him damage. More likely, her vet boyfriend, Louis: he's probably on methadone, writing poetry during the afternoons, or worse. He's just some guy who never even made it through boot camp.

"Tell her I'm dangerous," he says to Freddy. "Tell her I'm really a cop. Tell her anything, Freddy."

"I'll fire her."

"Play hardball, yeah. That would be nice."

From the back, coming through the storeroom, Ray sees Olivia-Margaret. Tonight she's wearing the Indian outfit. "Professor!" she calls.

"For you," Freddy says to Ray, "anything. Anything and on the house."

•••

Drunk, somehow and again by accident, he calls Jenna. Eventually she answers the phone and he doesn't know what to say.

"Hello?"

"It's me," he says. He's thinking he's being sly. He's thinking if he doesn't say too much then she won't know how much he's drunk. Also, he's not sure what she wants to talk about.

"Ray?"

"Ray. Yeah. Ray. What's up?"

"Me. I'm up. I thought you'd call."

"Just being nice. Trying to be nice."

"He didn't have to do that. Jazinski. He didn't have to do that, Ray. It's not a coach's fault just because one of his kids screws up."

"Would've done the same thing."

"He was upset, that's all. He and Edith—they broke up."

"He did the right thing. You know what, Jen?"

"What?"

"I don't love you. You know, the big *L* word. Four letters."

"It's late—"

"I know that too. I just thought you might want to know, so you don't feel bad or anything. I've been bad, Jen. Bad."

"What are you talking about?"

"Bad. I'm gonna write a book about it. A textbook, you know? One that tells people how to know what they're supposed to do. One that keeps them from being bad. Bad. I'm gonna have pictures, and quotes by famous people: Ty Cobb, even. I'm gonna have all these things inside this book and we're talking about something you can utilize here. We're talking about something people are going to goddamn want to fucking utilize. With real words, too. Ones that start with *F*. And *L*."

He thinks she should say something, it's almost funny; he can't remember where he's put his beer. His drink is somewhere on the floor, spilling. He waits and says, "Am I being out of line here, Jen? Telling you all this? Just telling you I want to write a goddamn book? I mean what the hell's wrong with Ty Cobb?"

"Nothing, Ray. It's fine. It's a great idea."

"That's 'cause you don't want to talk about it. I'm not blind you know. I can see the writing on the wall. I'm gonna write that too. Writing on the wall. I'm gonna call it *Ray Writes on the Goddamn Wall*."

"Ray, are you okay?"

"I'm lonely. I'm lonely and Merle-Bob's dying in a trailer park. I'm not crazy, though. I mean, don't worry. I'm not Walker fucking Miller. I won't make you feel bad."

"Get some sleep, Ray."

"Come over. Come over, okay? Promise. I promise I won't remember."

"Sleep, Ray. We'll talk. We'll talk, but get some sleep. Sleep on your book, Ray."

"On the wall," he says.

"Sleep."

If it's not anybody's fault, then whose fault is it? Even too much fear will cause a man to dream. When Cathy arrived at the meet alone, she was wearing more clothes than Ray had yet to see her wear: jeans that actually reached her ankles, a cardigan sweater, a silk scarf, as if she'd recently been to Italy. She walked in front of the stands; she stopped to say something to Howie Bently, who looked up at her longingly. Ray knew exactly what he was longing for, and Cathy smiled, and then she wandered over to the stands behind Ray. After a moment, she said softly, "Hey, Teach."

She climbed into the stands while Ray pretended not to notice. Michael Owens was asking Ray questions and Jazinski was stretching out. Ray went to Jazinski and asked him how he felt.

"Good," he said.

"Good?"

"I'm gonna kick his ass, if that's what you mean."

"I don't want you to kick his ass, Jazz. I want you to win."

Jazinski walked out to the mat, slowly, letting Danny Ernest watch him while the stands fired up. Ernest was taller by three inches; he had a longer reach. They tied up, the whistle blew, and Jazinski rolled Ernest over his shoulder into a fireman's carry, the boy rolling over Jazinski's shoulder while the crowd broke loose *... Jazz! Jazz! Jazz!* ... and Jazinski, pivoting, spinning and trying to work Ernest into a fast cradle, who broke loose, muscled himself out, and by the end of the first round they were knotted up on the mat, each going nowhere. By round two, Ernest had scored ahead of Jazinski, an escape which turned into a reversal, and then a takedown, Jazinski on his belly, inching himself and now he was flipped and he was bridging, lifting himself by the knots in his neck, saved by the whistle. Jazinski was two points behind, and into round three he was losing bad. Ray was up now, pacing, watching, not saying a word. Jazinski was slow and they were deadlocked on the mat, the crowd suddenly silent. You could hear it, breathing, things were that tight, and now a little kid's voice yelling *Smash 'im, Joe!* and Ernest flipped, lifting Jazinski and reversing him once again. Jazinski scrambled, a panic escape, and he must have seen Ernest's arm, locked into the mat, holding Ernest's weight, and somehow, as Ray saw the arm, just waiting to be of use, he knew what Jazinski was going to do. He was going to go after that arm.

Danny Ernest's arm, and Ray saw the hand, open, coming from the inside of Jazinski's body until it blew through the joint. The elbow. And Ernest, wailing.

"Oh my God!" Michael Owens screamed.

The ref was on the mat, holding the kid down. Nurse Henderson ran onto the floor with Ray and the Cholla coach, and Jazinski, standing, walked across the mats and out through the double doors, which swung shut behind him. Ernest had bones sticking through the broken skin of his arm. Even Buckner was on the floor; the ref remembered to call time, and Ernest was carried away screaming while all the people in the stands stood still and listened.

In the showers, Jazinski was sitting on the floor, the water spraying into the center of his suit. Ray stepped into the showers, avoiding the spray, which was impossible. Jazinski's headgear was caught in the whirlpool going down the drain.

"What happened?" Ray said.

"Nothing."

"What happened?"

"Nothing!"

"You just broke that kid's arm. You just ruined that arm for the rest of his goddamn life and you tell me: 'Nothing'?"

"I didn't mean to."

"Bullshit."

Jazinski sat there on the floor, his head between his knees. The laces on his sneakers were knots, and now a little kid, his brother, came hobbling into the locker room on crutches. The floor was wet, a crutch slipped and Spencer fell.

"Ouch!" Spencer yelled. He picked himself up and hopped over the gutter into the shower—the crutches long, slender stilts, pointing.

Ray turned to leave when Joe said, behind him, "I was afraid."

"Of what?"

"To lose! I was afraid I was going to lose!" He sat there, the shower beating down overhead while Spencer looked for a towel.

"Boy, Joe," said Spencer, looking around. "Boy."

The water was running fast, and Ray knew somebody should really turn it off.

"Hiya," Spencer said to Ray, pointing. "I'm not supposed to get my cast wet."

Because Life
Is Like a Window

Faith is a handful of flesh. Once joined to the bone, the human life begins to rip: lip to rib, breast to bone. It's enough to take your breath away forever. In Phoenix, the light is mostly white.

She thinks we start with a bang, a bang we call *theory,* and so too must we end with a bang—Armageddon, deconstruction, chaos, environmental warming, any and all related conflagrations: this, the history of love and sorrow, world without end until it ends, and she thinks we need to keep our eyes open. She thinks we've all been here before, on the stairs, carrying up the groceries while asking a lot of questions. She's carrying her groceries up the seven flights, the groceries just now beginning to slip; she's feeling slightly revived from her trip to Sedona, and her visit with her aunt Nicky. She stumbles, shifts her weight, catching her balance. She hasn't bought this much food in months, and she's been thinking recently that maybe she wants to buy a dog.

The door to her apartment swings open; it is already open. The key she keeps over Bill's lamp is hanging from the lock. Inside her apartment it is clear that things have been moved around. Not torn up, but gone through nonetheless: rearranged, like morning traffic. Books are lying scattered on the yellow carpet. She sets her groceries onto the counter and checks under the sink where she keeps a faded jar of brass cleaner. Inside the jar, along with two diamond rings which once belonged to her grandmother, is four hundred dollars cash. Aside from a CD in a bank in New Hampshire, this cash represents her only savings. But the money is still here; standing, she realizes someone has gone through her cabinets and the refrigerator. Three beers are missing, and for the rest of the morning, as she goes from one small place in her apartment to another, she takes inventory. Her journal is in the drawer of her nightstand, and it is clear that this too has been discovered—those things she's written across the pages. Later, in the shower, beginning to cry and still putting off what she's most afraid to know, she feels as if she just can't get away: everyone here keeps watching her, going through the quiet parts of her life, probing the details. The water in the shower is treated with salt; she tastes the salt and considers her closet, in her bedroom . . . *No!* . . . and now, with a fresh towel wrapped around her body, she leaves the shower running and runs to her closet, forcing open the door.

History, packed up inside a box. Each year, the box gains just a little more weight—letters from Sammy, and Nicky and Claire, and then the long, solitary letters from Nicky. And other documents: her birth certificate; her high school and college diplomas; an M.A. from U.C. Berkeley; portions of an incomplete and ill-considered dissertation proposal; several years' worth of income-tax reports; plane tickets to Paris and Lisbon, to Madrid; a concert ticket, her first; and the photographs . . . *the photographs!* . . . but at least the photographs are safe. The box was originally designed for oranges, with slits to permit the fruit to ripen while in transit, and here all the things in her box have somehow been overlooked. She thinks someday she will need to destroy this box; the statute of limitations must be drawing to a close . . . *When?* . . . and now she looks at the bed. She stands over the bed and lifts the mattress.

Her vibrator is still there, beneath the mattress, and now she picks it up, gently. The switch has been turned on, the batteries are dead.

She drops it onto the floor and screams.

• • •

Her parents died when she was twelve, a plane crash over Australia, and Jenna was raised in northern California by her aunt Nicky, who worked then as a probation officer for adolescents. Claire's illness was long and drawn out; Jenna would fly to California from New England and visit during vacations, visiting, talking about what she was doing—teaching at a boy's school for dyslexics; the boys taught her how to ski, and how to shoot baskets like a boy; and then one day, it all stopped. Claire died, and Nicky took a cruise to Alaska. Afterward, Nicky said she wanted to see the desert; maybe she'd move to a place with sunlight. A constant source of radiation, maybe it could prevent the need for more. Possibly it would be a safe place to live.

"So," says the cop, one Jenna recognizes from the night she drove her neighbor to the hospital, "anything valuable missing?"

"No," she says. "Not valuable."

That night he wore yellow rubber gloves. Today, just his uniform—a bulletproof vest and a gun. The vest puffs out his chest like a blowfish. He cocks an eye, and she asks him to sit down, if he'd like some tea.

He takes coffee, lots of sugar . . . *Lots, thank you* . . . and she realizes he must like this part of the job: taking reports, talking to people, to women in distress. She explains that nothing seems to be missing except a couple of tapes and a man's sport coat. She's never thought of herself as being that way. In distress.

"Somebody knows you, sounds like," says the cop. He writes something in a notebook and closes it up.

"What?"

"Oh, not like that. Probably, but maybe. You never really know, do you? This town has more peepers than drug addicts. Really. All the women in bikinis. All the people out beefing away in their swimming pools. Excuse me, didn't mean to make you blush. Do that all the time, really." He sipped his coffee, nodding. "It's a city full of perverts, though. I get two, three of these a week. All in the same neighborhood, too. Same block. We go catch Tom, we miss Dick and Harry, if you follow. Excuse me. There I go again, doing that."

"But I haven't seen anybody."

"Could be an old boyfriend, eh? Some guy still snotting on his sleeve? Keep your blinds closed, okay? Keep them closed. Remember, Miss—"

"Williams. Jenna."

"Remember, Jenna—can I call you that?"

"Yes."

"That's a plant, right? Jenna? I'm Jim," he says, rising to shake her hand. He fumbles in his pockets for a cigarette; he cups the match, lights the cigarette. He's looking for a place to put the match. There's a ring on his finger, and the ring makes her smile, unexpectedly—he's bound legally to the joint. If she wanted to, she could make him break some laws.

She feels wrong, knowing she could do that. The smile fades, and looking up, she understands that he knows she's seen the ring. He sits down, exhaling. "As I was saying . . . Jenna?"

"Yes?"

He adjusts his belt and says, "As I was saying, the point is, the point about your blinds and keeping them closed is—"

"Yes?"

"Well, if you can see yourself, then so can somebody else."

"The windows?"

"The windows," he says, nodding. He looks her in the eye and says, solemnly, "The windows."

He walks to the door, opens it to take a peak. Apparently his cruiser is still double-parked. He takes another drag, exhales. The smoke chokes the light rushing through the open door. He turns now, gesturing to the window. "Life's a mirror, Jenna. A big mirror. Especially at night."

"I'll keep the blinds shut," she says. "I'll run the air-conditioning, nonstop."

"Be careful, is all. Be careful, okay? We'll fill out a report, sure, but you gotta be careful."

She feels a rush of panic. Startled, as if by a ghost.

"Okay?" he says. "You okay? You're the high-strung type, I guess. Eh?"

"I'm fine."

"Remember," he says, pointing his cigarette. "Life is a mirror. And sometimes, sometimes you have to remember not to break the rules."

"The rules," she says, nodding.

"Life is a mirror and you know what happens when you break a mirror, Jenna?"

"Bad luck. Lots. A lifetime."

He looks at the ring on his finger, checking to see if it's still there, and says, regretfully, "You gotta remember all the rules. Okay? No more bikinis down by the pool. No more walking around in your skivvies at night. I don't mean to make you blush, Jenna, but keep that bedroom window closed. You know, at night? I mean, if—"

"I've never had a gun in my home."

"Oh?" he says, reaching for his holster snap. "Would you like—"

"I mean, I don't like it," she says standing. "Life is a mirror," she says. "I got it."

"Oh."

"I think I'm going to buy a dog," she says. "A Doberman."

He shrugs, just nearly catching her drift. Maybe he should call for backup. He flicks his butt through the open door and says, "That's not a bad idea."

Now he's looking for his car, the one with all the lights; he turns and smiles at her body, various parts at a time, saying good-bye, fare thee well. He says, "That's not a bad idea at all, Jenna." He steps out the door, turns again, smiles, and says, "Now you're really thinking, if you don't mind me saying so. You're really thinking now."

She thinks a woman wants love, not a pistol.

Ray comes over to help her install a new dead bolt, along with another dead bolt and two chains. While he works at the door, drilling holes, she reads through the instructions and makes jokes about living in New York City, where she's been only once but has seen enough about on television to get the general idea. There's a lot of crime. There people rob each other out of need. Or greed. The richest city in the world. It's all so incomprehensible.

The room is full of plants, recently sprayed; they make the place breathe oxygen and help clear out the smoke.

Ray turns and looks at her. "I know what you're thinking," he says. "But it wasn't me. Just in case I've got to say that. It wasn't me, Jen."

"I know that."

"Then why are you looking at me like that?"

"I think you've got a problem. That's all. I think you ought to do something about it."

"My carpentry?"

"No. And you know what I mean."

"You mean what you're not talking about."

"What *you're* not talking about. I mean you ought to try and get some help. It's a disease, you know? People die from it. People you care about."

"Right."

"It's something you can get taken care of. If you want—"

"People," he says disgustedly. "They always want to talk about it. They always want to smear their faces in the shit."

He drops the drill onto the carpet, and she knows she's violated some private territory. She knows he's trying not to be angry with her. He's rolling up his sleeves, and she thinks he is the strongest man she's ever known. His arms are thick as beams, holding up a ceiling, the sky.

"What we're assuming here," Ray says, "is that I have a problem—"

"Yes—"

"And if I do in fact have a problem, I think you'd be kind enough to let me goddamn work it out myself."

She thinks she knows what he means, even if he's wrong. "If

you weren't worried about it," she says, "you wouldn't be talking about it. You wouldn't be calling me up in the middle of the night, Ray."

"I said I was sorry. I'm sorry I did that."

By the look on his face, she understands that she should let it rest; they know each other pretty well. She thinks Ray is most afraid of being embarrassed, that she is most afraid of not being in control. She thinks each is the same, and that she should save it for another time, approach the subject slowly, try a metaphor . . . *you gotta watch the flags, you can't break the rules, if a country wants to lay down and get fucked* . . . and she can tell he's going over their conversations slowly, trying to remember the parts where he's done things embarrassing. If he hadn't called her, then he wouldn't be embarrassed, and she's glad he called her, she just wishes he hadn't needed to be drunk in order to do so.

Now he shuts his eyes, tight, and she's seen this before, too: Walker Miller. When she visited Walker Miller at the hospital— the way his eyes would snap shut, locking all the doors. Trying to be safe. Trying to keep things from getting in.

Or out. Maybe he's trying to keep things from getting out?
"No," she says.

"No?"

"No, damn it!"

"It's my mess," Ray says, warning her. "It's my fucking mess, Jen. It's my mess and I'm going to have to clean it up."

"No. It's everybody's mess. It's everybody's mess who loves you—"

"Love?" he says. "Love? Keep trying," he says, unrolling his sleeves. "Keep trying, Jen, and you just might save the whole fucking world."

He starts out the door, but he has to return because he's forgotten his keys. Now, when he picks them up off the stereo speaker, he stops. He shakes his head and says, looking at his sleeves, "It's stupid. The whole thing is stupid. I'm just not good at any of this anymore."

"Ray—"

"Look. It was a mistake. I'm sorry, okay? Call a fucking carpenter, Jen. Get yourself a handyman."

And he leaves, down the steps, two at a time the way he always leaves. He's going down the flights, two steps at a time, and she's wishing right now he'd come back and finish what she's started—the locks on her door, all those brass bolts and chains. If he were the way she wanted him to be, she wonders if she'd even want to love him. And maybe, maybe if she'd known better, maybe she wouldn't be sleeping alone at night. She knows it's not the alcohol. The alcohol is the flag—recently rediscovered, but still just a flag which is breaking all the rules: namely, Ray, who's beginning to break under the strain of carrying around so big a flag, and the pole beginning to slip through his hands. It's not the flag you fear, it's the country, and what the people who live inside of it are capable of doing. Going into your house, taking off their pants and maybe rummaging around, running down the batteries, having a smoke, maybe, while they stand there looking in the mirror, posing, thinking, *So what's a little bad luck? What's a little extra time on my hands all by myself?*

Sometimes, it's possible to lose the desert for the sky, or the stars. After Ray dove into her pool, splitting his head on the cement stairs, telling her it was his own fault . . . *It's my fault!* . . . she lead him up the seven flights to her apartment. She didn't have any clean towels; they were all soaked with blood, tossed somewhere into a hamper at Maricopa County. Hospital waste.

She gave Ray a fresh sheet to dry himself. When he took off his shirt, she saw the gash in his side strapped together with thick silver tape. It was the kind of tape people use on boxes and pipes.

"Door," he said, pointing. "Caught myself on a door."

She cleaned the wound—two fingers deep, long as her hand; she cleaned out the cut over his eye. It was something she'd never done before, dressing a man's wounds. She used a Kotex on his side and wrapped him in another sheet. She gave him a glass of water with five aspirin and put him to sleep on her couch, saying, "I don't want to make this a habit."

"Uh-huh."

Twice, while still asleep on the couch, he'd decided to try and leave, and twice she stopped him, stopped him while he stood and looked around the room, blinking, still asleep. *Daddy?* he said once. *Daddy?* and she knew he was simply too drunk to sleep. Maybe he had a concussion, which meant he shouldn't sleep, though she couldn't remember for sure. The problem with first aid was that you could never remember just how you were supposed to use it; she stayed up the entire night, listening to him breathe. She sat up in her kitchen chair, watching the airplanes make their approach into Sky Harbor—the lights, blinking. After Ray began to snore, a sound she recognized and almost enjoyed, she popped her last Fiorinal, then the one she kept for emergencies; she drank two more glasses of wine. Sitting there, drinking her wine, floating on the Fiorinal, she told herself this is what it meant to feel nothing. Nothing, except for what you think, and it frightened her, drifting this way while watching the sky, and the airplanes, flying, and the way she liked the way it felt . . . *drifting*. It felt so good she was afraid to sleep and miss the voyage, which she knew would pass, as it did, slowly.

Eventually she understood that several hours had passed, and she made tea, in case Ray woke, and when he did wake, near six, he went right on by her into the kitchen, knocking at the cupboards, searching for a glass. He couldn't find a glass. He opened the fridge and took out two beers.

"Thirsty," he said, nodding.

"Drunk," she said, still weak and slightly numb. She felt as if she were listening to someone say that . . . *Drunk*.

"Jesus," he said. "Jesus, you ain't kidding."

He stumbled into the bathroom, and she listened for him falling, knocking his head on the sink, the tub. He took forever to pee, and when he returned to the couch with only one beer, he lay down, shivered, and tugged at the sheet wrapped around his waist. He fell asleep, shivering, and she wanted to wake him up and make it stop, touch his ears, his neck, the parts she had at one time been familiar with enough to kiss. She left the beer sitting there at the foot of the couch so he'd find it when he woke, one more time, the beer a tepid and stale reminder of everything that happens. After a while, she moved to her balcony and fell asleep watching the morning traffic. She felt the sun finally begin to rise.

Even on Sunday, the streets were busy and important: people, rushing off to attend to the needs of their particular Lord. After Ray left, apologizing, shy and suddenly angry both, she went to Saint Christopher's ten o'clock. There Jim Lawson gave a sermon on the need for faith. Whenever he said that word, he seemed to capitalize all the letters . . . *FAITH.* Clearly, he was a man who believed in things he could say loudly. After the recessional . . . *O Paradise, who doth not crave for rest? . . .* afterward, Father Lawson gave the blessing.

But on the balcony, before leaving her apartment, Ray stood leaning into the rail. He stood leaning into the rail looking down into the water.

"You could have killed yourself," she said.

"Yeah," he said. "I guess."

So he was just beginning to remember, which seemed likely, and maybe unkind: remembering something you shouldn't be able to forget, ever, which is what nightmares were. The parts the soul wouldn't let the mind forget. Sammy Coughlin went tripping into the ocean and drowned. Or Walker Miller, sitting on the lawn. Or your lover, bleeding into a chlorinated swimming pool.

During the following week at school, she watched Ray spend a lot of time trying to be nice—saying hello to people in the hallway, being cheerful with the kids. At heart, he must really want to be Catholic, because only Catholics seemed to understand the need for grief, for guilt and absolution. Something to make you feel better, even if you've lapsed and joined up with the Episcopalians. Anything to make you feel better, one catholic and apostolic church bent on sending out the blessings.

Bill, Jenna's neighbor, gave her ten dollars for gas and bought her a new set of towels from an expensive department store Jenna would only drive by. She'd never even stepped inside, the merchandise was that expensive. Bill had the towels wrapped in a box with ribbons and apologized for not having them monogrammed; he didn't want to make her have to wait. He stopped by after the break-in to say hello and to explain that he hadn't heard a thing. He should have been paying more attention, he said.

"How do you like those towels?"

She was grading papers, research papers on either the effect of Reconstruction or the Marshall Plan—for extra credit, the Monroe Doctrine. The papers were lying in separate piles on the floor according to topic; a few students had managed to spell most of the words correctly, some had even cited their encyclopedias— all that accidental thought, colliding here in front of her. Bill said that the best way to buy a dog was to go through the want ads.

"It's where people advertise. The purebreds," he said, sitting down on the floor beside her. "The ones that cost a lot of money. Some people live on it. On the dogs, I mean."

"I'm not ready to buy," Jenna said. "I just want to start maybe looking. You have to make a big pet deposit here. Maybe I should move somewhere else."

"Dog's a dog," he said. "They like it wherever you are. All you have to do is play with it a lot." He grabbed the newspaper from Jenna's couch and spread it open. "Cars," he said. "Looking for a good buy on a Desert Romper?"

"Not really."

"How 'bout just a good time?"

"Do you see any spaniels? I really want a springer spaniel. I like their ears. I've wanted one all my life."

"Big," he said. "They listen good."

"I never knew that before, really. That I wanted my own dog."

"John," Bill said, looking over the paper. "I put an ad in the Romance. I never thought it would work. I couldn't believe it."

"It worked," Jenna said, smiling.

"Not really. His therapist says it's something he can change. John's all worried about his family and everything. If you ask me, he just can't forgive me over that window thing. I shouldn't have done that. Do you have any tea or anything?"

She stood, went to the kitchen and put water on the range. Bill said, following, "No. I mean, iced?"

He had a glass of water instead. He looked out the kitchen window and said, "I don't know. I've always been partial to cats, myself. Cats—they've got a mind of their own. They do what they want. The real problem with men is that we're always such goddamn pricks."

"God love 'em," Jenna said, smiling. She thought of Ray, and his prick, and the way she'd hold it sometimes while he fell asleep. When he was sleepy, she could fit him entirely in her palm.

Bill shook his head, waved his hand. "It's a big world, Jenna. A big world. Lots of . . ."

She knew what he meant, and she wondered if he closed his eyes, if she could do it. If she could keep Bill in the dark and still bring him comfort.

"You know," Bill said, waving. "In the sea. All that. Thing is, it's not the kind of thing you go and change. It's not like there's anything broken in the first place! Jesus, you fix a dog! A cat! You fix a goddamn broken window!"

But what about her? What could this man do for her?

He could love you, and that might never be enough.

"It's okay, Bill," she said. "Really, it's okay."

"I'm sorry," he said, convincing himself. "I should really just go and keep my mouth shut. Every time I say something, I say something wrong."

"Really. You should talk to someone who knows what she's talking about. I mean, I know what I think. But I don't know any answers or anything."

"Yeah," he said, knowing exactly what she meant, meaning he'd already thought of it. Probably, he already had. He said, "What do you think?"

"I think love will break your heart. Each and every time."

"That's pretty grim."

"I also think it's the only thing that can fix it, after."

"Oh," he said. "Kind of yin-yang, I guess."

"It's not any kind of answer, though."

"I guess, yeah."

She blinked, and she knew that she had made her decision. Once decided, she knew what she wanted to do. She thought all you have to do is make up your mind and blink; it doesn't take a lifetime.

"You can come with," she said, stepping into the living room. "Where?"

She snatched up the want ads and said, "You can come with and help pick him out!"

It's not his weakness that she fears. It's his strength—his voice and the way he always knows what he means to say. It's his will, and the enormous weight of all that discipline he lifts, each day, stretching across the back of his neck and arms in order not to become the person he might really think he is. And it's the possibility that she might need to be someone else just to spite him, six years later, or twenty-seven, just to have him need her— someone who needs taking care of. If she needs taking care of, maybe he won't want to take care of her. Need, and what she needs—love, which is just a matter of knowing what you want and being brave enough to try, even if it kills you, which she thinks it always will. The true root of history: *love,* and what you want, and what then must always happen next after you try to give it all away, or take it back, as if by accident.

Nicky would say, *There are no accidents. Only other plans we don't know too much about.*

Jenna once bought Nicky a subscription to *Arizona High-ways* so Nicky could plan what it might look like, living in Sedona, Arizona, among the retired and the tourists from California, or Paris—among all the advocates of a new and excessively impassioned age. Now Nicky really does live in Arizona, and Jenna has listened repeatedly to a number of well-intentioned people try to explain to her just what the New Age is. Often, they use words like *vortex* and *center* and *energy,* and phrases like *channeling along the astral plane.*

Her parents died in a plane, it makes no sense. The land north of Verde Valley is mysterious and intent. The landscape invites speculation. Here, the sky changes often—an uncertain altitude, as if considering apology. It invites people to channel along the astral plane, or to wander up Highway 89A to Oak Creek Canyon and an unpolluted vision of the world—an anomalous plot, there beneath the railing overlooking all that space. It is a territory fraught with geological transition and painfully clean air. It will make you whistle, breathing it, and Nicky has made new friends. She lives alone on a street called Ranch House Circle, along Oak Creek.

Nicky said, in Sedona, Arizona, "Tell me about your life."

"My life . . ." Jenna said, laughing. "My life."

They sat in the big room with Nicky's Labrador, Albert. He was too big a dog for an apartment; he needed a house like this with a fireplace. Behind Nicky's house was a golf course. Each morning, Nicky and Albert walked up the road to the swimming pool, where Albert napped in the sun while Nicky led a water-aerobics class for widowed men and women. Nicky believed in exercise and plenty of long walks.

"The good things," Nicky said. "The lousy things. Tell me what you're doing."

"What I always do," Jenna said.

"You've stopped seeing that man, Raymond?"

"Ray," she said. "There were some bad things."

They walked along the creek past the house a famous movie director was supposed to have lived in; people said they had to use a crane to get him across the creek, he was so heavy and slow.

"I knew it," Jenna said, stopping. "I knew if I came up here I was going to have to talk about it."

"Then you must have wanted to talk about it."

"I don't know what to do."

"About what?"

"I don't want to be there anymore. I don't want to do it."

"School?"

"School. Everything. Nicky, sometimes I don't know how people do it. I don't know how they keep doing things every day. Washing the dishes. Every day, you've got to wash the dishes. Sometimes I think I just can't wash any more dishes. I don't know how people stand it!" She buried her hands deep in the pockets of her shorts. "Ray," she said. "He drinks. You know? He's screwing everything up. I mean, it's getting bad, and I know I'm not about to save him or anything, but he didn't start screwing things up until all this shit started happening. And then he gets wasted and almost kills himself in my swimming pool. It's crazy," she said, wiping her eyes, almost laughing. "I mean, I didn't even think about him when I saw him, and then everything just happens!"

"What do you want to do?"

"I don't know if I can keep doing this. I don't know, Nicky."

"Quit," Nicky said. "Buy some paper plates and take a cruise. Take a cruise off to Alaska."

"I don't want to go to Alaska."

"Do what you want, Jenna. Consult the I Ching. Drink some herbal tea. Water."

"I want Ray to want me, I think. I want him to need me and I want to be able to need him back."

"Ray?" Nicky said.

"Yeah. Ray. I want . . . Nicky?"

She let her aunt take her, smother her in her vast arms, Nicky's breath drifting down her neck while Jenna wept. Standing here, in her aunt Nicky's arms, she felt as if she could weep for days, and after a while Jenna began to feel better even if she knew she wasn't ever going to know why. Walker, Ray, the way she'd been such a bitch to Edith—kicking her off the team, and maybe she just really needed to try a little harder.

"He might have done it!" Jenna cried. "He might have really killed himself!"

"There. There now."

But why? Why'd he have to do that?

• • •

Sitting on the floor in her apartment, surrounded by plants and furniture you put inside an apartment, and her students' papers, she thinks now that it's another question she will have to keep on getting used to, like:

—*Why is water heavy?*

—*Why does ice float?*

—*Why'd he have to do that?*

Influence, history, and the enormous weight of time, and Walker Miller and her neighbor Bill. He is at her door, knocking softly, even if it is still partly open. The late-afternoon light is vaguely warm, and Bill's carrying another newspaper. He says that there's a litter of spaniel pups somewhere out in New River.

"New River?"

"As in Brand New. Brand New River."

It's a place she's only heard of . . . *New River* . . . beyond a town called Carefree. She makes a call and a woman answers the phone. The woman is abrupt, almost rude, and gives her instructions; she'll take a check only with a bank card. She prefers cash. She says the dogs cost two hundred dollars each, *pet price.*

The drive up Scottsdale Highway is long and eventually begins to turn pretty. The sun is setting. Riding inside Bill's car, an expensive sedan with thick seats, Jenna gazes out the window. Bill has offered to drive so that Jenna can hold the dog on the way back, in case he gets sick, which according to Bill is what dogs are supposed to do.

"Dogs," Bill says. "They like to be held. Especially when they're new."

A half hour north of Scottsdale, they turn west into the sun. They begin looking for a dirt road, and a sign, WONDERLAND KENNELS, and Bill turns onto the only dirt road for miles. They drive over the dust, slowly, avoiding the potholes; after several more slow miles, when they pull up to a small mobile home, they can hear dogs barking and they know that they've arrived. The dogs, barking—all kinds—and around the car swarm five or six. A small man steps out onto the porch of the mobile home. He's wearing a white T-shirt and waving a broom. He smiles thinly, and Jenna sees the man and realizes simultaneously that there is not a single river in sight.

He steps off the porch and calls, "You the people come to see about a dog?"

"Yes," Jenna yells, through the window.

"Well," he says. "You best come inside and have a look!"

"No way," Bill says, inside the car, looking at the dogs, swarming. "No fucking way."

The man smiles and waits long enough for Jenna to see that he understands. He can't weigh more than a hundred pounds, if that.

"Dogs!" yells the man. "Dogs come!" And the dogs stop leaping at the car. They turn and trot past the gate the man is holding open. All except one, a German shepherd.

"Sam!"

Sam's too busy drooling on the window, barking at Bill. The man lifts the broom and throws it at the dog. His aim is good; Sam yelps and turns, running for the gate. The man walks across the dusty driveway and retrieves his broom. He takes out a cigarette, sticks it into a black plastic filter, like the twenties, and lights. He scratches at his head—his thin black hair is held in place with gel, or oil—and says to Bill, puffing, "You don't like dogs?"

"What?"

"Most people drive all the way out, they tend to like dogs."

"No," says Jenna. "We like small dogs."

"The old lady, she goes for Danes herself. Beats the hell out of me. You best come inside," says the man, frowning. "Come inside and meet the old lady."

The old lady was even smaller than the man. In California, Claire used to call Nicky *the old lady,* a private joke Jenna never ventured to understand. Nicky had said that a dog would be good to have. A kind one that needed you to be kind back and taken care of. The problem with most people, *with a lover,* Nicky said, was that people wanted to try always to take care of them.

"You can take care of a dog," Nicky said, patting Jenna's arm. "But you can't take care of a lover."

"I know."

"Unless she's dying, of course. Then you have no choice."

When Claire was dying, Nicky took a leave of absence. Nicky and Claire spent the days reading to each other until Claire could no longer concentrate on the words. Then Nicky simply read by herself, in the same room, reading long thick books about things which were purportedly simple—life, death, the passing of grief. During the increasingly brief moments Claire was strong enough to concentrate, Nicky would summarize, and after a while they simply moved on to poetry: it made more sense, waiting for death, because poetry removed entirely the need for summary. Jenna thinks Walker didn't even wait for death. He confronted it. The next world, people called it. As if it were just another day. As if things were really going to be any different someplace else.

She thinks heaven is where you make it. When Jenna's parents died, she was at a picnic. She was wearing a white dress and talking to a boy, Sammy Coughlin, from her church—Sammy, whom she later lived with, and loved. And who could have told her then, at that picnic with orange punch and oatmeal cookies and chaperons, who could have told her then? The punch was warm, it left the rim of your mouth sweet, and who was there to know?

"When in doubt," Ray says, "punt."

But people, after you came to know them, they died. Or worse, they did something stupid—went swimming on acid. Alive or dead, you couldn't just kick a body off into the distance. Sammy wanted to be a rock star like Walker Miller, and Sammy wrote songs about peace and love and death until, one morning, she felt a lump on his chest. They were nineteen and in bed; she was nursing his cock, swollen with having just risen, and when she reached her hand up for his chest, she felt the lump—hard as a walnut, there in the center of his chest. At first she wasn't sure if she should finish, and later that afternoon, she made Sammy call a doctor, and later Sammy spent the rest of the day drinking sun tea and going through his journals. He wrote her a song, "Jenna in the Morning," inspired more by Leonard Cohen than by Jenna herself, and later that night he played her the song on his guitar. She liked the song; she used to hum it often, until one day she forgot the melody, it had been that long since she'd heard him sing it.

"It's probably nothing," she had said. "Just a little bump."

And it was nothing. It was nothing caused by a rib separating from the sternum.

"It's a hunk of bone," Sammy explained to her later. "Just bone. Like tectonic plates. You know, those things that shift. Nothing to worry about at all."

Earthquakes, she thought, the secret and always unexpected, and sometimes, when she thinks maybe Sammy tried to drown himself in the ocean, she remembers the look on his face when he explained that—just a piece of bone, shifting out of its joint, as if the lump in his chest were simply a logical extension of the San Andreas. And she remembers his look of unequivocal relief: Sammy, standing in his purple boxers, in the kitchen drinking his iced tea. A week later he took a road trip with some friends. He was going to visit his old girlfriend. He kissed Jenna on the cheek and told her to be good.

"No," she said. "You mean, *Do good.*" She said, "Do good, Sammy," and then he drove away.

Later, stepping out of the library, she met a thin man on the quad, Frederick Aliston, who offered her 350 dollars. He was a tall man with discreet clothes. She thought Sammy might like it, a picture of her that he could show his old girlfriend and say that Jenna had made just for him. Thinking about it made her want to do it. She thought, So what if he's fucking his old roommate? He's going to live; he's going to have to write some songs. It's something he'd want me to do.

Aliston asked her if she had any lotion. *Some aloe?* He started shooting on the beach, and he told her to cover herself, slowly, with the aloe and to pretend first that she was here alone. Then he told her to pretend he was someone else. "Pretend I'm your boy-friend," he said. Eventually they slid into Aliston's car and drove to her apartment, and she closed her eyes, and she thought about how stupid this was, being a model. She thought about Sammy, and what her mother might think, who was dead, and she thought about how she was going to have to remember this. Aliston, setting down his Nikon, unzipping his fly, began to explain.

"I'm in your hands now," he said. And later, on the morning after, "Roll over."

She thought he might have wanted something more tradi-tional, and she remembers, finally, not being very surprised except for when it hurt. She remembers thinking he might not pay her, and she remembers his voice, coming from behind, brushing past the cool sweat on her neck.

Easy. Easy now.

There were others, after Sammy. Artists, mostly, who said they admired her form—a couple of photographers; a Rastafarian who did mostly landscapes; a native of Italy who was *really into film.* By now she was doing too many drugs; she'd moved upstate, floating in and out of grad school. History, of course, because it was something nobody could ever make sense of; to make sense of history, you had to know first what it was going to bring you: you had to know that Walker Miller was going to blow himself away, and you had to know that another was going to follow—a storm you know is coming, even though you're never ready when it hits.

It could be anybody . . . *me?* . . . even if you weren't looking for the signs the way you knew you should be. You had to look and look and look. Finally, after confronting the need to develop a worthwhile dissertation on a subject remotely connected to Pan-Americanism not yet beaten to dust, paging through the *DAI,* day after day, she applied for a job in New England. New Hampshire. As far away as she could get from California, or Pan-America, without a passport. In two months the state of New Hampshire would be smothered in snow. She packed up her books and stored them in Nicky and Claire's garage; she kissed Nicky and Claire good-bye, and Nicky told Jenna to learn something about herself.

"Dyslexia," Nicky said. "That's an interesting problem. A lot of my kids are dyslexic. They tend to see things differently."

"I know."

"No," Nicky said. "It's not that simple."

And it wasn't. It wasn't just a matter of spelling your letters upside down or backward: the source of confusion lay far deeper in the mind. The confusion reached beyond the bounds of that for which the retina alone might possibly account; it wasn't just a matter of seeing, of being *word blind*. For the dyslexic, *sea glass* could very possibly be just another word for *window*. And ADD, Attention Deficit Disorder, which was now being treated with Ritalin—clean, pharmaceutical speed for boys who couldn't look out the window and feel homesick without first popping fifteen milligrams of speed. Everything was backward, not just their spelling, and in New Hampshire, watching these boys all learn to think, however difficulty, Jenna felt homesick for California for the first time in her life.

Like all these boys, she'd never before been away from home: the Pacific Coast, and as a girl growing up in California, waiting for her body to develop and trying not to wonder where her parents really were . . . *somewhere in Australia, where there was a lot of dust* . . . Jenna would walk along the beach looking for sea glass—the detritus of a civilization bent on picnicking, preferably on the beach. She'd collect the glass—the smooth blue and green and silver pieces of glass to place later in the bottom of her aquarium. The glass had been made smooth and round by the sea, and the salt, rubbing against the glass, polishing, and the man Jenna bought the dog from, she realized, was from New England. She could tell by his language, his accent and attitude.

Laconic, she thought. She wondered if he'd ever seen the Pacific. Maybe Arizona was as far west as he'd ever made it. The thought made her sad—all that water, polishing the glass, just waiting to be discovered. Clearly, the man knew a lot about maple syrup. Sap, which you had to bleed from trees.

"Maine," said the man, after she had written out a check.

"Paris, Maine. 'Course, we don't really need a bank card. The old lady just says that."

And standing in the backyard of that mobile home in New River, Arizona, surrounded by chain link fence, this is what she saw:

A tiny woman lying in the sun on an orange lounge chair, drinking soda from a can with a straw, and holding a fly swatter. Behind the woman, a view of the desert, dark and full of shadows, and the saguaros and the sweet dusty smell of sage and mesquite. There sat an old pickup on granite blocks, its black paint oxidized white. The yard was full of dust and flies and dogs—a kennel, WONDERLAND KENNELS—and in the corner of the fenced yard stood a stack of used tires and ten-gallon water bottles. The old man and the old lady had to bring their water in by truck, and inside a small swimming pool, the type young parents inflate for toddlers, one breath at a time, inside the dry pool slept a litter of pups. Six of them, tangled up and breathing, dreaming about the rest of their lives.

Jenna wondered, right then, just what it was they were dreaming for. She watched the pups wake and sniff and scramble to the side of the pool for her to play with, and she picked the one in back, pissing on all his brothers and sisters, pretending not to pay attention. The man said that he and the old lady were from Paris.

"Paris, Maine," he said, to avoid confusion.

"My sister married a black man, too," said the tiny woman, winking. "They live in Tampa, Florida."

"Yep," said the man, looking at the dog. "He's got a mind of his own."

In the car, before driving off, Bill said, laughing, "It always happens, you know. Really, I've got more wives than most people ever dream of. 'Specially you white bitches."

"They were nice," Jenna said, waving to the man.

The man held the broom in his hands and told the dogs to *shut that up!* When they didn't, he threw the broom at the fence. The dogs kept barking, and she knew they were going to keep barking until Bill drove the foreign car away. He turned the car around and drove away, slowly, avoiding the potholes, and she listened to the barking dogs, their voices fading into the dust behind them. She held the puppy in her lap, feeling him breathe against her chest. She scratched his ear and rolled up a handful of skin.

Jenna named the dog Paris.

Paris, the boy who stole Helen and started the only war ever worth writing about. A story worth even the attention of the gods. The stuff of myth, finally—this dog now in her car, two days later, sitting on the floorboards, no bigger than a football.

She pulled into Edith McCaw's driveway and let Paris out, taking his leash, which he kept twisting in his paws. Jenna had decided to come visit after swim practice; she thought it would be good to bring Paris, her dog, who had spent the day pissing all over her kitchen. A dog shouldn't be kept too long inside a kitchen. A dog could help break the ice.

"Hi," Edith said at the door, uncertainly.

"Hi. I thought I'd stop by. If you're still angry with me, I'll go away."

Edith shifted awkwardly. She looked down at Paris and smiled. She stepped outside the door and knelt to pet him.

"His name's Paris," Jenna said. "He's a very famous dog."

"Famous?"

"You're looking at the guy who started the Trojan War."

Edith flinched, then giggled. "The one with all the Greeks," she said, smiling.

"And Penelope."

"Penelope," Edith said, looking at the dog. "I always want to say Pineapple."

They went into the backyard and Edith brought Jenna a glass of Diet 7UP. Jenna let go of the leash and let Paris wander around the swimming pool. Looking into the water, it was the first time he'd ever seen himself. He yelped a greeting.

"Have you been swimming?" Jenna asked.

"No. Not really."

"I shouldn't have gotten angry," Jenna said. "It was wrong. I shouldn't have done that—"

"That's okay."

"No. It was wrong of me. Sometimes, sometimes we don't always do the right things. I didn't want you to be late. I didn't think you were trying hard enough, and I wanted you to know that. Sometimes when people get angry at other people they're not really angry at them."

"I know."

"Probably," Jenna said. "That doesn't make it any easier. My aunt Nicky," Jenna said, laughing. "After something like this, she always says, 'Are we through with it?' "

A car pulled into the driveway, a door slammed shut.

"My dad—"

"I'm blocking the driveway. I should go, anyway," Jenna said, looking for Paris. "Paris," she called. "Paris!"

He was in the flower bed, sniffing. When she approached, reaching for his leash, he scampered off across the flowers, past the yuccas and barrel cactus. He tripped over a sprinkler head. He stepped on his leash and choked himself, yelping, and now Jenna decided to try the friendly approach, on her hands and knees, across the putting green, slowly. Behind her, she could hear voices.

"Just a second, Dad," called Edith. "I'll pull it in later."

"Right," said a voice. "You and A. J. Foyt."

Jenna stood, rising, wiping the grass from her knees. She was still forming an explanation—something about her dog, about him still not knowing his name . . . *Paris, the most famous name in history* . . . when she saw the heavy splint. And then his hair, and the line of his jaw and the way he looked that night bleeding on her landing like a hose. Behind him she could see a palm tree, swaying, and she looked at the palm tree while Edith said, "Dad, this is my teacher, Ms. Williams. She's the coach."

"Hi—"

"Hi," said John, holding his splint. "I think we must have already met."

• • •

The present, she tells herself, is where we'll always all end up. It's the gift we have to give ourselves, and Jenna said hello to Edith's father and pretended not to know him. This life was more complicated than she thought, and lonely, and knowing John McCaw, and Edith, and her neighbor Bill—knowing all their lives made her feel sad, impolite and uninvited. It made her feel complicit, and the bad things she's done in this life are simple and remarkably commonplace, even for a girl raised by her lesbian aunt to challenge the catechism: some stealing, some lying and cheating, a lot of sex and adultery combined. An insufficient amount of birth control which led, of course, to an abortion— absolute and, she tells herself, when needing a hit of remorse, unforgivable. She's neglected to pay her parking tickets and she's even tried to hurt people on purpose, and these are the things she remembers, most of which she knows she never should have done, but then it's not as if there were a lot of possible choices. Maybe there really are no choices. Maybe there's only what you do and having to wake up sometime the next morning to fix a cup of coffee, so what, then, is the point? Why did someone break into her apartment? Why did somebody want something that belongs to her? Why? And how do you explain forgiveness? Responsibility, and the need for something to hold on to? When Ray needs something, he reaches for a barbell, or a beer; she, for the warm spot in the small of a man's back, and maybe faith is nothing more than an attempt to extend your reach. And maybe somebody was out there now, looking through her blinds, wondering what she was thinking about right now. Outside, with the lights of the city washing through the blinds . . . maybe someone was out there now? Watching her. Watching a woman's hand rising, finding the warm spot, the spot among the unfolding of the flesh. The spot that if you practice on long enough is enough to make you even stop thinking. Enough to make you leave your senses far behind you, drifting in the sheets, because need too is enough to make you come when you feel you really need to. Even if you know it's hopeless. Even when you know you need to most.

The Theme of Your Life

The heart is big as a fist. And shame is the greater part of gravity. It's what keeps the race still and here on earth, because shame is what you have to learn to carry along with everything else. The heart, for example, weighs in at approximately twelve fluid ounces.

After he works out, Joe feels his heart pumping hard against the walls of his chest, and he knows this means it's working. This means it's strong enough to be working hard, and when he makes a fist, he tells himself this is what it feels like: his heart, pumping blood through the veins in his wrist. This is what he's meant to do, and right now he's sweating on the couch, something his mom never let him do: *No sweating on the good furniture!* He's finished lifting and now he's cooling down, looking at a book his father left on the couch last weekend before he left for Miami. Right now, Joe needs to write the theme of his life for Mr. Rolf.

Tomorrow, Spencer gets operated on: the doctors are going to remove the plate in his leg and Brad Jazinski is flying in from Seattle to make sure everything *goes as scheduled.* Joe is going to pick his father up at the airport in his hearse, which is almost as big as a limo; if it weren't for airplanes, it would take his father days to get anywhere at all. This spring his father wants to send

Joe on a trip by himself to visit colleges, all of them in New England, which means Massachusetts and Connecticut and one even in Rhode Island. His father says that's where all the expensive schools are. He says for education, money is no object. He says, "You get what you pay for, kiddo."

Joe's never even been to New England. He sets his father's book aside and goes to fetch the atlas. He reaches on his toes up to the top shelf. He could do curls with the atlas, it's that big, and now, sitting on the floor, the book in his lap, looking at the United States of America, he realizes that New England is no bigger than the state of Arizona. If Edith goes to college in Boston, like her brother, probably Joe will have to bump into her. Maybe they'll bump into each other at an airport, during Christmas vacation, or at graduation. Still, *he'd* have to recognize *her;* otherwise, with her eyes, she'd walk right on by him in a terminal. He thinks maybe they could sit together on the plane and order some drinks. They could talk about people they're dating now, and after a while, he could lean back and shut his eyes, tired from all his exams. Or maybe he'd turn on the overhead light and crack a book—something she's never even heard of, maybe something in French.

"No," he says, because he has just decided that when he goes to college, in New England, he's not going to date anybody. He's not even going to wrestle. He's through with that shit. Karate, he thinks, looking at the freeways outside of Philadelphia. There's a sport. Maybe he'll join a karate team and really learn to kick some ass; if he hadn't broken Ernest's arm, he might have been able to get a scholarship to Iowa, which everyone knows is the best school for wrestling. According to the atlas, Iowa really is in the middle of the country, and his father says Iowa is full of corn and farm equipment.

"It's not a place you want to be," his father says. "It's worse than Nebraska."

Joe remembers wanting to ask his father how you knew where it was you were supposed to be. His father said you wanted to be as near an airport as possible, and looking at the state of Arizona, Joe looks at all the space between the names of places—

Wickenberg, and Nogales. Years ago, Arizona was a place he'd only heard of, and now he turns the pages to look at the long state along the coast—California, a territory full of drought, computer chips, Hollywood and San Francisco, which is the place where all the gay people live. And the earthquake, in San Francisco. It's a place where people surf all day in the ocean and do chemicals. A place where, tucked behind Los Angeles, a naked girl lies on a piece of Japanese furniture, looking at a camera, almost smiling. Her name is Ms. Williams, only it's not the same Ms. Williams whom Joe used to take notes from, in American History, and on the back is written *I'm thinking you should be here with me now.* He recognizes the handwriting, and the polite look in her eyes; in the picture, her hair is long as a highway. Once, Jenna Williams had really long hair, and she looks sad, as if she really is thinking about someplace else.

Spencer wants to see the Grand Canyon.

"You are going to see it. This summer, with the Boy Scouts."

"No. I mean, I want to see it now. Mr. Moose, too. We want to see how big it is!"

Spencer finishes pouring milk into his cereal and reaches for a doughnut. Now, with the cereal and the doughnut, he seems uncertain how he's going to get himself over to the kitchen table. Even if he is allowed to use crutches, he still needs two hands. He puts the doughnut into his mouth, sticks both crutches under one arm, because he's always supposed to use *two,* and looks at his cereal. He shakes his head.

"Here," says Joe, getting up to help.

"Nuh-uh," Spencer says through the doughnut. He lets the crutches fall to the floor, grabs his cereal, and begins to hop to the kitchen table. When he finally makes it, the floor is covered with spilt milk. He takes the doughnut out of his mouth and looks at the floor. He says, "It was an experiment."

"Great," says Joe.

"Dad says I can go if I want to. He says you'll take me."

"I can't take you."

"Why not? You got kicked off, didn't you?"

"I'm still busy, Spencer. I'm busy. I got things I gotta do."

"Like what?"

"Like things. I got homework and I got to study for the S.A.T."

"S.A.T.—yeah, okay. Uh-huh. Edith said she'd take me."

"Edith doesn't even know how to drive."

"You don't like her anymore, that's all." Spencer chews on his doughnut and looks at Joe's orange juice, thinking. "I do," he says, nodding. He takes a drink from Joe's orange juice and says, "What's the S.A.T.?"

"A test. The biggest you ever have to take. If you do bad, you can't go to a good college in New England."

"Oh," Spencer says. "Are you going to be there? Tomorrow?"

"Sure."

"Is Dad?"

"Yep. Dad's going to be there. We're all going to be there."

"Not Mom."

For Thanksgiving their mom wrote a letter saying she was going to get married to a lawyer named Wallenstein this summer in Portugal. Their father was *tied up,* he couldn't make his flight, so he faxed the letter from Minneapolis. Mrs. Amato read them the parts their father had told her to read aloud. They were sitting down on the furniture, wearing their good clothes, because they were supposed to have Thanksgiving dinner with their father downtown; they were drinking root beer, waiting, and then Mrs. Amato brought the fax in from their father's office. She read the *serious news,* and then explained to Spencer that their mom still loved them very much and that this was how people *experienced change.* She read some more of the paragraphs out loud, and after she told them that their father was going to be tied up longer than he thought, they all climbed into Joe's hearse and drove downtown and ate Thanksgiving dinner, anyway, because they had reservations for three.

"She'll probably call," Joe says to Spencer, meaning their mom, who's getting married in Portugal.

"It's going to hurt, you know. That's why they put you to sleep, so you don't feel anything. Mr. Moose, too."

Joe can tell Spencer's about to cry. Joe gets up and grabs another doughnut. He says, "Want one?"

"Nuh-uh."

"I gotta work on my car, Spence." When Joe says that, *my car,* he feels as if he's twenty; he thinks somebody's going to have to wipe up the milk on the floor, but he's not going to do it.

"I know," Spencer says.

"Wanna help?"

"I want to go to the Grand Canyon. Everybody gets to go to the Grand Canyon!"

"Mrs. Amato's coming over. Maybe she'll take you."

Joe intends this to be funny, and he thinks Mrs. Amato can clean up the milk. She's going to mop the floor, anyway. When she mops the floors, Mrs. Amato sings in Spanish. She makes meals and leaves them in the refrigerator in containers with instructions. Mr. Jazinski says she's *dependable;* for Thursdays, Mrs. Amato makes macaroni from scratch.

"Mrs. Amato," Spencer says, concentrating. He pushes away his cereal. "She's goofy."

"Come out and help," Joe says, reaching for a rag.

"No."

Outside, in the garage, Joe listens to Spencer singing with the TV. After their father learned that Spencer could hike down the Grand Canyon next summer, he ordered Spencer a backpack, and a tent, which came in boxes shipped from Minnesota, and after, after Joe drove Edith home that one night, that one night at Fountain Hills, Joe decided that he was in love. It wasn't all that complicated; it was something he'd just decided, *to love.* The next day, working on his car, sanding the front quarter panel, he could smell her on his hand. He turned off the sander and sat on the floor of the garage, smelling the space between his fingers, the skin on his hand. He wanted to know how long it was going to last.

That night, when she had sat up in the back of his car, looking at him, she had put her hand on his chest. "The heart's a muscle," she said. "It's the most important muscle in the body."

"It's okay," he said. "I'm not going to tell anybody."

"What?"

"I won't tell anybody, that's all."

"Oh," she said. "I'm really, really happy. But could we go now?"

And that's when he knew it had been wrong. The day after the match, trying to cheer him up, Howie said, "Hey, it's high school. No big deal."

Howie said Danny Ernest was a prick, anyway; Howie said he had something special.

"Special," Howie said, popping open a beer. "We got secrets to learn, Jazz. We got things we gotta know!"

"Places to go," Joe said, though he didn't have any particular place in mind. He was thinking about the way his hand fit over certain parts of Edith's body, and he was thinking that nothing like that was ever going to happen to him ever again because now they were *friends*.

Howie and Joe sat on the roof of Mrs. Bently's station wagon, the kind you carry children in, and dogs, though Howie was an only child. The car had a pretty good stereo. They sat on the roof drinking beer and looking at the sky, the place where airplanes took you; the sun was going fast and the sky was lit up purple and orange, close enough to reach if you closed your eyes and thought about it, which Joe didn't, because he had places to go . . . *things to know*. Edith had told him he shouldn't call her anymore because she was busy studying for the S.A.T. She said maybe they could get together next month and practice analogies.

Spencer hobbled outside, carrying three beers from a six-pack, the beers hanging by a plastic strap from his teeth. Joe would have nearly a week before he had to worry about replacing the beer.

"Beer," Spencer said through his teeth.

"What?"

"Beer!" he said, and this time he let go, the beer falling on the asphalt. "There's still lots inside." Spencer pointed at the beer with his crutch and said, "When I go to the hospital for surgery, I'm gonna ask Dr. Ripley if I can get a permission."

"Prescription."

"Yeah, uh-huh. That's precisely what I mean."

"We gotta go," Howie said. "Spence, you watch the fort, okay? Don't drink all the beer."

"You betcha," Spencer said sadly. He said, looking around, "I hate beer."

"Anyone comes by," Howie said, "you tell 'em the troops are gone. You tell 'em we're out getting provisions. Ice cream, Spence. We're off to get some ice cream."

"Raspberry," Spencer said. "That's Mr. Moose's favorite."

"Don't tell anyone where we've gone," Joe said, though he didn't know where they were going.

"You mean Edith," Spencer said. "Can I call Edith?"

"No way," Howie said. "Edith's gone to California. We're gonna go find ourselves some naked women! This is man stuff, Spence. Don't call Edith, and we'll bring you back some ice cream. Strawberry."

"Raspberry," Spencer said.

"Raspberry," Joe said. He thought, Howie doesn't even know. *He doesn't even know we're just friends* . . . and then Spencer said, "Don't forget to take pictures!"

It's something their mom always used to say to their dad, when they loved each other, before, and Howie and Joe leapt off the roof of Mrs. Bently's car and drove south, blasting the pretty good stereo, sucking down their beers. Howie explained that when a guy gets fired, or kicked off a team or something, he needs to get himself laid. It's what the Navy SEALs always do after a mission, *they get laid, Jazz.*

When a convertible full of girls pulled up alongside, Howie stretched his long body out the window, yelling. Joe reached for the wheel, to steer, and one girl with curly black hair lifted her sweater, which made Howie yell even more because she wasn't wearing a bra, while Joe paid attention, hanging on to his beer, thumping his foot to the stereo blasting with a girl in a convertible nearby flying down the highway and her sweater halfway off. Eventually they turned off, yelling, waving, and Joe and Howie headed deeper south, Howie saying, *This way, this is the way* . . . until they were crossing Curry, into the river bottom. Tempe, and the fringe territory of massage parlors and naked women.

"Women," Howie said, pointing. "This is the place!"

"Where?"

"Here. Right here, big guy. The River Bottom."

At the door, the bouncer who was kind of huge checked their fake IDs, smiled, and told them to have a nice day.

"Have a nice day," he said.

The bar was full of men all of whom were bigger than Joe and Howie put together, and the little men, who looked even worse. They looked like they carried knives, or were psychos; the music was heavy metal and the place smelled like an ashtray, and then Joe saw a girl—a woman, he told himself—wearing a black see-through shirt and underwear. It was the kind of underwear his mother kept in one of her drawers before she moved away to get her hair fixed—black and itchy-looking. Joe thought girls must not be allowed to wear black underwear, at least not until they graduated from high school, and the woman could have been from the cable movies, late at night, drinking a Coke and looking at him, except she had a space between her teeth the width of a pencil. Howie and Joe sat at a small round table, front-row seats, and Howie said, "How 'bout it?"

Meaning everything, Joe thought. Another lady wearing something purple and uncomfortable approached their table. She put her hand on Joe's leg, squeezed, and said, "Ooooh, what a pretty pair!"

"Michelob," Howie said, smiling.

"Michelob, of course," she said. "I'm Olivia."

"I'm Howie," Howie said.

Olivia kept her hand on Joe's leg, and he felt a hard-on popping up. She was half-naked; her skin looked dirty and pale, covered with soot, or maybe it was just the light; if he looked at the dirt on her skin, then maybe he wouldn't get a hard-on. Olivia squeezed again, for emphasis, and said, "You boys, I just don't know about you! You just get prettier and prettier every day!"

"I know what you mean," Howie said.

Joe knew she was older than his mother. He wondered if his mother had ever been in a place like this—worse, his father—and now all he wanted was for this woman to take her hand off his leg and for his dick to go down and behave. Up on the stage a girl was straddling the toe of a man's cowboy boot. She had short yellow hair and a tattoo in the center of her chest.

"Hey," Howie said. "See anything familiar?"

"What?"

"Cathy," Howie said, pointing. "Cathy. You know, Walker's squeeze at the psycho ward?"

"Jesus."

"She'll blow you for a twenty, if you want."

"How do you fucking know?"

"I'm Howie," Howie said. "And I know everything."

It started again, his cock, and the idea of being blown for twenty bucks, while Olivia who was old enough to be his mother brought them their beers. Howie paid and told her to keep the change, about five dollars, and then she smiled and yanked open her fragile-looking underwear, flashing them both. She didn't look at all like the girl waving in the convertible.

"Oh," said Joe.

She left, laughing, ruffling his hair. Howie held up his beer and said, "A toast!"

"Toast," Joe said.

"To discovery," Howie said. "To the unknown."

"Okay," Joe said, and then he got drunk.

He'd never been this drunk. Twice now he'd thrown up, *tequila sunrises*, because he liked the name. And beer. He was going places and now he was drinking a beer from his History teacher's refrigerator, laughing, and Howie . . . *No, look, this is where she keeps her key! Honest, she's gone for days* . . . and now he was wondering why he'd never done this before, and he was thinking that the unknown was all the places you had never gone before—California, or college. It was something you hadn't yet touched with your own hands. They found Jenna Williams' vibrator beneath the foot of her mattress. It was three inches long and had a battery inside.

"This," said Howie, holding it up to the side of his head, vibrating. "This is dangerous!"

Joe still didn't know what it was, and they finished off the beer, started into a bottle of wine and watched TV for a while. There were a lot of plants inside, and Cathy said, once, "So, this is where Ray's squeeze lives?"

"Mr. Morrison," Howie said, raising his beer. "To Mr. Morrison!"

"I'm gonna take a shower," Cathy said. "Anybody wanna watch?"

"Come here," Howie said to Joe. "You gotta see something."

Joe followed Howie into the bedroom. The vibrator was laying on the mattress. The pillows were in dark green pillowcases and there were candles everywhere: small candles, the kind in a church. A hairbrush sat on a wooden dresser, strands of dark hair caught among the bristles. One of the drawers in the dresser was full of underwear—bras and slips, socks. Swimming suits. Joe was looking at the underwear, understanding that there was a pair of man's underwear in her drawer, the same brand he used, when Howie pulled out a large box from the closet. It was the kind of box with slits in the side made for oranges.

"Here," Howie said. "Take a look here. I'm gonna take a shower."

The box was full of papers and spiral notebooks and college degrees. He was trying to read the calligraphy when he discovered in the corner of the box a photograph. It was as if she were spying on him, and then he saw the others. Most were of her, some of men. One of the men had hair past his shoulders, but he was also going bald. The hair hung from the sides of his head. Another man looked vaguely like his father, if his father were naked and standing in a flower bed with a guitar.

But the pictures of her, of this woman who used to teach him History—in one she is holding a flower, probably from the flower bed, and in another she is sitting on the toilet, her legs squeezed together, as if she were embarrassed. Only she isn't embarrassed, because her eyes are looking straight into the camera. As for the man in the flower bed, he doesn't even have a hard-on, and at the bottom of the box Joe finds a picture the size of a paperback: she's lying on a Japanese bed, a futon, with a sheet tossed over her waist. You can see her breasts, and the start of a double chin, and the way the light is pouring through the window, and Joe decides that this one is his favorite. He likes it because of the light, and because of the sheet, and because of the way her hair is falling back behind her, revealing her ear and a small hole for an earring. He can see the fuzz under her arms; he listens to the water from the shower and the voices: inside Cathy, and Howie; and beyond the bedroom wall he listens to the voice of a man weeping. Water, running from a tap, and Joe takes the picture and tucks it inside his shirt. He can feel it against his skin, the photograph, and he's looking in the drawer—lace, and cotton, and argyle socks. He's taking the man's underwear and beginning to wipe away everything he's touched. The pictures, the notebooks and diaries.

Once, he forgets what he's doing, and where he is, and when he remembers, he's afraid to give himself away. Now he's going over all the furniture in the bedroom, the hairbrush, the vibrator, which he slides beneath the mattress. He shoves the box into the closet, with his foot, and covers up the box with a pair of jeans and a hooded sweatshirt; the man on the other side of the wall is still crying, and outside in the living room, Cathy is kneeling naked on the floor, Howie is sitting on the couch, his hands on her head, and Joe knows Howie's going to come. He knows he's going to come and he knows he can't ever come back here because beyond the wall a voice is wailing, and Joe knows that this means trouble. He knows that he's been caught.

Standing here, eventually someone is bound to notice. Cathy is kneeling on the floor, and Joe can see a horse, with wings, flying along the side of her ass. This is what it's doing . . . *flying*. The skin on her ass is stretched tight as a sail and now he knows he's heading out the door, the briefs still in his hand, and he's wiping at the doorknob and running down the stairs. The wind is blowing hard now. The sky is gray and everything looks filtered, the still light of dawn, though he doesn't know this is what it really looks like: Phoenix, and this boy, running through it. He thinks everything looks like Phoenix, gray and dirty in the hot white light. He thinks in the parking lot he's going to be sick, and he throws the briefs into a Dumpster. A man is standing by the Dumpster, going through a trash bag, searching for cans, or breakfast, and now Joe is running hard. He is running east, down Indian School Boulevard, toward New England, a place he's only read about in books.

Joe needs to write the theme of his life, for Mr. Rolf, and if Joe can convince himself he didn't do anything, then he can also convince himself that he has nothing left to be ashamed of. The problem is, while he tries to convince himself he hasn't done anything, he knows that he has broken Danny Ernest's arm, *on purpose,* and that he has also broken into Jenna Williams' apartment. He has even let Edith McCaw break his heart, which is the size of a fist, and if he hadn't come inside her mouth, then maybe none of this would ever have happened. Maybe he and Edith would be driving Spencer to the Grand Canyon, and maybe they'd be sitting on the lip of the canyon, looking at the sky, and the color of the rocks, which is always different. Maybe Spencer would be telling them things about the canyon that he's read in books. The canyon, he would say, was made thousands and thousands of years before anybody even came here.

Tomorrow, which is Monday, the day school begins for an entire week, seven days, which is how long God supposedly took to make it—tomorrow, Joe will have to go back to school and walk around the hallways and look at all the school newspapers lying in the hallways, and Roxanne the Retard's column, which is going to be all about the way Joe broke Danny Ernest's arm because she thinks she knows *the rest of the story.* And tomorrow Spencer has to go to the hospital, for surgery, and Joe is going to pick his father up during lunch at the airport, and Joe is never going to talk to Edith again. He's not even going to go to school, because he knows what Roxanne the Retard's going to say, and he knows by now the cops are really looking, and he knows his father is having dinner with a woman in Atlanta, or New Hampshire, and that his mother is asleep beside a lawyer in Portugal, halfway across the world, and Joe knows that he's done something wrong.

Worse, he knows just what it is. He knows exactly what he's done and he knows he's never going to forget it, because you're not supposed to come inside the mouth of somebody you're supposed to love. You're supposed to hold it back until you're married, or until you're inside her, properly, but not in her mouth because that's what whores do. They even swallow it, and even Edith swallowed it, and if he hadn't done that, if he hadn't made her swallow it and do something terrible, if he just hadn't ever done that, then maybe Edith wouldn't have called him up. Maybe she wouldn't have called him up and said, "I'm sorry, but I really think we should just be friends."

It's not something you forget. Spencer is in his room, taking apart his twisted-up bicycle. When he sings with the radio, Spencer tries to sound as if he were a rock star, and once, while reading a book about what whores do, Joe was pretending he was with one, and doing it. He was reading in bed, pretending, when Spencer banged into his room.

Spencer was only six, he forgot to knock a lot, and he said, "What'cha doing, Joe?"

"Nothing."

Even then Joe knew it wasn't the kind of thing you were supposed to talk about, pretending, with your hand down your pants. He tried to pretend it was the normal thing to do.

His father liked to be alone, and Joe knew there were reasons why men had to be by themselves, because of what men did and how they had to be ashamed. Perverts whack off, they have acne and smell bad, and if a guy is going to have to whack off, then he's going to have to keep it quiet and shower often so people won't know that he's a pervert. Once, Joe did it nine times during a single afternoon. There had been a Tarzan movie on TV, and Jane, and after he was so sore he could hardly walk. That night he cried for the very last time.

He always thought vibrators were long, and thick, like bananas; when he first saw it there, beneath Jenna Williams' mattress, he didn't know what it was. He thought it was a flashlight, for emergencies, and Edith can read her own books all by herself because he's never going to talk to her again. He's going to take his brother to the hospital and pick up his father at the airport. Next month, he's going to take the S.A.T. and he'll get the highest scores in his entire class and be asked to apply for early admission at Harvard, and someday, he'll be able to tell his children all about it: how he got into Harvard, the only one from his entire high school, while he was ducking out from the law . . . *breaking and entering, of course* . . . and how Edith McCaw, his high school sweetheart, spent the rest of her life by herself reading books.

Pretending . . .

The problem is, it just doesn't work. During the match, wrestling Danny Ernest, from Cholla High, Joe knew he wasn't going to win. He didn't know why he wasn't going to win, but he could feel it: something inside told him it was over before they even tied up. He wasn't breathing right, and he kept making mistakes, like when he slipped and Ernest caught his wing and gained his first reversal, because Joe wasn't paying enough attention and something, something inside of him was saying *It's okay. You don't always have to win* . . . but he didn't believe that, either. He needed to win and he wanted not to always have to, and he knew if he didn't win then he was going to lose, and everybody would know because he would lose and because Edith dumped him, because she wanted to be *friends* and he knew he never lost. He was the Jazz. He was the guy who was going to be famous and he was going to win, only he wasn't going to win: he was going to lose, even then, and even then, while Ernest was shoving him into the mats, while Ernest's bar arm was slamming into his face, even then Joe knew he still didn't really have to win. He could lose. And he wanted to be able to lose, to be able to stand up and say, *Hey, okay, it's a bad day, I'm tired, my girlfriend hates me. Okay, I lose* . . . and then he saw his slot, and he sat and spun the way he always did . . . *fast* . . . and he spun again, and now he had a wing, and his hand, opening, and he knew the moment he hit it that he had snapped the motherfucker in half.

He thinks Walker Miller would understand what it means to do something stupid, except that Walker Miller is dead. Walker Miller shot himself in the eye with a .45 automatic he stole from Howie Bently's garage. Last year, in the garage, while his father was at work and his mother was also at work, at the public library, ordering books and doing what librarians like to do, Howie showed Walker and Joe the gun.

Mr. Bently kept the gun under wraps in a woodpile, under the third log from the right in the second row. The rags smelled like oil and there were wood chips sticking to them. Howie showed them how to load the gun with a *clip* full of bullets. His father had let Howie shoot it once. He said you always had to check the *snout.*

"That's the chamber," Howie said. "He didn't want me to find the gun and kill myself by accident."

"By accident," Walker said, laughing. "Yeah. By accident!"

"Accidents happen," Howie said.

"Look at me," said Walker, nodding.

They all looked at Walker. Howie said, "My dad thinks I think it's in the bedroom closet underneath the *Playboys.* That's where he tells me he keeps it."

"It looks heavy," Joe said.

"It is," said Walker. "It really is."

"Because," Howie said, "if I think it's in the bedroom, then I won't go looking for it and kill myself by accident. Psychology, you know."

Walker took the gun and held it with two hands, like a cop. He said, "Don't make a move."

And then it really did go off. In Walker's hands, the recoil kicking him back into the woodpile.

He shot a hole in Howie's basketball, which sat on a shelf by bottles of turpentine and used paintbrushes. After the shot, everything was quiet, except for the leftover air hissing through the basketball. You could smell the smoke, and afterward, Joe thought *These things really do go off* and he thought they were louder than you'd think . . . *loud* . . . and all at once. All you had to do was flex a muscle in your finger, and the muscles in the top of your hand and, bang, and the rest was history.

They had to remember to throw the basketball away in case Howie's father found it. The bullet was stuck in a two-by-four, a purple wad of lead stuck inside the wood. Apparently, it had gone through lots of other things, including a brick, and Howie covered up the hole in the two-by-four with sawdust and wood glue. Howie wiped away their fingerprints, in case the gun was ever involved in a murder case, though Joe had never touched it. Joe's father wanted him to be a stockbroker, or maybe a lawyer, and the only problem was the missing bullet from the clip and the empty casing. Howie threw the casing away with the basketball and said, "We're just gonna have to hope the old guy doesn't notice."

Howie meant the missing bullet, and his father never noticed. Later, they would tell one another the story and laugh about it. The look on Walker's face when the gun went off. They waited days for Howie's father to find out. Howie put a hair on the rag, underneath the log, to see if Mr. Bently ever even checked the gun. Howie said that he wanted to be prepared.

"He was a loon," Howie said, after. "I should have never showed you guys. He was a loon, and now everybody thinks it's my fucking fault!"

They were driving to no place special, just driving, in Joe's hearse, cruising along the edges of the city drinking beer and listening to the stereo. It was just Joe and Howie now, driving, and Edith was baby-sitting Spencer, and Walker Miller was dead. The city was dark and full of traffic accidents and Joe was driving his big long car.

"It's not your fault," he said to Howie, meaning it wasn't *his* fault, either.

"God, Jazz, I know it's not *my* fault. I mean, everybody's going to *think* it's my fault."

"Fuck 'em."

"He shouldn't have done that," Howie said. "He shouldn't have done that without telling us."

"It's nobody's fault, Howie. Nobody's."

"He went on ahead, though. You've got to give him credit for that. And I thought joining the navy was a big deal."

Joe translated: *I thought my wanting to be a Navy SEAL was supposed to blow everybody away.*

Joe asked Howie to roll down his window, and Joe thought, *He never even got to see my car.* He thought Walker shouldn't have done that, *period.* "No," Joe said, making up his mind. "He didn't go anywhere. He's dead."

"Nah. He went on. He went on to the next frontier, Joe. We're just too pansy-assed to go along with!"

"Everyone knew he was crazy," Joe said. "Everyone."

"His mother was crazy, too. Maybe it's inheritable."

Joe began to pass a car full of teenagers. He said, "I don't know."

"Just tell me, Joe. If you're ever going to do it, tell me first."

"I'm not going to do it, Howie."

"Just tell me. Swear to God you'll tell me first."

And maybe it was *inheritable,* and you could kill yourself with anything. You didn't need a gun. You could use scissors from art class. You could stick a blue ballpoint pen through your ribs right into the heart or spleen. You could jump in front of a bus, or tie a brick around your neck and dive into a riverbed. Sometimes perverts would put a leash around their necks and whack off and die that way: in New York City, which was weird, and you could do anything, really. You could even go to your best friend's house and steal his father's gun and kill yourself in front of everybody so everybody would know exactly what it felt like. And even though Joe never saw it, he has dreams:

Walker, sitting on the mats in the wrestling gym, waving the gun and saying, *Hey, Jazz. Hey, it's really pretty heavy, you know?*

And *shame* is what you get when it's time to give up before the whistle blows, and the hand, slamming. That morning, running away, east, down Indian School, Joe ran all the way home—eight miles—and once home he stood on the patio sweating beer and tequila sunrises and took off his clothes. He dried the sweat off the photograph and buried it beneath his sweatshirt and dove into the pool, where he told himself while he held himself beneath the ice-blue water that things were going to be okay, that things like this happened only on TV, and you could always turn that off. His ankles ached, and he knew nobody really knew what it would look like if you stuck your face into the fan blade of your car while the engine was running hard. People always said that kind of thing always happened, but they didn't really believe it, and now, sitting at his desk, thinking about the theme he has to write for Mr. Rolf, Joe knows what he believes is absolutely true.

Blood, he writes, *does not look the way it does on television. . . .*

He's thinking about animals that have to kill every single day in Africa or South America, and Joe's watched enough nature specials with Spencer to know how animals look just before they kill. They look thirsty, like Mr. Rolf in class, just waiting for the bell to ring. Spencer's blood type is AB negative, the rarest type on earth, and tomorrow, when Spencer goes in for surgery, the doctors will have to make sure they have special bottles in stock just in case. Sitting at his desk, looking up at the place where he used to keep a picture of Edith from her sophomore year, and the way she used to smile, Joe is thinking about the theme of his life. He's thinking his life is more dangerous than he wants it to be, and he is listening to the phone, ringing. He thinks it must be his father, or the police, beginning their investigation. He thinks that he is sitting at his desk, watching the phone, making calculations.

Sometimes, he writes, *one can even smell it, like animals who prey.*

• • •

Once, at Fountain Hills, after they had washed his car and split an ice cream cone, Edith asked Joe if he believed in God.

"What?"

"You know, church. Do you go to church or something?"

She was wearing a white T-shirt and Joe could see the outline of her bra beneath. She smelled like the shampoo she always used, and he was uncertain how to answer, because maybe he was supposed to believe in God, and so he said, "Sure. You know. We're Baptists."

"Really? We're Catholic. At school we had to wear skirts. Our teachers were nuns."

"We don't have school, just church. You know, on Sundays, but we don't go anymore. I mean we used to be Baptists."

"Do you still believe in God?"

He put his arm around her shoulder. Outside, they could see a man playing with a golden retriever. The dog was running over the long lawn. The dog wasn't jogging, like some dogs, but really running fast, back and forth in long wide circles churning up the grass. When the dog tried to stop, he'd slide on the grass for seven feet and bark.

"I don't think so," he said.

"I do," Edith said. "I mean, I know my mom doesn't, but I do. She just made me be Catholic because then I'd go to Catholic school and learn to be polite. My dad is Existentialist, so he doesn't believe in anything either. But I do."

Joe thought, *Existentialist,* and he understood all this to mean that Edith was *good,* because she believed in God and was Catholic, which meant that she was going to get married and didn't believe in abortion or, for that matter, sex. It meant that the best he was ever going to do was hold her hand, and then he said, "Oh. That's good. I mean, I guess that's really good."

"Yeah," she said, and then she took his hand and looked at the dog. "He's so pretty," she said. "Running like that."

A woman had joined the man. She was tall and thin with brown hair and long, tan legs. She kissed the man on the neck and then kneeled down on the grass, calling to the dog. Probably, they were married.

"So does this mean you have to confess a lot?" Joe asked.

"Sure. But to myself. You know, and at church. But mostly to myself."

The man and the woman were on the grass kissing each other; probably they weren't married. Once people were married they didn't kiss each other often. Joe never saw his parents kiss anybody but Spencer. His father kissed Joe once when he was ten, and Joe was embarrassed, and his father said, "Well, I guess we're old enough to shake, then," which is what Joe did now every time he met his father at the airport. He shook his hand.

Joe squeezed Edith's hand and said, "So what does he look like?"

"Who?"

"God."

She laughed, and then she said, holding his hand, "Like me, I guess. Only older."

He'd thought she was going to say *Jesus*, who died on a cross after bleeding a lot. Actually, what killed Jesus was all that weight pushing his lungs against the rib cage—he suffocated, like people with asthma, because even Jesus had to breathe, and sometimes, Joe can't even breathe because of all the dust, which is why he always likes the windows down, and he thinks God is who you're going to have to face up to even if you don't believe in God. He thinks if Edith has confessed, then he's going to have to explain why he came inside her mouth, even if he doesn't believe in God . . . *because Edith believes* . . . and because maybe God knows and because most likely she's going to confess. He thinks someday he's going to have to explain why he's done all the things he's done. Up until now, Joe has spent his life staying out of trouble and getting good grades and not being a pansy ass, and now that part of his life is finished. Spencer is standing at the door, knocking.

He's still in bed, and Spencer is knocking; Spencer's old enough now to remember that he has to knock, and the sky outside is still and dark because it's winter. In the winter, it takes the sun longer to warm things up, even in Phoenix.

"What?" Joe says.

Spencer stands in the doorway, straddling his crutches, with his new backpack on. Strapped onto the top is Mr. Moose who is wearing his camping shorts. Spencer has been crying, Joe can tell, and now Spencer says, "What'cha doing?"

"I'm thinking."

"It's time," Spencer says. "It's time for me to have surgery."

"Okay."

"I put the heavy stuff of top," Spencer says. "It disturbs the weight. Dad's not coming."

"What?"

"He's in Newark City. He says Mrs. Amato will come and that you're supposed to be my guardian and sign the papers. Then you're supposed to go to school. He sent us a *fax*."

"Fuck school."

"Mrs. Amato's goofy. If you stay, I won't tell Dad."

"Go away and I'll get dressed."

"Did you finish your homework?"

"Go away."

"Can I read it?"

"Spence, go make us some cereal, okay?"

"I'm not supposed to eat anything. Besides, I want to read your homework."

Joe thinks his homework is something he can never let anybody see, even Mr. Rolf. He thinks he'll have to start all over and write about something unimportant and safe so nobody will know what he is really talking about; Mr. Rolf might read it aloud in class, and then everybody will know, and if he gets out of bed right now Spencer will see his hard-on, and then Spencer will say something to Mrs. Amato or their dad during dinner next month when he comes home if his flight's not delayed. Joe's essay is lying on his desk, and he can see Spencer, squinting, trying to read the capital letters.

"Spence, go away."

"You can't have privacy now," Spencer says. "We're late!"

"Okay," Joe says, "Okay," and now he's swinging out of bed, turning, looking for his jeans.

Spencer says, "Boy, Joe. Boy, you really do have a big dick—"

"Go away!"

"Now you're being sensitive and you're supposed to be nice to me because I'm going to the hospital where people die every single day just like *Marcus Welby*. I'm the one going to the hospital. Me!"

"You're not going to die."

"I don't think it's very funny," Spencer says.

"Uh-huh," Joe says, reaching for his sneakers.

"You're supposed to unlace 'em first."

Joe pulls on a shirt and walks past Spencer, down the hall and to the kitchen. He can hear Spencer behind, puffing.

Joe says, "Cheerios, or Wheaties?"

"Cheerios!"

Spencer sits at the kitchen table, with his backpack on, waiting. He says, "Except I'm not supposed to eat anything for twenty-four hours. When you have surgery, you're not allowed to eat anything. That way, they don't asphyxiate you." He folds his hands on the table and says, "I'll pretend."

While Joe eats, Spencer lifts up his arms and tries to flex. "Cheerios," he says, looking at the cereal, "makes you the most strong."

When Joe was little, their mom still let them eat cereal with marshmallows in it. Then she decided to buy black underwear, and she decided that health food was an important part of the day, and she started buying bran muffins and squash and candy bars without any candy in them. Joe has been eating Wheaties for six years now, and he thinks that's a good thing. It's something he has always done. *I eat Wheaties. . . . I use a blue ballpoint pen. I wear jeans with button-down shirts and never wear a belt.* And he thinks that if he tries hard, someday he'll be able to say, *I never do anything wrong, ever.*

"Remember that health food?" Joe says.

"It sucked."

"It sucked bad," Joe says.

"It sucked bad, oh boy." Spencer lifts his bowl, pretending to drink, and says, "Know what I'm gonna do?"

"No, what?"

"I'm gonna play football. In high school, I mean. After I grow."

"Yeah?"

"Uh-huh. I wanna be a tackle. Mrs. Amato says a tackle is a very unusual position. A lot of astronauts played football, you know."

Their mom would never let Joe play football, for all the violence, which she didn't believe in, and Joe drives to the hospital. He takes the fast way, which is through subdivisions, because cops never wait for you in subdivisions where everybody's all asleep. He drives fast and lets Spencer pick out the music.

At the hospital Joe says to the woman at the desk that he is Spencer's guardian. The hospital is quiet and full of old people sleeping in chairs. The colors are green and orange.

"Are you eighteen?"

"Of course," Joe says, lying, which means he will have to start all over again and that he can no longer say *I never do anything wrong, ever.*

Spencer asks, "Where's Dr. Ripley? I didn't see his car."

And now Joe signs a dozen papers . . . *Joseph Trevor Jazinski* . . . and the nurse, a woman who looks like a real nurse, and not a nurse on television, because those are always beautiful, puts Spencer in a wheelchair. She says Dr. Ripley will be here *momentarily* and asks Joe to carry Spencer's backpack, which weighs nearly as much as Spencer.

"Jesus," Joe says, "what have you got in here?"

"Oh, bicycle parts. My travel Legos. Mr. Moose's chess set.

The history of NASA, General Patton and Jane Addams. She went to college in Illinois," he says to the nurse. "She was a very famous social worker." Spencer wiggles in the chair, adjusting, and says, "And my stove and hiking boots, and dehydrated tuna casserole and blueberry tarts. Lots and lots of sodium."

The nurse is wheeling Spencer down the hallway, and now Spencer says, "Oh, and my compass."

"Your compass," says the nurse, stopping for the elevator. "That's so you won't get lost?"

"You betcha."

III

Apology

A secret is always true, which is why we must always keep it secret. Because somebody just may find out. *Truth,* the part deep inside the bone—the marrow, which is fluid and changing all the while we keep on discovering just who it is we are and what we know.

It's the skeleton you have to stand on, and walk on, because some parts you've been taught to bend: the knees, the shoulders and hips; you learn you're going to have to carry your own weight because it's always there just the same, just beneath the skin so secret and deep, and Edith thinks she has enough secrets now to last her a lifetime. Worse, she doesn't want any, because she wants things to be clear . . . *lucid* . . . and she wants to know why everything always has to be kept secret, while her mother asks her to hand her the shoes, the blue pumps, inside the closet beside her father's tennis racket.

Edith can't play tennis, though she likes hitting the balls, and the noise they make when she sometimes hits them. Her mother hasn't lived at home for nearly two weeks; she's been living in a hotel, and now she's come home to carry away more of her things. It's December now, and raining.

"It will be better this way," Ellen says. "We'll all be more free
to live our own lives. Everything will be out in the open."

"You mean you and Dad."

Her mother stops folding her gray pleated skirt . . . *the power
skirt* . . . and raises her eyes. She looks at Edith and says, "No, I
mean all of us."

"Then why are *you* moving out?"

"Temporary. Just till the divorce and we sell the house and
then you'll come live with me before you go off to college." Her
mother lifts her head and smiles sadly. "Like sisters, Edie. It'll be
fun."

Edith knows she will have to live with her mother because the
court will never allow Edith to live with her father, who is gay, and
who is also suing for divorce on the grounds of *sexual infidelity*,
because the courts don't need to know that he is gay. In Arizona,
it is illegal to be gay, and the gay part is the part that's secret, not
the *sexual infidelity*. The *sexual infidelity* is normal and something
the whole world can know about; if her father tries to fight over
Edith's custody, then the truth will be known, and she will never
be permitted to visit her father on weekends which suits her just
fine. She doesn't even like tennis.

The rain is pounding on the roof, loud, and Edith says,
"Where are we going to live?"

"The shoes," says her mother, stuffing them into a trash bag.
"Always wrap your shoes in plastic when you pack." She tucks the
shoes into a corner and stands upright, stretching the muscles
along her spine, which is huge because Ellen is so tall and big.

Ellen says, sighing, "I'll find a place. And everything will be
fine and then you'll go off to college next year and all of this mess
will be over with."

It's been raining hard. The water in the pool is rising over the
deck; the sky is gray as winter, in Michigan, only there is supposed
to be no winter here. This is Arizona, where the sun is supposed
to shine all the time because people wear sunglasses. On weekends
her father wears sunglasses and polo shirts and sneakers because
he thinks they make him look younger than he is, which is pa-

thetic. Tragedy involves choice, and Edith thinks there is nothing worse than having a father who chooses to be *pathetic*. In three days, Edith, along with most of the senior class, is scheduled to take the S.A.T. The S.A.T. is to be held the day after the Christmas dance. The theme for the dance is "White Christmas"—a joke, sponsored by the senior class, because in Arizona it never snows, because here old people wear sunglasses in the white sun while they look tan and pathetic. Here the sun will blind you, no matter how blind you already are, unless it's raining. Last week, with Mr. Morrison, Edith wore a pair of her father's sunglasses, over her contacts, while she took her driving lesson *On the Road*.

Mr. Morrison explained that this was also the name of a famous book by a guy who took a lot of drugs and died long before he should have. Personally, Mr. Morrison thought the book was pretty immature, but he said people should judge a book by the cover for themselves even if the cover is kind of ugly.

"Uh-huh."

"Edith," he said, kindly, "two hands, ten and two. Easy with the brake."

They still hadn't made it out of the parking lot. She was nervous and Mr. Morrison kept the window down, like Joe, staring out the window and talking about things she'd never heard of in order to keep her from feeling nervous . . . *talking* . . . which made her more nervous because she thought she was supposed to listen. She couldn't have a conversation and drive all at the same time. The parking lot had three cars in it, and Mr. Morrison told her to try parking first, just to get the hang of being near other cars, even if they weren't moving, and her father's sunglasses kept slipping over her nose, her contacts were dry because she hadn't cleaned them the night before; she was wearing them for the fifth time this week . . . *over the limit, way*. Also, she knew this was the kind of car her grandmother would drive if she had a grandmother. The car may have had special gauges, but the paint still looked like a grandmother. The only relatives she's ever had are all dead, and her father says he's finally discovered who he really is.

Well, what took you so long, Dad?

"Edie," says her mother, in the bedroom. She's closing up the suitcase, pulling across the zippers. "I want you to be nice."

"I am."

"No. I want you to be nice to your father." Ellen is opening another suitcase. She's tossing in her socks, her hose and underwear. Edith's mother has more lingerie than a department store, which Edith thinks is sad because nobody ever gets to see you wear lingerie.

"I don't want to be," Edith says.

"He loves you."

"Yeah," Edith says . . . *sure* . . . and now she's rearranging her mother's lingerie, picking it up, folding—a slip, a camisole. Her mother says the thing about pretty underwear is that just because you can't see it, that doesn't mean you don't know it's pretty. She says underwear makes a girl *feel* pretty, and Edith's brother, Anderson, who wears boxers, still doesn't even know, though Anderson and Edith have always known; in Michigan, they would listen to their parents argue, and what they were arguing about, and Anderson would always shrug and talk about his girlfriends to try and change the subject. If he was talking long enough about his girlfriends, then Edith wouldn't think he was going to grow up and be just like their father. In the car which looked like a grandmother, Mr. Morrison told her sometimes people just don't seem to get along, no matter how hard they try.

"Some people just aren't ever going to be friends," he said.

He was referring to Howie Bently and McGregor, whom Howie Bently had beat up in the parking lot last week. Howie had beat McGregor up so bad that he was suspended for the rest of the term, meaning Howie Bently wasn't going to graduate in time for college. McGregor was sent to a plastic surgeon to get his nose fixed, and Howie did it because, according to Carol Cunningham, Howie said, *I just never liked the fat prick.*

Edith was still in the parking lot, with Mr. Morrison, parked, and she was practicing the over-the-shoulder double check. If you *parked* with a teacher, it meant something different, or illegal.

"Sometimes," said Mr. Morrison, "people are just unwilling to try and work things out."

She knew her mother had talked to Mr. Morrison, *especially*, which was why Edith was being permitted to take *On the Road* even though everyone knew Edith was never going to be able to get her license, and she knew Mr. Morrison was trying to be subtle. Now Edith was thinking about Ms. Williams and the way everybody knew she had dumped him, or he her, or maybe they never really were friends to begin with so nobody's feelings had been hurt. When students go out, they are friends—*boyfriend* and *girlfriend*—but adults have *lovers,* which can be either a boy or a girl, male or female, friend or foe. Her mother told Mr. Morrison all about the divorce, too, and if Ms. Williams and Mr. Morrison were lovers, that meant they did what everybody else did. Edith glanced over at Mr. Morrison for a moment, imagining, and she realized that it really wasn't that big a deal. Everybody did it, even people who taught you how to drive.

"Sometimes," Mr. Morrison said, "it's tough to get along."

She thought, Now he's talking about me and Joe . . . *Who's he talking about?* She shifted her weight under the steering wheel and said, "Were you ever married? Mr. Morrison?"

"No," he said, laughing. He sounded for a moment as if he lived in Kentucky. He looked out the window and said, sadly, "You can spend your life being a kid if you really work at it." He said, pointing to her neck, "If you keep twisting your head like that, you're going to break it off."

She blushed, and he said, "I think it's pretty clear the traffic out here is pretty safe."

"Okay."

"Why don't you try pulling out onto the freeway? Pretend that's a freeway," he said, nodding to the access road.

The access road fed into the school parking lot. Across the road, the Communication Church of Christ was building a new church. Before, anybody could park their car on the lot, even Joe, though the dust from everybody parking there would make your car dusty and then you'd need to wash and wax it if you wanted to take care of the paint. The paint on Joe's car was perfect now. Smooth and even and shiny with wax—*Angel White*. Sometimes, she watched Joe drive it through the parking lot while she stood on the curb waiting for the bus. Behind the church, she could barely see the Christmas decorations on the houses, not even the huge Santa Claus, holding a candy cane seven feet tall, or the reindeers. It made her think of Michigan, looking at all those hazy decorations, and she drove along the access road, slowly, until she turned into the parking lot, using her blinker, and parked all over again.

Edith said, putting the car into *P*, "Seventy percent of all people get divorced, which is why most people shouldn't get married. It's all very statistical."

Mr. Morrison smiled and said, "You think so?"

She nodded. "I think so."

"How's your oil pressure?"

"Check," she said.

"Your alternator?"

"Check."

"What's behind you?"

"The football field."

He reached his arm along the seat, the way Joe did when they used to drive together in his long car. Mr. Morrison's arm almost touched her shoulder, but not quite, and when she was with Joe, he would pull her into his side and steer with one hand, sometimes one finger, because of power steering, and now Mr. Morrison leaned back into the vinyl seat. He sighed and kicked his foot up on the dash.

"Edith," he said, "can you keep a secret?"

"Sure," she said, elated.

"I think all that's a hill of horseshit. I really, really do."

She hasn't talked to Joe in two weeks. Once, by the lockers, he was standing by Diana Vanderstock and Colin Houston, and when she walked by, Joe didn't say a word. Everybody stopped talking until she recognized who they were, and then Edith said,

"Hi, Joe," and Joe looked away, and Colin Houston said, "Hey, Edith."

She was late for her ride with Ms. Williams, and the problem with being legally blind was that you were always going to be embarrassed by what you couldn't see. Her mother said that when people fell in love they wore *rose-colored glasses,* but this can't apply to Edith. Her vision is decorated with scar tissue, not roses, because of all the damage on her corneas—a birth defect, just not quite as bad as Roxanne's, the retarded girl. Even sunglasses won't help, and sometimes she thinks her birth defect may just keep her from falling in love, ever, because in order to fall in love you have to put on rose-colored glasses. When you see things as they really are, says Ms. Williams, then things are bound to be very bright.

They were driving down Scottsdale Road, to Tempe, where they were now holding practice in the university's aquatic center. It was before the rains came, and the sun was bright as a light—billions and billions of watts—and the pools here were outside and long: Olympic regulation. The water was heated, warm as bath water, and they practiced now with the university team; Jenna had said that if Edith did well at the sectionals, then Edith could expect invitations to try out for schools as big as this one in places she'd never been before. In North Dakota, or Pennsylvania. Or Florida.

Edith said, thinking about truth, "What do you mean?"

"Truth. Truth—the way things really are, the truth is always bright. It's why Tiresias was blind. And Milton. And Ray Charles. Because they always see the truth."

"Oh," Edith said. She knew who Tiresias was. She said, "Will Milton be on my S.A.T.s?"

"No, but Tiresias might."

"Who was Milton?"

"You tell me, kiddo."

Edith looked out the window; without air-conditioning, she was beginning to sweat, even if it was December. She thought about Jenna's classroom, the travel poster of France and the maps of North America, and said, "An explorer?"

"Poet," Jenna said. "But don't worry, he won't be on there.

Just remember, seventeenth century and Adam and Eve. You'll be fine, but he's not going to be on there anyway. Analogies," said Jenna. "Now those are going to be on there."

Edith looked at the palm trees passing by. She said, "A tree is to water as an engine is to gas."

"God," said Jenna, laughing. "Can you believe that? I mean, can you believe that somebody actually got paid to think that up?"

"Invariably," Edith said. Then she smiled; it was a word she'd never used out loud before. It made her feel old, like a teacher, and she said, "I've been practicing."

"*Lucid*," said Jenna.

"Clear and logical. Like water, or sentences."

Jenna adjusted her hands on the steering wheel and said, "How about *ubiquitous*?"

"Everywhere, I think. Like palm trees."

Jenna said, "That's the kind of word only stupid people say in public. *Unctuous*—"

"The kind of people who say *ubiquitous*," Edith said, showing off.

"*Equivocal*," Jenna said. "It's one of those that means the opposite of what it sounds like. Like *pithy*."

"Going both ways," Edith said. "I think."

"Good. I didn't know what that word meant until I was twenty-five."

Edith looked at the dash, and the windshield. She made up a sentence because that was the way you had to learn how to use a word; you had to make it one of your very own. . . . *Before he knew who he really was, my father was very, very equivocal.*

At the light on Van Buren, Jenna turned and smiled. She was tapping her fingers on the steering wheel, all eight of them, and she said, "You're going to do fine, Edith. Fine."

It's the same thing Joe told her. The very same thing: when she called him up one night and asked him if he wanted to get together sometime and maybe study analogies, or antonyms, and he told her he was busy—finishing up his car, taking care of Spencer—and he told her, "You're going to do fine. Really. Everybody knows you're the smartest person in the whole school, anyway."

Like a computer geek, she thought; if she were smart she wouldn't feel like calling him up all the time. At the pool in Tempe, she went into the huge locker room and suited up and went out to the pool. The sun was bright and warm and she swam in the long pool doing her warm-up. Jenna paced the deck, yelling, and the rest of her team was swimming, too, and Edith knew Joe was never going to watch her swim again. Up in the bleachers were college kids, laying in the sun, getting tan. Some of them had books on their laps. The college kids were older, some lived with each other, or medical students, and she told herself if she didn't talk too much then people would think she was in college, too. And she couldn't talk too much because she was in the pool, swimming freestyle, with not enough time or air even to talk. Still, whenever she swam, she always talked to herself. The water was warm on her arms and her back, and she could feel the hot sun pouring down through the sky, through the hole in the ozone, heating up the water.

She never saw Howie Bently beat up McGregor, but she heard about it, from Carol, after school while riding home on the bus. Now that Edith and Joe had broken up, Edith always had to ride the bus. The bus smelled like corn chips and old sneakers and dust, and made her feel like a freshman all over again, riding the bus, sitting by all the computer geeks; and sitting there, on the bus and looking out the window, Carol told her what it had been like—McGregor, lying on the asphalt, his face full of blood; and Howie, screaming. He was screaming like a lunatic.

"He really needed to cool out," Carol said. "You know?"

Like this, Edith thought, in the pool, swimming laps and cooling out, though actually she was just warming up. She was warming up for the sectionals, where she had a shot at the fifty and one hundred breast, and if she improved, Ms. Williams might let her swim the fifty free, which would be amazing for a blind person: swimming freestyle in competition. In the water everyone had to see through the same water, which was blue and made your eyes burn. Edith's eyes always burned; they would feel hot for hours and hours after every single practice, and she would drown them with eye drops, man-made tears, and then she would try and keep her eyes closed until they would finally grow cool and she no longer thought about how much her eyes hurt. The chlorine kept away disease, but it ruined your eyes, and your hair, which would feel like straw if you didn't use conditioner. Conditioning is what you did to increase your heart rate, and your heart rate was how your body kept in time, one beat at a time, while you swam through the water trying to keep it in condition. And if you kept trying then you knew you were going to be able to keep on trying no matter how much it made your eyes hurt.

Outside the rain is hard and she thinks it's going to keep raining for days. It's the storm everyone has been waiting for—impatiently, to get it over with—and she is sitting at her desk, reading over her word lists and taking notes. Normally she would be asleep by now, but now she can't sleep and she doesn't know what's wrong with her: why she can't sleep when she wants to, and why she can't make herself stop feeling so sad.

The rain is pouring and it's been days. It's filling up the desert, and her mother is driving across town to a hotel where she will stay until it is time for Edith to join her, sometime next term, before Easter, and Edith doesn't know where her father is. Maybe he is on a date. It makes her feel sick, the thought of her father, dressing up; *antonym* means opposite, and you're supposed to date the opposite sex, not the antonym: boy and girl, love and hate. Her father says it is impossible to hate anybody whom you do not love, and when you find the correct answer, you're supposed to fill in the bubble, completely, with the lead from a No. 2 pencil. Choose the *antonym* which seems most right now.

When she told Joe she thought they should just stay *friends,* she did it in order not to explain. They were sitting on the hood of Joe's white car in the school parking lot, talking, and she said, "I just think we have lots of stuff we have to do now, you know?"

"Yeah," he said, squinting into the sun. "Sure."

For a moment, she thought maybe he might understand. She thought maybe he would still be nice to her and say things to her in the hallway; she thought maybe she might really tell him, about what her father did . . . *My dad, see, he's a homosexual?* . . . and she knew she wasn't ever going to tell Joe that, even if she loved him, and she thought, *Do I love him? Is that what this is?* . . . and she thought, later, that maybe after she had moved out on her own and went to college, that maybe they could visit each other during long vacations and start all over again and maybe even get married, maybe. After they'd made a lot of money, of course. Maybe they could go to the same college and start all over again without anybody ever having to know.

Joe said, sitting on his car, squinting into the sun, "Sure. I mean, I know what you mean."

"How's Spence?" she asked, brightening.

"Spence?"

"Yeah, you know. Your brother?"

And then Joe said, sliding off the hood of his car, which he had recently waxed, "What the fuck do you care?"

And she suddenly understood that he wasn't going to forgive her. He wasn't going to let her still be his friend and he was never going to say anything nice to her again in the hallway. He wasn't even going to talk to her. Instead, he was going to stand here, leaning on his car, waiting for her to get off his hood and walk away; and when she did walk away, she walked away slowly. If she walked away slowly enough, then he was going to have to watch her walk away, and he was going to have to remember what she looked like walking away: her khaki skirt, her blue cashmere sweater, and the good bra beneath, which was the only one he knew how to unhook properly, and the sandals she always wore because you could wear them with anything and always take them off in class. He was going to watch her walk right on out of his life.

But before she did walk away, she said, "Bye, Joe," and she kissed him on the cheek.

He wiped his cheek, which was smooth and salty, and she did it fast in case he tried to pull away. Still, he wiped it off, and then she gathered her books, slowly, and walked away. She didn't even know where she was going.

She thinks, and not for the first time, that she just doesn't know enough; she thinks a tree takes a lifetime to grow, and by the time it's grown, nobody can even explain the way it happened. She puts away her word lists, which are made out of trees, and stands to stretch. Her back is sore from sitting hunched over for so long, and on her desk beneath the dictionary is a letter she has been writing over the past few days to Anderson, though she also understands that she will never send it through the mail.

At first, she wanted to cheer Anderson up, for being dumped by his girlfriend, Laurie Something, and instead she talked about Joe, and the way he hated her. She thinks that the last thing her brother is going to want is a letter from his little sister in Arizona. When boys have something terrible happen to them, the truly worst thing is for somebody else to know; otherwise, they think people know they are weak, or stupid, which is why she knows Joe won't ever talk to her ever again. Which maybe means he loves her . . . *does he?* . . . because if he talked to her, then that would mean he didn't care about what she did and *you can only hate the people you love most.* If Joe hates her, then maybe he loves her too. Her mother says boys remember everything you ever do to them, and girls just simply forget.

Stretching, Edith sees herself in the sliding glass door which leads outside to the backyard and the pool. She feels excited by the thought, that maybe Joe really doesn't hate her, and she stretches and goes to the window and looks outside at the rain, and her reflection, and all the water running down the window. She looks at her body the way girls do in the bathroom when they think nobody else is looking, because she knows it's safe, and her legs . . . she has strong legs and shoulders, but she's never going to be perfect; she's built too much like a boy, and the water is running down the glass, over her shoulders and arms and legs, and now, when she sees the shape of a man entering her very own silhouette, her ghost looking through the window, it takes her a moment to understand that she's no longer looking at who she thought she was.

She screams, and the man covers his ears, smiles, calling . . . *Hey. Hey!*

It's Howie Bently, standing behind the glass, calling. He's knocking at the window. He is knocking at her window, saying . . . *Hey! Relax!*

Edith slides open the door. "What?"

"Hi. How's it going?" Howie says. His clothes are drenched—his hair, his face, the rain streaming into his eyes.

"What are you doing?"

"Just thought I'd come by. You know. See how things were going and everything." He points to her nightshirt and says, "Hey, I really like that one."

"Huh?"

"Your shirt. That's cool, that's all." He takes her hand and says, "Come on!"

"Where?"

"Come on," he says, pulling her outside.

She thinks she must be wrong; Joe could never love her. She thinks it's going to be cold outside, which it is, and the rain is cold and hard and she feels it slapping against her skin, her nightshirt, which is beginning to hug her body like a swimsuit. And she's not wearing a bra, which means everything is there, just beneath the fabric, because everything is cold and Howie isn't even looking. He's pointing to the Jacuzzi, and the steam rising up into the rain and all the palm trees and yuccas, which look like shadows, caused by all the rain and foreign light.

Howie says, "When was the last time you took a walk in the rain?"

"It's cold!"

"You get used to it. Really. I mean, the rain is great. When it's raining like this, you know things are going to get really wet. You know why men go off and join the navy. In the navy, you never get used to it, it's that good."

He lets go of her hand and jumps into the Jacuzzi. "It's okay," he calls. "Nobody's home!"

She stands there, looking at Howie sitting in the Jacuzzi with all his clothes. He reaches over to the box and turns on the switch; with the air blowing, his clothes float up all around him, and now he turns on the other switch, for the light, and the light floods the small pool.

"Come on," he says. "It's warm!"

She giggles now, sliding into the Jacuzzi, her nightshirt billowing all around her. She presses it down against her body, expelling the air, and Howie is right, it is warmer in the water. The air outside above her head and shoulders is cold, but the water inside is hot, and the air shooting from the jets is almost cool . . . antonyms, she thinks. *Hot and cold.*

She slides deep into the water and says, "How's Joe?"

"Beats me."

"He's mad at me," Edith says, thinking about him.

"He'll get over it. He's the kind of guy who always gets over things. You know, he's not half as tough as people think."

"He did that—" She hesitates, blinks. "He did that thing at the meet."

"Piece of cake. If he hadn't, somebody else would have. That guy's an asshole. Shit, if it'd been me, I'd have snapped the motherfucker's neck."

She thinks Howie's pretending to be tough, which he already is. He sent McGregor to the hospital *just for kicks,* kicking his nose into pieces so that McGregor had to go to see a plastic surgeon, and she knows Joe wouldn't have done that . . . *maybe.* She puts her hands underneath her shirt, on her belly, and closes her eyes. She never saw what happened at the meet, but she heard about it, and the parts which were in Roxanne's column, and the way Roxanne had explained what happened and how Joe was responsible.

"Crack!" quipped the arm painfully. "Crack!" . . .

Edith says to Howie, "How come you did that?"

"What?"

"You know, beat up McGregor? How come you got yourself kicked out of school?"

"School," Howie says, thoughtfully. "School is the place you go when you don't already know where you're going. What's it going to teach you, Mathematics? How to buy some stocks? If Bob has seven apples, how many does his dog want to eat? Fuck school, Edith. Fuck it. I mean you think school means anything? You think *I* mean anything?"

"Yeah," she says. "Of course."

She presses her hands against her skin and thinks about the way that feels. She thinks she's being pretty mature and sensible; this is something adults do—talk about problems, in the Jacuzzi, even if it's raining. She thinks maybe she is even being helpful, like a counselor.

She says, thinking about school, "I like it. And I want to go to college—"

"Yeah, yeah." Howie wipes the water from his eyes and says, "Great." He looks over at her, smiles, and says, "Hey, how's the old man?"

"Who?"

"Your pop. How's the old man doing these days?"

She feels her heart flutter, beneath her nightshirt. She looks at him and sees that he's still smiling. He can see right through her nightshirt, and she knows it, and she can feel her veins flush.

He says, shrugging his shoulders, "Hey, I'm Howie. I know everything."

Edith says, carefully, "That's why you don't go to school."

"Because I know where I'm going. I'm going where we all go, only I'm getting a jump start. I did it for you, you know. McGregor. I kicked the shit out of him, yeah. But I did it for you even if you don't believe me. Here," he says, "put your hand over your heart and repeat after me."

Her shirt is billowing; her hand feels cool against her skin, her breast, which fits neatly inside her hand.

Howie says, "Come on."

"Okay." She says, "I am, you just can't see."

"Good. Okay, now repeat after me."

"Repeat after me."

He laughs, almost, and says, "I, Edith McCaw, promise to keep what I hear a secret. To love and protect that secret until death does me apart."

"What?"

"Come on. Say it. *I, Edith—*"

"No."

"What do you mean, No?"

"I mean I'm not going to." She can feel her breast, which feels almost swollen and full of blood, and the way that feels. The way it makes her feel something deep inside her navel, and her hand, skimming. She says, "You want to say something, go ahead."

He looks away. He shifts his weight in the water and says, "If you tell anyone . . . If you tell anyone, Edith . . . I can do anything I want."

"Then don't tell me," she says, angry, and sitting up. She puts her hand against her navel, anchoring herself. "Don't tell me anything, Howie, because I don't want to know!"

"Hey," he says, laughing. He puts his hand on her arm, squeezing. It's something Joe used to do, sometimes, and Howie says, "Hey, it's not that big a deal, anyway. Just that I'm going to be a Navy SEAL. That's all. I've already signed the papers and everything."

He pulls back his hand and folds his arms. "They say I don't even need to graduate! It's like they just can't wait to get me, see?" He laughs and shakes his head, the way people do in movies about the army, acting.

He says, "It's like living on a shoelace, I'll tell you. I mean the SEALs are the first to go. But man, what a fucking way to go! I mean, it's pretty fucking radical, you know?"

"What are you talking about?"

"I mean I'm gonna go away for a while, Edith. For a long while, you know. Because when you go out to sea, sometimes you stay out there for years. And if you're a SEAL, you're not allowed to tell anybody where you go. You're always in a state of preparedness, you see? You're always ready to do what it takes to do what's got to be done. You're always ready to have to do it, at any moment, you see, so you never get to see anybody you used to know ever again. . . ."

She wonders if Joe knows. She wonders if Joe has told him that she dumped him. Of if he dumped her. She wonders why Howie's telling her any of this, and says, "You're leaving?"

Howie takes off his watch, which is soaking, and says, "Yeah, and so I just wanted to tell you, I'm going to join the navy. Only my folks don't know, okay? I want it to be a surprise, kind of, and once I'm in the navy I'll never get to see you ever again. But it's not that big a deal or anything."

He holds the watch up into the light from the porch, and says, looking at it, "It doesn't work anymore. I mean, it's not water-proof, but I'd like you to have it, Edith. Here. I'd like you to have it. It used to be Walker's, a friend of his gave it to me, but I thought, Hey, it doesn't work anymore, and in the navy you can't have a watch that isn't waterproof—"

"Maybe you can fix it, Howie. Maybe you can get it fixed."

He looks at her, as if he is angry, or disappointed: as if she's just turned him down for a date. Howie Bently has never once asked her out on a date, and now he tucks the watch into his jeans, saying, "Okay. Fine."

"I know where you can get it fixed."

He reaches over to her, sliding his hand over her shirt, over her breast. His hand is hot and she can feel it squeezing her ribs. She thinks, *Howie Bently is touching my body.* She thinks he doesn't want to get his watch fixed. She thinks, *This is what it all means. . . . This is what it means!*

"Howie—"

He's pinching her nipple, saying, "Hey, you know what happens when men go off to sea?"

Because of Joe and what he's been saying about her. "Don't—"

"Come on, Edith. Come on—"

"Don't, Howie."

"Hey, I'm not going to tell anybody. Joe will never have to know, you know?"

Now he's unzipping his jeans—one hand, leaning into the water, trying to get the angle so that they'll unzip, only his jeans have buttons, not a zipper, and his hand is twisting her nipple hard. The rain is steady, the water hot, and she knows what's going to happen. She can see it in the sky. She can feel it in her breast, and the pain, in her nipple, which hurts because the sky is full of clouds and the clouds are gray, which means somewhere the moon must still be out, making them gray, even if it is still pouring rain. Or maybe it's the city lights, making the sky gray, and she thinks he means it, and she's pushing him, punching him screaming *Stop it! Stop it!* and now she's climbing out of the pool, skinning her knee on the deck. She's standing in the rain, catching her breath, almost. The rain is freezing and she's standing on the lip of the pool, screaming, "Would you please just go away? Just go away!"

"Hey, Edith," Howie says, looking up from the pool. "Hey. You really are a bitch, you know?"

"Just go away, Howie! Go away!" And now she knows she's crying. She has never cried before in front of someone she knows who isn't in her family, in front of a boy who wants to fuck her, like date rape, only she's never even gone out on a date with him, and she knows Joe never wanted to fuck her because he never even tried to go inside her which is why she hurt his feelings . . . *because he loves me!* . . . and now she's screaming Go *away! Go away!* and she wants to know what Joe has said to Howie and what Howie is going to say to Joe because maybe nobody loves her . . . *nobody!* . . . and the way that felt, his hand, twisting like that and the way it hurt because the sky is ice and nobody is here at home. Nobody, and the sky is full of ice, and she is screaming hard.

Go away! Just go away now!

And now he's running across the lawn, vaulting over the wall, slipping into the rain.

Go away!

•••

Words mean what people say even when they don't want them to: words like *I hate you*, like *okay* and *be careful*. Like *fine, you're going to be just fine,* even when you know you're never going to be fine for the rest of your life. Words simply make things more confusing because they are never going to be sharp enough to cut through all the space between yourself and the people you're supposed to love. After Walker Miller died, he never said another word, and Edith has been giving her father the silent treatment, because she understands the weight of words, and because if she is silent, then she can really hurt her father's feelings. According to Mr. Rolf, her English teacher, only words can perform miracles; only words can turn water into wine. Only silence can truly pierce the heart.

"I want you to be nice," her mother said, just before she left.

They had finished packing and Ellen wanted to clear something up. They were sitting at the kitchen table, drinking sun tea, though it wasn't really sun tea because it had been raining for days, and Edith said, "He doesn't deserve it."

"Everyone deserves it. Everyone."

"He's gay, Mom. He's gay and he's my father. What's that supposed to make me, Mom! Me?"

Ellen nodded, sadly, meaning she was trying to show how much she understood; she lit a cigarette and said, "It means that you are his daughter. You are his daughter biologically. It also means that you are my daughter, and it means that we love you very much because we fed you vegetables and watched you learn to talk. It means we are your parents—"

"But—"

"No. I don't think you get it, Edith. I'm not mad at your father because he's gay. I'm mad at your father because he doesn't want to live with me by the rules we once made. I'm mad at your father—"

"Because he's gay!"

"No. No!" Ellen waved her cigarette. She stopped, checking herself, and looked at her sun tea. She took a breath and said, calmly, "The issue is fidelity, and nothing, nothing is ever easy."

It's something her father always says . . . *Nothing is ever easy, except taxes and death* . . . and Edith knows what fidelity means. It means not being *promiscuous*. She knows nothing good is ever easy.

She said, "He won't even let me see Joe."

"That's because you were a little snot and he's still mad at you. He told me what you said."

"It doesn't matter."

"Yes, it does, and I certainly hope you are being careful." Her mother raised her eyebrows, the same way her father did when he was pretending to know everything about her, his daughter, because he was her biological father. He used to be like normal biological people who had kids, only now he didn't like to do it that way because he's just realized who he really is.

Ellen said, "You know what I mean."

Edith reached for her tea, thinking she wasn't sure. She wasn't sure and didn't want to talk about it because it didn't even matter anymore. Some secrets were worse than others. Everyone knows Diana Vanderstock is on the Pill.

"It doesn't matter, Mom."

"Of course it matters. And if you don't think it matters," she said, exhaling, "then you are going to spend the rest of your life hiding from what does." Ellen rose from the table. She tamped out her cigarette in the ashtray, BOSTON UNIVERSITY, and said, "Help me load the car, okay?"

" 'Kay."

Ellen said, "Someday, someday you'll be glad we know all this."

They carried out the suitcases and loaded up the car in the carport. Outside, the rain was pouring hard, and her mother set her iced tea on the roof while she loaded up the car; she always liked having something to drink in case of traffic, which there always was. Ellen stepped around the car to the passenger side and opened up the glove compartment. She handed Edith a brown paper bag. Then she hugged her before Edith could even look.

Ellen said, hugging her, "If you keep them in your ice skates, they aren't going to do you much good."

Ellen began to cry, softly, meaning she wasn't going to cry for long. She said, "Be careful, Edie. Be careful."

"Mom—"

Ellen pulled away and looked at Edith. She said, wiping her eyes, "Are you going to the dance?"

"Joe won't even talk to me, Mom."

"Then talk to him, Edie. Talk to your father."

And then Ellen kissed her on the cheek. Ellen wiped her eyes, stepped inside the car, and drove away. If she hadn't driven away, she would have spent the night in her own house . . . *her bed* . . . where she belonged. Inside the house, Edith put her new box of condoms—with a little carrying pouch to fit inside your purse, or ice skates—on top of her desk where her father would be sure to look. The little blue pouch, on top of the dictionary and word lists.

She is swimming in the rain. She is swimming her laps in the outdoor pool at the university where people become famous swimmers if they are fast enough. She thinks if she tells Joe what Howie did, then maybe Joe will know why Howie did it . . . *why he's acting so crazy!* . . . and she wants to know why Howie thought he could just come over and do that: jump into her Jacuzzi and do that, because even if she does have condoms, she's not going to do it with just anybody who jumps into her Jacuzzi. And maybe Joe never will talk to her again, but if he does, then maybe she'll know what she is supposed to say. *I'm sorry,* maybe. *I lied.* "Come to the dance," Carol said. "You can dance with Colin Houston." And what makes Edith truly not want to go to the dance is the thought of having to watch Joe dance with Diana Vanderstock. Diana is tall and pretty. Her father is president of the biggest corporation in all of Phoenix; Edith's father helps people get jobs there all the time; and because Diana Vanderstock drives a red Mercedes to school, and because whenever she sees Edith in the halls, she always says *Hi!* She says *Hi!* because Edith goes out with Joe, or used to go out with Joe, and Diana Vanderstock flirts with teachers. If Joe wants to dance with Diana Vanderstock, then he is going to dance with Diana Vanderstock even though he is never going to talk to Edith ever again. This morning, at breakfast, she talked to her father and tried to be nice for the very first time in weeks: she tried to talk to him because you can only love the people you hate, because antonyms mean nothing is ever easy. Because nothing is ever easy, and because you can only hate the people you truly know you love, and because the water is full of rain, and now she knows she's really swimming fast.

Today, before swim practice, she and Carol went to the gym and cut out snowflakes. On the record player, Bing Crosby was singing, to help establish the proper mood, and the girls from the Senior Class Social Committee and Mitchell Hemly, the kid with acne in Mr. Nadolny's History class, were busy spreading white streamers along the walls of the gym. Just before, they had helped Diana Vanderstock set up chairs and tables, and then Wiz the security guard came into the gym carrying the disco ball. He lowered a cable to the floor, attached the disco ball, and then he made the cable lift the ball up into the rafters. Mr. Buckner kept the disco ball locked inside his office because people liked to try and steal it.

After, when Wiz was finished, he said, "Looking nice, girls. Looking mighty nice!"

It's the kind of thing men say when they think you'll do it with them. Mitchell Hemly, the kid with acne, looked hurt. He was the only boy on the Social Committee; if you were on committees, you could make friends, even if you did have acne and always smelled bad. Mitchell Hemly didn't play sports. Sometimes, Edith knew he was just waiting for her to talk to him, to ask him about his homework or maybe something he'd read about recently at the library. He was always in the library sitting by himself.

Carol, who was snipping snowflakes, said, "So, did you ever use 'em?"

"No," Edith said, shaking her head. "Never."

"God! Why not?"

"It never came up," she said, laughing. "I hid them in my ice skates. I knew my parents were going to find them. Which they did. At least my mom did. My mom knows everything."

"Like Howie Bently," Carol said. "Good thing she's moved out, yeah?"

"I guess."

"God. I can't believe you never even used them!"

"Believe it, Carol. Besides, if I did I wouldn't tell you anyway."

Carol blinked. She looked at Edith's snowflake, which was screwed up; Carol held up her scissors and looked across the gym at two fat girls sitting on the floor. Because they were seniors, and had more self-confidence, it wasn't so bad for them being fat. Carol whispered, "I tell you everything. Everything!"

"Some things you're not supposed to tell," Edith said. "I'll go if you go."

"Then you did do it!" Carol said, laughing. "I knew it. You really did?"

"If you keep asking me, then you're going to make me lie, because I won't tell the truth. You're not supposed to know the truth about some things, you know?"

"No. I don't know. What's it matter? I mean, look at Diana Vanderstock. Look at Mitchell Hemly. Everybody knows he's fucking queer."

"What?"

"Hemly Schmemly. He's queer, everybody knows. Big deal!"

She snipped at her deformed snowflake; she thought Mitchell Hemly liked *her*. "It matters," she said, "because if I did it, which I'm not saying I did, or if I didn't do it, which I'm also not saying I didn't do, even if I've never used them . . . you know, the condoms . . ." She said, trying again, "It matters because no matter what I did, I didn't do or not do anything by myself. I mean, I'm not the only one who knows, you know?"

"Don't get snotty, Edith. And no, I don't know."

"I mean you shouldn't tell secrets if somebody else is going to get hurt. I mean, Joe wouldn't do that to me, even if he does hate me."

She looked at Carol and thought, *Except for Howie.* He told Howie. He must have told Howie *something*, and she threw her scissors onto the table, which ripped the paper tablecloth. She said, holding up her white snowflake, "This is not really how it's supposed to look."

"I kind of like it," Carol said. "Even if it is a little bent."

She was about to say, *What do you mean, Mitchell Hemly's gay?* when Roxanne, the retarded girl who thinks she is a journalist, began to cross the gym. If it weren't for the tape recorder, Edith would never have recognized her, and she wondered who Roxanne and Mrs. Hoffman, the Journalism coach, were going to say mean things about this time.

Carol pointed to Roxanne and said, loudly, "We better get ready for practice!"

Roxanne said, "Hi. Hi, I'm doing a story." She picked at her hair, which was greasy and long; once, Edith thought, she must have washed it. Roxanne said, "I was wondering, just wondering if maybe you'd tell me a story."

"What kind of story?" Carol said. It's what you always said. *What kind?*

"Any kind of story," Roxanne said. She licked her lips, because when she spoke she tended to spit all over everybody, especially herself, which always made her lips chapped.

"Just some kind of story," Roxanne said. "Some kind I could write about. I've got to do another column, and the more stories I have, the more columns I get to write. 'Roxanne's Corner,' which is where I'm writing all my columns, in 'Roxanne's Corner.' Would you please tell me a story?"

"We're kind of busy," Carol said.

"Please? Please? I mean, I've been trying to do an *investigative feature* about Walker Miller. The two-month anniversary is coming up, you know, but nobody will talk about Walker Miller just because he killed himself!" She took a breath and said, loudly, "Do you think it's true he was really crazy?"

"No," Edith said, setting her lip. "Just retarded."

Roxanne blinked. She turned off her tape recorder and began to cry, instantly. "I'm not retarded!" she screamed. She breathed in spasms, screaming. "I have brain damage and it's not my fault!"

The fat girls, seniors with self-confidence, stopped talking. Probably, they were looking, and Carol said, "Hey, Roxanne, are you going to go to the dance?"

Roxanne stopped screaming. She wiped her face with her sleeve, smiling, halfway, because her mouth didn't work quite properly for all the brain damage.

Edith said to Carol, definitively, "I'll go if you go."

Roxanne turned her tape recorder back on, smiling, and Carol said, "So what if he's a sophomore? He's still really cute."

Roxanne said, "Just for off the record, who do you think is really cute?"

Carol meant Colin Houston. She meant Edith should go to the dance and she meant she was still mad at Edith for not telling her things. She meant Edith wasn't being a proper best friend.

"You are," Carol said. "I think you're really cute, Roxanne, but Edith and I have to go to swim practice.

Edith said, "I have to go talk to Ms. Williams."

"Aren't you going to ride with me?" Carol said.

Roxanne said, "Can I come?"

Ms. Williams is driving Mr. Morrison's car.

"I had to borrow it," Jenna explains, and driving to the university, Edith thinks maybe this means they'll get back together. She says, "You know what Roxanne asked me? The retarded girl?"

Jenna is slowing the car for a small flood washing across an intersection; the water is sloshing at the doors, and Jenna says, "No. What?"

"She wanted to know if Walker Miller was crazy. She wanted to know why Walker Miller killed himself."

Jenna slows down even more to keep the car from stalling. "What?"

"Why did Walker kill himself?"

Jenna is quiet for a moment, staring at the traffic, which means she doesn't know what to say, either. Or she does know, but she doesn't know if she should really say it. They are through the deep water now, the traffic is accelerating, but maybe Edith is too young to understand. Finally, Jenna says, turning up the heat, "I don't know."

"But he liked you. He talked to you all the time and—"

"And?"

"Did you know he was going to do it? I mean, did you ever really think that he would do it?"

"Edith, what are you asking me?"

"I want to know if you knew Walker Miller was really crazy."

They're following a bus now—yellow, which is the highway symbol for *Warning*. In the back are kids staring out the window. The windshield wipers on Mr. Morrison's car don't really make the windshield any more clear, and now Jenna says, shaking her head, "No. No."

"Roxanne—"

"It wouldn't have made any difference, Edith. Walker was already in the hospital. He was under supervision. It's not something anybody can stop once somebody's made up their mind."

Edith thinks maybe this is like homosexuality, or early enlistment. She says, "How do you know if somebody's mind is made up? I mean, maybe you can still change your mind?"

"Can?"

"Could. I mean, maybe you could—"

"Maybe, maybe. I don't know," Jenna says. "I do know there's nothing better than this," she says, pointing to the sky. "I do know it doesn't get any better than this!"

The sky is gray and wet, because it's been raining now for

days, and Jenna says, "How could anybody give this up? I mean, when will this ever happen again?"

Edith thinks they are both missing the point. She says, "I don't know . . ."

"God!" Jenna says, almost laughing. "How could anybody give this up?"

Later, and now in the pool at the university, talking to herself while swimming her laps . . . *fast* . . . Edith thinks Ms. Williams thought she was talking about herself.

Me! She thinks I'm going to do it!

And she thinks this is because of words and what people don't mean when they don't necessarily say them, because Ms. Williams thinks Edith is thinking about doing it, and now Ms. Williams, who's real name is Jenna, is looking at the bright side even if there hasn't been one in days. It has been raining for three days straight. Edith thinks even if her father is gay, and even if Joe hates her, and even if her parents are never going to be happy again for the rest of her life, that still she isn't ever going to do it. Even if she's mean to retarded people, Edith isn't about to kill herself: at least she knows *this*. She knows the water's rough because it's raining. They are swimming in the rain and she is headed for the block and she thinks she should have kept her mouth shut.

She thinks she must be to blame. If she hadn't stepped outside, last night, then Howie Bently would never have tried to do the things he did; they're lining up along the blocks and it is really cold. Cold, so that everyone is shivering, even Ms. Williams, who's wearing sweats and a windbreaker and purple mittens and is pointing to the clock. The clock is huge and going fast, timing them, telling them they're not going fast enough . . . *Because it's freezing!* . . . and cold makes the blood in your veins thick and slow, and it's freezing and raining and Edith wishes they'd cancel practice just this once and let them all go home and sleep. She wants to sleep now and she knows she can. She could fall asleep even in the rain, where Howie Bently lives, because when it's raining people you don't even know come visiting, and if you're sound asleep then you don't have to answer. In the rain, people come knocking at your door, telling secrets and promising not to and running away just before everything has to start all over again until you have to start looking up because you know it's all your fault. Because looking up, looking up at the thick sky, she realizes it's not really rain after all. It's not rain at all and the sky is simply full and heavy and all around them white. They are standing behind the blocks, shivering, and looking all around them at the white sky. And Mr. Rolf, standing on a block, waving at the sky.

"It's snow!" he's yelling, waving his arms. "It's snowing just for us!"

It's snow, and Edith knows exactly what she means.

It's something she will have to live her life with. Because her father is *agnostic,* meaning full of doubt, and because her mother, who is lapsed, no longer lives at home, Edith goes to Mass by herself: fifteen minutes by bike, which is always dangerous; thirty-five minutes if she walks. And for now she goes to Mass, and sometimes afterward she bumps into people she knows: Michael Owens, the undercover cop who everybody says carries a gun inside her purse and pretends to be a college counselor, or Mitchell Hemly, who Carol says is gay. If Mitchell Hemly is gay, then he should not be going to church, because the pope says gay people are bad; if the pope changed his mind, maybe her father wouldn't be so agnostic. Always, always at church, Edith sits by herself, and when it comes time for the Our Father, where the priest leans forward and always asks the celebrants to join hands, she quietly refuses. Instead she holds her hands together and sings by herself, and during the homily, she tries to pay attention, and when she takes Communion, she prays for everyone she's ever known be-cause, according to Mr. Rolf, *only words can really turn water into wine,* and only words can make people feel better about who they really are, and when she prays, she never prays for herself because that is *selfish*. Instead, she prays for everyone she's ever known and hopes, maybe, that someone she knows will pray for her, too. Tomorrow, during Mass, and after she's supposed to take the S.A.T., she knows she's going to have to pray. She knows she's going to have to try and make things right and she's going to have to start going to confession even though she never will believe in it. It's not as if God doesn't know already what you've done wrong. God knows all the secrets already, and secrets are made up of words, like *God,* and God knows all about her father and all the things she's said. God knows she has condoms in her ice skates, and on her desk, and now even two inside the pocket of her jeans.

And God knows what she let Howie do even though she didn't let him do it, because deep down, deep in the secret place, she isn't sure if maybe she didn't really want him to do it, which makes it worse: her being so uncertain. The idea seems not as bad as the way she knows she'd feel if he really did it to her, in the Jacuzzi, because sometimes she thinks about doing it in the Jacuzzi, sometimes, with all types of people, and she knows she didn't have to slip inside with him. According to Christ, just thinking about something bad is as bad as doing it, which means she's just as wrong even if she didn't do it. Which means, she's always going to be wrong which is the opposite of right. She thinks *No* means *No* unless you're not sure what you really mean when you slip inside the Jacuzzi. She thinks words mean what anybody wants them to.

Go away, Howie. Just go away!

Tomorrow she will go to Mass, and she still doesn't know that it's a record: snow, in Phoenix, the first in years and nearly an inch. The city is full of traffic accidents and ice, underneath the snow, the rain freezing on the long flat white highways with people sliding all over the ice into one intersection after another. People in four-by-fours are driving around in four-wheel drive, happy for the excuse to use four-wheel drive, because of all the snow, and that's what four-wheel drive is for: to get you through the elements. Snow, up to your toes, there's that much killing off the bougainvillea and the lemon trees and all the lawns, the long green lawns which are covered with snow. Carol is driving her father's Bronco, in four-wheel drive, and Edith is staring out the window, sipping on a bottle of champagne, staring at the snow lighting up the headlights and the path they make going through the snow. They are listening to Angelica . . . *KSTM, The Storm.*

"It's like Michigan," Edith says. "Kind of, but without the trees."

"It's perfect," Carol says. Carol is wearing Edith's blue cashmere sweater and one of Edith's bohemian skirts. When Carol put the sweater on, she dabbed some perfume on her chest, saying, "Just in case." Then they each drank half a bottle of brut, fast. Edith likes to pop the cork.

And for a moment, when Carol said that, *Just in case,* Edith wondered what it might be like to kiss her. She wondered if she'd go to hell if she kissed her, the way Walker Miller was going to have to go to hell because he'd committed suicide without saving anybody else's life. According to the catechism, you could only go to heaven for killing yourself if you saved somebody else's life in the process, like the martyrs, or a guy who falls on top of a hand grenade to save a baby who will grow up to write plays about how bad war really is. Edith thinks she could go to hell even if she's not sure she wants to kiss Carol because she's just thought about it. She's thought about it . . . *twice* . . . and she thinks if everybody killed themselves, especially when they thought about things, then there wouldn't be anybody to hang around and put money in the collection plate during the bubonic plague or other bad times. The church would go broke and the pope would have to find another job. Maybe he could change his mind, just occasionally, and maybe Walker Miller did save somebody's life once.

Just once?

In the parking lot, taking their time to the gym, Carol and Edith slide along the snow. People are outside, making snowballs, and throwing them. A group of boys are making a huge penis out of the snow, and you can see the grass sticking up through the places on the lawn where the snow has already begun to disappear.

"By tomorrow," Edith says, "it will all be gone."

Once inside it's the same band from the Halloween dance; the singer is wearing the same pants and hairdo. He looks as if he wants to be on MTV, but he looks made-up, fake, and not like the real thing on MTV.

He yells, "Is everybody ready to pahh-ty!"

Carol laughs, and people stand in groups by the punch bowl and cookies, looking up at the guy in leather pants. It's impossible to party at a high school. You have to have alcohol and drugs, and the only thing you can do at a school dance is sneak outside and drink something that maybe you brought. Inside Carol's father's four-wheel drive is another bottle of brut, and she thinks maybe they should go outside and have another glass. Only they don't have a glass, and when they drink it, they have to drink it from the bottle.

She thinks wine makes the mouth lonely and sweet. The band is playing a song now, and people are dressed up: the rich people in fancy clothes, and the people who don't really give a damn are just wearing the same kind of clothes they always wear. Edith's hair is still damp from washing, and the snow, and she wishes she could see exactly where people are and what they're doing.

And when she feels someone brush her arm, she knows who it is. It isn't Carol, and then she hears the voice, and she knows exactly who it is.

Hey—

She turns and knows just who it is before she even turns, saying, *Hey, Joe,* and she can't tell if she sounds happy or scared.

"Hey."

They stand there, looking at each other, and the lights dim. Somebody has politely dimmed the lights and they are suddenly standing together in the dark with the disco ball spinning overhead. She can't see him, but he can't see her, either, and she can make out the shape of his body and the way he's shifting his weight on his toes. He's turning his head, having a look around, and now the disco ball is spinning faster and the singer is yelling all over again.

I say, Are you ready to PAHH-TY!

Still nobody is dancing. It's still too early for people to start dancing. People only start dancing once they know the dance is almost over, once they've missed out on all the time they could be dancing, and she can smell the perfume she's put on her neck, and her chest, like Carol . . . *just in case* . . . and she's worrying that maybe she's put on too much. That maybe Joe will know why she's put so much on, and now she's giggling, softly, and he is saying, "So, how's it going?"

She can't really hear him because the band is playing loud, the disco ball is spinning, and now she has his hand and she's leading him outside, out past the doors of the gym and outside where all the snow is falling even if it's going to melt, *fast,* because by tomorrow the snow will all be gone. Once outside, she keeps walking, holding on to Joe's hand, almost running but not quite because she knows where there's a bottle of champagne and that's what you're supposed to drink when you're in love. Finally, in the middle of the parking lot, beside Carol's car, she stops.

The snow is falling on her hair, and she says, shifting her weight, "I drove to school today. Mr. Morrison says if I'm careful I can be just as safe as anybody."

"That's great," Joe says, and she can tell he's smiling by the way his voice lifts, the way it does when he's nervous, and by the way he's still holding on to her hand. Sometimes, he squeezes it; you're supposed to do something while you hold somebody's hand, Joe still hasn't let go, and this morning, over breakfast at the kitchen table, while her father was still eating his cereal and looking at the paper, she said to him, "Hi, Dad."

The kitchen was tidy, warm from the heat being turned on all night. He looked up from his paper and said, "What's this?"

"I just said good morning. Okay?"

"Indeed," he said. He folded up the paper and pretended to frown. "You forgot to turn the Jacuzzi off," he said. "You really shouldn't be using it in the rain. Especially by yourself."

"I'm not going to drown. I'm on the swim team, you know."

He sat there, looking up at her, and then his watch, and then the newspaper. He sat there and she thought he was going to yell at her all over again, and then he said, looking out the window, "I know."

Outside the window the day was cold and still full of rain because it wasn't going to snow until later on.

Her father said, "The bridges are going to flood out if this keeps up."

"Uh-huh."

He said, "Eat some breakfast."

"Maybe they'll cancel school," she said, later.

She drank a glass of milk all at once while she stood at the counter. It was the same way her mother always had her breakfast—milk, or orange juice, depending on what was available in the refrigerator, always standing at the counter and having your breakfast all by yourself.

Her father said, chuckling, "You might have been electrocuted!"

"Can you give me a ride? To school?"

And later, in the garage, he stopped and put his hand on the hood of his green sports car. You could hear the rain beating on the roof of the garage, and he was looking at the wall where he kept all the gardening tools, and then he said, remembering to yawn, "I'm kind of tired, Edie. Why don't you drive."

"No," she said. "For real?"

The Pythagorean Theorem

What we see is what we know, but what we feel is who we are. What we feel is what nobody can ever take away. We can only give it up, freely, if we want to feel differently than we do right now.

Joe's been reading the *Metamorphoses,* by Ovid, because Mr. Rolf is making his class read it in preparation for the twentieth century, which means *modernism,* and the book is all about myth and how things came to be. According to one guy, Pythagoras, *nothing ever dies.* Pythagoras, who was also a vegetarian, says that *what we call birth is the beginning of a difference.* He says that while the parts may vary, *the sum is always constant,* which is also what you learn in geometry, because everything is always going to add up to some kind of answer especially if it's in a triangle. If you're lucky, maybe you can use it on a test, the answer you come up with, and even now, while Joe is still in high school studying for his S.A.T.s, and for Mr. Rolf's exam on the *Metamorphoses,* Joe understands a test to be a device inadequate to measure what you know. Each day Mrs. Fullerton gives her Economics class a quiz, after she takes attendance, and when you take the S.A.T.s, your entire future depends on your ability to pick only the correct answer. And the correct answer is the answer you always have to work out for yourself, even if there may seem to be more than one, because:

   —*if nothing ever dies, then Walker Miller never died;*
   —*if and only if the sum is always constant;*
   —*because nothing can ever be removed.*

Nothing can only be given up freely, into the sky, which is big enough to hold it. The sky is where the wind blows and turns into rain, or snow, and the sky is where the differences learn to gather all by themselves—the weather, the satellites and space shuttles, or your little brother, looking up at the sky, going *Oh Boy. Oh boy, someday, Joe . . . Someday!*

Spencer was conceived when Joe was eight years old, and Joe thinks this too was the beginning of a difference. One day, before she got her hair fixed, Joe's mom came home from the doctor's office and said, "Well, Joseph, it looks as if you're going to have a little brother." Then she pointed to her stomach, which was already beginning to swell, and she said, pointing, "Here. Do you want to say hello?"

Joe no longer remembers saying hello to his mother's stomach, because it's embarrassing, just as someday he will no longer remember stewing over his S.A.T.s. He will barely remember having taken them. Even so, right now, he does remember watching Spencer slowly learn to walk, slowly, because even then Spencer kept having accidents: *foreshadowing,* like bumping into walls, and sticking his finger into sockets, and Joe remembers listening to his mother tell him to be nice and not to break his little brother's Big Wheel. And if Spencer lived inside his mother's stomach, for nine months, then so too did Joe. He lived inside his mother, who now lives with a lawyer named Wallenstein in Portugal, and Joe hasn't spoken with his mother in two years.

The beginning of one difference is the beginning of the world, over and over again, and Joe is beginning to understand that he is going to have to find some answers. According to Mr. Rolf, the answers aren't in the textbooks; the answers are in the myths you are raised to believe . . . *Why is narcissus such a pretty little flower,*

Mr. Jazinski? . . . and Edith, she believes in Jesus Christ, the only son of God, not Zeus, and Joe has never once gone to church because his parents do not believe in anything. But if a person doesn't believe in anything, then how is a person supposed to live a life? How is he supposed to know what he believes in? Mrs. Amato fixes hamburgers on Saturdays, chicken on Mondays, and the Greeks made up gods to explain the weather, and love, and why things came to be the way they did . . . *Zeus, acting like a nice bull, or a swan, just biding his time . . . Mr. Jazinski, what's old Mr. Zeus busy waiting for now?* . . . and the Buddhists invented a quiet little bald guy to sit cross-legged and speak in paradoxical phrases, which are the kind of phrases which always contradict themselves. Mr. Rolf always says, *Contradiction is a fine and sometimes necessary thing,* and he says the answers lie in myths and in the questions these stories raise. *So why does Icarus allow himself to be singed, Mr. Jazinski? Why must he fly into the sun?* . . . and even if Mr. Rolf always answers your answers with a question, at least he's still giving you an answer. At least Mr. Rolf's not scratching at his head, looking over his class and saying, *Gee, I don't know. But let's have a quiz, shall we?*

What Joe wants most right now is the ability to know. He wants to know why he broke Danny Ernest's arm when he knows he should have never done that; and he wants to know why Walker Miller thought he was supposed to kill himself when everybody else knows it was a crazy thing to do. The hero, says Mr. Rolf, must always undergo a series of tests, as well as a descent into hell, where he has conversations with all the dead people, like Tantalus and Sisyphus, though Joe always gets the two confused, and he thinks if a test is always going to be a device inadequate to measure just what it is you know, then maybe there can be no more heroes. Maybe there's only all the people you're going to have to say good-bye to before they go away and die.

Last year, once, Walker and Howie and Joe snuck inside the girls' locker room. Joe and Howie had been working out in the gym, and Walker was playing coed volleyball, and later they decided it would probably be a pretty good idea. After Diana

Vanderstock left, her purse full of birth-control pills, swinging like a pendulum, they slid in through the door. The girls' locker room had the same layout as their own—the one for MEN—with showers on each side, like wings, and here there were showers with stalls for shy girls, but the shy girls never showered anyway, because they were shy, or something, and then Walker and Howie and Joe walked along the front row of lockers among the scattered towels and the benches girls sat on when they tied their sneakers. The air was wet from all the showers, and they could hear one running, and a radio playing softly, and while the air smelled wet and full of mildew, it still didn't smell like piss and Desenex. It smelled like girls—perfume, and shampoo, and fresh laundry detergent, and the smell girls make when they sweat a lot and get their periods. It was different.

"Hey," Walker said. "Over here!"

They followed him into a closet full of towels and basketballs and badminton rackets. They shut the door and hunkered down to wait.

"This is crazy," Howie said.

Walker said, "Shhh!"

"This is truly crazy," Howie whispered, and then they began to laugh, softly at first, until it was so funny they couldn't stop laughing, and then they began to howl: three wild guys in the girls locker room! They were going to have some serious stories *Whew!* and they were going to tell *No, seriously* the entire school that they were in the girl's locker room, and they were going to have some stories to tell . . . *You fucking betcha!* . . . *Whew! Jesus, man. Whew!* . . . and Howie, snorting, and Joe trying not to because even this was serious. You could get caught, especially when you were laughing. Still, he couldn't help it.

Walker stopped first. "This is serious," he said, snorting. He stood and said, "Come on. We gotta do some recon."

He opened the door slowly; he thought for a moment, then slid down onto his belly. He began crawling along the tiled floor, seriously, and Howie followed suit in his jeans and T-shirt, crawling on his belly, commandos in a foreign conflict squirming along the floor of the girls' locker room. This was truly a dangerous place for a guy to be. This was where a guy learned what it is girls do when they know there aren't any guys around to watch them do whatever it is girls are supposed to do. Here in the girls' locker room, a place Joe had never been before, here Joe stood in the aisle, watching Howie and Walker crawl along the floor. They turned the corner, slowly, and began a new row of lockers, Walker's huge sneakers winking as they turned the corner, and Joe simply went the other way: to the right, on his own two feet, following the direction of the music. A radio was still playing music and he could hear a shower running, and now he turned a corner and saw a girl, in the shower, dancing.

She was standing beneath the water dancing by herself. Not fast, but moving anyway, beneath the spray, and the music was so low and the shower was so fast Joe knew that she couldn't possibly hear anything. She was listening to something else, a heartbeat, dancing. It was the first time Joe had ever seen a naked girl.

He stood by a stack of fresh towels looking at the naked girl, telling himself *This is a naked girl.* And maybe this was a thing worth getting caught for—seeing a girl dancing in the shower—and someday, years from now, he would be able to tell the story of his first naked girl, probably in prison, because he didn't even care if he got caught now. She was the very same age, and she was naked in the flesh.

"Ow!"

And Howie, laughing, and Walker Miller crying, "Ow! My head! Ow Ow Ow!"

Who are you?

"Shut up," Howie yelled, laughing.

She turned and saw Joe, standing there by the lockers. He could almost make out the color of her eyes . . . *green, and kind of blue* . . . and she didn't even cover herself. She just stood there, under the water, looking at him, and she had moles on her shoulder and maybe she was telling herself something, something which was going to make her believe it someday, later, when she might have otherwise not bothered to remember . . . *This guy, this wrestling guy, looking at me . . .* and then she turned off the water. The music became louder and she stood there with all the water dripping off her body, and they could hear Howie laughing, and Walker Miller saying, "My head! Jesus, I'm blind!" and Joe stood still, counting the moles on her shoulder, smelling her shampoo and looking at her skin.

"Hey," she said, easily. "Toss me a towel?"

This is a naked girl talking to me!

"You okay?" she said.

"Huh?"

"You look a little lost."

"Oh, yeah. Sure."

He reached for a towel from the fresh pile on the bench, reached for another and tossed her both. Before she caught them, she held out her arms, waiting, and then she said, without even looking, "Thanks."

When she did look up, he was gone, so he was never sure if she ever did look up. He ran along the rows of lockers until he found Walker and Howie. Walker had his hand over his eye, which was bleeding; he'd crawled right into a combination lock, swinging from an open locker, and Joe understood that the open locker belonged to the girl in the shower.

Joe said, "Come on, let's get out of here."

"No way!" yelled Walker. "No fucking way!"

"In here," Howie said, heading into the office.

They shut the door and Howie threw Walker a towel for his eye, which was going to keep bleeding for a while, the gash was that big, just over the brow, bleeding and splattering thick fat drops onto the tile floor. In the office stood a desk, just like Mr. Morrison's, and on the desk were pictures of famous students who had almost become famous: swimmers, and volleyball players, people who won the trophies kept out front in the trophy case the custodians never bothered to dust. These were the people who had their pictures in the newspaper and graduated. There were history books, too, and stacks of papers waiting to be graded. Walker sat in the chair behind the desk, holding the towel up against his eye, while Joe shut the door and Howie started going through the drawers.

"Wow," Walker said. "So this is where Ms. Williams grades her papers. Imagine, sitting here, grading papers every night and we never even knew it." He put his hand on the desk, feeling it. "I mean, this is where she goes!"

"Yep," Howie said. "That sure is something, Walker."

"Wow," Walker said. "This is totally unbelievable!" Now he put his feet up on the desk, teacherlike. He leaned back in the chair and said, touching the bump on his head, "Wow. I really bonked myself."

He sat there, feeling the bump, and Howie began looking through the shelves and drawers and cabinets. Joe stood still behind the closed door, thinking about what he'd seen, and about how good that had been. He told himself he wasn't ever going to tell anybody, ever, and he told himself it was just a matter of time . . . *It's just a matter of time . . .* and Wiz, the security guard, bellowing:

"Locking up!"

Then a girl's voice, calling. "Just a sec!"

Howie leapt and Walker looked right at Joe. "No way," Walker said, shaking his head. "No unbelievable way."

Joe drew his finger to his lips and blushed. They listened to the girl's feet running across the tile, and the big doors, swinging shut. And then the sound of the lock, turning.

They ended up drinking a lot of water.

On the morning of Spencer's surgery, to remove the plate from his leg, Joe went into Spencer's hospital room and watched cartoons with him. The cartoons were on a small television the size of a shoe box, only smaller and less rectangular, and they watched cartoons while Spencer played marbles with Mr. Moose. The marbles were really ball bearings from his bicycle, and Joe knew that their father was going to buy Spencer a new bicycle. He was going to buy Spencer a three-hundred-dollar bicycle just as soon as Spencer could walk again without any crutches, and eventually the nurses came into the room to give Spencer an I.V., which made him dopey and slow, and then more nurses came in and put him on a bed with wheels in order to roll him down the hallways into an elevator, and then into a room with green-and-pink tile on the walls, where he would be operated on.

"Oh boy," Spencer said. "Oh boy."

"You'll be fine," Joe said. He tied a paper mask over Mr. Moose. "He'll be with you the whole time, too. Giving instructions."

"Where's Dad?"

"Dad says he's going to buy you a bicycle. Any color you want."

"I don't want a bicycle. When you play football, you're supposed to drive a car. Like you. I want a car just like you, Joe." Now Spencer clapped his hand over his forehead, the way actors do on daytime television, and said, "Oh boy, Joe. Here we go."

A nurse reached down and examined Spencer's I.V. Joe could tell the nurse wanted to say something nice, but he could also tell the nurse had no idea what to say. Straightening herself, she pressed her skirt and said loudly, "That's a big boy!"

But Spencer wasn't a big boy. He was a little kid who was going to be picked on for the rest of his life even if he did want to play football. He was a little kid with legs made out of twigs. Just as the nurses began to wheel Spencer out of the room, Spencer spread out his arms, like an airplane, and said, "Joe?"

"Yeah?"

"You're the best."

Seven hours later, they brought Spencer back. They flipped him into his bed and Joe stayed in the room, watching TV with the sound off. When Spencer began to wake, he was sick, which made everything hurt, and he began to cry until he fell back asleep, crying. He couldn't cry for long because he still had to sleep, and Joe knew the crying was just going to make everything hurt more: the stitches and scars, the ankle the doctors had to break one more time because the joint had been misaligned. They used a small sledgehammer to break it. When a young nurse only a couple of years older than Joe said that Joe should go home, get some sleep, Joe didn't want to go home; he didn't want Spencer to wake up alone, and so he drank coffee, with the nurse, who was still a nursing student and had bright yellow hair, like flowers, and it was something he had never done before—drank coffee. The nurse asked him if he'd like some cream. She asked him questions about college.

"Spencer," Joe said once. "He's my little brother."

"He's a sweetie," she said.

When she said that word, *sweetie,* he couldn't tell if she was flirting with him, and then he felt guilty for wondering if she was, and he knew she knew the same thing he did: that he wanted her to be flirting with him.

He talked about colleges, in New England, and he knew he was supposed to be worried about Spencer, his little brother with the broken leg because he had been hit by a car while riding his bicycle. A man had broken Spencer's leg, by accident, and Joe had broken Danny Ernest's arm . . . *on purpose?* . . . and now Joe was ashamed because of what he'd done. If Spencer knew what Joe had done, he would be ashamed of Joe, and this was something Joe suddenly realized he could never bear: Spencer, being ashamed of him. Spencer had a broken leg and it was going to be years before he would walk without a limp, because when Spencer was hit by a car traveling forty-seven miles an hour, he was thrown onto somebody's front lawn; the sprinklers were running, and the man took off his shoe in order to cover up one of the sprinklers. At first, Joe wanted to kill the man. He wanted to hunt him down and find him and break his neck; he was going to break his legs, one kneecap at a time, and then, thinking about what that meant, about what he knew he wanted to do and why, he felt ashamed. Everybody drove fast on that street; in this world, there was a lot of room for accidents, and it *had* been an accident; anybody could get hit by a car. Anybody, and Spencer is going to grow up and face his own life, and sooner or later Spencer's life will belong to himself, because when you're a kid, you can only own your very own toys—your bicycle and your moose. As for shame, that's something you have to wait for. The first time you see a naked girl, or the next time you see a normal girl and imagine what she, too, might look like naked.

After Spencer woke, for real, Joe ate breakfast with him at the hospital. Then Joe told Spencer about the nice nurse with yellow hair who was going to look in on him later, and then Joe went home. He hadn't slept for twenty-four hours, the third time *ever,* and he had drunk his first cup of coffee . . . *I like it black, actually* . . . and when he drove home, through downtown Phoenix, slowly making his way up toward the edges of the valley—24th to Lincoln, to Tatum, over across Doubletree—as he drove, rising up through the city interior and smog, he drove with two hands on the wheel, slowly, and he told himself to stay sharp. He told himself anything can happen.

Anything.

Once home, he parked his car in his father's parking place in the garage, and he left his keys in the ignition, which is what his father always did whenever he parked his car inside the garage. Joe went inside the house and thought about making a bowl of cereal. Instead, he went to the bathroom, thinking about the pretty student nurse, and the yellow hair; it took less than ninety seconds, probably, and she had cheeks the color of flowers. He never got to the other parts, and what they might have looked like. He was that fast.

In the kitchen there was a note from Mrs. Amato, on the fridge, explaining what was for dinner . . . *meat loaf?* . . . and then the doorbell rang.

Mrs. Bently stood at the door, wearing a peach dress and sandals and a halfhearted smile. If your smile was really *half-hearted,* said Mr. Rolf, then that meant you had low blood pressure, or were really sick. She was carrying a basket. For someone as old as Joe's mother, Mrs. Bently was still sort of pretty, though she did look tired and halfhearted.

"Hi, Joe," she said. "I brought you some food."

"Oh. Thanks, Mrs. Bently."

"May I come in? Just for a minute?"

He thought it dangerous, talking to a woman after doing what he'd just done in under ninety seconds in the bathroom. He wiped his hands on his jeans and said, "Yeah. Sure."

Inside, he asked her if she wanted to sit down, in the living room, which is where all the good furniture was that he was never allowed to sweat on, and the bookshelves, and the atlas, on the top shelf, and the picture he had swiped from Jenna Williams' apartment with Mrs. Bently's son, Howie. It was the first time he'd thought of the picture all day. The picture, and what he'd done.

"How's Spencer?" said Mrs. Bently.

"He's in the hospital."

"I know, but how *is* he? Did everything go okay?"

"Fine. He's fine, really. He wants to play football, before he becomes an astronaut. Everything went fine as scheduled."

She pointed to the basket, which was full of fruit and a package with a bow—a book, since all books looked the same when you wrapped them up, with or without different-colored paper. Librarians always gave books for presents.

Mrs. Bently said, pointing, "I brought him a present, too."

"That was nice. Really."

"Howie says you two had a fight, Joe. I know it's none of my business, but—"

"We didn't have a fight."

"Oh," she said. She felt her chest, the center, and took a breath. "Then why don't you come around anymore?"

"Well, I've been studying. And Spence. And—" He was about to say "wrestling," and now Mrs. Bently looked up at him, her eyes huge; she was a mom, even if she wasn't his. She was still a mom who was supposed to make that look.

"Is it about what happened?" she said. "At the meet? Everyone knows it was an accident, honey."

"Nah. Really, I'm just busy and stuff. Spence is really going to like this," he said, nodding at the basket. "He likes books a lot."

"I thought he might have been with you."

"Howie?"

"He hasn't been home in two days. I thought at first, well—boys will be boys, especially you two. I thought you two were camping out or something, the way you used to, with Walker, before . . . I thought maybe he was at the hospital with you and Spence. But it doesn't make sense Joe if you two have had a fight. It doesn't makes sense that he would—"

"We didn't have a fight—"

"Because if you two are fighting, then it just doesn't make sense that he wouldn't come home! It's not as if he doesn't have a nice place, Joe. It's not as if we nag him too much because, you know, we were kids too. Bob and I were kids too and we had the same kinds of things. Not so many drugs, maybe, but when I was a kid, people had the same kind of problems, and if he can't even come home and tell us what's going wrong, Joe, then I don't know what's wrong! I don't know and I think he'd have the decency to come by and let us know just what's going on!"

She was crying now. Joe went into the kitchen for some paper towels. When he returned, he gave her one and asked her if she wanted to sit on the good couch. She was still crying, shivering in her peach dress, looking at the food.

She said, wiping her face, "Is that too much, Joe? Is that just too much for me to ask?"

"I don't know, Mrs. Bently."

"I wish you'd talk to him, Joe. He listens to you. He's always listened to you because you're so mature."

He thought, I am not mature . . . *am I?* He thought maturity is something *parents* respect, not your friends, especially when you've stopped talking to them.

When it was time, finally, Joe walked Mrs. Bently out to her car, the way his father and mother used to escort their guests back in the days when they had some. They'd walk the company outside, and Joe walked with Mrs. Bently down the brick path to her car—a blue station wagon with a pretty good stereo. The station wagon had recently been washed; he said thanks again for the presents and headed back inside, and Mrs. Bently sat in the car a few minutes, probably thinking, before she started it up and drove away.

Back inside, Joe shut the door; he turned the lock, then the dead bolt. He looked at the room with all the good furniture. This was the room in which his parents would drink coffee or scotch with people they used to know and admire . . . *These are our friends, the Ripleys* . . . and sometimes Spencer would come in and read a novel he'd been writing about astronauts, and afterward the company would clap and admire all the pictures, but that was before when their parents still had friends. Now the living room was just a room stuffed with pretty furniture you still weren't supposed to sweat on. It was the place their mother always insisted on keeping neat and tidy, and on top of the bookshelves, above all the pictures of Joe and Spencer in brass frames, stood the atlas, and Joe stood there, going up on his toes to reach, pulling down the atlas. He pulled it from the shelf, thinking the book weighed more than any other book he'd ever lifted, except maybe an encyclopedia; the atlas weighed more than the dictionary; and there behind the state of California lay the photograph: Jenna Williams, with hair longer than it was now. Joe dropped the atlas onto the fancy couch with flowers and took the photograph into the kitchen. He turned on the gas range. In December, just before she left two years ago to get her hair fixed, Joe's mom had seen that the kitchen was *completely redone* with new wallpaper and ceramic tile, with new appliances, all of them avocado green, which was truly an ugly color, and now Joe held the photograph up against the flame. It took only a moment to ignite, and before he set the flaming photograph onto the kitchen table, he found a plate to match the décor, and then he took his place at the table. Sitting there politely, he watched the black smoke begin to lift.

When Howie beat up Johnson the Drug Addict, back in October, it made perfect sense: Johnson was an asshole, and Howie was feeling a little crazy. After what Walker had done, killing himself like that, Joe was surprised that more people weren't going crazy. Mr. Horn, the Bowling and Chemistry teacher, seemed to think everybody was going to go crazy right off. He bought a bulletproof vest from a Peace Outlet and wore the vest to class for weeks beneath his lab coat. You could tell he was wearing it because it made Mr. Horn look bigger than he really was. It also made him walk a lot more slowly, it was so heavy—the kind of bulletproof vest that had been made during Vietnam for generals.

And then it began to rain. Rain, for days on end, washing away the dust, and the sky, and all the people outside wearing windbreakers and coats. Howie had been kicked out of school; he'd been spending a lot of time alone, and other places, and now they sat watching the rain from inside Joe's car. They were stuck in the center of Mockingbird Lane. When Joe tried to drive the car through a stream pouring across the street, the engine choked and died. At home, Spencer was eating dinner with Mrs. Amato, and the distributor cap in Joe's car was full of water. The distributor cap was something Joe had read about in some of his auto-repair books. Also, Howie had been doing a lot of coke.

"You should slow down," Joe said.

"Not us, Jazz. Not us. We sure as hell didn't get caught with our pants down."

"We should have. We still can. It was stupid, Howie. Stupid and we could have ended up in prison. Jesus—don't you ever think?"

A pickup truck approached from the other side of the road. The driver stepped outside. He was wearing a yellow slicker, and now he was walking into the water, the water rising up past his boots and his knees. He was measuring the depth and from this distance looked as if he were only a few inches tall, he was that far away across the water. Joe knew everybody gets caught eventually. It's called *perspective,* the way people look so small so far away.

"You're fucking up," Joe said.

"What?"

"You're fucking up." He set the hearse in neutral and stepped outside into the rain. "Come on."

Outside, they began to push the car through the water, but the car was long and heavy; it had been designed to carry a lot of weight. Howie said, almost yelling over the rain, "What the hell do you know?"

"Your mom. For Christ's sake. You should at lest tell your mom—"

"Yeah, right, Joe. Sure. You and that sweet little piece of ass of yours. You think Walker—"

Joe stopped pushing. He knew Walker Miller was dead, that Howie was fucking up. He knew that it was raining hard, and he stood here in the rain, wiping at his eyes and yelling at his best friend. He stood, yelling at his friend, yelling, "Walker is dead, Howie. He's fucking dead!"

"No."

"He's dead, Howie. He fucked up!"

"No. You fucked up, Jazz. You!" And now Howie was crying. He was crying and Joe knew Howie was never going to forgive Joe for watching him cry. Joe knew he should have hit him, hard. He could have given Howie an excuse to hit back. Instead he stood in the rain, watching him cry, and then there was this guy in a yellow slicker wading through the water carrying an orange tow rope. He was wading through the water, calling out, "Hey! Hey, you guys need some help?"

"Just get me home, Jazz. Just get me fucking home."

Spencer is dancing. He sits in his wheelchair, in front of the television, watching MTV and dancing—his arms flying through the air, his chest bopping back and forth, with his chin.

Joe says, "What are you doing?"

"Dancing," he says, watching the television. "It's good exercise."

"You look like a goof."

Spencer stops. He looks up at Joe and says, "A goof?"

"Yeah, you look like a goof, Spence. A weird-ass goof."

"Oh."

"Yeah."

Spencer picks up the remote and turns off the television. He says, "How was your day?"

Joe knows he's hurt Spencer's feelings, by accident. He says, "Okay. What's to eat?"

"Macaroni and cheese, from scratch."

In the kitchen Joe fixes himself a bowlful. The macaroni is cold, which is the way he likes it, and he knows he doesn't know how to dance. He's never even been to a dance, and Spencer has turned the television back on. The music is loud, coming through the door; when Joe goes back into the TV room, where the pool table is, he sees Spencer staring at the television rock-still. He doesn't even blink.

Joe says, "Did you help make this? With Mrs. Amato?"

"Nuh-uh."

"Oh. Well it's pretty good, you know?"

"She made it herself. Last night. From scratch."

"It's good."

On the television a group of people are dancing on the beach. There are cameras moving around, following them, all these people on the beach in swimming suits dancing, and Joe says, "So how do you think they learn how to do that?"

"Do what?"

"That," he says, pointing with his spoon. "You know. I mean do you read books? Do you take lessons? How come when they do it they look so cool?"

"I don't know," says Spencer, shrugging.

"Well, you look cool, too, Spence. I mean, it's tough when you're in a wheelchair."

"That's why I'm a goof."

"Nah. Just for a while, till you get out."

"Paula Abdul is best," Spencer says. "Boy, she's really the best."

The VJ appears on the screen. He's talking in a foreign

accent, probably fake, and he's talking and saying things like *cool* and *hey, dudes, this is really radical,* and Spencer says, "I like it better when they just play songs. That's the best way to practice."

"Yeah?"

"Yeah," Spencer says, thinking about it. "You want to practice? I'll show you how, Joe?"

"Turn it up, okay? I like this one."

"Look!" Spencer yells. "Look!"

"What?"

"Outside," he says, pointing. "Look outside! It's snowing!"

He pushes at the wheels, swings his chair to the door and down the ramp. He rushes past Joe's car in the garage and says, "Look! It's snowing!"

Snow, Joe thinks. *Snow.*

"I've never seen snow," he yells. "Not for real!"

It's thick enough you can't see through. Big white flakes floating down from the sky, and Spencer, wheeling his chair in circles, catching the flakes on his tongue.

"Oh, man, just wait," he yells. "Oh, man, just wait till I tell somebody. Man, they're never even going to believe it! It's snow, Joe! Snow!"

Before, when they lived in Chicago, before Spencer was even born, Joe used to love snow. This is the first time Joe's seen snow in years, and he's forgotten what it looks like, and what it feels like on your skin when it begins to melt, because your skin is warm, usually *ninety-eight degrees point six,* unless you're overheated. Their mother hated snow. They moved to Phoenix to get away from snow, and in Phoenix there wasn't ever supposed to be any snow, and from inside he hears the phone, turned on extra loud so Spencer will pay attention.

Spencer says, looking up at all the snow, "Phone's ringing!"

Joe picks it up in the kitchen on the seventh ring. It's Carol Cunningham, Edith's best friend, just wondering if Joe was planning on going to the dance.

"No."

"Oh," says Carol Cunningham.

Outside, the snow is swirling over the palm trees, melting in the swimming pool, and Joe says, "Is it snowing there?"

"Of course."

"Oh. Well, no, I'm not going to the dance."

"Well, that's too bad. I mean, we are. You know. Me and Edith. I'm driving."

"That's good," Joe says. He wishes he had something more to talk about. "Well," he says, thinking. "Well, have a nice time, Carol."

He hangs up, and Spencer comes wheeling in through the door with Mr. Moose, who's in his football clothes. Spencer stops and throws a snowball at Joe. The snowball falls apart midair, breaking up over the kitchen tile, which was completely redone in avocado green before their mother left.

"That's a snowball," Spencer says, pointing. "I've never made one before. Who was that?"

"Who?"

"On the phone!"

"Nobody."

"Oh."

"Nobody, Spence."

"Probably just one of his girlfriends," Spencer says to Mr. Moose, who nods vigorously. Now Spencer looks up and says, "You know, Joe, you should really learn to dance. When I have girlfriends, I'm gonna be a great dancer. You know, lots of football players have to dance. It keeps them *limber,* and if you're not *limber,* you're not ever going to be able to be an astronaut, which is exactly what I'm going to be after I become a doctor."

"Uh-huh."

Spencer squeezes Mr. Moose's head, just a little, and says, *Me too!*

Now Spencer is wheeling himself back into the TV room, and for a moment, just for a moment, Joe wants to make him stay. To make him stay in the room and look at his snowball melting on the floor. In Phoenix it's only going to snow once in a lifetime, and this is something that is never going to happen again, and now his little brother is rolling out of the room, saying, "Okay, Mr. Moose. Okay, let's see who's up next."

"Where you going?" Joe says, but this isn't what he means to say.

"To practice," Spencer says, not even looking. "We gotta practice!"

When you practice, you do the same things over and over again. But some things only happen once: your birth, your life, your time to die. But that's not very specific, really, and according to Mr. Rolf, *specificity* makes the difference between *food* and *apple pie* or *goat cheese;* specificity marks the difference between *woman* and *Ingrid Bergman,* whom Mr. Rolf admires deeply. And there are other things which will happen only once, things meaningful and important as any other, and usually they involve the idea of *the first time:* the first time you see *Casablanca,* or a naked girl, or the first time you say you love someone; and other fatal accidents, like suicide, car wrecks and all those planes, crashing. Robin Mendelberg and his girlfriend, Suzy Dribble, drove off the big curve on Tatum Boulevard last year. Robin Mendelberg had his arm around Suzy Dribble, and they were driving fast, and then a dog crossed the highway, a big black rottweiler, and Robin Mendelberg tried to avoid killing the dog and instead he drove off the highway and killed himself and his girlfriend. He killed the dog, too. The dog's name was Biff, and they found parts of him smashed underneath the front axle.

It was the first time Joe ever understood that people his age could really die. And there are other first times: like the first time you touch a girl's breast and she doesn't roll her eyes, or hit you, which means this is the first time that a girl *wants* you to touch her breast; or the first time you drink a beer; the first time you bench your weight; the first time you get a flat tire, and fix it, because you know how; the first time you wash your own clothes without turning your underwear pink and blue; the first time you lie on purpose and do it anyway; the first time you turn sixteen, and then seventeen; and the first time you decide maybe you really don't need your parents, anyway . . . *fuck 'em.* In class Mr. Rolf says *coming of age* is just a phrase tired English teachers make up to explain what they've forgotten to understand. All it really means, says Mr. Rolf, *this coming-of-age schtick,* is that you eventually come to understand that some things are beyond your control *. . . like the grades you're going to get, Mr. Jazinski, when you take Physics . . .* or like the weather which just might rip your roof off on your birthday, or Halloween, or like the people you are bound to fall in love with. Mr. Rolf says you know you've come of age when you fall in love and think you're sick and are glad, anyway. He says, *To come of age is to understand that no man is an island, and no island is a man. You can lead a horse to water, but you cannot make him swim. You can lead yourself to water, Mr. Jazinski, but . . .*

But your parents are never going to understand why.

Even . . . ?

Even if they say they love you?

And why? Just why's that, Mr. Jazinski?

Because nothing is ever lost.

In the locker-room office, with Walker and Howie, Joe had finally asked Howie, "What are you looking for?"

"You know," Howie said. "That picture!"

And then Walker smiled, as if he owned the world, and took out his wallet. The picture had been folded into squares, and he set it on the desk, smoothing out the wrinkles. Up until then, Joe had never even believed it. He had thought it was a story, like the time Mr. Rolf climbed up onto the roof of the gymnasium and began reciting the *Aeneid;* or the time the gay kid, Mitchell Hemly, was caught whacking off underneath the bleachers during a wrestling meet. The time Joe's father met his mother, at a basketball game in college, and they fell in love. They fell in love and had a couple kids, and if no one knew the story, would he still be alive to prove it?

Looking at the snow, taking a breath, Joe is on his way to his very first dance. The White Christmas dance, and truly it is white outside, because it is snowing and everywhere all around them is snow. Snow, and the way it keeps drifting all around the cars in the parking lot: his car, under the snow, the snow sticking to the paint he's spent three months putting on his car; and the wipers, beating at the snow. Across the access road, behind the Communication Church of Christ, Santa Claus is standing on a roof, smiling. He's big as life, lit up in the snow, and some of the decorations have been rearranged. Instead of holding on to his seven-foot candy cane, he's got it propped into his belly, and it's reaching across the roof, to Rudolph, who is apparently blowing him off. Rudolph's going to blow Santa off the roof, suspenders and all, and now Joe's turning, setting the car into park. The windshield is broad and he's looking out at all the snow, and night, which has fallen. The night of the White Christmas.

Before, Joe was going to give Edith a necklace made out of *twenty-four–karat gold,* whatever that meant—a thin necklace he was going to give to her for Christmas. Now, thinking about it, he hopes she's here. And maybe he should have bought her something nice. Maybe she isn't here, and if she isn't here, then he has no reason whatsoever for being here. Joe thinks Edith's skin is white as snow. He's seen her skin, and her body, and the way she used to look at him, before, and thinking about it, about the way she used to look at him, he tells himself he's stupid. If he waits here long enough, eventually it will melt, and now he's outside, walking across the long lawn to the gym under all the snow. Halfway there, he stops, turning to admire his car. He thinks it looks nice this way.

He sees Mitchell Hemly standing by himself. Mitchell is looking at the house with Christmas decorations—Rudolph, and Santa; Mitchell's hands are buried deep in his pockets. When he sees Joe, he almost holds Joe's eye, and Joe thinks maybe Mitchell is going to wave, only he doesn't. Mitchell just keeps standing there, turning away to look at the roof, and the snow, and all those Christmas decorations.

At the door Mr. Rolf is selling tickets.

"Mr. Jazinski," says Mr. Rolf. "And how are you?"

"Hey, Mr. Rolf."

"Yes. Yes," says Mr. Rolf, breathing something, maybe gasoline. Mr. Rolf is looking into the gym. The music is playing, and they can see the shadows of people standing in groups under all the lights, and the disco ball, spinning.

"Yes," says Mr. Rolf, nodding. "And how are you?"

"Okay."

Mr. Rolf smiles and pulls out his flask. He unscrews the cap, pours some dangerous fluid into his coffee and takes a nip. He says, "How old are you, Mr. Jazinski?"

"Seventeen."

"Seventeen, eh? Seventeen?" He begins to screw the cap back on. He says, sadly, "Someday, Mr. Jazinski. Someday we will have to have a drink together."

"Uh-huh."

Mr. Rolf unscrews the cap. He passes the flask to Joe and says, "A toast. If you're old enough to write a theme, you're old enough to make a toast!"

"No thanks, Mr. Rolf."

"Ahh," says Mr. Rolf, nipping. "The spirit knows the flesh it must consume!"

Joe looks at Mr. Rolf and smiles. "You make that one up?"

"Oh, no. No. That one comes from a former fellow denizen of the great Northwest, Mr. Jazinski. The great Northwest!"

"Washington," says Joe.

"The state of, yes indeed."

"I've never been there."

Mr. Rolf smiles, halfheartedly, because his heart no longer works properly. Joe understands for the first time that maybe Mr. Rolf likes him. Maybe that's why he's always picking on him in class . . . *because he likes me?* He thinks Mr. Rolf is probably the smartest and the saddest man he will ever meet.

Mr. Rolf says, "Are you going to stay out here in the snow with an old man? Or are you going to step inside and attend to this celebration properly?"

"It's snowing," Joe says.

"That it is. It's snowing, it's snowing," Mr. Rolf says, flushing. "It's snowing just for us!"

Joe can see a lone girl, dancing. She is wearing black: boots, jeans, a T-shirt, a black bow in her yellow hair. She is dancing and Joe knows she is Lacy, the girl he saw in the locker room, almost a year ago, and he knows there are still others he knows inside: there, where the music is playing, while Mr. Rolf stands outside taking tickets.

"You're all right, Mr. Rolf. You know? You're really okay."

"Go on, Joseph," he says, pointing. "The world is for the living."

Mr. Rolf has never called him anything but Mr. Jazinski, and inside he goes: past the lone girl, Lacy, who is dancing; past the table full of cookies and punch; past Jenna Williams and Mr. Morrison and Mr. Buckner; past Wiz, who is standing there all alone looking at the girls who are wearing dresses and the girls who aren't wearing bras; past everybody else Joe has ever seen before, walking slowly and wanting more than anything to be truly *anonymous,* which means unknown, here under the spinning lights which are passing by anonymously. If nobody knows who he is, then nobody is ever going to know just what he's done, or what he's even going to try and be, *good,* especially when it's dark.

Joe and Edith, he will write, in the snow. *Joe and Edith . . .*

They will be oblivious, and still slightly dizzy, and they will be on top of Camelback Mountain when it happens, sitting in the back of the hearse, the doors swung open wide. They will be sitting in the back of the hearse, finished with all the explaining, looking at the sky, and the snow, all the city lights, and Edith's sweater will be slightly askew because she has recently put it back on, leaving her underwear and shoes and socks in the front seat, by Joe's underwear and socks, and they'll be drinking champagne, too, from the bottle. It's a bottle that Edith has brought along *. . . What people in love are supposed to drink, you know? Here, I want to pop the cork . . .* and Joe will be sitting there, one hand up beneath her sweater, right beside her heart. It would be nice if she didn't have to put her sweater back on, but the snow is kind of cold, even now. Still, it's okay, because he knows what she looks like, and he can remember, and he's got his hand where something counts; his hand, here on her breast. The cold will cause his ankles to ache, just enough for him to notice, and they will feel the snow . . . *It's like Michigan all over again!* . . . drifting down on their toes, and they'll keep staring at the sky . . . *Yeah, I guess it is* . . . and the lights from the city, and the snow falling on top of the city lights . . . *Phoenix* . . . and then Edith will reach for the bottle of champagne. She will take a big sip, wipe her mouth and set the bottle by the tirewell, and then she will draw her finger over the lines in Joe's hand, the hand that's not beneath her sweater. Her lips will be wet from the champagne, and almost chapped, and she will be looking at the calluses on his hand. The calluses are from lifting weights, which he has done a lot of . . . *Lifting. It's something I know how to do, lifting* . . . and then Edith will say to Joe, squeezing his hand, hard, "You know what I really love?"

"No, what?"

"Things that light up. You know, from the inside."

Under the Influence of Ice

If we live alone then we are going to have to learn how to be lonely—that space we all must learn to travel in order to reach the other side: a cloud full of silver, a white-sand beach lying in wait just there behind the ocean. The people we can learn to truly love, waiting on the beach, waving.

In Phoenix there is no ocean. When Ray was a kid he read books and played football and thought about girls. He could distract himself by thinking about things he didn't yet seem to know enough about. But now, when the distractions seem increasingly fewer, and less imbued with meaning, life often seems at times to him an illness—drawn-out, complicated and, finally, terminal. And he knows when he is feeling this way that he is merely feeling the need for medication, and he wonders if without this need he would understand so clearly what he's up against: the world, which is now sophisticated enough to destroy even itself, one life at a time, or a billion. Sometimes, when he needs to get out of bed, he's not even sure he can.

But still he does, every single day. Once, when he was a kid, nine, he had to stay after school for not completing his math. His father said he would pick him up at five, and it was raining, and cold, and his father never picked him up. Instead Ray stood outside in the rain, holding his math book over his head because the janitors came by to lock up the doors, with chains, and he told himself, looking at the chains, *Sooner or later . . . Sooner or later, he'll come . . .* only he never did come, his math book became severely water-damaged, and he waited there in the rain for hours thinking that his father was dead or maybe worse. That maybe he was supposed to be here, standing in the rain, freezing, which is why his father wasn't ever going to come pick him up. He thought for the first time in his life that he was meant to die, and he was standing in the rain, freezing, going over his multiplication tables *. . . Six times six fell on the floor, picked it up and it was sixty-six . . .* and he kept thinking them up, making up the new ones to fill in all the gaps, like his father, these gaps he was waiting any moment to fill in: to arrive and take him home, dry him off, tell him, *There, it's okay, Raymond. . . . It's okay . . .* because he wanted to get out from under the rain. He wanted to get out now.

This he eventually understood to be the true force of time: the waiting you had to do to watch it pass right on through you—a thunderstorm, or river. Had he known back then about its usefulness, back when he was still only nine years old, he would have had a beer. He would have had six or eight, maybe, because the enemy wasn't the rain, or the cold, or the $D-$ he had in Math, or even the fact that his father, drunk, had simply forgotten once again to pick him up. This time it had just happened to rain, the rain eventually turned to ice, and the enemy was, and is, time.

The enemy is time and knowing, finally, that it's inconsiderate enough to kill you. It's everywhere: up close and far away: the sudden moment of living with yourself with no possibility for distraction: no stories, no whiskey or love. And Ray is just beginning to realize that without distractions life for him is simply unendurable; and waiting for time to pass, to blow over you like a cloud, is the same thing as knowing deep in the core of your bones that you simply have no control over the weather: it makes you feel small and hopeless, and laughed at by someone who does. What the body needs, he tells himself, is a wanting to be involved with something meaningful.

His parents both are alcoholics, now divorced, one recovering for the past twelve years: recovering, it lasts forever, like time, and the only way to destroy time is to destroy yourself, which is like saying *If you blow up the entire city, there will no longer be any crime. . . . If you destroy the planet, you will no longer have to worry about the environment. . . .* Sooner or later you're going to have to face the day, and while Ray is smart enough to know he is not an alcoholic simply because his parents are, he does know that this is why he doesn't want to be an alcoholic. He's seen what it's done, and what it makes people do, and it frightens him, living in a dream with something . . . *a wrenched heart? a needy liver?* . . . which will impel you toward something you simply do not want. Something as simple as not drinking a beer. Each morning he makes up his mind and, until recently, each evening he changes it; he thinks no man ever liked a beer more than one who needed it. He thinks often he wants a normal life. He wants to be able to get excited about the weather, because sometimes it really is very pretty, and he wants to know how the Broncos are going to do, and what Jenna just might say to him next . . . *Hey, big guy!* . . . and sometimes, after waking, looking out the window, sometimes he tries. He tries and tells himself maybe something is going to happen today. Try. Try, and maybe it will be worthwhile. Go out and buy some hot dogs, maybe. Work out. Take a drive. Maybe you can watch it rain.

Loneliness is something even a glassful of bourbon will not cut, and time is always going to be there, nagging, eroding away the spirit into some space vague and empty as a canyon. Or else time will disappear completely, and you'll run out before you even know it: you'll merely understand that something big has been lost by its very absence, a tooth you used to worry fondly, and as Ray understands the process, it's either use the day or let the day use you; conservation is a matter of deciding to conserve your resources—your water supply, your strength and your energy, and Ray is not going to be used any longer.

"If you want to win," he tells his wrestlers, "you've got to want it. You've got to make up your mind what it is you really want."

Even if you lose. He's running now, trying to figure it all out. Each day for the past seventeen, running. When his alarm strikes 5:00, he slips out of bed, quietly, in order to surprise the sky, still sleepy and quiet. He looks out the window and puts on his shorts, his sneakers, a sweatshirt and then he begins to run. He thinks his life's intention is simply to run the sweat out of his entire body: running, a twelve-mile course around and up along the canals, up through Papago Park, up past McKellips, into McCormick Ranch, which was named after a guy who made chain saws, and later turned into a subdivision . . . up through the ranch and over to 68th Street and then back down, running along the bicycle trails which lace the interior of suburban Phoenix.

And today, like the past three, it's raining hard. He's running through the rain, the sweat mixing with the rain while Ray is running hard because discipline is a matter of the will, one foot in front of the other, carefully, and sometimes while he's running he comes across people he knows. Tina, who wears the leopard-skin outfit at the River Bottom, a place he's been known to frequent; or Michael Owens, the undercover cop, who rides her bicycle along the bike trails. Usually Ray and Michael Owens meet up around Indian School, exactly seven miles east of Jenna's apartment, and Michael and Ray will nod, and she will be smiling, pedaling along on her blue-and-green bicycle, and Ray will admire the shape of her chest and her legs while he keeps on running by, tempted to pause, to turn and have another look.

After, after he finishes his run, Ray showers, slowly, in cool water. Then he will dress in his school clothes, the same school clothes he's been wearing now for years—teacher's clothes, bought by a teacher's salary with its three-percent annual raises, sometimes less; the kind of clothes affluent people with bright children never even notice, and after school he will change out of his teacher's clothes and work out with his wrestlers, and then by himself, finishing up in the weight room alone until he can barely move a muscle.

Today is back and bis; tomorrow, legs and shoulders. It is raining hard now and Ray is on the road, running, and thinking that if all goes well he should be able to fall asleep by nine o'clock, tonight, without having to read or think about what it is he's still trying to avoid. Up ahead, he sees Michael.

"Ray!" she calls, applying the handbrakes, gingerly. The rain is spilling off her wheels as she rolls tentatively to a stop. She's unhooking her feet from the toe clips, balancing.

"Hey," he says, slowing, jogging in place.

"It's raining!"

Ray looks up at the sky, behind him, gazing. He says, "Sure looks it." His accent . . . *hillbilly* . . . has just slipped out fast.

She laughs, maybe at the accent, or maybe she's embarrassed for saying something so obvious. She says, "I thought only the crazy would be out—"

"Just me."

He's wondering why it is that every time he comes across her she wants to try and save him. In three weeks she is going to enter her first biathlon, near Saguaro Lake, and she's asked Ray if he wants to come along and watch, carry her water and towels, maybe, and Ray knows Michael Owens is the kind of woman that magazines call *responsible,* and he knows that she has never done anything wrong in her entire life: which is why she is a cop and social worker both, and why she is pretty, and has perfect skin, and why she is absolutely without any problems whatsoever.

"Do you want to get some coffee?" she says. "Breakfast?"

"No," he says, waving, still running in place, but picking up the speed, growing nervous. "I've got to set a record."

"Well," she says. "One of these days, okay?"

"Yeah," he says. "Sure." The rain is pouring down his face, his sneakers are soaked, and it's cold. Cold as ice water, and he heads off, up the path, wondering why it is she always wants to save him from what she can't possibly understand.

"Ray!"

He stops and turns: in the rain, she is pretty as a picture, only more so, because it really is raining, and because she is really there, breathing, wiping the water from her eyes. He says, nearly annoyed, "Yeah?"

"All you gotta do is say so, Ray."

"Say what?"

"I'm not stupid, okay? I'm not blind. I can read the writing on the wall. Problem is, sometimes you gotta pull back the curtain."

He smiles; it's something he might say: *writing on the wall.* "Lunch," he says. "Lunch, okay?"

"Okay," she says, brightening.

"I'm freezing, Mike. I gotta go."

He goes. Now, just two miles from home, where he's eventually going to make a pot of coffee and sink into his tub full of bubbles and steam . . . *no cold shower, not today* . . . he can't keep from smiling. He's actually happy. He can't remember even wanting to be happy for a long time. He's happy, and it feels good . . . *good.* The way you sometimes need to pinch yourself, because it feels good: a woman looks you in the eye, exploring the possibilities, assessing the damage, and she asks you out for breakfast . . . *What could be more simple?* . . . and running up the street, past the cheap housing, into the even cheaper housing with swamp coolers and chipped paint, it strikes him clear as the pain rising deep from within the center of his chest.

Maybe she wants me to save her!

It's something he could never do for anybody, even Jenna, though he tried. He actually tried. If Ray has ever wanted to save anybody—his father, himself—then he also wanted to save Jenna Williams. After he left her apartment, after partially installing the dead bolts and locks, he was convinced he had a problem, and he was convinced he understood the immediate source of trouble: Louis, the crazy poet-vet with the rifle, just longing to shoot Ray's nuts off.

Next day, cleaned out and running, the day was promising to

be clear and bright. He was running through the early light of dawn and behind him a car was following slowly. The car was pacing him, watching him, and at the light on Curry, Ray slowed and began to run in place, waiting. When the car pulled up to the light, Ray yanked open the passenger door and screamed, "What?"

Inside, an elderly couple. The woman screamed back incomprehensibly and the man cried out, "We're lost!"

The man had a hearing aid and was looking at a city map. He was breathing through a tube, from a green oxygen tank in the backseat, and Ray apologized. He gave the couple instructions to Fountain Hills; he shut the woman's door and ran away.

That night Ray went to school and worked out. Afterward, he drove to Jenna's parking lot and began to wait. Sitting there in the dark, waiting for Louis, falling asleep, almost, he heard a tapping at his window.

He turned and looked. It was Jenna, tapping. For a moment, just before he turned his head and saw her, tapping at the glass, he had thought he was going to die.

"Ray? What are you doing?"

He rolled down the window and said, "I did not break into your apartment."

"I know you didn't."

"But he's going to come back. He's going to come back and I'm going to be here."

"What are you talking about?" she said. "Why don't you come inside? Come inside." And then, looking at him, she said, "You can stay on the couch?"

"No. Thanks."

"You can meet my dog! Come in, Ray."

She looked nice, dressed up as if she'd been on a date, and he went in, following her up the seven flights. She led the way, offering a pleasant view he told himself it was now time to avoid. Inside her apartment, Paris jumped onto his leg and peed. It was a cute dog, he said. Full of piss and vinegar, and her neighbor was having a party, a small party with quiet music and lots of voices.

Ray sat at Jenna's kitchen table and listened to the voices. He drank a cup of tea. Then another. Jenna asked, *What do you mean, he's coming back? . . .* and thinking about it, he understood that some things were simply impossible to explain. He sat there on that hard kitchen chair, thinking, and Jenna looked over at him and smiled sadly.

"What are you thinking about?" she said.

"Nothing."

She shifted her weight, crossed her legs. "Want to try?" she said.

"Try what?"

"Want to try again? Sometimes I think maybe we should try again. Maybe I didn't try hard enough."

"No," he said, shaking his head.

"Maybe Walker, all that—"

"No," he said. "You'd made up your mind before all that, Jen."

"Oh." She sipped at her tea and said, "Are you going to meetings?"

She meant AA, not faculty. "No. Not yet."

"There's nothing wrong with meetings. If you need a sponsor, Ray, I'd like to do that. You know, a kind of coach. I'm a good coach. You know that."

"The hard part's over with," he said, hopefully. "What did the cops say?"

"Nothing. That one cop, he comes around. He says nothing's really going to happen. He tells me to stay away from the window and asks me if I'd like to hold his pistol. Same old gig, you know. *Wanna touch my pistol?*" She laughed. Then she said, apologizing, "He's just a cop, Ray."

"I'm tired," Ray said. "I'm gonna go."

"I'm sorry he did that," she said, pointing to his pants leg.

They were old pants, he thought, not particularly fashionable.

Jenna said, "He still gets excited."

•••

It was too late to save Walker Miller: he'd been freaking out for months, it was in his genes . . . *and yours?* . . . and so he sat in his car, drinking mineral water and waiting. He didn't want to yell at old couples lost in traffic; he didn't want to have to keep looking over his shoulder. It slowed down your pace, and he decided to speed up the waiting. He drove to the River Bottom, waiting for the cars to thin out, because he had made up his mind.

Cathy. Waiting for her to step through the back door of the River Bottom in her torn jeans and faded shirt and step inside her car. She drove a car older than Ray's, and when she finally did leave, he followed her across town. He felt like a private eye, or cop; he followed her down Van Buren, straight through the center of the city, the junkyards and stockyards and used-car lots, the hookers on 24th, the shiny and sealed-up glass-and-steel buildings . . . *downtown* . . . and then, once past, into the avenues as they began to click on by, westerly, one after the other, she finally turned onto the freeway. He almost lost her on the freeway, because she drove fast, her car could go faster than his, and he kept following her and watched her take the ramp leading to L.A. The road to L.A. was quiet and still, recently repaved, and she drove fast until she eventually turned off somewhere past Buckeye, near the nuclear power plant, Palo Verde. He cut his lights and followed the dust down a dirt road, and then another until she stopped in front of a lone house sitting just beneath the moon. He pulled off into a ditch, grabbed his baseball bat, and stepped outside.

He made his way slowly up the road. He thought he should be wearing camouflage, not his teaching clothes, and there was a dog, barking. He could smell horses nearby and a chicken farm. The traffic from the highway was marked by an occasional lone semi, delivering goods to L.A., or other places in California, and he stopped for a while to watch the traffic. If he smoked, he would have had a cigarette, to slow the waiting, and he wished almost for a moment that he did smoke because now was a good time for people to smoke. Instead, he looked at his watch, often, and then, making up his mind once again, he stood and walked into the yard where Cathy had parked her car—in her own front yard, right in front of the door. The yard was brimming with tumbleweeds; the grass, dead, rose up past his ankles. If he dropped a cigarette, he could start a brush fire all the way to California, and he could see lights on inside the house, and the blue-gray nuclear glow of a television lit behind the drapes. Holding his breath, counting, he kicked in the door.

A woman, not Cathy, screamed. He stepped inside with the bat, took aim at the television, and swung. The set exploded.

He said, calmly, "That's something I've never done before. You know? I've always wanted to do that."

The woman screamed again. She was old, withered, and drunk—a bottle of vodka between her legs, beginning to tip. She looked at Ray and decided to stop screaming.

"What?" she said.

"Where is he?"

He heard the click—a pump shotgun, a shell sliding into place. The woman decided to scream again. It sounded like the thing to do. She was on the floor, covering herself, duck and cover, 1963, and Ray was standing behind the wall, holding the bat, waiting. He was used to a different uniform and more sophisticated weaponry. At the same time, this was something he'd been trained to do.

He waited. The woman was lying on the floor, screaming again, her dress hitched up around her thighs; the carpet was full of potato chips and stains. It smelled like beer, like the trailer Ray had been raised in, in Kentucky, like fast-food chicken and beer cans and peanut-butter sandwiches. Ray swung the bat around, took aim, and headed down the hallway. The light was off in the hallway and he picked a door. Inside, the bathroom, with a tub stopped up and full of brackish water, dirty clothes, and then another door: he flipped a light and stared into a shallow closet filled with quarts of motor oil and household products—the type with price tags on the box that people sell to build a fortune. He went to the third door and tried the handle. He swung and knocked the handle right off.

He took a breath and stepped inside.

Cathy sat on the bed, shaking, a shotgun pointed dead center. She said, "You move and you're going to die."

"Where is he?"

"I'll kill you. I swear to God, Ray. I'll fucking kill you."

"Where is he?" He swung the bat and smashed a mirror hanging on the wall. The glass fell in pieces and he stepped closer. Cathy dropped the shotgun. She put her head into her hands and began to weep.

"It's not even loaded," she cried. "I forgot how to fucking load it!"

"Where's Louis, Cathy? I want him now."

"Louise," she said.

"Louis. Louise. Where is he?"

"You fuck," she cried. "You stupid simple fuck!"

He stood there and thought about what he'd been doing. He dropped the bat onto the floor and sat beside her on the bed. It was a big bed with a pink bedspread and stuffed animals on top. It had been recently made.

"What are you going to do, Ray? Kill my mother? You going to kill my mother? What are you going to do, Ray?"

She was laughing now and hitting him. She was swinging her fists and laughing and now she stood and began kicking him, and hitting, and laughing and screaming *You stupid fuck! You stupid goddamn fuck!* and she kept screaming and punching him and then she leapt and picked up a piece of the broken mirror and held it to her throat. She stood still, lifted her head, and let out a long, tender scream. Now she let go of the glass, which splintered at her feet. She fell onto the bed and kicked off her shoes. After a while, she asked him to close the door on his way out.

"I'm going," he said.

"I thought you were different," she said into her pillow. "I thought maybe I could love you."

"I'm sorry."

"You are one stupid fuck, Professor," she said, turning for a last look. "You really are."

"So long."

"Just shut the fucking door."

On the way out, he stepped over the woman's body, passed out on the floor. She was snoring, so Ray knew that she was still alive. It wasn't heart failure. He had thought when he hit the TV set there might be flames, but instead there was just glass, and the sound of a small, minor explosion. The kind a kid makes with a paper bag.

When he arrived home, he had to piss. It was almost dawn and he wanted to take a run. He stepped out of his car, unzipped and pissed on a lamppost. Standing there, pissing outside in the rising sunlight, he didn't have a headache.

He thought, *What goes in, must come out,* and still he doesn't have a headache. He hasn't had a real headache for seventeen and a half days. Sometimes, he takes aspirin anyway, because it's what he's used to doing. Sometimes he even misses not feeling fucked up: a long lost brother, or shoe, and when he realizes this absence, he sits back and admires the veins in his hands. The blood in his hands is clean as ice water, his hands steady as slate, and he remembers his father, after his father married his second wife in a tavern in Paducah, Kentucky.

His father, Merle-Bob, leaning on the barstool, his one suit full of cigarette burns, raising a finger, gently, unexpectedly, as if suddenly amazed at the prospect of this brief and conciliatory gesture toward parenthood—his father said to Ray, raising his fine finger, "If you're a fool at thirty, you're a fool for life."

When his father slid off the stool, Ray caught him. His father embraced him tiredly and said, beginning to weep, "Don't be a fool, Raymond. Don't be a goddamn fool."

"Okay, Daddy."

"And never, never get married in a fucking bar."

Ray has spent his life avoiding his parents, his life in Kentucky, and who he is, the son of two fucked-up hillbillies . . . though he knows this is unkind, and maybe even wrong . . . and next week, Ray will turn thirty-six, and on that day he will write his letter of resignation. Buckner can find a new coach, and a new driving instructor, and while Ray is still uncertain what he's going to do with the rest of his life, he knows that he no longer belongs here in Scottsdale, Arizona. Teaching, only the faces ever change, the faces and the fashions; it's time for change.

In the hallway, walking along with Marcia Taylor, Michael Owens sees Ray and nods.

The hallway is empty of kids. Michael offers some closing remarks to Marcia Taylor, and now Michael pulls away from Marcia. She meets Ray just outside the doors of the main office, and Ray thinks he doesn't know what to say.

"Hey," he says.

She's wearing a skirt and sweater and her hair is pulled back into a knot. A small knot, because she doesn't have too much hair, which is pale yellow. Her earrings are small, silver, and match, unlike Jenna's. He's thinking he's never before looked at her ears. They are nice ears. *Nice,* and he says again, "Hey."

"I can't, Ray."

"What?"

"I know I've been nagging but I can't." Now she's looking at her watch, brushing a loose strand of hair behind her ear, and she says, "My purse, Ray. Somebody stole my purse. From my office—somebody just went inside and took it!"

Ray thinks he has lost his wallet three, maybe four times in his entire life. He once drove his car with illegal license plates for twenty-seven months. He says, "Okay. I'll buy."

"You don't get it," she says. "I've got to talk to Cal." She opens the door and says, turning, "And then I've got to run downtown."

Ray thinks, *You don't really keep it in your purse, do you?* . . . but he knows she wouldn't keep a gun in her purse. She's never even once made a bust.

Ray says, "Do you need to borrow my car?"

"I was gone for half a minute. I swear. I was doing conferences, and Mitchell Hemly came in and sat down, and I said, 'Just a sec, Mitchell, I need to use the ladies' room,' and when I came back, Mitchell Hemly was standing outside talking to Carol Cunningham and when I sat down and called him in it was gone! I always leave it hanging off my chair, Ray. And it was gone!"

"It's okay," he says. "The keys are under the mat."

"Oh, thanks," she says, shaking her head. "I still have my keys."

He follows her back into the office. Now she takes his hand, squeezes it briefly and leaves him feeling dizzy; it's the first time he's ever touched her, and it feels familiar, and dangerous, the way a woman touches you for the first time. Now she is swinging shut Buckner's door, and Margaret Knudson is unwrapping a chocolate, popping it into her mouth, smiling. Margaret has recently had her hair done, and it looks expensive, the way it's been carved so neatly into stone.

"Hello, Ray!" she says, beaming. "Have a seat!"

Chocolate, he thinks. *Chocolate.*

After the coke addicts Robin Mendelberg and Suzy Dribble were killed in a car accident, on Tatum, while trying to avoid running over Nurse Henderson's rottweiler, Ray drove home the importance of safety belts with a baseball bat. He brought it into class, along with five watermelons, and then he lined the kids up outside the classroom door. For each class, he set a watermelon on his desk and invited each kid into class, one at a time, and then he asked each kid to grab the baseball bat, with two hands, and swing. It was important that each kid get a chance, alone, without anybody else watching. By the time Mitchell Hemly came in, there was nothing left to strike: just seeds and the pink juice of watermelons skimming along the desktop. The juice looked like blood, watered down, and on the blackboard Ray had written LIFE IS NOT A WATERMELON. The next day Buckner called Ray into his office, a *colleague* had complained about the noise, of course, and later that week Ray lectured on just what could happen—what Jenna would call *The Violence of Acceleration and Neglect.* She meant unfastened safety belts, worn tires, bad brakes, and Walker Miller had been in one of those classes. He was the kind of student who asked a lot of questions other students always thought were dumb.

Do cars really explode, Mr. Morrison? You know, when you drive into them?

When Michael leaves Buckner's office, she leaves carrying with her some documents—legal documents, with seals—and Ray thinks he's been sitting here waiting long enough to make up his mind over and over again.

She says to him, stepping forward, "I've got to go downtown, Ray. It's probably nothing, really. But—but I'll see you tonight?"

She means the dance, because as designated undercover cop of Gold Dust High, Michael must attend all the dances, and because Ray and Jenna and Andre Langousis and Jeffrey Nadolny and Robert Horn are all monitors this year for the school dances, then they too will be there. Nathan Rolf always goes, anyway, in order not to feel lonely. Now Michael leaves through the glass doors, and Ray steps into Buckner's office.

Cal is sitting behind his desk, his head in his hands, sweating. The disco ball has been removed from the top of his filing cabinet. It's the kind of thing you notice, the disappearance of a disco ball.

"Ray," Cal says. "What's going on?"

Ray nods, has a seat. "Everything okay?"

Cal laughs and lights a cigarette. "I used to not smoke," he says. "I quit, but never forgot. The whole time. The whole time I wasn't smoking I always remembered—it's like your first girl. Every time, you always remember, even when you're trying to forget."

"I won't take long."

"What. What is it."

"I just wanted to let you know I won't be coming back next year."

Cal looks up, exhaling. He says, waving his hand, "You guys starting up some kind of club?"

"Club?"

"Jenna came in here Monday and said the same thing. Only she's quitting midyear. She's quitting soon as her grades are in."

There is no ashtray on Cal's desk. He drops ashes onto the floor and smears them into the carpet with one of his expensive sneakers.

Cal says, looking up from the floor, "You are at least going to finish out the year?"

"Yeah, Cal. I just thought I'd give you some notice. You know?" He looks at Cal's cigarettes, sitting on a blotter, and wonders what it tastes like: giving something up so obviously foul—smoke and ash, in your lungs, and what it does to you. He thinks he had no idea Jenna was quitting. She never told him, and now he's angry, almost, but not quite. He's thinking maybe he's supposed to be thinking, and he's thinking . . . *Good for her. Good for her!* . . . because you can't be wrong for making up your mind. At the same time, he's thinking he's supposed to be angry.

"It's not like you're going to get a raise or anything," Cal says. "You want to quit, quit. Fine, I think it's wonderful."

"Okay, Cal."

"Go start up a car wash. Go take up plumbing or day care. You could do a lot worse than Gold Dust High, but no, no—you guys come in here full of ideas, dance around a little, and once the grind really starts to wear you down you hold up your still lily-white hands and say, 'Hey, Cal, I think I'm gonna quit.' "

Cal stands, drops his cigarette onto the floor, and says, crushing it, "So great. Great. Tell me another, Ray. Tell me another—"

"Why are you so pissed?"

"I'm not pissed, Ray. Not a bit. I'm happy for you. I think it's great. So great. You want me to write you a letter? Great. Tell me what you want me to say, Ray. Tell me, I'll say anything. I'll say you never fuck your students and I'll say you always turn grades in on time and I'll say you never show up hung over and that all your students love you. I'll say you always wear a tie, even. You name it, I'll say it, stick it in your jacket and send you on your way. Anything, anything, Ray—"

"But?"

"But for now why don't you get the hell out of my office."

"I don't get it—"

"You never did. Your timing sucks and now is not a good time to talk about your career."

Ray stands and says, looking at all the papers on Cal's desk, "You're the principal, Cal. You're the man who swings the paddle."

"That I am."

"See you."

Outside, Ray leans down to kiss Margaret Knudson's cheek.

"Merry Christmas, Maggie."

If it hadn't been for his teacher, the crazy guy with dysfunctional hair who was always nice to him, even if the crazy guy did sleep with one of his students, a sorority girl Ray took out sometimes for ice cream and a movie, then maybe Ray wouldn't have wanted to be a teacher. One thing Ray always knew was that he wasn't meant to date a sorority girl, and maybe teachers just wanted to be like someone who has taught them something, and he thinks you can't teach anybody anything if you don't like what you're doing: you either become severely damaged, like Robert Horn, or you become an administrator: the guy who swings the paddle and dresses badly. At Gold Dust High Marcia Taylor and Robert Horn are the saints, even if they live pathetic lives, because they have each accepted the bald truth: they are going to spend the rest of their lives encouraging people to do things that they never will; they will be teaching for the rest of their lives—saving people, even if it kills them. Ray thinks he's been close enough to death to know what that means, to kill yourself, no matter how you do it. He thinks if a man worries about being fired, then he will never be free to do anything right.

He leaves the main building, taking the long ramp outside. The ramp rolls gently down to the lawns, the rain is pouring, and he ducks his head beneath his tweed coat, the only one he owns, and runs along the ramp down to the gym. He looks like a nerd, running in the rain, like a schoolteacher afraid of getting wet. Inside the gym he passes his office and sends Lacy into the locker room to fetch Jenna. When Jenna steps out, wearing sweats over her swimsuit, a whistle hanging from her neck, she says, "Everything okay?"

"Why didn't you tell me?"

"Tell you what?"

"Why didn't you tell me you were quitting."

She takes his arm and leads him outside. They stand under a ledge watching the rain. Jenna zips up her jacket and says, "I was going to. I was going to tell you first. Who told you? Cal?"

"Not really."

"Oh. I thought—" She buries her hands in her jacket, pivots the way she always does, and says, "We're practicing now at the university. I'll finish the season out."

"Jen," he says, "if you want to quit, that's fine."

She smiles vaguely; he thinks he's never said anything more stupid in his entire life. He laughs and says, "I just thought you'd tell me. Hell," he says, laughing uncertainly, "why would you?"

"Ray—"

"Okay, really. I think it's great. The kids will miss you, but it's great. What's so funny is you just beat me out."

"I thought you'd be upset. That night, at my place—I was going to tell you, but I don't know. You were acting so weird. . . . I was afraid you'd be angry. Or hurt."

"You know, I'm tired of being angry. Of being pissed off all the time." He smiles badly. He thinks he always looks stupid when he smiles, like his father, who never smiles at things you are supposed to. He says, "My father . . . daddy, as we say back home . . . my daddy used to say, 'What goes in must come out.' He'd say that after getting sick, you know? He'd come home, puke, and then start in again all over, and every time, Jen, every time, he'd say that. He'd say, 'Raymond, what goes in must come out.' "

"Uh-huh."

"That," Ray says, pointing to Belinda Fullerton, trotting down the ramp with her umbrella. "That's bigger than me. It's bigger than me and the odds aren't fair. Some things you're born with, like your daddy. Okay, it's not good, but it's a fucking given,

Jen. You can't change a clubfoot. You're going to have to learn to limp, so okay. Fuck it. But I'm not going to bother getting angry. You do what's right, Jen. You don't need me to tell you that."

"Ray—"

"I'm sorry you thought I was angry. I wasn't, really. I mean I was, but not at you."

"I think—"

"An enemy can only be something big enough to kill you. It's the first rule. If it can kill you, you're going to have to be careful."

She's looking at him, the way she used to, sometimes. He thinks it could start all over again if he let it. Maybe. Probably not, it's absolutely freezing. He's done some stupid things. She wipes a stray drop of rain off her cheek and says, "Ray, can I borrow your car? Just for a couple hours?"

The crazy brilliant professor with perplexed hair died shortly after Ray graduated—an aneurysm, which exploded, and dropped him like a mule. Ray read about it in the papers and sent the university twenty dollars for a scholarship fund for people who liked philosophy. At first, it made Ray sad, the guy dying so young like that. And then after he thought about it off and on, for months, even years, he thought, *What a way to go.* A brain problem, for someone like Einstein, who invented physics. Ray had nearly failed Integrated Science, which didn't even mention physics, but Ray does believe that the crazy guy would have referred to his own death as *ironic,* and sometimes Ray wonders if the guy was ever really brilliant. Maybe he was just full of disease and disrespect. Maybe he was just another guy waiting for his life to explode before his very eyes.

After swim practice, when Jenna returns his car, Ray drives south through the snow to the River Bottom. He's never seen snow in Arizona, the traffic is confused and complicated, and once he steps into the bar he thinks you'd never even know it. He thinks, now he's in a bar, what's it matter? The bar is full of stale smoke and spilt beer. The doorman, who's tending bar, says, "You having a nice day?"

"It's cold out," Ray says. "Cold. It's a nice change."

"Mm-hmm."

"How about you?" Ray says. "What kind of day you having?"

Freddy steps out from the toilet, hitching his pants. They are less fashionable even than Ray's, baggy and full of stains. "Ray," he says. "If you're looking for Cathy, you gotta know she's split."

"Split?" In this context, it's a word he hasn't heard in years. He says, "I thought she might be here."

"Nope."

"She tell you?"

"Tell me what?"

"Nothing."

"She come in, asks for her check. Says she's going off to California. Her mother lives there. She says she's going to take her mother to a hospital and start her on methadone. Who knows?" Freddy says, rubbing his hands. "She has tattoos. She's fucked up, anybody can tell that."

"Yeah."

"A shot? A beer? What'cha need?"

"Coke, actually—"

"Coke," Freddy says loudly. "You want a Coke, you get a Coke. Jeezum. You want your old job back, you get your old job back. We make you manager. Give you an office, even."

"You're serious?"

"We're opening up another place in Glendale. Gonna call it The Harem. You know, like those harems people have all the time? We're gonna require ties, inside, so only rich people will get to come. It's going to be nice, Professor. Think about it. Good money, even. No brawls. Just the right kind of place, like Las Vegas. Ever been to Vegas, Ray?"

"I don't know, Fred—"

"Think about it, okay? Think about it?"

"Vegas," Ray says. "I can imagine."

• • •

He thinks if he were a good person, he would go home, visit his daddy—his stepmama, even. Take them some cactus plants or sombreros. Ray has close to nine hundred dollars in his savings. If he works hard at it, by the time he quits he could manage two thousand. With two thousand dollars, a man can go almost anywhere in this country if he doesn't stay in hotels. He once went without for seventeen months, and it was hard only for a little while. Then it was better, though still he knows it's going to be hard. He's going to have to be careful, and he knows he hasn't really paid all his bills. Nobody is ever free and clear.

At the dance, the White Christmas dance, in honor of Bing Crosby, he's looking at the snow outside. He is standing just inside the main doors with Cal Buckner and Nathan Rolf and Jenna. Inside, Buckner's disco ball has been attached to the rafters of the gym, and Ray knows he still has certain obligations and that those obligations are going to take a lifetime to repay: Walker Miller and Joe Jazinski and Howie Bently and Cathy and Jenna, and his parents, who are still alive, one in a trailer park in western Kentucky, just ten minutes from a store that sells lawn mowers and spaghetti sauce. Wal-Mart.

Just inside the gym, he sees Jazinski, who is standing by himself.

"Ray," says Buckner. "Have a snort."

The snow is still falling: down through the lights, onto the ramp cutting across the lawn. It looks nice, all this snow, and Nathan Rolf is passing around his flask: to Buckner, who is passing it to Michael Owens, who has joined them and is now passing it to Ray. Robert Horn, Bowling and Chemistry, is waving, and the flask is full of peppermint schnapps. Michael is carrying a new purse now—big enough to hold a shoe, or seven sets of car keys—and in the gym somebody is speaking into a microphone. Ray is still holding on to the flask.

"Hey," Jenna says, smiling. "You look like you've just seen a ghost."

"Are you ready to pahh-ty?" somebody screams. "Are you ready to rock 'n' roll?"

Ray returns the flask to Nathan and says, "Thanks."

"So," says Nathan, twisting on the cap. "The world is too much with us?"

"Late and soon," says Buckner, flushing with the schnapps. "I remember that one, Nathan."

Ray smiles stupidly; he has no idea what people ever talk about. The professor with descriptive hair said people always remember things they never intended to. He thinks his professor was a man who knew a lot about philosophy and never bothered to worry about his hair. Unless of course he left it like that on purpose. He thinks Nathan Rolf used to be like that guy—a college professor. He used to be brilliant, too, and Ray steps inside the gym, looking for Jazinski. He has some things he'd like to say. The band is singing now, without instruments, everybody inside singing "White Christmas," the band and the kids, all together now. It's a dreamy song, wishful of snow, and tonight they've got good reason. It really is snowing, even in Phoenix, and the kids keep singing. In a few hours, all this will be over with, and then he will finally be able to go home. He will boil some water for tea, maybe cocoa. Tomorrow he and Robert Horn will be proctoring the S.A.T., which pays, and maybe when he goes home tonight he'll take a bath, to soak, and look at one of his books. He has a new one on hunting in Alaska. In Alaska snow is a normal part of the landscape, like seasons, and he's thinking about snow and what Jenna has just said to him, that part about seeing a ghost, and there is the unmistakable sound of music: of all these kids, singing. Jenna has gone off somewhere by herself.

He wanders past the kids who all are singing. Lacy, the famous dancer who always wears black clothes, is standing alone, waiting for a fast song so she can start dancing like a maniac—her hair, and her body, completely going crazy. She's even been on TV. The kids are still singing, and he's looking for Jazinski—they've got some things to settle up—and just when the singing stops, the band starts up—a loud long noise with three or four notes. Rock 'n' roll.

He's looking over the crowd, looking for Jazinski, when he hears a scream.

A girl, screaming, which is different from a woman. Longer, and far more inexperienced. A girl is running from the women's rest room until she stops. She pulls her hair, sits on her heels, and screams. She keeps screaming and he sees it's Carol Cunningham, the girl with red hair, screaming. She's screaming and even the band notices. It stops playing, slowly, and Buckner is waving at the back doors, waving and yelling, "Stay calm. Just stay calm!"

Buckner's trying to cross the gym, the kids ignoring him, and now Carol stops just long enough to take a breath.

He's got Ms. Williams!

Ray's going through the crowd, fast, shoving the kids out of his way, and he knows he can make it, he can make it fast enough, and he can hear Buckner, yelling, and Carol screaming *He's got a gun! He's got a gun!*

When he hits the door, he hits it hard, slamming it open, and Buckner is outside, somewhere, yelling, and there's Howie: standing against the sink with a .38 in his hand.

He has Jenna, kneeling. She is kneeling in front of Howie on her knees and the gun is pointed to her throat.

And Michael Owens, out of nowhere, saying, "Calm down. Just calm down, Howie."

"Fuck you."

Ray steps closer, past Michael, and says, "What are you doing, Howie?"

"Fuck me?" he says. "Fuck me, Teach."

Jenna screams, and Howie lifts the gun, points it at Ray, and says, smiling, "Big fucking bang, Coach."

Jenna screams again and Howie whips her with the gun. The barrel cuts a ridge across her cheek, and when Buckner comes running in, Howie fires. He fires into a stall and screams, "I know, I'm expelled! Now get the fuck out of here!"

Michael's pressing behind Ray. He can feel her breath on his neck, her hand pressed into his back, and her gun; she really does carry a gun. She's holding the gun in the flat of her hand, pressed squarely into the small of Ray's back so he can feel it. She says, "Jenna, you okay?"

"Jen," he says.

Howie yanks her by the hair. He yanks her face to his crotch. "Come on, Teach. Why don't you fuck me?"

Michael is pressing the gun harder into Ray's back, and she's saying, "Leave. Leave."

"No," Ray says. "No fucking way."

He can feel her gun pressed up against his back—a .38, same as Howie's, police special—and now Howie's pointing the gun into Jenna's face and Howie is saying, "I was going to do it by myself. By myself, Coach. I didn't ask for her help. What time is it?"

"I don't know."

"I didn't ask her to suck my dick."

"Howie—"

"Do you think she would have? Do you think she would have done that?"

"Stop it, Howie."

"Did you? Did you ever ask her to suck your dick?"

Howie hits Jenna again. Then again. He's shoving the .38 into her mouth. "Suck on this, Teach."

Michael presses harder, her hand pressing toward Jenna. Jenna is choking on the gun. Michael whispers, loudly, *Leave!*

"She ever do this to you, Coach?"

"No. Howie. No."

"Liar! You are such a fucking liar, Coach. I'm Howie—"

"And you know everything. I know. Just calm down. Calm—"

On three, Michael whispers. *Three!*

"On three!" Howie yells. He pulls Jenna's face into his crotch and yells, "One!"

"Howie," Ray says, "this does not have to happen. This does not have to be happening now."

"Did you, Coach? Did you?"

One.

"Yes. Okay, yes. Now put that thing down before it goes off. Put it down!"

Howie's shoving the gun into Jenna's face, her face, she's bleeding fast. She's shaking and delirious, the gun in her hands: both hands, she's holding him, screaming . . . and Michael pressing, *Two!* . . . and Jenna, screaming, *Howie, Howie, please! It's okay, Howie! Just stop, okay!* and *Howie! Okay? . . . Okay?* and Howie, no longer screaming, lifting the gun to his mouth, lowering it . . . *Okay, okay. Then fuck me, too.*

It takes less time to count to three than it does to take a life, even if it is your own. Some things truly take a lifetime.

In the morning the news will be full of gossip and unconfirmed reports: two shots fired at Gold Dust High. A teacher, Ms. Jenna Williams, was severely wounded by a distraught student troubled over the recent suicide of his close friend Walker Miller.

Jenna Williams will be reported to be in critical condition with a punctured lung at Scottsdale Memorial. As for the student, Howie Bently, he will be pronounced D.O.A., and the reporters will interview several students, and Cal Buckner, and Nathan Rolf. Even Roxanne, the retarded girl, will have her moment to appear on camera. Roxanne will be smiling and waving her tape recorder, and she will talk a lot about *teamwork,* and then Michael Owens, the officer on duty, will explain that they never exchanged any fire . . . *I did not pull the trigger* . . . and a team of forensic specialists will examine the ballistics, though it will be clear that Michael Owens never once fired a shot. She will be standing in front of the gym, snow will be falling, and she will be saying, *There wasn't a clear enough view.* The snow will be falling on her pale yellow hair and then she will say, *I couldn't see a thing* or *I would have dropped the little fuck cold.*

But it was your gun, Ms. Owens. Was it not?

Yes. It was my gun.

After Howie Bently shot Jenna Williams, he put the barrel into his mouth and fired; the sound technicians will be certain to delete all profanity, and Michael Owens' career will simultaneously be ruined. Captain Miller, retired, will be in a foreign country, unavailable, and the reporters will move on to deliver the news to Mrs. Bently, live and in her front yard. The reporters will also camp in front of Ray's house, the cheap house with the swamp cooler and bad paint, and wait to ask him leading questions. The shooting will also inspire a local investigative documentary—*Suicide in Our Schools: An Adolescent Investigation*—and the local ratings will increase, which will justify additional reports, because it's not the kind of incident the people of Phoenix are likely to forget, not for a while, and because it's going to be worth some mileage: the double suicide, and who it is that will be held accountable.

Just who exactly is to blame.

Sea Glass

In the beginning was the word, and the word was made flesh, and once passion turns to shame, our lives become apology. It's something even Christ could believe in: mystery, while we're still here on earth, and what it truly means to live a life.

If none of this had ever happened, then nothing would ever happen. But *cause*, Jenna reminds herself, is not *effect*. Sequence is not explanation. There is something bigger in the air than chronology. Something random and coincidental and terrifyingly real, something in need of embrace nonetheless. How else can you admire the sky? The way the clouds swell up in the west?

How else can you know?

It will take her a while to recover fully; and she will wake in the I.C.U. to find Ray, standing over her bed, holding her hand. Later, they will say good-bye to the kids, and he will help her pack up her car and move to Sedona. There she will live with her aunt Nicky. She will read often and swim in a heated pool and, sometimes, she will write Ray letters, until the letters grow thin in the telling. Until there is nothing left to say.

The light in Sedona is pretty, she will write. *Sometimes I still miss California. The water, and all those waves.*

And Ray will write back, *The snow in Alaska is deep.*

• • •

Once, in California, while she was still living with Sammy, they watched a late-night movie. Before cable, or VCRs, and the movie starred John Wayne and Jim Hutton: *Hellfighters,* about oil-fire fighters. John Wayne and Jim Hutton put out fires that terrorists or lightning bolts had unexpectedly ignited; there was a lot of drama, and color, because the film was shot in color—a relatively new invention—and the premise seemed to be that if you had to put out a big explosion, you made another: you dropped a case of nitroglycerin into the flames, and after the nitroglycerin exploded, the flames would suddenly be extinguished. It had to do with oxygen and the way fire required air to breathe, and you had to be careful, approaching the flames with all that nitroglycerin. You had to be careful not to trip. It's one of the few movies starring John Wayne that Jenna remembers clearly—she's not a fan of the Western—and Sammy, while watching the movie, had explained to her the parts she didn't know were coming because he'd seen it so many times before.

Just wait, Jen . . . Just wait . . . I'm gonna write a song about all this. . . .

She thinks oil is something you spill inside the ocean, on top of the sand; she thinks life goes on, even into the past. Sammy, and the movies they used to watch on the TV, in bed, fed by a bowl of popcorn, maybe some ice cream. They smoked a lot of marijuana back then. In Sedona, on Ranch House Circle, just last month while she stood quietly in front of her car, preparing to return to the city and wanting to say something decisive, she couldn't think of anything to say.

Instead, Nicky spoke. "Melodrama bores me," said Nicky. "It just downright bores me, Jenna. I don't tolerate it in myself, and I'm not about to tolerate it in someone I love."

Nicky was wearing her swimming suit, the pink one, and her thongs. She had a towel tossed over her shoulder, and Jenna said, smiling, "I know, Nicky."

"I figure we're all entitled to a crisis, say, every seven years.

Seven, that's a biblical kind of number. Seven. But after that, it's time to buck up, kiddo. It's time to get back on the horse."

Jenna looked at her aunt, standing in front of the sun, and said, "I think I'm going to quit teaching."

She said it just to see how it sounds—a pebble, dropped into a still pool of water. In the yard, beside the coiled garden hose, lay Nicky's Labrador, Alfred, scratching. He looked so content, scratching; it was something that made him feel good. In a few minutes, Nicky would be late for her water-aerobics class for widowed geriatrics. Later, Nicky would go alone to the public library, which is what she always did.

Nicky said, "Ph.D.?"

"God, no," Jenna said. "No. I could be a lawyer, though. Or a nurse, maybe. I don't know. I don't know, Nicky, but I'll let you know, okay?"

"Let me know, honey. And be kind. Be kind to yourself."

And then Jenna stepped inside her car, which started on the third try, and she drove away, lurching, because, as Ray had explained, the clutch was getting thin. The only thing she knew about a clutch was that it was something you pushed with your foot, preferably the left, and she drove down the highway, past Bell Rock, which was ringing silently through the air: all those colors, ringing. The air was bright enough to paint with, though Jenna knew she had no talent for art—she could see, but she couldn't make—and perhaps this was going to be her role for the rest of her life: observation, with occasional bits of analysis tucked into the side, and she knew she wanted to do something. She wanted to do something meaningful and just, right and so to be, and she wanted to be of use. Sedona was full of starving artists, as well as rich artists, because even now, thanks to irrigation and student loans, foreign debt, trickle-down economics, homelessness . . . what better time for an artist to make a living? To save the world? Because amid all this horror even that had become ostensibly possible: to rewrite the laws of gravity, of history and light. If you wanted anything bad enough, all you had to do was figure out what it was you really wanted to take and hold for your very own.

The problem was, how did you figure out what it was you wanted?

"I want a dog!" she told herself, passing Cherry Highway. There was a cop, waiting beneath the bridge, where he always waited. Her car couldn't go fast enough to merit a real speeding ticket, and she waved as she passed by, and he waved back, tipping his hat, and then she said, "A friendly dog. Like Alfred."

Like Alfred, to have and to hold. If she'd had a radio that worked outside the city limits, she probably wouldn't have spent so much time talking to herself, and now she had a dog. His name was Paris, and together at night they took walks in the park. When she lay on the floor grading her papers, he sneaked up under her arm to look. In the tub, he'd want to join with. He'd sneeze at the bubbles and yelp; his voice wasn't developed enough for a true bark. He was still just a pup.

Looking at him, it was hard to believe he could ever start a war, especially the Trojan War, and she decided she wouldn't have him neutered, which really meant *castrated*—to have his balls cut off. Instead she was going to find him a friend, and they could have puppies, when the time was right, and she would find a home for those puppies. The idea was still far enough removed to be pleasant—raising a family, and what she might in fact end up doing with it. If she had a child, she wouldn't necessarily have to get married, but she didn't want to have a child by herself. Ray could have a child. If he could learn to love himself, he would be a good father, fair but kind, forgiving and always kind; she understood now his strengths, and the weaknesses, lingering near the joints, and the way he would always have to shift his weight to compensate. Balance, and the awkward grace with which he would always struggle to conceal those weaknesses within himself . . . and what that would mean, watching. This year, he was going to receive the Senior Class Teacher of the Year Award, because his students loved him, and because he was kind and always fair. Cal had told her this in his office, two weeks ago, when she went in to tell him she would not be coming back next semester.

"But don't tell him, Jen. We want it to be a surprise."

"I can't stay, Cal."

"I know. And I understand. Really. You'd die before you let yourself become defeated."

She thought that a strange remark, however complimentary his intentions. Cal said, tugging on the sleeve of his aloha shirt, "We have more defeated teachers here than we have failing students. Than we have passing students. Even the defeated know how to *pass,* Jenna. That's what makes some different."

She thought of Marcia Taylor, and Belinda Fullerton, and Robert Horn, Chemistry and Bowling; she thought, I'm a good teacher. I know what's important. I know what I believe. *But what if you stop believing? What then?* . . . And she knows she can still teach, and she can still teach well and remain undefeated. Cal Buckner once taught English in the Bahamas.

And she wanted to say to him, *Cal, what do you believe in?*

But she already knew the answer. It would be the same for everyone . . . *survival.* People just used different words to say what they mean.

It's snowing, Nathan Rolf had said. *It's snowing just for us!*

Last year, when she walked into the locker room and discovered Howie, Walker and Jazinski, sitting in her office, leafing through her magazines, she had said, "What are you doing in here?"

And Walker said sheepishly, "Exploring. We've been exploring, Ms. Williams. But right now we're really kind of hungry."

She thought, boys will be boys, until they grow up, and now she thinks it's time for her to grow up . . . *I've got to grow up.* To celebrate her decision, she dressed up and went out to dinner by herself. She took herself to a restaurant with cloth on the tables— ordered wine and vegetables stir-fried in peanut oil; she ate slowly, as if she had all the time in the world, which she did. After, she drove home, lingering here and there, admiring the city lights and knowing that she had no special place calling her home. She knew that after Paris fell asleep, she was going to be there, sitting in her kitchen, looking out the window at the dark. When she finally pulled into her parking lot, underneath the carport, she saw Ray's car. It made her feel happy, seeing his car there, the way she used to. He was sitting alone in his car asleep.

She knocked on the window and he panicked—the way a man will check his fly, or pick himself up after he trips. She apologized and invited him up. Once inside, Paris jumped on his leg and peed.

"His name is Paris," she explained, apologizing.

"I know, after the Trojan War. Everybody's talking about it."

"Oh," she said. "I didn't know that."

He was sitting at her kitchen table, and he said, "You look nice."

He sat there, drinking his tea, and she was about to tell him the news—Senior Class Teacher of the Year, which would mean a bonus to his salary, over two hundred dollars, just enough to celebrate in Reno, or at a steak house with three of your closest friends. She wondered who Ray's friends really were. Michael Owens, the cop, and maybe someone else . . . *Who are mine?* . . . and she was about to tell him . . . *Hey, guess what?* . . . but she checked herself midthought not to spoil his surprise. She thought, not for the first time, that people who give away secrets want power as much as those who keep them. She hadn't asked to be told. She doesn't want power . . . *I know it's not that* . . . and she looked at his arms, the veins spilling into his wrists, and she wanted him to stay. His eyes looked sleepy and clear, she wanted him to take her to bed, and to kiss her, and she wanted him to want her to kiss him back. Next door, Bill was having a party; the walls were full of music and gentle conversation. People were laughing, and in love, and instead of saying what she meant . . . *Hey, Ray . . . It's really been a long time, you know?* . . . instead of placing her hand on his knee, or his wrist, she tripped him into feeling self-conscious. She asked him if he was going to AA.

Later, after Ray left, she fell asleep on the couch, weary from so much exhausted effort.

• • •

She woke, startled, beneath the harsh bulb of her reading light. A tapping outside, against her window. Paris was yelping, and she yelled, "Go away! I have a gun! And a dog!"

When she turned on the outside light, she couldn't see a trace. She'd never even touched a gun, a real gun, except for the one Walker Miller had held in his hand. It was large and full of bullets, and she dropped it, after holding it, screaming. She had dropped it onto the grass and screamed while the paramedics tried to feed her oxygen. Her swimming suit was laying on the grass, empty, still damp, just waiting to be filled, and she had thought the worst was over. She had thought maybe there was something she could do.

Sammy, after drowning in the ocean while tripping on acid, at the funeral, what Sammy's mother had said was "God never closes a door without first opening a window."

Or a vent. At Sammy's funeral, Jenna had worn the uniform of a girl in mourning: a black cotton dress, her hair tied into a knot; she wore her dark sunglasses, behind which her eyes were lit with tequila and hashish. Sammy was buried in jeans and a sweatshirt, though the casket was closed; it had taken days for his bloated body to wash up onto the beach. As one cop had said, *Not a pretty sight;* and Walker Miller died with his sneakers on—hightops and purple laces—and just last spring, before he was committed to the Superstition Mountain Care Facility, he had freaked out in a supermarket.

Jenna was in the supermarket, shopping. Milk, orange juice, tampons, pasta, basil, a pint of rum-raisin ice cream—she had barely enough to fill a grocery bag. Walker Miller was bagging groceries, and she stood in line, watching him. He was wearing a green tie, and his face hadn't yet begun to break out. She recognized him from school and thought he was Howie Bently.

Walker said, "Hiya, Ms. Williams. What'cha doing?"

The ice cream was cold in her arms, beginning to slip. She balanced herself and said, "Hi, Howie."

Walker pointed to his name tag and said, "Walker. I'm Walker. I'm in your Sports for Life class. I really like it."

The name tag said WALLY, and this confused her. She was embarrassed for not remembering his name. When he played volleyball, he never dressed properly; he'd play in jeans and a dress shirt, getting himself all sweaty, swinging at the ball. Sometimes, he would actually hit it. He had the grace of a boy who knows that if he could just hit the ball, just once and maybe make a winning point, then for the rest of his life maybe some girl would like him. Maybe she would even let him ask her out on a date. He could save the team.

There was one girl, Iva Polanski. Often, she'd be sitting on the lawn underneath the orange trees with Walker, smiling, because Walker was in the school choir, for which Iva Polanski was accompanist. Walker Miller's mother had committed suicide by slitting the veins in her thighs after swallowing a bottle of Percocet. Somebody found her in a Jacuzzi, the water bubbling and full of blood, and even before that, years ago, during Jenna's first year at Gold Dust High, she knew a young teacher named Fennerstrom who had an affair with a student. The teacher had driven his car off a cliff over Camp Verde. It was the kind of scandal the newspapers adore—pictures, letters between the student and the teacher, a quiet man named Fennerstrom who drove his car off a cliff, and died, according to the coroner's report, seventeen hours later. At first, everyone had thought it was an accident.

Until the press learned of the affair—teacher in love with student. The teacher was a quiet man, the student desultory and wise, the letters simply tragic. Love letters, written by a literate and lonely man; and the girl's letters, the more heartrending, with grammatical errors and misspellings, her script loopy and bold. The paper had reproduced two of the letters on the cover of its issue breaking the scandal, and in one the girl had written, *I don't care what they say, what they know, nobody can know, Fenny. Nobody. Nobody!*

And Fennerstrom had written back, gently . . . *If these be days, then these be ours. And who will be there to forgive us? Who, and why?*

Later, while Ray is visiting her at the hospital, night after night, while Jenna's lung slowly begins to heal, she will begin to tell Ray the story. She will tell Ray the sad, tragic story of Mr. Fennerstrom—a man she knew distantly, as if they were related. She will tell Ray how, after first learning what had happened . . . *seventeen hours!* . . . she had cried, because she knew the man, slightly, they each taught a similar class, and over the coffee machine sometimes Fennerstrom would stand sipping at his coffee, looking out the window. Often they would smile at each other, briefly, in the hallway, or at meetings. His eyes were always heavy with sleep, and tired; like Ray's, actually. Always tired . . . *Like yours, Ray, only not as clear . . . and more sad . . .* and she would tell Ray how, when just this past fall Belinda Fullerton and Andre Langousis started launching accusations about Ray and Diana Vanderstock, their assignations in the parking lot . . . Jenna would explain to Ray how she had used the accusations as an excuse for making contact, and how she had tried to warn Ray.

"Be careful," I said. Remember, Ray? I said, "Be careful, these things happen. . . ."

Though she knew even then, even as she said it, that Ray would be careful: only a romantic could believe in love, and Ray, for all his discipline and strength, Ray could never be so savagely and pointlessly romantic. For Ray love was something to be endured, like betrayal or unexpected weather; it wasn't something you gave yourself away to. It wasn't something you let yourself drown in . . . *Love, deep enough to drown you . . .* and in the hospital, recuperating, Jenna would laugh, and cough, because it was going to take a while, a very long while for her lung to heal, and Ray would show her pictures of Alaska.

The kids. We've got to talk to the kids!

Once, a long time ago, at a checkout stand in a crowded and air-conditioned supermarket, Walker Miller began to freak out. He was bagging Jenna's groceries, and he had asked Jenna, smiling, always smiling, "Regular or double strength, Ms. Williams?"

"Regular."

"Doesn't matter," he said, catching himself. "Not really. Even our regular is really double."

Inside, it was cold—the refrigeration turned on high to save the produce, and outside the sky was bright: the white light of heaven, she thought. Spring, with summer pressing, and Walker Miller, pushing her grocery cart, smiling, stumbling over his huge feet . . . she had tried to think up some conversation. She praised him for his serve, which was almost improving, and then a car came passing by. It was a long, heavy station wagon; inside were boys, and as the car passed by, someone yelled out to her, "Hey, nice tits!"

Walker leapt, instantly. "Fuck you!" he yelled. "Fuck you!"

The car stopped; a boy jumped out. "What?"

Walker charged, his body electric and sudden, lifting the cart over his head. He threw the cart onto the hood of the car, screaming *Fuck Fuck You!* and he charged into the boy, swinging, screaming, swinging his fists into the car, the shopping cart, the boy, and now people began pulling him off, pulling and yelling and Jenna was screaming, a random elbow popped her in the nose, she began to bleed. The three boys held Walker down; he was breathing, gasping. His fists bloody stumps.

She told the boys to let him up . . . *Let him go!* . . . and she pulled him to his feet.

"I was doing it for you, Ms. Williams. I was protecting your honor!"

"Walker—"

He looked at her in sheer, terrific horror. He stood on his toes, as if beholding a vision of the next world, or the last; he raised his fists to his eyes, cried out, and ran. He ran into the supermarket, past the automatic doors, and there, once into the produce section, he took the produce hose and let loose: on the housewives, the children, the bag boys all in uniform. The cash registers. He was flooding out the entire store and then the water stopped. Someone had shut the water off, and he stood there, holding the empty hose. He let it go and turned to the yellow grapefruit behind him. That sweet, yellow grapefruit—bombing the customers, each fruit squeezed to a pulp, and Walker, never taking any real aim, just lobbing the grapefruit through the freezing store, screaming *On sale for today only! It's sweet! It's good! It's got no seeds!* and the fruit landing on the floor, in the aisles, the blood from his hands staining all the aisles.

"Walker?" she said, softly, opening her arms. "Come here, Walker."

And then he collapsed. He lay on the floor, and in the quiet of the air-conditioning, you could hear him, sobbing.

This morning, while listening to the rain, she called the cop, that same cop who has repeatedly advised her. She explained what might have happened, last night, the tapping at her glass; maybe, *yes,* maybe she might have dreamed it, and afterward she decided to check the oil in her car. She thinks the oil is something which should be checked regularly, two or three times a year at least. Preventive maintenance. Once, Ray had told her where the dipstick was, and while going through her drawers, looking for a rag, she thought she'd use the underwear Walker Miller's father had stuck onto her radio antenna, that day he was so tired and drunk, cleaning the windows of his empty house with a pair of boy's briefs—Walker Miller's briefs, made out of cotton and elastic— and she went through her drawers, her closet, knowing they should be here, somewhere, though she never did find them . . . *Maybe you really threw them out?* . . . and she decided instead on a yellow sock with a hole in the heel, and climbing down the stairs, aiming for her car, she saw the windshield, spattered white. Snow, all across her windshield, only it hadn't yet begun to snow. Arriving closer, the rain pounding on the breezeway, she realized that the windshield had been completely shattered.

The interior was showered with splinters of glass. Hundreds of dollars worth, but the windshield still seemed to hold together. Sagging into the center, still holding itself together, and it made her angry, all that waste; really, really angry. She ran up to her apartment, angry, and at the same time feeling slightly vindicated: somebody had vandalized her car, she had parked in a safe and considerate spot, *my spot,* and when she returned with a broom, she understood that she was going to have to break out the glass entirely. For a while, it actually made her feel better, breaking all that glass. She stepped back to take long, even swings . . . *It's not my fault, it's not my fault* . . . and she sent the remains of her windshield flying. It was something she could get used to, being angry, justifiably so, and after a while she discovered she wasn't all that angry. She had kept up on her insurance; it wasn't that big a loss. She swept off the seats, the dash and rubber mats, then the pavement, because she was responsible . . . *but not for everything, not everything* . . . and sweeping up the remains of her windshield, she remembered the oil, which was black, just the way she always remembered it. Probably, she should just move away.

The rain was coming down fast. She ran across the street to a convenience store, what Ray always called a Stop 'n' Rob; she bought two quarts of oil in plastic bottles, but when she returned, standing under the carport, dripping, looking at her yellow sock, and her car with the big gaping wound, she decided that this was something that could wait . . . *to hell with it* . . . The sky swollen and full, the rain not about to let up, and she dropped the hood of her car. She watched the water wash across the gutters of her building; she sat on her heels and began to laugh. It was a ridiculous situation, somebody should bother to take notice, and after, after she was finished, she took Paris for a quick walk in the park. She was walking in the rain, something you were supposed to do with a lover, or perhaps a close relative, and it felt oddly exhilarating, walking alone in a park full of rain. She thought, while walking, *This is what matters. This. Yes, this* . . . and then she began to run, with Paris following, running across the wet grass, home to her apartment, and she understood that, given enough time, anything was possible. You could change the way you chose to live. You could choose someone to love. You could even learn to try all over again because you knew you had to.

•••

Given enough time even the sharpest of moments will begin to fade: the tide of history, washing away the edges, following a course already laid out by the moon. Day in, and day out. She thinks there will always be time to fix your car, and to apologize, and outside the snow was a record. The deepest snowfall in the history of Phoenix, de facto and still coming down. Nathan Rolf passed his flask to Ray, and she leaned up against Ray, warm and happy, his body giving off heat. She could feel it rising through the space between them, and she wanted to take him home. While he stood there, looking at the flask, blinking, she said to Ray, "Hey, you look like you've just seen a ghost."

Ray smiled and returned the flask to Nathan, who said, "The world is too much with us. . . ."

"Late and soon," Cal said. "I know that one, Nathan."

And later, after the dance, after they had helped the band load up its truck and after they had helped the senior class put away the tables, and after they had folded up all the tables the senior class neglected to put away, she would ask Ray, one more time, if maybe they could . . . *You know, maybe?* . . . and then there would be, of course, another time to ask . . . *Hey, big guy. Give me a ride home?* . . . and another, which is what she was going to do. She knew exactly what she was going to do, and she flushed, thinking that way, and saw Robert Horn, gazing unabashedly. Robert Horn, no longer wearing his bulletproof vest, looked as if he'd dropped twenty pounds.

She saw Howie Bently. He was wearing a loose T-shirt, his hair damp from the snow, his arms long, gangly and white, and she drifted off to follow, to say hello, something, and she was following and she could hear the voices there behind her: Ray, saying something to Michael Owens, who so clearly wanted to fall in love with him. It made her jealous, and what that felt like—ice, caught in her throat. Overhead the disco ball was spinning fast.

"Howie!" she called.

He kept walking.

She called to him again. "Howie?"

He stopped by the rest rooms, spinning on his toe. He smiled tensely and looked at his watch. "What time is it?" he said.

"I don't know, Howie."

"I gotta know. What time is it right now?"

"Howie—"

"Ten-fifteen," he said. "That's my birthday. October fifteenth."

"Howie, are you okay?"

"Fine. I'm fine!"

The band stopped, pausing for a moment of contemplation, and now they began to sing "White Christmas," a capella, and Jenna said, "Are you sure?"

"What? Am I sure? Of course I'm sure. I know when I was born. What do you mean, *Am I sure?*"

She was looking at his watch and now, looking up, she met his eye—distant, and very, very close. No, she thought. No. *No!* . . . and Howie, pushing open the girls' rest room.

She stood there, watching the door come to a close, slowly, its hinge bringing the door slowly home. And she knew that she'd been here before . . . *You don't have to do this. You do not have to do this. . . .*

And the entire school, singing "White Christmas," a song she used to know the words to.

No. I do not have to do this!

"Howie?" she called, pushing open the door. "Howie?"

Heaven

The blood of faith, the body of hope. Blessed be the day.

What else is there to know? That love will lead to grief? That grief must always give us cause to love? We enter into this life by taking first a breath, then another, and for every breath we take, it is impossible not to give one back. This is something she can feel now—her breath, in the cool morning light, just now beginning to rise. She is sitting on the lip of her parents' pool, which is now for sale, like the rest of the house. Lately she comes out here to watch the water, the water and the sky; when it's cold, she brings along a blanket. The pool is full of blue water, ruffled by a breeze, and inside her bedroom, Joe is fast asleep. He is fast asleep beneath the big green quilt her mother bought to match her eyes.

Sometimes, when he sleeps, it's almost as if he's about to wake. He takes a lot of medication now, which is supposed to be *temporary,* and sometimes, his dreams are dangerous. Sometimes he'll even wake up screaming, and then she'll hold him, and then he'll fall asleep. Usually, he won't remember all the details . . . *just the feeling* . . . and today, after he wakes, they are going to fix English muffins and drive Spencer up into the mountains—a trip to see the canyon, and snow which will last for an entire season. Spencer says his resolution, *for this year,* is to learn to ski.

"Fast," he said, nodding. "Really, really fast. Think Mrs. Amato will let me?"

"Sure," Joe said. "Probably."

They were standing in Joe's driveway, beside his car, and Spencer was showing off on his new bicycle. Spencer was riding in circles around Joe's car, steering with one hand, giving explanations. He had a cast on his ankle, which made pedaling awkward. He stood on the pedals and said, "Now I'm going to jump!"

He accelerated toward the landscaping, a sloping, minor hill, decorated with small boulders, and fell.

Joe reached for her wrist. "Spence," he called.

"What?"

"You fell."

"Nah," Spencer said, brushing off his knee. He rolled over on the hill, beside his bicycle, and giggled. "It didn't even hurt!"

"Mrs. Amato," Joe said. "Tell Mrs. Amato we'll be by to pick you up. Tomorrow."

"First thing," Spencer said. "We'll make sandwiches!"

"First thing."

They left Spencer in the front yard, *practicing,* and drove to Desert Bloom, which was a nursery. She thought it was a peculiar name for a place that specialized in flowers and plants. Behind the store stood hundreds of trees, in barrels and pots, and they walked among the trees looking for a nice one. In Michigan the trees were tall, and made of hardwood, but this was a different kind of place. She wanted to find one that might fit in.

"A paloverde," Edith said. "They don't need much water."

At the counter, Edith asked the man how much water a paloverde would need to keep growing. "I mean, all by itself?"

"Beats me," said the man.

The tree cost over a hundred dollars, which Edith paid for with a blank check her father had left for her on the kitchen table. Her father was on vacation now. Edith had the house to herself, this time for an entire week, and her father was on vacation with his lover, which was the word your parents used to mean *the person I love most,* or *sleep with.* Kids, like Spencer, were too young to have a lover. Spencer would have to sleep alone for several more years at least. Her father was going to find himself a nice apartment, maybe a house, and she could visit on vacations when she came home from college. She still didn't know which one, and it was nice, sleeping with someone, someone you really liked to sleep with, but it also took some getting used to. Where to put your arm, for example. When to actually fall asleep. Sometimes, it was hard not being by yourself.

Her mother says you spend a lifetime, getting used to it, being by yourself even if you're married. She lives across town in a big building with an exercise club, and three swimming pools, and says she's making friends. She says if you stop making new friends, then pretty soon you won't have any left, and Edith understands exactly what she means. People sometimes vanish, into thin air, even when you're looking. Joe says that's what he dreams about. Vanishings, and then what's left behind. The empty spaces.

They loaded the tree into the back of Joe's car, with the man's help, the dirt spilling out through the burlap. The roots were wrapped, soaked with vitamins and water. Handling a tree, said the man, you had to watch out for thorns, which are sharp, really. "Really sharp," said the man, helping, waving good-bye.

Driving, Joe and Edith listened to the radio. The tree took up a lot of space, and Edith slid under Joe's arm while Joe brought down his power window. Then he steered with one finger, the way he always did, and pretended to relax. It was a big car, it didn't take a lot of effort. On the way to the mountains, tomorrow with Spencer, she might even drive part of the way. It made her feel happy, knowing she could drive, even if she didn't necessarily always want to; of course, there couldn't be a lot of traffic. She didn't want to kill anyone. By the time they arrived at school, which was still closed for vacation, she thought it looked pretty, but also lonely: a school, shut down for vacation, and all those empty buildings. She reminded herself to remember what this felt like: sitting here, beside Joe, and the light beginning to fall across the lawns, the parking lot and tennis courts. The parking lot was empty except for one small car, a blue car, which belonged to Ms.

Williams. The car was full of boxes and furniture, and she was standing next to Mr. Morrison, who used to be her lover.

"Hey, Coach," Joe said. "Miss Williams."

"Jenna," Jenna said, nicely. "Hello, Joe."

Mr. Morrison hugged Edith, briefly; then Edith hugged Jenna, which was difficult, because Jenna was still very sore. Jenna stood quietly, her arm in a sling, not because of her arm, but because of her breast. When a bullet enters a woman's breast, it does irreparable damage; even the thought will make your ribs hurt. It will make you ache, each and every time, and after, Edith visited Jenna often, and Mr. Morrison. Joe was going to counseling now, his father's idea, who was in Baltimore, and Edith still hasn't said a word about what happened—that night, in her Jacuzzi, and what happened there. And she knows that this will be her secret, her own private grief. Truth is tender, and always private, which is why Joe has nightmares and goes to counseling, and why her parents will divorce, and why, at the memorial service, she didn't say a word.

Jenna said she understood; after she came home from the hospital, they cried a lot . . . *like sisters* . . . and later, while taking walks, getting to know each other. As adults now, which was different. Sometimes they played with Paris in the park. Eventually, Edith helped Jenna pack her things into boxes—books, mostly, and some dishes—because Jenna was going to move away, but not with Mr. Morrison. As for the tree, that was Edith's idea, even if it was illegal, to plant a tree without permission, and standing here in the parking lot with her boyfriend, Joe, and with Jenna and Ray—standing here in front of Joe's car, she hoped secretly that they might. That Ray and Jenna might stay together and make each other happy.

They lifted the tree, which was almost heavy, even Jenna. They carried it onto the lawn, looking for a place, then another, behind the library. It didn't take long to dig the hole, and Ray said the tree would do well because of all the sprinklers. The sprinklers ran on automatic timers, they could have bought an orange tree, or a lemon, and after the hole was dug, Jenna insisted that they each say something, now, to make it meaningful. *Our own special service* . . . and she listened to Jenna, who said nice things, though Edith knew Jenna was saying them for Edith. Jenna was saying things for Edith, and for Joe, and then even for Ray, who kept shifting his weight. When it was Joe's turn to speak, he began to cry. She knew Joe didn't want to cry, you could tell by the way he kept trying not to, and Jenna put her arm around Joe which made him cry even harder. It made her ache, watching Joe, and everybody else, everybody she was ever going to know, and love, and after a while she knew it was going to be her turn. She was going to have to say something, and *Good-bye,* and that wasn't what she had to say . . . *Go on, Edith* . . . and before, before when she knew she had to cry, she knew it didn't necessarily have anything to do with her. She knew some things just happened, and that they could be fixed; she could go to her parents, who would understand, especially if you were really crying hard. Everything could be set right. You could get a bandage, or a couple aspirin, or your mom might call you pretty . . . *pretty as a piece of heaven* . . . which is why you had to do it. You had to learn to make yourself feel better, and she stood in front of the tree, beside her boyfriend, looking at the sky. She stood all by herself looking at the sky.

"This is for us," she said. "You know? This is just for us."

About the Author

T. M. McNALLY received the Flannery O'Connor Award for Short Fiction for his collection of stories, *Low Flying Aircraft*. He lives in Chicago.